HUNT FOR
UNDERSTANDING

Onoma Series Book 4

Alisa Hope Wagner

HUNT FOR UNDERSTANDING

Onoma Series Book 4

Hunt for Understanding
Book Four of the Onoma Series
Copyright © 2021 by Alisa Hope Wagner
All rights reserved.
Marked Writers Publishing
www.alisahopewagner.com

Scriptures taken from multiple translations of the Bible.

Author photo by Lori Stead of www.wetsilver.com
Cover images designed by Muhammad Ahsan Ayaz
Cover designed by Alisa Hope Wagner

ISBN-10 :1733433384
ISBN-13: 978-1733433389

DEDICATION

Daniel, my high school sweetheart and soul mate.

Isaac, my first-born son and prophet.

Levi, my brown-eyed boy and shepherd.

Karis Ruth, my cherished girl and graceful companion.

Christina, my amazing twin.

ACKNOWLEDGEMENT

Writing the finale to the *Onoma Series* was a daunting task, causing me to really press into God and His imagination. One afternoon, I went into my backyard and wrestled with the Lord about how to finish the series. I didn't want a simple conclusion; rather, I desired a gripping end with many plots colliding into a single purpose. I wanted every character to shine and have a hand in accomplishing the climax of the story. I can say with enthusiasm that this feat was achieved, and I'm blown away by the conclusion of this series. It is truly a story that I will always look at with both endearment and relief that I finally finished it well after fifteen years.

I couldn't have written in excellence without the support of my husband and children. They are always on my mind when I write because I hope they will be proud of me. I also want to thank my sweet editing team: Patricia Coughlin, Cynthia Faulkner, Faith Newton, Jennifer Smith, Daniel Wagner and Bernadine Zimmerman. They find those pesky typos that always seem to wiggle their way into my story. Finally, I am so honored by God and His call. I pray that I have been a faithful steward of His giftings in my life.

INTRODUCTION

Randall Hunt doesn't want to live in the shadows, but he soon realizes that he has more to live and fight for than simply a wealth of oil. The plot to take down the World Government by attacking the Regional Integrated Banking System (RIBS) is underway, but fear of Neil Elder using the Kill Switch is causing the Colonials to understand less and trust more. As Ada Armel dazzles the world with her *Grand Opus Gala*, Bear and his pregnant wife, Ruth, are confronted with decisions that may save the world from evil but destroy their growing family. Tensions climax on New Year's Eve, and Jonah, the city bodyguard gone rogue, seems to have an ulterior plan of his own.

"We humans are a hungry lot. We are driven by a craving to know who we are. Yet who we are is embedded in the heart of a holy God. Unless we seek for ourselves in the epicenter of God's grace, we will be forever condemned to walk the arid edges of self-understanding."   – Calvin Miller

CHAPTER 1

"Is this all the men you could get me, Tal? I count only fourteen. I will need at least three times that amount," Randall said, staring down at the young man wearing worn, dirty jeans and a disheveled t-shirt. Randall knew that Tal couldn't be more than twenty years old. He was of Middle Eastern descent and claimed to be a non-practicing Jew. Whatever that meant. Religion was new to Randall, so he had very little understanding of the various religions and their beliefs. He was still trying to understand his personal encounter with this Jesus who forgives. Something inside of him had changed, but he would have to get to that later. Right now, he had an army of men he needed to organize.

"Yes, sir," Tal said. "But I promise I will find more. These men here follow me and are trustworthy."

Randall extinguished the snicker that had suddenly risen in his throat. Tal called these boys lining his living room *men*. They were all boys, even younger than Tal. But boys were easily trained and controlled. This is just the group he needed to start his oil enterprise. These boys had loose family ties and were at the age when they needed to fend for themselves. Randall knew that desperation created loyalty to the right leader.

Randall quickly adjusted the eyepatch over his left eye. Then he paced the living room floor to the right of the line of young men, looking into each face as he passed. White faces, black faces, tan faces—all desperate and all in need of guidance. They would be a piece of cake compared to leading the group of self-important bodyguards back in the city. He walked back to Tal and crossed his arms.

"How long have you worked for my grandfather?" he asked.

"I have known him since I was a boy. My mother cared for him before she died. I took over her duties," Tal said, staring assertively into Randall's eyes.

Randall liked Tal's confidence. He would need it. "Then why is my family's estate in shambles?" Randall asked, sternly.

Tal didn't drop his gaze. "I've had many ideas, but your grandfather would not listen. He only wanted food, water and books—nothing more."

Randall nodded. "Yes, my grandfather is old and stubborn. But I will be running this estate from now on, and we will be expanding. We have only one oil rig working, but there are more that can be fixed." Randall turned his attention to the entire group. "My name is Randall Hunt, and you will call me Sir. I was the lead bodyguard to Neil Elder and Eve Pallue until I got so powerful that they tried to have me killed. You all have heard of me?" he asked, raising his eyebrow.

The young men straightened their stance. Their breaths sucked in, and their eyes shot briefly side-to-side to see the expression of those next to them.

"Good," he continued. "I will not tolerate disobedience of any kind. I have killed worthier men for lesser reasons," he said. "Do you understand?"

The men vigorously nodded their heads.

Randall knew that the men would have eventually found out that he had worked for the World Government and had been declared dead by a factory accident. His family line was easily connected to the World Government. He took a risk by being so forthcoming, but he wasn't about to hide behind a false identity. He was Randall Hunt, bodyguard to Eve Pallue and Neil Elder, and top advisor to the North American Magistrate. In fact, he wanted the World Government to find out that he was alive. He could just imagine the expression of shock and dread on Neil Elder's face when he discovered the truth. A factory accident could never kill Randall Hunt.

Randall continued. "On the other hand, if you work for me and become part of my team, I will make sure you have plenty to eat, a place to stay and you will garner the respect of all the towns around us and beyond. I will teach you how to fight. I will teach you how to get your skinny, pathetic bodies into shape. You will want for nothing. You will be an elite team of soldiers, and everyone will know your names. Is that something you would want?"

Again, the men nodded their heads.

Randall turned his attention to Tal. "Do you have the room assignments for each man in the workers' quarters out back?"

"Yes, sir," Tal said.

"They have today to get settled in. We start drilling tomorrow. Find me men who can fix the oil rigs that are sitting on my land doing nothing. There is a lot more oil out there, and we need to start pumping it."

"I've kept one running," Tal said.

"I know. My grandfather told me," Randall said. "Get your men situated and meet me back here in an hour. We'll drive to the working rig. I have some questions for you."

"Yes, sir," Tal said. The young man turned at the others. "Men, follow me to your new home."

Randall watched the young men pick up their meager belongings and follow Tal through the backdoor of the living room to the old working quarters on an acre of land several hundred feet behind the house. He noted their excited expressions, especially Tal's. He knew the young men anxiously wanted to be a part of something big and important. Randall was like that at Tal's age, and maybe he still was. He was not born to live a simple life. Either in the city or the colonies—he would be a leader of something big. He never thought he would own oil, the only commodity that truly had unlimited value. His old life was gone, but this new life was starting to look up.

"Randall, you really think you can control those boys?" John, his grandfather, asked from the top of the stairs.

Randall looked up. "Did we wake you?"

John slowly walked down each step. "No, my bladder did that."

Randall watched his grandfather make his way to the bottom of the stairs and into the living room. "The boys will be easy to lead. Tal is desperate to be in charge. He'll be a good assistant."

John nodded. "He's a good boy. His mother helped me after your grandmother passed away. You know, it seems like your grandmother only died a few years ago, but it's been closer to ten years now that she's been dead. Tal's mom passed almost two years ago. Time is going by so fast that everything has become a blur."

An image of Randall's grandmother came to his mind. She was a quiet woman, but always treated him kindly.

"Those boys staying in the old quarters out back? You know they're in terrible shape," John admitted.

"From the look of those boys, they'll appreciate any roof over their heads. But I'll tend to every inch of this estate once I get the oil flowing. The first thing on my agenda is to get the security of this estate up to my standard. We need to mend the perimeter walls, get the watchtowers rebuilt and rewire the fence around this property."

"You won't change the inside of the house, will you? Your grandmother prided herself on her interior decorating. It's exactly as she left it," John said.

Randall looked around. "It's exactly how I remember it too. I'll clean it up a bit, but there's no reason to change anything. It's a big house. I'll need to find someone to maintain it."

"Randall, why don't you just find yourself a wife?" John asked. "It's surprising that you're not married yet. But all you Efficientists are strange on families, aren't you? I wouldn't mind seeing some great-grandchildren in my old age."

"I'm not looking to start a new relationship any time soon. I've got too much to do. I'll worry about that when I get our family estate running again," Randall said.

"You better be careful. The World Government is hard pressed for fuel. If they discover our oil, they'll kill us all and absorb our property. That's the only reason I hid the oil from your dad. If he would have discovered it, the World Government would have taken it all for themselves."

"They can't touch us. I know Neil Elder and the limited power he has. The World Government's control is restricted to people plugged into their LPSs and HMSs. They have no actual power except in small pockets. I will create an army that will surpass any mob of government workers they can put together."

John nodded his agreement. "That's true, and the World Government knows it too, which is why they are trying to wield more control over Colonials. They realize that we outnumber them. If we had a leader who would mobilize the colonies, we could easily shake off the government's shackles."

Randall raised his hand. "Grandfather, I'm not here to fight the World Government. The World Government is an idea with a little bit of weight to back it up. I'm not about to usurp that idea with a dictatorship. It's better to leave it all alone."

John walked closer to Randall. Randall could feel the tension in his grandfather's countenance.

"Not a dictatorship. A republic, like we once had in Old America before the fall of the public-school system that started the Second Civil War."

"That republic and its people were entitled. Everyone wanted everything for free and no one wanted to work for anything. They were fat, lazy and not willing to sacrifice an inch."

"But it didn't start that way," John insisted. "It started with sacrifice and belief that we could create a government that offered freedom in a country that respected individual rights. People gave their lives exploring and establishing Old America. I'm reading the journals of Lewis and Clark. These men traveled across unknown lands and documented what they saw and experienced. We live in a frontier once again. We can learn from our mistakes and start again. The future has endless possibility!"

Randall held up both hands this time. "Look, I haven't even established our estate, and you are talking about establishing a new government. You are a dreamer! You should have spent time maintaining this property instead of reading so many books," Randall said, gesturing to the office that held hundreds of books on the wall shelves.

John stepped back. "You sound like your father now."

Randall sighed and scratched his chin. He wanted to move his eyepatch, but he resisted the urge. He needed to get used to wearing it. "Grandfather, I am a man in transition. I'm leaving a lot of skeletons behind and starting this new life with you here. You seem to have no middle ground. You are either a self-absorbed recluse or a World Government saboteur. I just want us to have a good life here in the colonies with oil and a capable army. Let me re-establish the Hunt Estate, and then we will worry about taking down the World Government, alright?"

John stared at Randall for several seconds before speaking. "Maybe I am a dreamer, Randall. But I remember what Old America was like, and it makes this life sad compared to it. In fact, I mourn what I see now!"

Randall walked up to his grandfather and placed his hand on his shoulder. "Let me implement my ideas and see if you don't find the life that I provide agreeable to you."

"Okay, Randall. I'll go along with your plan, but don't forget that I own all this property. I'm not dead yet. And be good to Tal. I've known him since he was a boy."

Randall crossed his arms, so he wouldn't mess with his eyepatch. "Speaking of that, will you ride with us to the working oil rig? I need to learn as much about pumping oil as I can."

John laughed. "You've got a lot to learn. I saw you took a few of my books from the office about drilling for oil last night."

"I know a little bit from my time in the colonies, but I need to study more. Since we only have one oil rig running, I have time to get my bearings."

John hesitated. "I also noticed that you took your grandmother's *Bible*. What do you need that for?"

Randall's face showed no expression. "I lost my eye and almost died. A man who had every right to kill me saved my life instead. He told me about this God-man named Jesus. Something I can't explain happened inside of me. I need to know what that is."

John nodded. "Now you sound like your grandmother. She could never explain this faith thing to me either. Maybe when you figure it out, you'll let me know."

CHAPTER 2

Tal waited outside of the old storage room that Randall had converted into a gym. Randall asked him two days ago for free-weight equipment, and he had come through in record time. This man, Randall Hunt, was smart and confident as a leader. He gave commands fully expecting them to be obeyed. Tal was honored to be his right-hand man, and he would do anything to prove his faithfulness and worth. His loyalty to the elder Mr. Hunt had finally paid off. Tal knew that the old man had a grandson in the city, but he rarely talked about him. Now fate had brought him home.

He peered into the open door once more, seeing if Randall was done with his reps. He didn't want to interrupt him.

"You can come in now," Randall said, as he put the fifty-pound dumbbells back on the rack. "I need a large mirror to hang on the wall. I can't check my form in the window anymore."

"Yes sir," Tal quickly said. "I already know where I can get one."

"Good," Randall said. His shirtless body was soaked in sweat. He sat down on the floor and began to stretch.

"Were you a fighter?" Tal asked. "Only fighters look like you."

Randall laughed. "You can say I was a fighter." He looked back up to Tal. "Is the second rig working?"

"Almost," he answered. "The crew said that it should be working by the end of the day. We found two more oil storage tanks in a village about an hour out. I sent four men to retrieve them for us."

"How about that tanker truck?" Randall asked.

"We have it, but it's not driving yet. Got two men working on the engine now."

Randall nodded. "How are the repairs on the house and fence?"

Tal broke eye contact for a moment to think. "They ran out of paint, so they are making more. The fence has been repaired, and we are adding the razor wire to the top. We will start construction on the watchtowers in the morning. The damage from neglect won't take long to fix."

"I want both of them functional. The one behind the house and the one in front. I want them well-lit too. It's dark out here in the country, and we need to see everything and everyone trying to get onto my land," Randall said before moving his legs forward to stretch his hamstrings.

"Yes sir," Tal said. "I also found the housekeeper you asked for—" he hesitated. He needed to present his words carefully.

Randall looked up. "What is it?"

"Hear me out first. I know everyone in the area, and this woman can be trusted. Her name is Adella. She'll do her work and keep out of sight. She also won't discuss what is going on here. She's desperate for a job, so I know she won't let you down."

Randall got up. "Don't overstep your bounds. I make that kind of call."

"Sorry, sir," Tal said quickly.

Randall grabbed his hand towel and walked over to Tal by the door. "So what's the catch?"

"She'll have to be live in," Tal said.

"That's not a problem. We have plenty of extra rooms in the house."

"And—" Tal hesitated again.

Randall put his hands on his hips. "What is it?"

"Adella has two young daughters, but they are able to work and help her with the chores," Tal said and waited.

Randall crossed his arms and thought for a long moment. "How old are they?"

"Six and eight."

"What happened to their dad?" Randall asked.

Tal shook his head. "Sad story. Adella's husband, Robbie, owns an auto shop in the village. He started chasing other women several years ago, and a few weeks ago, he told his wife and daughters to leave. She's the one who's maintained the auto shop and did the books. I don't know how he's going to run the place without her. She's been staying with a friend and looking for work ever since then."

"She doesn't have family nearby?" Randall asked.

"No, she met her husband when she was young and moved here after they married."

"Where is she now?"

"She's waiting in the kitchen with her girls," Tal said.

"I'm building an oil empire here. Not running a Learning Life Center. I don't need kids getting in my way," Randal said.

"Like you said, you make the call, but you may want to meet her first."

Randall exhaled. "Let me wash off and then send her to my office. The girls can stay in the kitchen."

"I brought your water for washing up to your bathroom," Tal said.

Randall nodded. "Where's my grandfather?"

"He's in the kitchen," Tal said.

"What's he doing there?" Randall asked.

"It looks like he's making the girls lunch," Tal answered.

"Great," Randall said sarcastically.

"Before I leave, can I ask you about our weapon systems we will be using to protect the estate? An invasion may be inevitable."

"You are overstepping your bounds again, Tal," Randall said. "I am the one who thinks and plans. You are the one who carries out my orders. When I want your insight, I will ask you."

"Sorry, sir," Tal said, looking down. He tried to calm the heat rising in his cheeks. He looked at the floor, feeling Randall's stare bearing down on him. Finally, Randall spoke again in a composed voice. "No one will have a gun except me. Bullets are expensive," Randall said.

"Yes, sir," Tal said, keeping his eyes on the ground. "That they are."

"But," Randall began. "I will think of something else for you and the men to use for weapons. You are dismissed."

Tal nodded, never looking up from the floor. He exited the office and made his way to the kitchen. He needed to learn to keep his mouth shut and trust his new boss. This man knew how to command and lead people. He was comfortable making decisions, and Tal wanted to gain as much knowledge and experience as he possibly could. His mom died of ovarian cancer and there was nothing he could do about it except watch her slowly die. He would never allow himself to feel that helpless again.

"Mr. Hunt," a woman's voice said overconfidently.

Randall was looking at a diagram of an oil rig's systems. Simple design, but completely different than anything he's had experience with. "Come in," he said without looking up.

"My name is Adella. Tal found me for the housekeeper position," she said.

Randall looked up and stopped. He had learned long ago to cover up any expression of surprise with a look of disinterest. He said nothing as he stared at the woman in front of him. He was expecting a Colonial, mother type woman to walk into his door, but instead he saw a Spanish beauty. Her thick, curly black hair fell around her face and over her shoulders. Her belted pink blouse and long floral skirt accentuated her feminine curves. She had full lips the same shade as her blouse. More stunningly, though, he beheld large dewdrop-shaped, dark brown eyes. He composed his breathing before talking. "Are you able to clean, cook and mend clothes?" he asked.

"Yes, sir," she stated clearly.

Randall realized that Tal was right: desperation was motivating her out of her shyness.

"I can also garden and preserve food. I can raise chickens and cows and pigs and process them all."

Randall got up from his chair. He wanted a better look at this woman. "Tal tells me you also kept the books at your husband's auto shop?"

"Ex-husband," Adella corrected. "Yes, I did all the accounts."

Randall noted the rebuff and let it slide. He could tell she carried a lot of pain from her ex. "How many employees did you have?"

"We had anywhere from ten to twelve," she said.

"I have five times that many employees, and I will have more soon," he answered.

"I can handle it," she said. "I wanted my ex-husband to expand, but he wouldn't listen to me."

"Too busy chasing other women I heard," Randall said and waited for her reaction.

He watched as her cheeks became crimson. "A fact that became apparent to me only a few months ago."

"But I heard he'd been with other women for years, yet you did nothing," Randall said, pushing her resolve.

"A woman will overlook a lot for the love of her family," she answered simply.

"So you love him?" he asked.

"I loved the man Robbie used to be. I hate the man he is now," she answered.

"Strong words," he said.

Randall noticed that Adella extended her chin slightly. "I am asking the Lord to rid me of my bitterness. He hasn't done it yet."

Randall sat on the edge of his desk. "So you believe in God?"

Adella stared into Randall's eyes, and he could see the spark of determination he was looking for.

"My belief in God is the only reason I am here today," she answered.

"That's good. You'll need it here. I got a rough bunch of boys on this property. You alone are sole protector of your girls. I will tell the men not to touch or harm you or them, but there is no way I can be responsible for every man."

"I understand," she said.

Randall stood back up and walked around to his chair once more. "What are your daughters' names?" he asked before sitting down.

"Alexandria and Anastasia," she said. "But I call them Alex and Ana."

Randall could see a motherly tenderness flood her face.

"Do you teach them?" Randall asked.

"Yes," she answered. "I would like to teach them after my morning chores and before dinner."

"You will teach them as long as you get everything done," he answered. He looked back at the oil rig diagram on his table. He couldn't think about a woman right now. There was too much work to be done.

"So, I have the job?" she asked.

"Yes," he said. "So long as you keep those girls out of the way. You will start tomorrow. I want breakfast before the sun is up and dinner before the sun goes down. You will be preparing food for my grandfather, Tal and me. You and your girls can have what's leftover."

"What about the other men?" she asked.

"They are making their own arrangements. You are to serve this house only," he said, keeping his eyes on the paper.

"Where are we staying?" she asked.

Randall noted the shyness returning to her voice.

"There is an apartment in the basement with two rooms, a bathroom and a small kitchen. You will stay there. If your girls are not working, they need to be down there."

"Yes, sir," she whispered.

Randall heard her pause. "Is there anything else?"

"I have a German shepherd. He is housebroken and loyal and he protects the girls. My friend has said she would keep him, but I would like him to stay here with me. He is very protective of us."

Randall dropped the page and looked back at the woman. "You ask a lot. I am barely offering you this job as it is."

She straightened her shoulders. "I only ask because I think you will like him. He is watchful and will make noise if he hears any intruders at night. If he knows that I have made this place my home, he will protect it."

Randall sighed. "What is his name."

"The girls named him Favian," she answered.

"Fine," he said. "But if Favian messes in my house, I will shoot him myself."

CHAPTER 3

Tal leaned over his truck's engine and put the oil cap back on. It wasn't a new truck, but it was his. Randall bought it for him, so he could better do his job. Tal smiled to himself and swiped back his disheveled, dark hair from his face with the back of his arm. Randall was depending on him more and more. He had even given Tal a room next to his is grandfather's room upstairs. The old man was up all through the night, but Tal didn't mind. He was out of the quarters in the back where the rest of Randall's men slept. Tal was officially the second in command, and he would make sure that it stayed that way. He would outperform everyone else to remain Randall's right-hand man. It was an opportunity that he knew was a gift. His mother would be so proud of him if she were still alive. He would have bought her something nice to celebrate.

A brush against his leg startled him out of his thoughts. He looked down. It was Favian, the large German shepherd brought here by Adella. The yellow and black fur of the dog was thick, and Tal was sure he appreciated the cool wind that blew in this week.

"What do you want?" Tal said, kneeling and petting the dog. The dog had proven to be useful. His ears captured every noise in the house at night, and he would run up from the basement where he slept with Adella and the girls and bark the alarm. Two opossums had crawled through a torn screen of a kitchen window, and Favian attacked them before they created too much damage. Tal watched Randall's expression that night as he inspected Favian's work. He didn't say anything, but his nod of approval spoke volumes. That was another point for Tal, since he was the one who suggested Adella for the housekeeper position in the first place.

"We're bored," he heard a young girl's voice say. He looked down. It was Alex and Ana standing side by side looking expectantly at him.

"Where's your mother?" he asked, amused. They were never bored with their mom at home. She would have them sweeping the grass if it kept them occupied.

"She went into town with Randall. They're picking up stuff for the house—linens, towels—you know, boring stuff," Alex said. Out of the two, Alex looked most like her mother—tan skin, dark eyes and curly black hair. Tal guessed she was around seven or eight years old. Ana looked more like her father. She had light brown hair, blue eyes and pale skin sprinkled with freckles. She was about five or six years old. Both girls were pretty, and they had enough features in common to look enough like sisters.

"Grandpa John was supposed to watch us, but he fell asleep in the living room reading his book. Now we are bored," Ana chimed in. "What are you doing?"

Tal grabbed the hand towel he tucked into the waist of his jeans and wiped the oil off his hands. "You are not supposed to leave the house, but since you are here, you see this truck? This is mine, so I'm changing the oil and making sure the engine is running smoothly."

"Wow," the girls said simultaneously.

"Mr. Hunt gave me this truck because I am very important to him, and he knows it will help me do my job better," Tal said, straightening his shoulders.

"Mom says that she's known you since my age," Alex said. "I can't imagine you being so young since you are so important, but I guess important people have to be young at least once."

"Yes, we do," he said smiling. He looked up to see where the sun was. It was still high in the horizon. He had a little time to kill before Randall would be back. "You see the top of my truck there," he pointed.

Both girls nodded their heads.

"I'm going to put roof lights on it. I've already traded for them. Just need to pick them up and install them. And you know what else?" he said, eyeing the girls seriously.

"What?" they said wide-eyed.

"I've already installed the best speakers money can buy. You want to hear them? I just so happen to have my favorite CD ready."

The girls nodded excitedly.

"Listen to this," he said and walked to the driver's side door and got in. He started the engine, and music blared out of the speakers.

The girls squealed with delight and began dancing around the truck. Tal watched them and laughed. Maybe music would keep them occupied for a while. He watched them dance for three songs, wanting to join them but repressing the childish impulse. He was twenty years old and too old to be dancing around where anyone could see him. But he did enjoy watching the girls' free and exuberant movements. Favian trotted around the truck with them, yelping and jumping along. The scene reminded him of when he was young and without care, living here under Mr. Hunt's roof with his mother. He was finally back in the house where he belonged, but now he was not a kid. He was a very important part of an oil enterprise.

He looked back up at the sun and frowned. Maybe it was later than he thought. He needed to see about the cows and chickens that were supposed to be delivered this week. They had chosen the land behind the workers' quarters, and several men were prepping the area. He turned off the truck, and the girls' dancing abruptly stopped. He jumped out of the driver's side to sad, little faces looking up at him. Even Favian looked upset.

"Tal, please let us dance a little longer to your music," Alex begged. "We are having so much fun."

Tal hesitated.

"Please, Tal," Ana pleaded.

Tal thought for a moment. "I have an idea!" he said and went back to the truck and leaned in. When he retrieved what he was looking for, he walked back to the girls. "Here," he said, handing a shiny CD to Alex. "This is my music. Why don't you play it on my portable CD player in my room? You can take it to the basement and bring it back to me at dinner. Just don't listen too long. The batteries for it are expensive."

Alex took the CD. "We will just play the songs we haven't heard yet. Promise," she said, holding the CD carefully.

"And don't go snooping about my room," he said, looking stern. He didn't have anything to hide, but he liked showing his importance. He wasn't a kid anymore. He was second in command.

"We would never do that," Ana said, seriously. "Mommy says we can't touch anything in the house without permission."

"Well, you have my permission to get my CD player. Now go! I have work to do. And stay in the house and keep Favian close. Your Grandpa John doesn't seem to be in the babysitting mood today."

"Yes, sir!" the girls said and ran back up to the porch and into the house. Favian was right behind them.

Tal put his hands on his hips enjoying the moment. It felt good to be admired. He couldn't help but think of how lucky he was. His mother wouldn't have said it was luck. She would say it was God. Although she was of Jewish decent, she really didn't follow the rules. She always said that God would understand. Being poor and a single mother made following the religious rules almost impossible. Either way, he felt pretty good. Maybe if there was a God, He was repaying him for all that he had lost. He had lost a lot in his twenty years of life, but that was all in the process of changing.

CHAPTER 4

Ada stared down at her Portable, trying not to bite her lower lip. Her makeup was perfect, and she didn't want to smudge the lipstick. The camera could be brutal on a face not done up properly. She glanced at the entrance to the roped-off area for the paparazzi. Several people had left for lunch. The World News left a cameraman with a sandwich in case someone arrived.

Ada frowned and looked back at her Portable. She swiped through several pages of faces and bios on the screen who were due to come this week. The last several *Grand Opus* representatives had been boring mathematicians and scientists. The space scientist had amazing ideas and theories of space travel, but none of it could be seen visually, except with computer graphics. People were not interested in theories. They wanted a front row seat to the lives of fascinating people with extreme personalities. These mathematicians and scientists were too imbedded in the World Government to stand out.

Ada looked around her. The old, dated building had been transformed into the *Grand Opus Gala* building. The crew were still finishing up the finer details—and there were many of those to address—but the noise of construction was minimal. She had recently become an expert in the Regency Era, even discussing ideas with a historian who had been chosen as one of the *Grand Opus* representatives. His field of study was mainly historical monarchies, but he was able to give her some valuable insights.

The crew worked like buzzing bees around her. They were quiet because they knew she needed silence in case a representative showed up and she had to do an interview. She turned around and looked at the three crystal chandeliers that were donated by the European magistrate. Just looking at them cheered her up. They were the final piece in making her vision come to fruition. The hand-carved wood paneling from the African magistrate came in early that week. The crew were busily securing the paneling between the seams of champagne-colored wallpaper and gilded paint that she had chosen. Although Neil Elder had donated the building to the *Grand Opus Gala*, he paid for the gold and wine-colored window coverings. They were thick, multi-layered and lavish, costing tens of thousands of money points. They matched the large, elaborate area rugs and crushed-velvet furnishings gifted from the Asian magistrate.

Ada looked back at the entrance. Some of the paparazzi were returning from lunch. All the furnishings in the world would not maintain the popularity of the gala. She needed someone to boost her waning poll numbers. Less and less people were logging into their HMSs and LPSs to see what was going on. She had six weeks to change history and to open the way for wonder and beauty to come back into *Life Efficiency* and the World Government. Production left little to live for and making people pretty for PR events was no longer a satisfactory career for her.

"There's a Colonial truck coming!" one of the paparazzi yelled.

Ada strained her neck to see out of the entrance. A truck pulled up next to the curb in front of the building and came to a stop. She couldn't make out the people inside. She stared back down at her Portable. The only Colonial left was supposed to have arrived several days ago: the Shaman. Ada turned off her Portable and tucked it under her arm. She straightened her corduroy light blue suit jacket and fluffed her knee-length floral skirt. She was trying to blend textures in her ensemble, but she felt insecure with the floral and corduroy. She would make up for it in her show of confidence.

She heard the noise of the paparazzi grow louder and saw several reporters and photographers running from all directions toward the truck. Something was happening. She could feel the excitement coming from the growing crowd along the roped area of the entrance. She looked toward one of the bodyguards and snapped her fingers. "Stop staring and get out there!"

"Yes, ma'am," he stammered and walked quickly to the door.

Ada put on her best poised smiled and walked smartly toward the entrance. The cameras flashed toward her as she got closer. They were wanting to get her reaction, so she needed to milk every second of this moment. She reached the door and couldn't help but allow her smile to lengthen. There was the Shaman. His Mohawk had been replaced with smooth, black hair with strands of silver pulled back in a long braid down his back. *Perfect*, she thought. He looked angry. *Even better.*

The cameras were flashing in his face and he stood on the sidewalk with his arms crossed in front of the passenger door of his truck. He wore a charcoal-colored outfit that she had never seen before. It looked comfortable and loose enough to allow movement. *Probably for fighters*, she mentally noted. She would have a line of these outfits ready by the end of the week. The paparazzi moved around her like whirling wind, and she eased into the crisp, winter air of the city like a queen. She stood in front of the intimidating man and said nothing for several seconds, allowing the intensity of the moment to build. The Shaman's native American features had become more distinct as he had aged. He was still handsome and fit, but there was more of a matured wisdom to him that had replaced some of the boyish cockiness she had noticed in his fighting videos.

"You must be the Shaman," Ada said. She did not shake his hand. She could tell that he was in no mood for common niceties.

"My name is *Cabena Sa Ne'aw-ze*," he said without hesitation. "In the *Ka'to* language of my people, this means *Fighting Bear*. But you will call me Bear. I am no longer the Shaman."

Ada felt a chill run through her body. Mystery. Novelty. And confidence. Everything needed to strum the chords of people's curiosity. She knew if she could be wowed by this man then everyone would be. She wondered how many people were logging into the *Grand Opus Gala* site at this very moment to watch. She glanced briefly to the right, noticing that her own cameraman had made it back with lunch still on his shirt.

"My apologies, Bear. There has been very little information about your current life over the last several years. I will update my records. We were expecting your arrival three days ago."

Bear nodded. "Yes, my truck wouldn't start, and I needed to wait until I found the part I needed."

"Well," she smiled. "I know that things like that happen in the colonies. I am glad you made it despite the trouble. Would you care to make a statement to our live viewers?"

Bear looked at the cameras flashing around him like he was just now noticing them. "Yes," he said, staring at each camera in turn. "I am not here for fame or riches. I left that life behind. I'm only here because I was summoned by the World Government. Stay away from me and my family when I am not working or I will break you and your camera."

Instantly, flashes exploded, and paparazzi yelled out questions.

Ada took the moment free from the cameras to grin. Bear was exactly what she was waiting for. She noticed that the crowd included many Efficientists who had gathered on the street. They should have been working, but they were watching her work instead. She took her Portable into her hands and turned it on. The World News yelled out questions, but Bear did not answer a single question.

"I see that you are bringing your wife," Ada said when the crowd quieted their unanswered questions.

She watched as Bear's countenance became rigid. "I am trying to get my wife out of the truck, but the crowd needs to leave!"

Ada looked in through the passenger window for the first time. She couldn't make out a face. Something was blocking her view. If his wife was half as interesting as Bear, she had hit the jackpot.

Ada looked to the bodyguard, relieved that another one had joined him. She motioned them to come over. "Get the crowd back, both of you."

The bodyguards split up. One went right and the other left, waving their arms and pushing the crowd back. The cameras continued to flash.

"More!" Bear yelled. "Move back!"

Now this was interesting, Ada thought. He's protecting her.

When Bear was satisfied. He kept his eyes on the crowd as he reached back and opened the door.

The air in Ada's lungs instantly left her. A masked woman exited the truck. Ada's eyes scanned her outfit and promptly analyzed the fabric, stitching and textures. There was so much to take in. Her face was completely hidden behind a mask which made Ada think of Italy during a time long passed. She would have to resurrect the theme. She saw exquisite beading, ornate textures and exotic feathers. The wife wore a long black chenille skirt. Ada squinted her eyes and stared at the material. The thick fabric was bustled in the back with gorgeous, gold stitching. The woman's top was black lace over solid gold fabric. It was shining in the afternoon light. Ada went through a list of fabrics in her mind. *Wool satin*. It had to be wool satin. She could spot cheap polyester in an instant. Ada stood speechless even as the woman stood next to her husband.

The cameras flashed in her face, and she knew the paparazzi had captured her amazement. Hopefully, that would turn out to be a good move. She quickly smiled.

"Welcome—" she floundered. She had forgotten the woman's name. She didn't think the Shaman's wife would be of much importance.

"Her name is Ruth," Bear said. "Now please show us to our room."

"So pleased to meet you!" Ada said. She walked over to the woman, surprised at how small she was. Ada wrapped her arm around the woman's slender arm and began to lead the way. "Will you join us, Bear?"

Bear nodded and walked on the other side of his wife. "Everything in the bed of the truck needs to come to our room."

"I'll get my men right on that," Ada said and turned to the woman. "Ruth, let me show you what we've done so far to the *Grand Opus* building. I can tell a woman with your tastes will appreciate all the effort, time and money that has been poured into the *Grand Opus Gala* so far. I must confess that I adore your ensemble. Who created it?" Ada asked. She needed to know if someone from the city or colonies created such an amazing outfit. She didn't think she had competition in the city, but the professionalism of the outfit had her second-guessing herself.

"I designed and sewed it myself," the woman said in a proficient, yet soft voice that did not sound very Colonial.

Ada smiled. "Perfect," she said smiling to herself. Now she could manufacture and sell this ensemble on her own line.

CHAPTER 5

Ruth and Bear allowed themselves to be led by Ada into the building. Ruth looked at her husband. His face was stoic, but she saw him fidget with the pearl strung with nylon around his neck a few times. The pearl represented their wedding vows. She felt for hers too. It seemed like a lifetime ago when she was at the World Bank with Jonah, and the pearl necklace broke. God knew what was about to happen later that very day. Her home and life would go up in flames, and those pearls would be like a deposit into her future. It was only fitting that she and her husband wore them now in the city during the *Grand Opus Gala*, the World Government's desperate attempt to appease the backlash to *Life Plethoricity*. She allowed a small smile to form on her lips. Her name would never be tied to that ridiculous life plan. *Thank you, Lord*, she thought to herself.

Ruth felt Ada's walk suddenly stop and she looked around the foyer of the building. As she gaped, her eyes took it all in, and her brain examined and categorized every inch. "The Regency Era," she whispered.

Ada grinned. "Finally, someone who truly knows and appreciates my work! Tell me, truly, does it resemble what a Georgian heiress would have done in her estate? I swear I was born in the wrong century. This New America is bland and boring. No beauty. No extravagance. Well, that is all about to change!"

Ruth stopped and looked at Ada from behind her mask. "Neil Elder has allowed this? It goes against *Life Efficiency*."

Ada tilted her head back and laughed. "Oh, I just love you already. If the cameras weren't watching us from outside, I

34

would take off your mask to see the expression on your sweet face. Positively shocked, I'm sure!"

Ada unwrapped her arm from Ruth's and stood in front of the couple like she was on stage performing a drama. She waited for a beat while they both watched her.

"The polls are everything. They are the only thing that truly give the World Government power. If the people aren't happy, they begin to walk away from their LPS monitors. Neil realized that we need something to get the people, Efficientists and Colonials, plugged back in, and I am giving them the splendor and grandeur of the *Grand Opus Gala*," Ada said, extending her arms in a theatrical wave.

She looked back toward them and leaned in like she had a secret to share. "You know, I was going to give the Shaman—I mean Bear—one of the small, bland rooms. You both being Colonials and all. But I can tell that you two are learned and cultured Colonials. I have a boring violinist coming in today with his wife, who is simply a snooze. How about—" Ada said, taking her Portable into both hands. "I swap his room for yours? It is double the size and oh so stunning!"

"We are simple people," Bear said. "We don't need anything fancy."

Ruth instantly turned to Bear. "But I would like to have the bigger room if available," she turned back to Ada. "I guarantee that I will appreciate the design, and I could use the extra space for my sewing equipment."

"Will you be sewing more while you are here?" Ada asked.

Ruth hesitated. "I would like to make another masquerade mask and a wardrobe to fit the themes of your events. We will be here for more than a month, and I would not like to wear the same outfit more than once."

Ada shot her palms to her face with a gasp. Ruth could see her eyes glistening tears. "Ruth! You are reading my very soul! We need that spirit. You are who I've been waiting for.

You are my muse for the First Annual *Grand Opus Gala.* The other Efficientists will see your creativity and dedication, and they too will begin to open their hearts and minds to the beauty of what I'm trying to achieve. Yes! Yes! The room is yours. You are more deserving," she exclaimed and wound her arm back around Ruth's and continued walking. "And I love the mask idea. It will add a touch of imagination. You are more alluring when we don't actually know who you are—probably a history teacher at one of those small Colonial schools or something," she said. "I could find no information about the Shaman's wife, but I am beyond thrilled by you so far!"

Ruth turned her head to look behind her and watched as Bear rolled his eyes and followed. She knew he did not favor the attention but coming back to the city had given her something she was not expecting. She felt free from the heavy constraints of her father. She no longer had to perform to keep rank. She could for the first time enjoy the city with no expectation or limits. She would indeed boost the poll ratings, but it would be on her own terms. Ruth was in complete control of her image, and no one—not even Ada Armel—could tell her what to do.

"The elevators are right down here. I have already switched your names to your new room. The view is breathtaking. You will be on the eighth floor facing the city— number 818. Just look into the camera and the security will let you in."

"What is in there?" Ruth asked, noticing a few workers enter through doors across from the elevators. She could hear construction noise coming from within.

Ada stopped and thought dramatically, biting her lip. "I guess I can show you," she said in a hushed voice. When she reached the double doors, she pushed them open simultaneously. "Come in. It's not done yet, but we are scheduled to have our first dinner and dance here next week. I call it the Gala Hall, and it is the most exquisite ballroom! I found a dance team from the colonies, and they do the most stunning performance. I doubt any of the other guests will dance, but I will have the dance floor ready. Maybe I'll add ballroom dancing lessons to get these boring Efficientists on their feet."

Ruth walked into the room. The ballroom emulated the foyer, but with more pomp and décor. "I recognize this building as Arthur Pallue's. He did not have this ballroom before, did he?" Ruth asked.

"Of course not! That old bore was completely opposed to dancing. I tore down some of the second-floor rooms and designed a ballroom that would make King George IV stand in awe," Ada said, crossing her arms and looking at the large, circular room with fresh eyes. "I amaze even myself."

Ruth looked down. "The floors are different from the foyer."

"They are mahogany wood," Ada squealed. "And I've hired an artist to chalk the floors with a stunning design for my VIP list. And that reminds me," Ada said, looking back at her Portable. "I need to add you and Bear's names to the list. You must be my VIPs!"

"White chalk only?" Ruth asked.

Ada looked up. "No, my design has many colors. Just white would be too bland."

"The ladies of the Regency Era would use white chalk so not to stain the dresses of the attendees," Ruth said.

"Really?" Ada asked, looking back at her Portable, scrolling through different images. "I don't have that in my notes. I must have missed it. White chalk only. That makes complete sense," she said, busily typing new notes. She looked back at Ruth. "I must pick your historian brain before I make plans. You know all about Old America! There is an LPS in your room with limited access. I will contact you there with questions that I may have if I'm too busy to see you personally."

Ada put her Portable back under her arm. "Well, then. I will take you to the elevator. It is getting late, and I have a PR event tonight. I'll let you two get settled in. I'm sure you want to take off that mask," she motioned to Ruth. "I think your allure will help your husband's chances at being picked as the most notable contestant of *Grand Opus Gala*! We shall see. It's all about the poll ratings, of course."

"Thank you," Bear said brusquely. "We will find our way from here."

"Yes, you're right," Ada said. "I am running out of time and the cameras are still rolling." She looked at Bear and replaced her smile with a firm, no-nonsense look. "Just so you know, I have planted surveillance cameras everywhere in this building, so no one comes or goes without my knowledge. My reputation is on the line, and I will have no one rain on my parade, as the expression goes."

"Don't worry. I'm not planning on doing anything besides getting this gala over with and taking my wife away from this city forever."

Ruth looked at her husband through the mask. She could see that he was tired from the travel, and the public relations duties were wearing on him. She wondered if he would last the several weeks they had left in the city.

"And you, my dear," Ada said turning to Ruth, "are my Gala Muse. I will write up a little article about you tonight to tantalize the palate of all our viewers. And I look forward to seeing your next ensemble. I am sure you will not disappoint me."

"Will there be cameras in our room?" Ruth asked.

"Of course not!" Ada exclaimed. "We value the privacy of our guests. We have cameras in the hallways, but never would we invade your privacy. I better go. Lots to be done! Oh, and Ruth, if you need any material for clothes or shoes or anything at all, contact me. I'll make sure to get you everything you need. I'm sending my LPS link to your LPS now." Ada held up her Portable and briskly typed a few keys.

"Thank you," Ruth said. "I will enjoy having more material to work with."

"I know you will!" Ada blew a kiss to the couple and turned, walking importantly to the door of the Gala Hall and disappeared into the foyer.

"They have cameras everywhere," Bear said, looking around.

"Everything we do and say will be monitored outside of our room," Ruth added.

"Let's get to our room," he said. "I'm exhausted and we only just arrived."

Ruth allowed her eyes to survey the ballroom once more. She wondered how her life would be different if her father had allowed beauty and creativity into her world. She felt a twinge of jealousy for Ada's accomplishments. She designed the most stunning room that Ruth had ever beheld. Ruth adjusted the mask on her face. "I am not exhausted," she said, allowing Bear to take her hand. "In fact, I am in the mood to design a new dress."

CHAPTER 6

Neil Elder held the short glass of amber liquid in his hands and listened to Matt Coughlin debrief him on the events of the day. He slowly sipped the whiskey, knowing his limit was almost up. He couldn't help but grit his teeth when Matt mentioned Ada's gala work. He may have to exceed Dr. Linton's restriction on his alcohol consumption that night. He almost wished he hadn't fed into Ada's superfluous ideals, but at least all the ruckus she was creating distracted the World News from the mess of the *Unum Vernum* debacle and *Life Plethoricity*. His ratings had actually inched up a few points from their plummeting decline—though, he now realized that he would probably never reach the zenith of Eve Pallue's ratings and money points.

He regretted having Eve killed so soon. He should have bided his time and watched to see how her new life plan played out. If he would have been more patient, she would be the one to blame for all the Efficientists dropping rank. Production among the Efficientists who stayed in the city was also low. He would have liked to see her squirm as she realized her life plan was based on speculative theory that had no basis in real life. Neil smirked behind the glass as he brought it back to his lips. She was supposedly the first native speaker of T-variety. What a lie. He remembered seeing her speak to her mother in Long English when she just two years old. Her entire life was made up of deceit *threaded* together by her father, Arthur Pallue, to make his ideal society seem as perfect as he claimed it to be. If every person was productive, all the world's problems would disappear. What a joke. Now where were his lofty ideas and his life's work? Burned up in a fire. Yet, the fire freed Arthur Pallue and his daughter from the responsibility of *Life Plethoricity*. That was now on him. Eve's premature death had backfired in his face.

It was all Randall's fault. He was the one who talked him into destroying Eve in the fire so soon. Randall had been dismissed by Eve in both love and work, and he used slick words to get his revenge approved. Why had he been a sucker for Randall's words of deception? Never again would he let his desire for control override caution. It wasn't worth it. At least Randall was no longer a threat. Neil had gotten the final say on him. Ted Stanton, the officer in charge of one of the colonial forced labor camps, assured him that Randall had been taken care of.

"Good riddance, Randall Hunt," Neil whispered under his breath.

"Pardon," Jonah said, stopping his stream of words.

"It's nothing. Just thinking about some other business," Neil said. "Now about Dr. Linton. He's been fairly close to me these last several months. Are you sure we should send him away? And where do you plan to send him?"

Neil watched Matt adjust his thoughts. He was an intimidating, watchful man with an innocence that belied his work. Bodyguards were not innocuous, yet Matt walked in integrity, which was rare. Matt had even risked his life to save him, taking a knife into the chest for him. Yet he almost seemed too perfect, but his background check came out clean. Actually, it was more than clean. It was immaculate.

"I want to send him to the factory at Trinity."

Neil hesitated. "The same factory that Zach Daniels worked at?"

"Yes, I believe something is happening in that village. It is close enough to the city that Efficientists may be gathering there. Charlie Liu must have met Zach Daniels in the factory there or somewhere around that village. I have a gut feeling that Trinity will lead us to the very people who have been attacking the World Government systems."

Neil gulped the last of his drink and set down the glass. "But the attacks have stopped. Ada's gala is distracting the masses. Even the incessant faith writings from the so-called Faith Movement have stopped. Should we worry about a threat that is no longer there?"

"I don't believe the threat is gone. It is only resting and building strength. Things are a little too quiet, which is why we need Dr. Linton's help."

Neil stared at Matt. His concern was evident. "Like the quiet before a storm. You are probably right. This gala could be a distraction for them or an opportunity, but how can Dr. Linton help us?" Neil reached over and poured another two ounces into his glass. With Dr. Linton gone, he didn't have to be so restricted after all.

"We send him to Trinity. He is an observant man who doesn't play sides, which will be to our benefit if he discovers a plot to attack the World Government."

"How could that benefit us?" Neil asked, taking another sip.

"All Dr. Linton wants is to live in his cottage outside of the city and retire. If he discovers a plot against the World Government, he will have the leverage he needs to leave *Life Efficiency* forever. I think that man worked hard all his life to get where he is now, but now that he's here, he wants nothing more than to leave."

Neil looked away and cleared his throat. He had similar feelings for being a magistrate. Not at all as powerful and attractive as he once believed. "How much of this plan does Dr. Linton know?"

"He knows nothing. He's merely the fish on the end of a long line. He may think he's free, but he's not. We'll reel him in eventually. Until then, he'll swim around and gather all the information we need."

"I didn't take you as a fishing man," Neil laughed.

The large, dark man stopped. A menacing expression spread across his face that caused the hair on Neil's arm to stand straight up. But before Neil could examine Matt's countenance further, his normal inoffensive expression swept back, causing Neil to question what he really had seen.

"I fished long ago in another life. But that's history. What we need to do now is focus on protecting the World Government from an imminent threat."

"Fine," Neil swept his hand and leaned back into his couch. "Dr. Linton is harmless. We'll use him as bait, but I seriously doubt Charlie Liu and Zach Daniels are still in Trinity. With all those jewels you let them steal from Eve Pallue's vault at the World Bank, they probably purchased a villa somewhere in Central America and are living in luxury off of cheap Colonial labor."

"Maybe," Jonah said. "But it's better to move with caution than assume too much. If we send Dr. Linton to Trinity, he'll find them if they're still there. And if they are, they are definitely planning something. We just need to find out how and when."

Neil eyed Matt momentarily. It's like they were both looking at the same puzzle, but Matt saw more of the pieces. Or did he see more of the puzzle? "If we do find an attempt to attack the World Government's systems, it would have to come from multiple sites around the world and hit all at the same time. There's no way those two have that much skilled manpower."

"Efficientists have been dropping rank ever since *Life Plethoricity* was established as the new life plan," Jonah countered. "All they have to do is recruit them. They're obviously disgruntled with the World Government at this point. I doubt it will take too much convincing."

"But most of them are lower Efficientists. They can't hack into our systems," he said irritably, not liking Matt's insistence.

"Yes, but they are easily trained, aren't they?"

"Then why don't we just send some men to kill them. If Randall were here, he would have Zach and Charlie gone by tomorrow," Neil said, getting up from the couch. He didn't like this conversation. It made him feel powerless. He waited for Matt's reply and examined his face. There was not an ounce of indecision.

"That's where Randall and I differ. If we take out those two men now, their plan can still continue. It is better to root out the threat, not the hands that carry it out."

"Fine. Tell me how and when they plan on attacking—if there is indeed an attack—and we will find a way to stop it."

"That is my fear," Jonah pushed. "What if we can't stop it?"

Indignation filled Neil's voice. "I will *always* have the final say. If there is an attempt to attack, and I find it serious enough, I will use the Kill Switch. It will reboot the entire system, and the attack will crumble."

Jonah shook his head. "But you can't use the Kill Switch. It's never been tested. We don't know what will happen."

"You see, that's where you're wrong," Neil said, savoring the feeling of power once more. He saw more of the puzzle than Matt, after all. In fact, he saw all of it. "Arthur Pallue did use the Kill Switch over fifteen years ago when the World Government's systems were weak and vulnerable. He had to use it because the Efficientist Christian Sect infiltrated the World News with their propaganda. Once the switch turned back on, the entire system rebooted like nothing ever happened. The Apostle and that despicable Sect lost everything they built because only what's approved by the World Government can remain once the system reboots. Everything else falls away."

"But there is no information about this incident in the World Government records," Jonah persisted.

Neil waited a beat, soaking in the memory. "I was the one Arthur Pallue ordered to pull the switch. I saw the system reboot with my own eyes."

"You were the prison director in charge of it?" Jonah asked.

"Indeed, I was. And I know it will work."

"But as you said, that was when the World Government's systems were weaker. Now we are strong, and we have the Regional Integrated Banking System under our jurisdiction. We don't know what rebooting will do to the money points."

Neil thought a minute. "If the RIBS are part of the World Government's systems now, they should reboot. But you are right. I wouldn't use the Kill Switch unless I had no other choice." He felt drained and his adrenaline was wearing off too quickly. "Plus, I'd have to get the okay from the other nine magistrates unless I had tangible proof that a reboot was absolutely necessary because of immediate threats. There's no sense worrying them about events that are only theory at this point."

He walked back to the couch and sat down. He'd have to call Ted Stanton in the morning. The Kill Switch was in the tower of the forced labor camp. Thinking of the prison sent a sudden surge of guilt through his stomach. He chased away the gruesome images that bombarded his mind and focused on what he needed to do next. Definitely, the security of the prison needed to be beefed up. Also, he would send out a small team from the scientists assigned to monitor the Kill Switch at all times. They needed to go to the physical location and ensure everything was in working order. He eyed Matt who was awaiting his next command. He was an asset, but he didn't need to know everything. He would keep the most valuable pieces of the puzzle to himself.

"Send Dr. Linton to Trinity and keep me informed of what he finds. Tell him not to waste time. The faster he gets that information for me, the faster he'll be able to go back to that petty cottage of his and to his small existence."

Jonah left Neil Elder's flat. He did not look at the video cameras mounted to the wall as he passed them in the hallway. He made his way to the elevator while watching his shoes step across the plush carpet. He feared the emotions on his face would belie the façade of indifference he kept fixed over his true feelings. Being called by the name, Matt Coughlin, conjured up painful images from his past. The real Matt Coughlin would be proud of what he was doing. However, Jonah knew that many more details needed to fall into place. If he thought about how impossible his plan really was and how many variables he needed to consider, he may be tempted to circumvent what God was wanting him to do.

The worst part of it was that he was all alone. There was no one he could trust—at least, not yet. He wished Christina Straight was still with him. She had been a pilar of patience and trust. But now it was his turn to be steady and remain faithful. He would never have it all figured out. Instead, he would ask God what he needed to do at the beginning of each day. And right now he needed to remember who he truly was.

He pushed the elevator button to go down. He waited as the elevator made its way up to the top floor. He muttered under his breath and only the discerning could read what his lips were mouthing: *I am Jonah Goodman the Third. I am Jonah Goodman the Third. I am Jonah Goodman the Third.* He continued mouthing his identity as he entered the elevator. Once the doors closed, he whispered the words repeatedly while no one could hear.

CHAPTER 7

Thomas Isaacs organized his desk for the second time. He had just turned off his HMS and was considering several correspondences he had read and quickly erased. He got up and began to pace. He once wrote all his thoughts down on lists that he would keep around his home and office, but he couldn't risk writing things down anymore. Someone could easily find his thoughts written out on paper and spill the information to the World Government. Instead, he had begun to recite his thoughts out every day. He memorized all the old details and would add the new ones to memory. The information that didn't matter anymore would be taken out of his memory list.

"Okay," he said aloud as he continued pacing. "Ruth has written stacks of articles that have created a faith movement within *Life Efficiency*, which continues the work of the Apostle—or Christina Straight—the Life Therapist who led Ruth to Christ. Many Efficientists have left rank because of her words and the implementation of *Life Plethoricity*—which Ruth also wrote." He stopped and smiled and looked up at the ceiling. "God, You always give us a chance to make things right."

He continued. "Then Neil Elder tried to force a World Religion on all of us, the *Unum Vernum*, the *One All*—or should I say the *One None* now. This abomination gathered bits and pieces of all the world's religions and tried to sew them up in a nice, tidy package. Well, that backfired in his face, didn't it?"

Tom stopped pacing and thought of Li, the other Elite Efficientist who God sent to Trinity. "Li just nabbed that atrocity right out from under Neil's nose. God knew we would need him. So to make up for the *Unum Vernum*, Neil gave Ada Armel the green light to create the first annual *Grand Opus Gala*. An event that brings a hundred of the most talented and interesting Efficientists from across the ten regions together. Well, only ninety of them because Ada surprised us all by allotting ten spots to Colonials—one of whom happens to be Bear."

He continued pacing again. "Bear and Ruth are in the city for the gala that's happening over six weeks, and there is a little over five weeks left. And Ruth is pregnant..." He shook his head and laughed. "I would have never imagined Ruth and Bear to be married and expecting a baby. What are the odds of the top elite Efficientist and a colonial circuit fighter marrying? Only God could have arranged that marriage."

"Next," he continued. "Esther has a house full of Efficientists who have dropped rank and now live at the ranch. The house guests are learning the basic skills of life in the colonies, and the sisters are doing a wonderful job at teaching them. Esther and Deborah's time as foster moms have really helped them with dealing with Efficientists who can be temperamental and not at all happy about cleaning, cooking and gardening. But there is a wealth of expertise and information there that we can tap into once they learn to trust us."

"What's next?" He paused and thought. "Pilar was kidnapped by Randall Hunt and brought to a factory where we discovered that Neil Elder has been using his power in the World Government to implement forced labor camps because of an oil shortage."

He leaned over his desk and placed his knuckles hard against the wood top. He felt his jaw tighten, so he rolled his head trying to relax the tension in his neck. "I can't let my emotions get the best of me. Now is not the time to lament. It is the time to plan."

He pushed off the table and straightened. "I think most Efficientists have no idea about the labor camps, but it won't stay a secret for long. It's just a whisper and rumor now, but I'll figure out a way to tell people the truth."

"And what about Randall? Zach saved his life and shared the Gospel with him. Don't know if he truly had a heart change, though. He took the truck and his gun and vanished. I researched as much as I could about him and discovered that his grandfather owns a ranch about two hours northeast of here." He scratched his chin, feeling the two-day-old whiskers rubbing against his hand.

"The World Government has declared him dead in a factory accident, so I don't think he'll be going back to Neil. But I don't know what he's up to. Knowing his history, he won't be hidden long. But until he pops back up on our radar, it's best to keep a question mark on him."

"Now for the new stuff. Pastor Rohan has returned home to his family with a few of the old-style computers. We'll have more points of access into the World Government's systems. Spreading out our signal to multiple connections will help us cover our trail."

"What's next? Oh, yes! Deborah and Pilar are at the colonial hospital outside Trinity with the sick that they rescued from the labor camp. Pilar is trying to find families for a few of the kids until their parents are released from the camp. Deborah says that the doctors don't suspect anything. They didn't even ask where the people had come from." He thought about Dr. Linton. "I can see why they don't ask questions. Better not to know too much, especially when your money points come from the World Government."

He began to pace. "Now Jonah is in the thick of it. He pulled off becoming Neil Elder's bodyguard by taking a knife to save him, which sounds crazy when you really think about it." He paused for a moment lost in thought. "And when he found out that Bear and Ruth were coming, he told Neil to relieve Dr.

Linton from working the gala. Don't know if I agree with him, but I guess he's trying to protect Ruth. He's ready to act. He said whatever we have planned needs to happen during the gala because everyone—including Neil Elder—is distracted. But we can't rush this. Taking down a corrupt World Government is close to impossible. But there are people dying in labor camps. We must do something."

Tom stood quiet for several moments, allowing his mind to gather up his thoughts. "Then there is Zach and Li…"

"What about us?" a familiar voice asked.

Tom looked toward the entryway of his basement office. There he saw Zach's lanky body leaning against the doorway. His face and arms were golden tan and his shaggy blonde hair hung past his ears. His blue eyes glinted mischievously. Li stood next to Zach and was almost as tall, and his black hair was just as shaggy. His dark eyes also glimmered with amusement.

"I found these two loitering inside the Trading Center," Cindy, his wife said, coming up from behind the two young men. "Are you hungry? I have lunch ready."

"Yes, dear. I'll be up in a bit," he answered. "Let me catch up with these two. We shouldn't be long."

His wife nodded. "I'll have lunch for you two, as well," she said.

"Yes, Ma'am," Zach said.

Li nodded. "Thank you."

She smiled and walked back upstairs. Pastor Tom watched her leave. So many changes and his wife has been right by his side. He silently thanked God for her.

"Just the two guys I wanted to see! Come in and have a seat. I was just talking out loud, trying to make sure that I have all the little details set in my mind. Why do you both look like you have something hidden up your sleeves?"

Li walked into the office. "Because we do."

Tom looked from one face to the other trying to read their expression. "What do you mean? Have you found a way to release the people from the labor camps?"

Zach shook his head. "No, we found something better— a way to take down the World Government."

Tom stood stunned. Then he slowly walked over to his desk, pulled out his chair and sat down. He placed his elbows on the wooden tabletop and stared at Zach and Li. "How and is this plan fool-proof?"

"We have just come from Deborah and Esther's place. We have the old-style computers ready. We have the brainpower we need. And now we have the perfect plan," Li said seriously. "There is only one loophole that would sabotage everything."

"What?" Tom asked.

"Have you heard of the Kill Switch?" Zach asked.

Tom nodded intently. "Yes, Arthur Pallue created it in case the World Government's systems got penetrated or hijacked. It's supposed to shut everything down, but when it's rebooted, the systems should go back to normal again. It's like a pause button until the threat passes. Other than that, there is not much information about it. The World Government keeps it under lock and key. You're not trying to use the Kill Switch, are you? Some speculate that it would erase everything, but it was created only as a reboot. Even the money points are theoretically supposed to stay the same."

"No, we don't want to use it. We want to prevent the World Government from using it," Li said. "Supposedly, it's never been used, but I remember rumors from when I was a kid that it had been used and it worked."

"I've never read research about it. Besides, it would be almost impossible to pull it now. Neil Elder would have to get approval from the other nine magistrates. Only if something were seriously wrong, and he had proof, would he be able to pull the Kill Switch," Tom said.

Zach and Li grinned.

Tom dropped the pencil he had been fidgeting with and leaned back in his chair. "You two have found a way to take down the World Government?"

"Not exactly," Zach said. "But Li has figured out the next best thing."

"What?" Tom asked, staring at Li.

Li's face became serious. "We are going to collapse the RIBS of the World Government."

Pastor Tom sat silent for several seconds. Finally, he looked at both men. "The Regional Integrated Banking System. It holds all the accounts of money points for all ten regions combined under the authority of the World Government," Tom said, thinking. "Ever since the World Government replaced tangible money with digital points, they've had complete control over us. That is when tyranny really began, and we Colonials separated even more from the government."

"Yes," Li said. "But now we've found a way to infiltrate the RIBS and erase all money points. I've confirmed with the other Efficientists. There are only five obstacles including the Kill Switch. First, the attacks on each of the ten RIBS must be done at the same time for the entire system to fall. Second, the attacks must come from multiple locations to create enough force. Third, the World Government cannot find out that we are using old computers to infiltrate their systems. Fourth, as many people need to be logged onto their LPSs and HMSs at the same time as possible..."

"And fifth, Neil Elder must not use the Kill Switch," Tom finished. "And if you can take down the World Bank, you will take away the World Government's power."

"Precisely," Zach said. "And our hope is that without power, they too will fall."

"We've already jumped most of those hurdles. Our old computers are going undetected. We just need to find a perfect time when we know all the Efficientists and Colonials will be on their LPSs—anyone who receives money points must be logged in," Li said, placing his palms on the desk and leaning towards Tom.

"The *Grand Opus Gala!*" Tom said, getting up from his chair. "That's it!"

"That's exactly what Pilar said when I discussed the details of our plan with her. She said New Year's Eve at the final show would be the best time to coordinate our attack. The more people tuned into the World News will create a bigger platform for us to hit. If we can get at least seventy-five percent of people who receive money points online, we can make the whole system self-destruct!" Zach said.

"I didn't know Pilar and Deborah had returned," Tom said.

"They came in a few days ago after finding families for all the kids we were able to take from the forced labor camps. You might want to pray for her. Seeing those people sick and enslaved has really gotten under her skin. She's staying at the ranch for a bit, so Esther can talk through her experience. I've never seen her so angry in my life, and she's been pretty steamed at me on several occasions."

"After we told her our plan, she said that we would need to think of a way to create a huge commotion to get the Colonials logged in. She fears the gala will bore most of them," Li added.

"I believe she's probably right. Most Colonials won't care about the lectures. I'll have to contact Bear and Ruth," Tom said, standing up and continuing to pace. "Bear isn't going to like it, but he needs to get the gala's ratings up. They were slumped for several days until he got there. He has an effect on viewers. They are fascinated by him, and he'll have to milk that intrigue if this plan is going to work. Ruth too. Her wardrobe and masks created a lot of intrigue from the viewers. I've read the comments. They want to know who she is, but no one can find information on her."

Zach's excited expression was replaced with concern. "I don't want anyone finding out Ruth's true identity."

"You don't have to worry about that. Jonah says that Eve Pallue is as good as dead. The only one besides us who knows the truth about her is Dr. Linton, but Jonah assures me that he will not say anything. In fact, he has been relieved from working the *Grand Opus Gala*," Tom said. He tried to sound reassuring, but he still did not trust Dr. Linton. A man who didn't choose sides can be more dangerous than a man who blatantly opposes you. His actions can never be calculated.

"Where are they sending him?" Li asked.

"I don't know," Tom said. "But let us hope that it is far away from the *Grand Opus Gala* and far away from Trinity for that matter."

CHAPTER 8

Pilar looked at the woman who sat in the driver's seat. "Thanks for the lift." She grabbed her backpack that rested by her feet and got out of the car. As she walked toward the side of the street, the car honked behind her.

The woman quickly rolled down the car window. "Are you sure you want me to leave you here?" she said, eying the road that led west. "This is no place to be alone. There's a prison factory close by and rumor has it that if you're found wandering alone, they'll take you and put you to work."

"Don't worry about me. My friends are meeting me here," Pilar said. "I'll be safe." Pilar hated to lie, but the woman would not drop her off if she knew her true intentions.

"I'm heading to town. Can't your friends just meet you there?"

"No, it's out of the way. They should be here soon."

The woman looked unconvinced. "Want me to wait here?"

Pilar realized that she would have to be firm or the woman would soften her resolve. "Look, I appreciate the ride, but I'll take it from here."

The woman looked offended. "Suit yourself, but don't say I didn't warn you." She rolled the window back up and drove off toward the small town.

After Pilar zipped up her jacket, she slung the backpack over her shoulders. "God help me. What am I doing?" she whispered. It was a frigid morning, and she hated the cold. Now here she was walking almost a mile with the chilly wind blowing against her face. At least it wasn't snowing like it had been when they were leaving the forced labor camp.

She remembered the images of all the starving children—the ones they had rescued just weeks before. Their faces stayed in her mind. She couldn't shake them. The forced labor camps needed to be exposed. Never had she felt such a burning passion to stop an injustice. It seared her to the core. She would go in there, take video and Li would figure out how to hack into the World News and play the clips on the final night of the *Grand Opus Gala*. At least, she hoped he would. They would have to do something with the images to expose what the World Government was doing to Colonials. Neither Li nor Zach knew about her plan, but they would find out soon when Pastor Tom tells them. She had visited him the day before she left.

She placed her hands into the pockets of her jacket and began walking down the street heading west. Pastor Tom didn't want her to go, but he reluctantly conceded when she said that the photos would help more people log into the gala. He promised to keep it a secret for a few days, so Zach and her dad wouldn't try to rescue her. When she thought of Zach, her shoulders drooped as a sigh fell from her lips. She had romanticized that their relationship was finally on the mend, but now he was consumed with taking down the Regional Integrated Banking System. She stayed at Esther and Deborah's ranch, hoping to have some quality time with him, but he instantly became consumed with his work with Li.

She saw herself fading behind the shadows of his plans. He would only talk with her if it was about the gala or how to collapse the World Government. She knew what he and Li were planning was important. Erasing the World Government's money points would take away its power and destroy the forced labor camps. But she was important too. And she finally realized that she would never be a true priority in Zach's heart. He would always find a way to place something of greater importance above her. She either wasn't the one for him or he would never marry. She suspected it was the latter, but the pain of not being able to love him still hurt.

She refocused her attention on the road and saw the factory in the distance. Tremors shot down from her chest to her toes. She stopped and quickly pulled out a slip of paper from her pocket. The name, Jordan Holten, was written on it in Pastor Tom's handwriting. Ever since they discovered the forced labor camp, Pastor Tom had been trying to find a way to infiltrate it to gain information. Holten was a young security guard who wanted out. Pastor Tom wrote him a note to his personal HMS. If he would help Pilar with taking her video, then Pastor Tom would find a place for him in Trinity.

The security guard said he would help her. She didn't know his plans, but he was expecting her today. She tore the piece of paper into shreds and let them fly away in the breeze. Then she took off her backpack and opened it. She had packed nothing that would verify who she was or where she had come from. She found the tiny digital camera that Pastor Tom had given her. She reached down the top of her shirt and slipped it into her bra. Suddenly, she heard another honk behind her. She briefly thought the woman had followed, but she realized the horn sounded lower. She looked back. A large security van slowed next to her.

A young man rolled down the window once the van came to a stop. "Are you Pilar Jones?" he asked.

Pilar could tell he was extremely nervous.

"Yes," she nodded.

"Hurry, get in."

She ran around the back of the van and got into the passenger side.

The young man had sweat dripping down his pale forehead even though the van was quite cool inside. He looked to be no more than twenty-three or twenty-four years old.

"And you are Holten?" she asked.

"Yes," he said, and turned back to face the road. "I have to keep driving or they will suspect something. I've added your name to our list of prisoners just in case someone stops us. Here is the plan. We will go in. I will escort you around with the other prisoners that I have in the back. We have protocols of getting the prisoners acquainted with the property and the rules."

"You have prisoners back there?" she asked, looking behind her.

"Yes, I picked them up today. You'll have to join them in about 30 seconds. Now listen. We can't make any mistakes. Where is the camera?"

"I have it," she said.

"I will need it. I will have to do the filming. Don't worry. I know exactly where to film. I'll keep it on my clipboard."

"Why are you doing this?" Pilar asked.

He glanced at her, and she could see anxiety imprinting his expression.

"I can't do this job anymore. The prisoners keep getting sick and more and more are dying. There is a virus spreading through the camp and even some of the security guards are getting sick. They need to just close the factory down, but orders from the World Government are keeping it open. Now they want us to take people without reason and give them criminal records to use them as laborers. We are supposed to take people who aren't connected to a community—people who live isolated. But in order to meet the quotas, some security guards are taking entire families. I'm telling you. The villages around us are not going to stand for it much longer. We will be found out, and there will be a revolt. Now, this pastor. Can I trust him? Will he take me in if I get this film for you?"

"He's the most honest person I know," Pilar confirmed. "When we go back to Trinity, he will make sure that you have a place there."

"Good," he answered. "Set the camera in the cupholder there."

Pilar turned away from the man and got the camera out of her bra. "I didn't know if I should hide it or not," she said, setting it down.

"Now this is important. If we get separated, they can't know that I'm helping you. If they find out, they will torture you for information and your pastor friend will be compromised. I've seen it happen dozens of times. You won't be able to keep any secrets. They must think you are just a prisoner I picked up."

"But we won't get separated, right?" she asked, resisting the urge to jump out of the van.

"We shouldn't unless someone gets nosy. We will take the tour. I will film. I will drop off the prisoners and then we will leave. I have hidden my car just off the road. I will dump the van and drive to Trinity. As long as you stay with me, we should be in and out before my shift is over."

Pilar nodded, reluctantly.

"Now get in the back," he said. Then he grabbed the handle behind his right shoulder and pulled. "One more prisoner coming in."

Pilar hesitated for a moment, but she set her jaw and grabbed her backpack. She squeezed her body through the narrow opening that separated the front from the back of the van. She saw the scared faces of several young men before the door behind her was shut and everything went black. There were no chairs, so she sat down on the cold metal floor. "God," she whispered. "Be with me."

They drove for a few minutes, and she sat quietly reminding herself that it would be all over soon. She would go back to living her normal life in Levington with her family. When the van finally came to a stop, she heard Holten get out and talk with another guard. Then keys jingled just before one of the van's back doors swung open. Light flooded in and she had to squint her eyes.

"Come out and line up," he ordered.

She waited for the others to get out of the van before making her way out. The moment felt surreal like another woman walked in her shoes, but a calm wrapped around her like a blanket. God was with her. As she climbed out of the back, she noticed Holten holding the clipboard flat between his hands. The camera was pinned under the metal clip with the lens pointing right. He would have to stand to the left of whatever he was filming to capture the images.

"Line up and face me," he said authoritatively. "I will be showing you around the grounds and telling you the rules. All of you were sent here by the World Government as punishment for your crimes. I will not debate your crimes with you, but if you work hard and serve your time and comply with all the rules, you will be released in due time. However, if you try to escape or if you disobey the rules, you will be punished. Now follow me."

Pilar jumped ahead of the line and walked directly behind Holten. She wanted to ensure he was keeping up with his end of the bargain. She noticed his hands shaking a bit. He was anxious. He was speaking a little too loudly, as well. He would probably be killed for filming the inside of the forced labor camp. If he was willing to take the risk, she needed to be strong too.

"We do various jobs here at the camp," Holten continued as he walked toward the factory. "But we mainly harvest and process cotton into textile. The cotton crop has already been harvested, so now we are processing and packing it. Once it's pressed into bales, we will begin the next process of spinning the cotton into thread, weaving the thread into fabric, dyeing the fabric and cutting it into bolts to be delivered. The electricity has been shut off, so everything is done by hand. But don't get any ideas. We aren't shut off from the World Government. Mr. Stanton runs this prison, and his office is powered by a generator," he said, pointing to an old tower in front of them. "He has direct communication with Neil Elder who has the World Police at his disposal."

Holten stopped and held the clipboard in order to film the fencing around the prison. Pilar wondered why the fence was important until she saw it. A body of a young man lay tangled in the wire and drooped over the edge of the fence.

"You see that body?" he asked, keeping the clipboard steady to film the gruesome scene. "He tried to escape several days ago, but instead he got stuck in the razor wire. He survived for over two days while screaming for help until he passed out from the pain. Mr. Stanton commanded that we leave the body there for a while as an example to the other prisoners. No one escapes from here and survives."

Pilar's stomach felt sick, and she had to look away from the mutilated body. She felt an urge to tell Holten never mind, but she knew it was too late. They would have to finish filming, and only then could she leave with Holten and return to Trinity.

Next, Holten began walking toward the large factory with huge glassless windows rimming the top of the building. "All the work is being done inside the factory now. We use large machines that are normally powered by electricity, but they have been modified to be powered by human power with crank and pulley systems. We tried to process the cotton by hand last year, but it took too long. So engineers modified the machines to be operated manually instead."

Pilar had seen Ruth working on her thread wheel, and she knew the process was tedious. She couldn't imagine what Holten meant when he said the machines were powered by people, but as they got closer to the factory doors, she could hear the loud grunts of men and women in strenuous work. She could also smell the foul stench of body odor permeating from within.

"Watch your step. The prisoners are doing their work, and they are not responsible if you get in their way," he said.

Pilar noticed that Holten turned left once he walked through the doors of the factory, which gave the camera he held a clear shot of the inside of the factory. The first thing she noticed was a band of armed guards standing at key positions on the first and second floor of the factory. She wasn't used to rifles being held in such close proximity. The next thing she noticed was the large machines being used to press cotton. Attached to the machines were thick levers about eight feet long. Five to six men held onto the levers. Once the cotton was forked into the rectangle container, they would pull the lever down and a large metal press pushed the cotton into a bale shape.

"This is the final stage of processing the cotton. The women and children are upstairs cleaning it. They pull the seed from the lint and get as much debris out of the cotton as they can. The seeds are collected for cow feed, which we will ship out once the cotton is done being processed. There are also a few lighter machines upstairs that do additional cleaning. They are powered by cranks that are turned by the women and some younger boys. It is exhausting work, so they try to make the cotton as clean as possible by hand first."

Pilar looked at the faces of the men as she passed them. Their faces were gaunt, and their clothes fell off them. They looked emaciated and hopeless. No wonder they were dying.

"Before we go upstairs, let me show you the prisoner quarters. He nodded to a guard as he continued to walk. Then he entered one side of a double door. Once everyone was through the door, he looked behind him to make sure he wasn't being followed. "The quarters are further down. Men sleep separate from the women and children. But let me show you where we put the sick first. There would be more of them, but several of them were taken a few weeks ago."

Holten reached to his security belt with his right hand and unclipped the large flashlight that dangled next to his gun. "Here," he said, handing the flashlight to Pilar. "Shine the light in the center, so we can get a good view." Then he opened the door and slightly angled the clipboard with his left hand.

When Pilar shined the light inside the dark room, her eyes opened wide from the horrifying scene. Dozens of bodies lay listless in rows on the ground.

"There is a fever spreading. We haven't had medical help in weeks. When someone catches a fever, they are brought in here, including security guards. They either walk out eventually or they are carried out. We check for dead bodies once a week and bury them in the graveyard behind the factory."

Suddenly, one of the young men standing next to her started backing away.

"No, man! I can't be here!" he started yelling.

Holten quickly let the door shut and turned toward the man. "Calm down. Do not run, you understand me?"

The man shook his head. "No, I'm not supposed to be here. I did nothing wrong."

Holten put his hand on his holstered gun. "If you run, you will be shot," he said firmly.

The young man turned and began sprinting down the hallway. He pushed open the door and ran out of sight into the factory. Pilar began walking toward the door, but Holten grabbed her arm.

"Don't," he said. "He's gone. And they will shoot you, as well."

Repeated fires rang out from different angles and screams flooded the hallway. She heard the young man's voice yell for a second before it was silenced. Although Pilar didn't see it with her eyes, she knew that the man was dead.

"Keep your head down," Holten demanded. "Just walk straight. We are almost to the van and then we are out of here."

Pilar continued to walk keeping her head low. Her stomach felt sick, but freedom was a mere few seconds away. She had seen the man's dead body lying on the floor. Blood flowed around him like thick red dye. She had to wait while Officer Holten was detained for questioning. Pilar looked toward the horizon. The sunlight was fading. They should have been almost to Trinity by now, but her escape from the factory was delayed. Instead of leaving, she watched as the young man's dead body strewn with holes was wrapped in a black tarp and carried through the factory and out the backdoor to a burial ground with countless, nameless graves.

She was trapped with the other prisoners from the van remaining to be assimilated into the forced labor camp. But she didn't belong there. For that matter, none of them belonged there. Finally, Holten came back to gather his prisoners. He dropped the others off, and the two of them were now walking briskly to the van. The light of twilight dimmed, as the sun hid behind the old factory.

"You must get in the back of the van until we reach my car. Then this charade will be over, and I will start my new life in Trinity with your pastor friend."

Pilar said nothing and looked toward his jacket pocket. Before he was summoned, he had recorded the dead body with the camera. Then she watched as he placed the camera into his pocket before disappearing behind a door. He must have noticed her stare.

"Don't worry. The camera is safe. I want to give it to your pastor myself and make sure he's good to his word."

She nodded. She could hear the desperation in Holten's voice. She realized that he hated this place just as much as she did—maybe more. She followed him as he walked to the back of the van and paused while he anxiously wrestled with his keys. Finally, he put the correct key into the door and opened it. Pilar wanted to jump into the darkness and away from the awful memories of the forced labor camp. Just as she put her foot on the bumper, she heard a brute voice.

"Holten, where are you taking this prisoner?" another officer asked.

Pilar stepped back down onto the gravel ground and kept her head low. She tried to keep a calm expression, but her heart rate accelerated. She didn't look up, but she could hear Holten fumbling with his clipboard. He wasn't talking.

"Did you not hear me?" the man asked louder. "Where are you taking her?"

Holten continued to delay speaking, and Pilar realized they were both about to get caught.

She held up her small backpack. "I think my water bottle fell out of my backpack. Officer Holten is letting me retrieve it."

She continued to look down waiting for his reply. She silently prayed that he would take her excuse and leave them.

"Fine. Get in there and get it," the other officer said.

She got into the back of the van and searched the area for a water bottle she knew wasn't there. She continued to look hoping the man would walk away, but she didn't hear his footsteps leaving. After over a minute, she knew she needed to give up the search. She crawled out of the van.

"Well," Holten said, finally catching on. "Did you find it?"

She shook her head. "No. It must have fallen out before I got in."

"You have wasted our time," Holten said, a little too severely. He looked to the other officer. "I'll take her back. Sorry to inconvenience you, Sir."

"Your shift is over. I'll take her back. You won't be getting any overtime for your carelessness today. You seem to be having trouble controlling your prisoners. Go home and think about whether or not you value your job here. Make sure none of this happens again."

"Yes, Sir," Holten said and hesitated.

Pilar wanted to plead with him not to leave her, but she knew that they would both be buried in nameless graves if she did. He needed to get the video back to Trinity. Once Pastor Tom discovered she was still there, he would make sure they found a way to get her out. Zach would find her. Just like he did after Randall kidnapped her. She just had to survive until then.

"Yes, Sir," Holten repeated. Then he walked to the driver's side of the van and got in.

Pilar was now a prisoner.

CHAPTER 9

D r. Linton went to clasp the doorknob, but he pulled his hand away. He glanced down at the baggage next to his feet. He could simply grab both handles and walk straight back to his car. He'd drive to his cottage on the outskirts of the city and simply see the factory patients via video chat. Why had Matt sent him here? And to this house? He was too overqualified to be a factory doctor.

"Do you need help getting in?" a young girl's voice asked.

Dr. Linton turned. A young brunette girl around eleven or twelve years old stood with one foot on her scooter and another on the uneven sidewalk. He stared at her and said nothing.

"The backdoor is unlocked, and the key is on the counter. I go in there to feed Ms. Naomi's cats. She lived there before she died several months ago. She was my friend. Do you have any kids?"

"Ah—no, I don't," Dr. Linton said after finding his voice.

"Are you married?" the girl asked.

He shook his head.

"Why'd they give you family quarters if you ain't got no kids?" she asked, disappointed. "I was hoping you had kids or at least a wife I could come visit. It's just me and my dad, and he's always off running stuff to the city."

Dr. Linton stared at the girl's dejected face. He knew what it was like to be the only child of a single parent. "You knew the woman who lived here before?"

The girl brightened and nodded her head. "Yes, Ms. Naomi was the sweetest lady. But she got sick and her son wouldn't let me visit her anymore. He moved away and left her cats behind. What kind of son would do that?"

He shrugged. "Maybe one that was grieving the loss of his mother."

The girl thought for a bit. "You might be right. He did seem really sad. Well, it's a good thing I'm still here. My dad won't let me take their cats to our house, but I take care of them here. Dad brings me home cat food from the factory. I guess he knows that they keep me company while he's gone. Here, let me introduce you to them."

The girl gently set her scooter on the grass next to the sidewalk. "I'll go around back and let you in. Just wait here."

He watched the young girl disappear around the corner of the house. He stared back at the front door. He had seen this front door before when Eve Pallue contacted him on his Portable to come check on her mother—Naomi. Now here he was again. Why had Matt sent him here? Did he also know that Eve Pallue was still alive? No, he couldn't have known it. He would have told Neil Elder, wouldn't he? But Matt did know that he had left the city to come here. He rubbed his temples. He had too many secrets hidden in his mind, and it was beginning to show on his face. He had dark circles under his eyes. It was like every second he was waiting to be found out. But he couldn't confess what he knew now. Neil Elder would wonder why he didn't say anything in the first place. He needed to figure out a way to get out of this pit of secrets, so he could finally live in peace.

The door suddenly creaked open. "Come on in. I'm going to leave the front door open, so we can get some fresh air blowing through the house. It smells dusty, but I've done a good job at keeping the cats from messing in the house. You see," she said pointing to the open backdoor. "I built a cat door for them. I did it all by myself. Took the door off the hinges and everything. Cut the hole and added the flap. It took a while to train them to go outside, but they figured it out. Now they mostly live outside, but I still feed them in the kitchen to prevent pests from taking their food."

Dr. Linton walked in and set his bags on the floor in the living room next to the small, run-down couch. He inhaled the musty air and felt his gag reflex almost push out his early morning breakfast. His gaze fell onto the kitchen. Layers of dust blanketed the tiled counters and the small round breakfast table. He quickly spied the appliances. At least there was running water, a stove and a fridge, but he couldn't imagine staying here long.

"Want me to clean up for you?" the girl asked. "I'm a good housekeeper. I keep my house clean for my daddy."

"Doesn't seem like you kept this house clean," he said.

"Well, I wasn't get paid now, was I?"

"You take money points?" he asked.

She shook her head. "No, the people of Trinity don't deal with money points. The only place I can use them is at the factory, and my dad already gets me stuff from there. You got anything you can give me? My dad has a workshop in our backyard, but he ain't got no material for me to use. I'd like to build something to sell at the bazaar, but I need something to trade for the material."

"Look, I'm a doctor for the World Government. I don't have anything to give you other than money points."

"Oh, yes you do!" the girl said excitedly. "You have medicines. People always be needing those."

"I'm not giving you drugs," Dr. Linton said. "Do you want me to get into trouble?"

"I don't want the dangerous drugs. Just the antibiotics. Those aren't addictive and the people of Trinity need them. Kids always be getting ear infections and fevers."

Dr. Linton looked at the girl skeptically.

"Look, give me antibiotics to cure just one ear infection. That's not a lot. And I'll clean your house for you. I'll wash the sheets, dust all the rooms. I'll make this place look like new."

He bent down and opened a suitcase. He pulled out his Portable and turned it on with his thumbprint. "What is your name and what is the name of your father?" he asked.

"My name is Melissa Canwell and my dad's name is Martin. But you can call me Missy, and he goes by Marty."

"Martin Canwell. Trinity Factory. Runner," he said. He flipped through several screens, reading the condensed words of T-variety. "Alright. Melissa Canwell. Trinity school." He continued reading the new windows that appeared on his screen. Once he was satisfied with his research, he looked back at the girl.

"So? What did you find?" she asked.

"Looks like you're a pretty good kid, Missy Canwell. Okay. I will give you what you ask for in exchange for you making this place livable. When you are done, unpack all of my things in the master bedroom. If I am satisfied with the work, I will give you the medicine in the morning. And I will think about having you come a few times during the week."

"I have school in the morning. Can I come after?"

"Yes, that is fine. However," he said, holding up his finger. "If anyone asks you where you got your medicine from, you must not mention my name. Think of anything else to tell them."

"You don't have to worry about that. When it comes to medicine, nobody asks. But if they do, I'll say my dad found them at work or someone in the city gave them to him."

"Good," he nodded. "Now, if you excuse me, I need to check into the factory and see about getting something to eat."

"There is a diner next to the factory. They take money points there," Missy said, grabbing Dr. Linton's luggage. "You ain't got nothing in these bags valuable, do you? I don't want to be blamed if anything is missing."

Dr. Linton shook his head. "Only clothes. I don't plan on staying here long." He held up his Portable. "I read on your father's files that he is on a delivery to the city right now. Do you know when he is expected home? I would like to introduce myself."

She thought for a moment. "Today is a short day. I'm supposed to have dinner ready for him this evening. He might even be at the factory right now. I better hurry up and get your house cleaned. I'll be back tomorrow afternoon for payment. Make sure to get your house key from the counter," she said and walked briskly down the hall that led to the bedrooms.

"I'll see you then," he said, watching her leave. He looked back at his Portable. He had discovered that Martin Canwell was a Runner with Zacchaeus Daniels. Maybe that was why Matt had sent him to Trinity. He wanted information about where Zach had gone after he robbed the World Bank.

"If information will get me out of Trinity and back to my cottage, then I will gladly find it," he said staring at the screen. "Maybe if I find enough information, Neil Elder will let me retire." He tucked the Portable under his arm and walked to the counter and grabbed the house key. "Maybe if I work fast enough, I'll even be able to make it back for the *Grand Opus Gala*," he whispered with a smile.

Pastor Tom pushed from his chair and stood up. He stared at his HMS disbelieving. He finally voiced it off and slowly backed away as if the dimming screen were to suddenly come back to life. When he was sure the screen turned black, he surveyed his office in the basement of the Trinity Trading Center. Had all of his thinking and planning been in vain? He looked at the old printing press hidden under the stairs that led to the main level of the trading center. It mocked him. He had taken it all the way from Pastor Rohan's home, thinking God was going to use if for something, but now his faith steps seemed ridiculous. In fact, all his steps up to now were useless in light of what he had just read.

Jonah sent a quick correspondence that flashed only briefly on his HMS screen before it was taken down.

I sent Dr. Michael Linton to Trinity Village. Be prayerful about what you do. God will lead you. – Jonah

And that was it. Why would he send Dr. Linton here? To Trinity? It didn't make sense. Tom tried to play out the scenarios of possible moves in his head, but Jonah's reasons for sending Dr. Linton to the very place he had discovered Eve Pallue was, in fact, still alive only led to the World Government finding them and discovering their plot to take down the RIBS.

Even the fact that Ruth was in the city now didn't excuse Jonah from sending Dr. Linton to Trinity. He could have sent him to any village in the area but why here? Tom began to pace the floor to help him think. Zach, Li and all the Efficientists at Deborah and Esther's ranch were here, working on a plan to take down the World Government. This was the worst place Jonah could send him. If Dr. Linton was sent to the Trinity Factory, he was sure to look around and ask questions. Zach and Li had successfully robbed the World Bank without repercussions. They could be found out.

"God, we need to hide them!" he yelled, slamming his hands on his desk. "Why is this happening?" Heated frustration oscillated in his mind without any resolution to land on. He felt like this once before—when corporate church had been banned. But God had given him a new way where there seemed to be no way at all. Tom allowed his hands to go limp. He looked back at the quiet HMS screen. *"Be prayerful about what you do. God will lead you"* is what Jonah had written.

Tom slid to his knees and pressed his elbows on the top of the desk and cupped his hands. "Lord, I have no clue why You are sending the very man who can't be trusted to Trinity.

Dr. Linton doesn't take sides, which makes him more dangerous than anyone because I cannot calculate his next move. He is a wildcard. Jonah has never led me astray before, and I must trust his decision to send Dr. Linton here. Please, God, show me what to do. Should I send Zach and Li away? That will most definitely delay our plans, and we have only weeks to prepare before the *Grand Opus Gala*. Show me what to do. I pray this in Your Son, Jesus's name, amen."

Pastor Tom rose to his feet. He noticed his *Bible* on his desk left open from his quiet time earlier that morning. He turned the book around and read the first verse he saw. "I wait quietly before God, for my victory comes from him" (Psalm 62:1 NLT).

Tom exhaled. He knew what he had to do. The vibrating thoughts in his mind ceased, tucking themselves quietly into faith. He had to do nothing.

CHAPTER 10

Bear walked next to his wife along the white-chalked ballroom floor as they circled the stage. He fidgeted with the white, stiff fabric that his wife had looped around his neck and knotted in the front. He had never felt so uncomfortable in his life. The great room was air-conditioned yet sweat dripped down his back under the layers of thick fabric. Ada had called him a Beau Brummell when she met them in the lobby that evening, and she had thrown her head back and laughed with her chirping giggle when he had no idea what she meant. Bear had grown to loathe her laugh. He had an image of hitting the voice box just under her pointy chin to shut her up, but immediately he felt a tinge of guilt...but only a tinge.

"It's a name of a character in an old movie portraying the Regency Era," Ruth told him. Ruth had been on the LPS all week. And if she wasn't there, he'd find her at the sewing machine—a convenient gift from Ada—sewing new outfits for every event. He was the one performing in front of the World News, yet his wife was the busy one. She made him wear ridiculous costumes, like the one he wore tonight, to this boring, drawn-out event. He looked around. At least he wasn't the only buffoon dolled up. Every man around him wore the same manner of clothing: thick white button-up shirts with high collars, strange-fitting pants, or *breeches* as his wife called them, with no zipper and a loose flap that buttoned at the front of the waist, tight-fitting jackets that were long in the back. Ruth had wanted him to wear ruffled sleeves and a large, black drum-like hat, which he had instantly protested.

He sighed and looked at the circular stage again. It was divided into three sections, and two men and a woman each discussed their area of expertise with visual effects shining on the white screens behind them. He was listening to one of the men speak about something called *physics*, but it all sounded like a different language to him, even though he was speaking in Long English. Ada had explained that all performers must use Long English to engage the Colonials, but Bear knew it didn't matter if they were speaking in Twin-Variety. Most Colonials would not understand nor care about what these Efficientists were saying.

He reached up and pressed a button on the headphones Ada had given everyone at the gala to wear. The channel changed, and he could hear the woman talking now. Something about stars. He tried to look at what she was referring to, but her demonstration was on the other side of the round stage. His wife's already slow pace stopped, and she drew closer to the stage where the man was talking about thoughts and layers of thoughts—whatever that meant. He came up beside Ruth and turned the channel on his headphones to see what had drawn her attention.

"So you see," the man said, noticing Ruth watching him from behind her mask. "Layered Thought Process has been deemed invaluable during a person's allotted sleeping time. The time of sleep is necessary for a person to process all the information they have produced and consumed during the day, which as Efficientists—even low-ranking ones—is a lot. We discovered that people who listen to the World News in their Sleeper will eventually begin to struggle with controlling their thoughts—though, if they are upper Efficientists, it may take some time for the lack of idle sleep to show. Eventually, however, they will have rogue thoughts that begin to cause an unwinding effect on the rest of their thought processing. We believe that was part of Eve Pallue's struggle after her Awakening, and we know now she sought a Life Therapist.

Thanks to Neil Elder's research, her problem occurred because she did not allow her mind to be idle. The Efficientists who successfully came through an Awakening with little to no downtime are the ones who did not administer Layered Thought Processing while sleeping."

Bear put his arm protectively around Ruth's shoulders, trying not to smash the puffy sleeves she had worked hard on creating. Although he couldn't see her expression, he knew first-hand what it felt like listening to information about yourself when you were a different person living a different life. The World News relished playing old videos of his life as a circuit fighter. They had even found and interviewed a few of his old girlfriends, who had nothing good to say about him. He had to remind himself of Ruth's words at the river when she fell in the water trying to run after him. He couldn't let unforgiveness back into his life, and that included unforgiveness toward himself.

Ruth looked up at him and smiled. She pressed the off button on her headphones and took them off being careful not to disturb her curled updo. Bear wished he could see her full face, but he knew her identity needed to stay hidden. Truth be told, he rather liked being the only one who could see her. She almost never wore makeup, which he also preferred. Ada insisted on makeup for all gala women, but Ruth needed none except for a lip gloss now and then.

"I have heard enough for now. The only performance even moderately engaging was the LTP lecture, but I had already made his assessments for myself," she said. "Do you mind if we sit for a moment?" she asked. "I know that Ada has more planned for this evening, so I want to rest."

"Of course," he said. He took her hand into his the way Ada had shown him, holding his palm up and allowing Ruth's downward palm to rest on his. He cautiously led Ruth toward the chairs that lined the walls, not wanting to step on her burgundy gown, like he had done entering the elevator. She wore a simple burgundy mask that matched the material of her dress, and it was rimmed with the same braided cordage that went around her waist.

He finally got her to a seat without tripping, and they both sat down. The ornately wooden carved chairs with high backs and flat cushions were uncomfortable, to say the least. He wanted to take his wife back to their apartment and pretend the gala was over with, but Ruth continued to press how important it was that they follow through because the World Government could make their lives miserable if they didn't play their game for a while.

He noticed his wife looking around. "Are you looking for Jonah?"

She nodded. "I have not seen him yet. It is probably for the best because I do not know how I will react. When I finally met my mother after all those years, I cried like a child. I do not think that will happen with Jonah, but I will be grateful to see him." She placed her headphones on her lap and rested her head gently against the back of the wooden chair.

Bear looked across the ballroom. "I would like to thank him myself for saving you and sending you to me." He saw no one that looked like the man he had seen in the World News article about Jonah Goodman, or Matt Coughlin as he is called, after he had saved Neil Elder's life. He saw some Efficientists still walking leisurely around the circular stage, changing the station when they made their way to the next lecturer. Others were sitting on the chairs like them, waiting and looking bored. And many were at the buffet table refilling their drinks and eating hors d'oeuvres. He noticed the bird of prey man holding a white owl on his leather-covered arm. He was one of the ten Colonials that made it as a gala contestant. Many of the Efficientists were taking turns petting the bird. The man seemed to genuinely enjoy the attention. Ada, of course, stood right next to him because that's where the News Media had camped out. She always gravitated to whoever was attracting the World News most.

Bear looked at all the faces around him. He once felt inferior to the Efficientist, but now they seemed ordinary to him. They were just people like him trying to figure out life and their place in it. Abruptly, Ada's voice rang out and startled everyone. She now stood on the stage as a crew behind her removed the wall dividers and screens from the stage. "Thank you to our three guest gala speakers. Your insights are invaluable to *Life Efficiency* and to production as our way of life." She paused briefly and gestured toward the lecturers who were now descending the steps of the stage to the ballroom floor. "Now, if you do not mind, will you take your seats in one of our Regency Era chairs donated by the British Magistrate and her district!" Light applause was offered, and an older woman with white swept-up hair and a glossy black gown waved.

Ada paused again allowing the World News to snap a few shots of the magistrate. Then they moved into photo range of the circular stage, as the other Efficientists took their seats around the room. Bear was glad he and Ruth were already seated, and Ada was directly on stage in front of him. At least, he would be able to see whatever she had planned.

She continued. "I have two more surprises for you tonight. First, a Regency Era presentation that will steal your breath away. And I will give the final surprise after the performance, so please stay seated when the music stops. You will not want to miss the exciting news I'm honored to share before tonight's Regency Era's festivities come to fruition. But first, it is my honor to introduce a musical genius and pianist extraordinaire, Boris Williams." Another round of light applause sounded as the middle-aged man walked up the stairs to the front of the platform and stood next to Ada. A cranking noise sounded, and Bear tried to scan where it was coming from. There were gasps heard from the seated crowd, as they saw something rise from behind Ada and the pianist. A long black piano turned slowly into view. Bear realized that it must have been hiding inside the belly of the stage. When it finished its ascent, Boris Williams sat down at the bench poised to play.

"And finally," Ada continued, "it is my privilege to introduce the Georgian Dancers who will be performing an actual dance from the Regency Era." She nodded at Boris and remained next to the piano as he began to play.

Suddenly, the great doors of the ballroom flew open, and couples swept into the ballroom with long steps and wide turns. They twirled around the dance floor, moving clockwise along the white-chalked wooden floors. Bear noticed Ruth sat up straighter, so she could take in the full view. He could tell she was enthralled by the way her breathing became more rapid. He looked back at the dancers. They wore clothes similar to theirs. Ada must have dressed them all with her designs. He noticed all the men's clothing were much more feminine than his with ruffled collars and sleeves. Maybe he shouldn't have given Ruth such a hard time for spending so much time doing research and sewing their clothing.

Bear found the dance to be moderately entertaining. He would see a man's foot land on the hem of a woman's dress. She would tug the dress just briefly before continuing the dance like nothing had happened. They all had fake smiles fastened on their faces. They seemed to look more at the audience than to each other. He wondered if it was common practice back then or just a trait for today. The World News flashed many photos, capturing every detail. The show was more for those who were watching from their LPS than for the contestants at the gala. There was always pressure to capture the attention of the World News. Bear remembered that spiral well. Doing more and more to please a never-satisfied audience. It had almost killed him. He fought not to win, but to entertain. Never again would he fight to please others.

The music finally died down, and the couples did the complicated bow and curtsy that Ada tried to teach him and Ruth earlier that evening. To Ada's frustration, they both were unable to grasp it. Ruth because she lacked coordination, and Bear because he lacked motivation. Now that he'd seen it done; however, he realized it wasn't that complicated of a move. He knew ground grappling techniques that were much more difficult to learn.

The applause for the dancers was much louder, and Boris bowed many times on stage. Ada beamed and continued to clap as the Word News flashed their cameras. After at least a minute of cheering and clapping, the dancers left the ballroom just as quickly as they had arrived. The pianist followed after them, and the piano slowly spun down into the belly of the stage once more.

Ada waited and looked at the crowd expectantly, waiting for a hush to overpower the whispers. She did a full circle, attempting to look at each face in the crowd from the stage. When all was quiet, she focused her attention back on the World News. "Now, you all know that one of our Colonial gala contestants has had an interesting history."

Bear felt something deeply wrong in the pit of his stomach. There were only nine other Colonial contestants, and out of them, his past had been exposed the most. Ruth must have agreed with him because she instantly clasped her hand around his.

"We interviewed some of his ex-lovers and discovered that his treatment of women wasn't the best. However, I can assure you, that he has made amends. He now has a lovely wife, and we all adore her designs, don't we?" she asked, nodding. "Of course, you know that I'm talking about our very own fighter, the Shaman or Bear, as we know him!"

Now every face turned toward him. Ada looked around dramatically before bringing her attention to him, as well. She continued. "But I want everyone to know that we wanted to

80

unearth some good news from his past, as well. So, I did a little digging and discovered a beautiful gem! Let me introduce her. Her name is Shayla, and she is Bear's long-lost daughter!"

CHAPTER 11

Randall walked behind the line of young men who were holding stretched bows with arrows ready to shoot. He wore a leather jacket and gloves that he found in his grandfather's closet. The weather had turned cold again and most of the men did not have warm clothing. Just like his home in the city, the area where his family's estate was located did not get very frigid in the winter. They were too far south in what used to be Old Texas. However, this week had been an exception. A cold front had come through that brought the temperature down to almost freezing.

"Fire!" he yelled, and arrows flew—many of them missing the spray-painted targets on the large bales of hay. He shook his head. "Tal, come here."

The young man with unkempt black hair walked up to him. His nose and cheeks were pink despite his tan skin. He too looked cold, but Randall knew he wouldn't admit as much. His skinny frame left no insulation to keep the cool breeze from getting under his skin.

"The men need jackets, hats and gloves. They're useless to me if they are too cold to do anything. And look at you. You can barely stand still."

"Yes, sir," Tal said through trembling lips. He moved his hands under his armpits to keep them warm. "I already know which people to talk to. It will have to wait until the morning, though. The shops in town will be closing up."

"That's fine," Randall waved. "Send the men to their quarters, but make sure that the watchtower duty still continues. I don't perceive any threat yet, but it's only a matter of time. Come see me in the house when you're done. We will eat dinner and then go over some plans I have."

Tal nodded and walked back to the line of men and began shouting orders. Randall smiled to himself and started to make his way to the back of his house. Tal had proven to be a dependable and resourceful young man. His grandfather had been right about him. As he continued walking, he found himself looking forward to returning home far too much. He wished he could say it was because of the warmth or even the food, but he knew it was a certain Latin female that would be busily working inside. Adella had only been working for him for almost two weeks, but just like the wind, she was getting under his skin.

He heard a deep bark that forced him out of his thoughts. He looked up and saw Favian, the German Shepherd, standing on the back porch guarding the patio door. The dog had seen him coming and barked to let him know that he was there.

"Great," Randall sighed. He discovered that although Adella hadn't actually lied, she hadn't told him the full truth either. Favian wasn't just a German Shepherd. He was a German Shepherd wolf mix. A *Wolf Shepherd* is what Tal called him. He was a massive yellow and black beast whose protective tendencies toward Adella and her girls ran strong. He now knew why Adella wanted him with her. None of his men would come close to the girls because Favian always had his eyes alert and his ears attentive. The fur on his back would bristle and his large canine teeth came out when one of the men got too close to the girls playing in the yard.

Randall walked more authoritatively toward the steps of the patio. He would not let this dog think that he ruled the estate. He was not intimidated, but just to be sure, he felt the cold steel of his gun on his right hip with his forearm. When the dog first arrived, he had given him endless low growls for several days. He only growled once at his grandfather, but that stopped after he'd fed the dog leftover bacon and eggs from breakfast that first morning. Favian had finally stopped growling at him, but he still eyed Randall warily.

As Randall made his way up the stairs, the screen door opened.

"Favian. Go to your bed," Adella said, holding the screen open.

Randall had seen the large pillow they brought in for Favian that rested on the floor of Adella's bedroom in the basement. The dog dutifully listened to the woman's command.

Adella looked at him and continued to hold the screen open. He could tell she was distracted. "Dinner is ready. I used the rabbit you brought me this morning along with some root vegetables to make a stew. Your grandfather will be down shortly. I left the pot on the stove and there is bread and butter on the counter," she said, wiping her hands on the apron she wore each day. "Will Tal be joining soon or should I save his portion?"

Randall walked into the kitchen. "Yes, he's on his way," he said and looked around. "Where are your girls? Are they still doing their schoolwork?" He glanced toward the stairs that led down to the basement. He could hear Favian whining below.

"No. They are with their father. He came just before lunch to get them. He said he wanted to buy them a few winter clothes and then take them to lunch." She looked through the hall opening toward the front door. "I was hoping they would be home soon, but it's still a little early yet."

Randall felt his pulse begin to race with an anger he hadn't experienced in a long time. "How did he know you were here?" he demanded.

Adella looked Randall in the eyes. "He is their father. I can't just hide them from him. Besides," she said, shrugging her shoulders. "They miss him. For all his flaws, he tried to be a good father until the last few months or so. I think maybe he is trying to redeem himself."

"I doubt it," Randall interjected. "More like he's trying to see what's in it for him."

Favian's claws could be heard coming up the steps. He trotted to Adella and pushed her hand with his muzzle and continued to whine. She bent down and grabbed either side of his furry neck. "I know you're worried. Alex and Ana will be home soon. Don't worry about them."

"I wish you would have informed me that your ex-husband had come onto my property," Randall insisted. "I don't know this man and I don't trust him." From what Tal had told him, the man was about to lose everything. Desperate people could do desperate things.

She began to untie her apron. "I didn't let him in. Everyone knows your grandfather. He thinks I'm just working for him. He didn't ask any questions. He should be back within the hour. Until then, I'm going to lie down. C'mon, Favian. Let's take a quick nap," she said, taking off the apron and draping it over her arm.

Randall watched her walk down the steps with Favian at her heels. She wore a long white skirt and a red knitted sweater. Her face was made up beautifully, like usual, except today she donned a deep red lip color. Although she was only a housekeeper, she dressed every day like she was working a storefront. He could tell she was worried, though. The makeup could not hide her emotions.

Randall heard footsteps coming into the kitchen.

"Was that Adella?" his grandfather asked. "Did the girls make it home yet?"

Randall shook his head. "No, they are not here. And it is none of our business," he said a little too firmly. "If she wants to give her girls over to a man who is self-destructing, that is up to her. Now, let's eat."

His grandfather looked out the window. "He was just going to spend a few hours with them and get them a bite to eat. It seems a little late. The sun is already going down."

Randall tried to calm his breaths. The anger he was feeling was not proportionate to the situation. He needed to distract his thoughts and consider his feelings when he was alone. He couldn't let himself get soft, especially not for a woman. "Come and sit. This is none of our concern."

His grandfather didn't look convinced, but he walked to his usual place at the table and sat. Adella had already laid out his stew, buttered bread and hot tea. He sat down and began to quietly eat.

Randall walked to the cupboard and got out one of the larger ceramic bowls and a spoon from the drawer. He ladled out several helpings of stew and tore off a big chunk of bread, sliding it firmly over the butter before sitting down. He began to eat quietly just as Tal opened the screen door and walked in.

"Smells good," Tal said.

Randall kept his gaze on his stew as Tal spooned out his portion and sat down.

"You two are quiet," Tal said after swallowing a big bite of his bread. He leaned back into his chair. "Adella sure knows how to bake bread." He looked around. "The girls ain't joining us for dinner? I haven't seen Alex and Ana all day."

Randall felt his frustration surge. Just another reminder that he was not keeping proper order in his house. His grandfather had insisted that Adella and her girls eat dinner with them. He should have said no from the start, but he was intrigued by the dark, sultry eyes of his new housekeeper. Adella dining at his table gave him more opportunity to look at her. Now look at him. Eating dinner void of a female's presence and being upset by it.

Randall slammed his fist on the table so hard that the bowls rattled, and his grandfather's tea splashed over the lip of his cup. "I don't want to hear another word about it! This is none of our concern!"

Tal and his grandfather gaped for several seconds until they finally recovered and continued eating their dinner. Tal looked like he was about to say something, but instead, he took another large bite of his bread, keeping his gaze on the table.

Randall forced down another spoonful of his stew. He had lost his appetite, but he wouldn't let Tal and his grandfather know. The girls were not his responsibility. They had only been there a short while, and the emotions he was feeling were totally unfounded. Suddenly, he heard the scratching of paws coming briskly up the basement stairs. Favian jogged to the kitchen table next to Randall, sat down and began to whine.

Randall stared at the wolf-dog mix and cocked his head to the side. He had been growled at by the animal, but this was new. He looked to his grandfather. "Why is he doing that?"

"Maybe he wants some food," Randall's grandfather said, spooning a portion of meat out of his bowl. "Here. Have a piece of rabbit." He threw the meat on the ground, but the dog didn't notice. He continued to look at Randall and whined louder. Suddenly, he got up and trotted to the front door. He looked back at Randall and barked.

"He's worried," Randall said matter-of-factly. He thought for a moment and finally let his spoon drop on the table. "Tal," he said looking toward the young man. "You know where Adella's ex-husband lives?"

Tal placed his spoon onto the table, as well. "I sure do," he answered.

Randall got up from his chair. "Then let's go for a little drive. Tal, go get your truck. I'll get Favian."

CHAPTER 12

Tal turned off his headlights and slowly crept the truck up the driveway. The small house almost disappeared in the trees surrounding it. Randall didn't wait for Tal to put the truck into park.

"Keep Favian in the truck." He opened the truck door, got out and marched up the driveway to the front porch. His smoldering anger accumulated like thick smoke in his mind. He could hear Favian barking furiously from the truck. The dog's anger was just as impassioned as his own. He could feel fury radiating from his palms. His entire evening had been disrupted, and he hated unforeseen disturbances that were out of his control. But his lack of control in this situation ended right now. Right here.

He walked up to the door and banged loudly. He heard nothing for several seconds, so he banged again.

"Who is it?" he heard a rough voice yell. Then the voice was cut short.

The man must have tripped because Randall heard a loud thump hit the ground and glass shattering. A string of loud curse words followed quickly after.

"I am John Hunt's grandson. I need to talk with you!" Randall yelled and put his ear to the door. He needed the man to get closer.

"What's that old man want with me. I ain't done nothing to him," the man yelled.

His voice sounded closer like he was right at the door. Randall took the opportunity. He stepped back several feet and rammed his entire body into the door. The hinges popped off and the door slammed the man on the other side. Randall let the door fall on top of him.

"Whoa," Tal said, coming up from behind. "I wasn't expecting that."

"Grab the door off of him," Randall commanded.

Tal bent over and picked up the door. Blood flowed out of the man's nose.

Randall reached down and wrenched the man onto his feet. "Where are Alex and Ana?" he yelled. He could smell the whiskey in the man's breath.

"What was that for?" the man screamed. "You broke my nose!"

"Where are Alex and Ana?" Randall repeated, pushing the man's back against the wall.

"They went home!" he yelled.

"You lie!" Randall yelled. He took his fist and struck the man deep within his belly.

"No, I swear. I sent them home!"

"What do you mean you *sent* them home?" Randall asked though he knew the answer.

The man rubbed away blood from his lips with his sleeve. "Those ungrateful brats. I took them to lunch. I bought them jackets. Then they wanted to go home. They wouldn't even stay at the house a bit and spend some time with me, their father! So they walked home."

"When did you start drinking?" Randall asked. "Before or after they decided to walk home."

The man said nothing, but the silence was disturbed by Favian's intense barking and growling that echoed down both sides of the street.

"So, you—their father—willingly let two young girls walk over five miles in the dark and cold because you didn't or couldn't drive them. You should be thankful all I gave you was a broken nose," Randall said. Then he pulled out his gun from his hip holster and held it against the man's cheek. "You better hope that we find them or I will be back to break every bone in your body."

The man winced.

"And how long have they been gone?"

"Only about twenty minutes ago. They'd be right off the main road. I was just about to go get them. I swear!"

Randall could tell the man had sobered up quickly. "Now listen very clearly. Adella and her girls live under my roof. They are my responsibility now. If you want to contact them, you must go through me first. Do you understand me?"

The man vigorously nodded his head. "Yes, sir! I do!"

"Good," Randall said, releasing his grip and letting the man drop to the ground.

Randall looked toward Tal who was grinning wide-eyed. "Let's go find the girls."

Randall walked back to the truck and got in. Favian jumped on his lap and began to smell him. "Get in the back seat. I took care of him," he said, hoisting the large dog to the back. The dog put his muzzle back to the cracked window and continued to bark at the house with the broken door.

Tal got in the driver's side a second later. "Favian knows that house. I don't think he likes his previous owner anymore." He started the truck.

"They are walking off the main road, so they won't be seen by the cars. We need to have some sort of signal to let them know it is us. They know your truck, but it's too dark to see it," Randall said.

"I have an idea," Tal said. He pressed a button on the dashboard, and his newly mounted roof lights shined brightly.

"Now we can see them, but how will they know who we are?" Randall asked.

Tal flipped on another switch. "Don't worry about them seeing us. The girls know my favorite album. I let them listen to it the other day. They'll hear us."

Music began to blast from the speakers and Randall jumped in his seat.

"Roll down your window!" Tal shouted over the noise. "With our lights and music, they'll know who we are!"

Randall instantly rolled down the window, thankful that the vibration of the music lessened now that it could escape the cab of the truck. He didn't like that the music had startled him, but Tal didn't seem to notice. In fact, Tal seemed to enjoy this little distraction, like they were on some heroic adventure.

Tal backed the truck out of the driveway and turned on the main road heading back to the estate. He drove slowly, and the loud music disturbed the noiseless atmosphere around them. Randall kept his eyes on the tree line that rimmed the road about eight feet back. They drove for almost ten minutes when Randall saw a figure peeking out from the woods.

"Stop here!" he yelled. He jumped out of the truck and tried to find the figure again. "Alex! Ana! It is Randall Hunt, your mother's boss. I'm here to take you home."

Randall opened the back door of the truck, and Favian jumped out. He began to sniff the air and instantly made his way to where Randall was looking and vanished into the darkness. Randall continued to call for the girls. He could hear Favian whimpering. Suddenly, two young girls burst onto the road with Favian jumping around them. They saw the truck and ran toward the music. As the two girls came closer, he was surprised when they each threw their arms around his waist and held onto him tightly. "Ah—be careful girls. My gun is on my hip."

The girls didn't let go. He could hear them as their hot tears began to soak into his shirt. Finally, the music and the lights from the truck turned off, and Randall could hear Tal walking toward them. Favian continued to circle and whine.

"I knew my music would work," Tal said. "And good job, Favian!" He exclaimed, bending down to pet the anxious dog. "You sniffed them out." He reached his hand toward Alex and

Ana. "Come on, girls. Let Mr. Hunt alone and get into the truck. Your mother is very worried about you."

The girls let go of Randall. The older one, Alex, looked up at him. "We prayed that you would rescue us, and you did!"

"Thank you, Mr. Hunt," the younger one said. "And thank you for playing the music, Tal," she said, smiling at him.

"No need to thank us," Tal said. "Now let's get you both home." Each girl grabbed one of Tal's hands, and Favian jogged behind them. Tal led them back to the truck and got all three comfortable in their seats. Favian sat between the girls, licking each of their faces and whining for attention.

When Randall got back into the truck, he looked at the trio sitting happily in the backseat. Favian sat contented next to the girls. Randall recalled the way the dog growled and barked at the window of his truck. He looked at Tal after he started the engine. "Do you think Favian would have hurt him if we would have let him out?"

"I don't know, but his barking was intense. He is protective of Adella and the girls, but I've never heard him bark like that. I have to admit, though, I think if he did get out of the truck, he would have done some serious bodily damage to Adella's ex-husband."

Randall nodded. "I think I agree with you."

CHAPTER 13

Randall listened to Alex and Ana whisper excitedly when they pulled into his estate. They had already claimed his house as their own. He wouldn't admit it, but it felt good to have people in his charge again. He had spent so many years protecting Eve Pallue, and although there were written attacks on her life, she never faced an enemy that he needed to save her from—well, except for himself.

He was the one who willingly let her experience an Awakening in her Sleeper. He had known that it had been tampered with on Neil Elder's command at the factory. Though, they didn't know at the time that it would actually kill some Efficientists. It was supposed to just slow them down, so their rank could drop a bit. He also orchestrated the fire that ended Eve's life. She had dismissed him so easily after years of dedication that he had given her. He was angry—and even happy when Neil asked him to do another job for the World Government. One that, if he were honest, he had pressed Neil to let him do. But now it felt like a boulder of heaviness landed on the bricks of guilt that already weighed him down.

Tal got back into the truck. "The fence is secure," he said, continuing the drive down the winding driveway that led to the Hunt Estate.

Randall was relieved for the distraction from his thoughts. He looked at the watchtowers. They were both lit. The estate had plenty of generators to go around and seemingly unending fuel. He could live his entire life here, like his grandfather, and be happy—or at least, in control.

"Tal, we need to set up gardens. And we should purchase some more milk cows and chickens. We have a lot more mouths to feed now. I want this estate to be able to maintain itself without reliance on anyone else."

Tal nodded his head. "I think it's a good idea. I know where to get more livestock, and I'll look into buying seeds and farming equipment for the spring. My mother would always ask Mr. Hunt to do these things, but he was content to stay in his room reading his books."

"Your mother sounds like a wise woman," Randall said. He didn't know why, but he felt he needed to reassure Tal on that matter.

"Yes, she was," Tal agreed, quietly. "She could have done so much more with her life. She was a very industrious woman, but she was comfortable taking care of Mr. Hunt." He paused. "I think she was simply grateful to have a safe place to raise me. Life was hard before we came to live here."

Randall said nothing. He could see the porchlight of his estate. His grandfather and Adella were standing under the light. Maybe if he could take care of those in his charge, the people on that porch, he could redeem his past sins. And maybe he could start to earn some of that forgiveness he had been given freely—maybe.

Favian began to whine from the back seat. He was ready to get out and stretch his legs. When Tal came to a stop, Alex opened her door and Favian jumped out.

"Stay in the car, girls. Let me help you out," Randall said. He didn't want to get them home safely only to have them trip in the dark on the uneven ground.

He got out of the truck, and Favian came up to him and licked his hand. "Move back, Favian. Don't want you to knock over the girls with your enthusiasm," he said, pushing his body in between the truck door and the anxious wolf-dog.

"Where were they?" Adella asked, coming up behind him. "I was worried sick."

Randall widened the opened door. "I'll let Tal tell the story when we get in the house." Randall didn't know if Adella would appreciate the damage he had done to her ex-husband's face, but after she found out that he forced the girls to walk home in the dark and cold, she may not mind so much.

"Okay, Alex. Let me help you down," he said, picking up the eldest girl and setting her down next to her mother. "Now you, Ana. It's way past your bedtime."

He placed both girls safely on the ground, and they grabbed hold of their mother.

"Oh, thank You, Lord! Thank You for bringing them safely home!" she exclaimed. After kissing each girl several times on the face, she stood and turned to Randall. "Thank you, Mr. Hunt. I don't know what to say. I didn't want to upset you with my problems, so I went straight downstairs to ask God to help me. Thank you! You were an answer to my prayer. And thank you, Tal," she said, turning to the young man. "I will cook you all your favorite meals for a week!"

"It was nothing," Tal said, awkwardly. "Favian also helped. He was able to smell the girls in the dark."

Randall noticed that Tal enjoyed the attention that Adella gave him. She probably somewhat filled the void left behind after his own mother died. Plus, Adella was stunningly beautiful, and any man would be drawn to her affection.

"What happened? Why were they gone so long?" Adella asked.

"It's best not to talk about it in front of the girls," Randall said, motioning for Tal to not talk. "Why don't you get the girls ready for bed? Then you can meet us in the kitchen, so we can let you know what happened on our end."

"I, for one, want to know every last detail of that man's negligence and what my grandson did about it," the aged man said from the porch. "Glad you girls are home safe. Would be impossible to get any sleep if you two weren't tucked safely into your beds."

Randall looked surprised at his grandfather. He was visibly upset. It was a wonder how fast Colonials bonded—

much faster than Efficientists. The Efficientists called it Community Lifestyle—or something like that. He had worked for Eve Pallue for years and hadn't bonded with her like this. There was always mistrust and a sense of triviality to relationships. But here in the colonies, bonds needed to be made to survive. Already his amassing army of young men were showing signs of loyalty and devotion that he had never experienced with the other bodyguards in the city. The relational webbing he was building around him was new, but he rather enjoyed it because he was the one in charge, and they all looked to him for answers.

Randall held his cup of coffee that Adella had given him. He watched her walk the length of the kitchen back and forth, slicing bread, grabbing butter and jam from the refrigerator and bringing plates down from the cupboard. She insisted they all needed a snack before the night's events were explained. She wore a long, blue robe over her full-length nightgown. Her hair was pinned up and face washed. A few curly strands brushed across her cheek. She had been crying, and her normally large eyes were puffy and pink. Randall thought she looked more beautiful now without makeup and in her robe than the first time he met her.

Tal had tried to help her with food preparations, but she insisted they all sit down at the table. Tal sat smiling, sipping his tea and honey. The boy looked like he had just conquered the world. Randall hid a laugh and looked at his grandfather who was sitting opposite him on the other end of the round table. The old man was petting Favian. The dog had run up and down the stairs to check on the girls. Whenever he heard one of them whisper, he would trot the steps down to make sure all was well. Finally, the girls had fallen asleep, and the dog sat next to his grandfather, knowing he would most likely sneak him a bite to eat from whatever was served.

Finally, Adella sat a plate in front of each of them and placed one down for herself before joining them at the table. Randall noticed her slice of bread was small, and there was no butter nor jam on it. He doubted if she would eat any of it.

She put her elbows on the table and cupped her hands together. "Okay, what happened?"

Tal looked at Randall and waited for approval, and he nodded the go-ahead.

"So we get to your husband's house," Tal began.

"You mean, ex-husband," Adella interrupted.

"Yeah, sorry. Ex-husband. And Randall, I mean Mr. Hunt, knocked the door down right on top of him. Broke his nose and all! Mind you, he'd been drinking a lot. I could smell it six feet away. Probably no other way to get into the house than to bust down the door," Tal said, watching Adella's expression. When she didn't react, he continued. "He said that he had sent the girls home because they didn't want to stay any longer. What probably happened is that he drank so much, the girls didn't trust him to drive. They're smart. So he made them walk home."

Adella took in a deep breath. Randall assumed she was taking it all in. "How did you find them?"

"Remember the other day when the girls wanted to borrow some of my music? That was the CD they took. So I played it hoping they would know it was us."

She nodded and pushed her plate away. Randall saw fresh tears sliding down. "Thank you both for bringing them home. I assure you that this will not happen again."

"I seriously doubt it," Tal laughed. "Mr. Hunt told your ex-husband that you and your girls were his responsibility now, and he would have to go through him first if he wanted to see you all."

Adella looked at Randall astonished. He felt embarrassed under her stare, but years of keeping his expression nonchalant helped hide his emotions.

"Why would you say that?" she asked.

"Look, I am a man of control. I don't like what happened tonight almost as much as you. Your ex-husband is a loose cannon and can't be trusted. I don't need to know your business, but as long as you are under my roof, your ex-husband must be monitored."

Adella's gaze fell to the table.

"It's just a form of protection, Adella," Randall's grandfather interjected. "You told me yourself that your ex-husband is not the man you married."

Adella began to weep. "He's nothing like the man I married. It's like he has become someone completely different. I don't even recognize him anymore. My girls don't recognize him. And from what you've said, Favian doesn't even recognize him! I keep thinking he is that man I fell in love with, but he's not. And I must let go of what he was." She pushed off from the table.

"Don't worry about the dishes, Miss Adella. I'll clean up for you," Tal said, getting up.

She smiled at him and gave him a hug. "You are truly a gem," she said.

He beamed under the compliment.

Randall watched Adella make her way downstairs. Favian followed her. As she disappeared into the basement, Randall wondered. If her ex-husband could change so completely to where he was unrecognizable, then Randall could change too. But instead of turning bad, he could somehow turn good.

CHAPTER 14

Randall squinted and continued to stare at the small words on the onion-thin page. He felt the strain behind his right eye build. He scratched at the eye patch over his left eye socket, wishing the gaze from that eye were still there. Everything was slightly off. If he wasn't careful, he sometimes knocked things over. His gun aim was slightly off. And he couldn't read the tiny letters on his grandmother's *Bible*. Nothing worked like it should. He kept reading the same words over and over again, but none of them made sense.

He closed his eyes in frustration and slammed the center of the *Bible* with his fist. How was he supposed to figure out this God thing if he couldn't understand the words?

"Would you like me to read to you?" a sincere voice asked.

He looked up. Adella stood at his office door holding a plate with what looked like his breakfast. "No, I can read!" he said loudly. He felt foolish. She looked beautiful and fresh, and he was a handicapped man trying to discern words from an old book. She continued to smile at him in her serene way. He appreciated that she didn't flinch at his harsh tone.

She walked over to his desk and set the plate down. Then she closed the large, worn *Bible* and read the cover. "Just as I thought, KJV. It's the King James Version. I've never read it. It would be like reading a foreign language to me."

He looked back at the *Bible*. "Is a translation like a variety?" he asked, thinking about the varieties that Efficientists use to speak condensed English.

"Kind of," she nodded. "Except this translation was written hundreds of years ago." She put her hands on her hips.

Her curly, dark hair was loosely pinned into a wide bun, and many of the tendrils escaped to frame her face. "I have an extra *Bible*. It's only the New Testament, but it will get you started. You'll never get anywhere with that one."

He looked back down at it. "It was my grandmother's *Bible*," he said, remembering the times he would visit when he was a child. He would wake up to the smell of breakfast and his grandmother sitting at the kitchen table reading the book in the light of the morning sun. "My grandfather complained about it too, but I would see her reading it constantly."

"I didn't realize it had sentimental value. I apologize if I have offended you. Maybe if you read my *Bible* first, you can come back to this one and it will make more sense."

"Maybe," he repeated. He didn't mention the fact that he had no idea what she meant by *New Testament*. He had already exposed his ignorance by not knowing what a translation meant. That was enough humiliation for one day. "Thank you for breakfast." He picked up the fork and began cutting the sausage. "I appreciate the protein."

She smiled. "You're welcome. I see you working out a lot. I don't know much about lifting weights, but I do know that you need to eat a lot of meat. I believe you would forget to eat if I didn't bring you a plate."

He shrugged and kept eating. "I'm busy."

Adella walked to the far edge of the desk and leaned her hip against it. "I've noticed," she said. "The property is looking better and better. Tal has done a great job at implementing your orders. I've already begun the garden, and we have more cows and chickens. It's nice not having to rely on others for basic things."

Randall didn't look up from eating. Adella's reaction to him ever since he helped bring her daughters home had changed. She definitely wasn't like the Efficientists he had known, but she also wasn't like the Colonials he had known either. She was no longer guarded or distant. In fact, she'd come and talk to him for a few minutes throughout the day whenever there was a break in her duties of cooking, homeschooling and cleaning. She was relaxed around him now and sure of herself. The anxiety and apprehension he had seen on her face and demeanor the first day he met her were completely gone.

When he didn't say anything, she continued. "In fact, I see you working too much. I'd say you need to take a break every now and then and remember that quality of life is an important aspect of living life. Life doesn't mean much if you're not enjoying it."

He stopped and looked up at her. Her face was made up. Her lips were painted a bright pink and her eyelashes fanned out from her dark-lined eyes. She wore a silky, cream blouse that accentuated her tan skin and a long shimmery, lavender skirt. "Are you enjoying life?" he asked, expecting her to look away in retreat.

She didn't. She leaned in closer. "I've spent the last ten years of my life simply trying to make it through each day. But here and now, every day is new. Every day is bright and sunny. All my worries have vanished overnight. I can't explain it except to say that I've been drowning for so long, and to finally breathe feels exhilarating. It is like I've been given new life."

Her words surprised and gratified him. He had only given her a job and a bit of protection, but those two things had transformed her. He wouldn't admit it, but his handicap seemed small now in light of what he had accomplished in her eyes.

He put his fork down and continued to stare at her. She didn't look away. It seemed that she actually enjoyed this time to look at him. Was it her transformation that really confused him or his own? He was relieved when he heard the knock at the door. Randall looked up to see Tal's worried face in the doorway. "What happened?"

Tal entered the office. "One of the men got his hand crushed working on the oil digger. We need to find him a doctor. His hand is swelling up pretty bad, and I'm sure he's broken it."

Randall stood up. "You don't know of anyone?"

Tal shook his head. "I only know of the colonial hospitals."

"No, that would put us on the World Government's radar," Randall said.

"I know the factories usually have a doctor or a medic. The closest one is near Trinity Village."

"I know that place." Randall thought. The world he had left, which seemed at the other end of the galaxy, was actually less than an hour away.

"It's a big factory," Tal continued. "They'll probably have a doctor on staff. I can drive there now."

Randall shook his head and got up. "No, I'll go. I know the place, and I'm better at keeping a low profile. Do you have something you can give the man until I return?"

"I think Mr. Hunt may have something. He hurt his back a while back and needed pain pills. But I don't know if they are still good," Tal said.

"That'll do. Make sure you give him what he needs and let him rest. Elevate his arm and take some ice from my freezer and put it on his hand," Randall said. He looked to Adella. "Would you mind coming with me? I would look less threatening if I had a wife."

"A wife" she asked, confused.

Randall saw her cheeks flush and let out a low laugh. The confidence she had faded quickly. "Just for a few hours. Don't worry. I'm not going to try anything."

"But what about my girls? They're doing school right now."

"I'll watch them," Tal said. "And I'm sure Mr. Hunt will help, as well. He finds the girls entertaining."

Adella still looked unsure.

"Weren't you the one just telling me you have to learn to enjoy life?"

"This is an emergency, not a date."

Randall looked at Tal. "Go get the man situated and tell my grandfather to check on Alex and Ana."

"Yes, sir," Tal said and left.

Randall walked around the desk to Adella. "So you're after a date, huh?"

"Did I say *date*?" she whispered, as the red in her cheeks deepened. "I just meant a fun outing or a trip."

"Look, Adella, what if it was one of your girls needing help? We are going to have to jump this hurdle anyway. It might as well be today. We need to have a medical connection if this community we are building is going to survive."

Adella stared at the ground for a moment. "You're right. Something is bound to happen, and we should have a plan when it does." She looked back up at Randall. "You think we will be back before dinner?"

"If everything goes my way, I want to be back in less than four or five hours," Randall said. He knew he had the means to bargain with a doctor. If he could just make that connection, he would pay the doctor well for him to visit their compound.

"Okay, I'll go with you to Trinity. I've only been a few times. It's a nice village, and I hear they have a huge trading center there. How will you know how to find the doctor?"

"Finding an Efficientist in the colonies is simple. They always stand out," Randall said. He had been sent on hundreds of surveillance missions in the colonies. It was second nature for him to read people by simply watching them.

"Maybe we can scope out the village for a future outing or trip. I bet your girls would want to go. They have a great restaurant there that makes delicious pies."

Adella swiped a few of her dark tendrils behind her ear. "You'd take all three of us?"

"Of course," he said.

Her confidence must have returned because she stared at him like she did when he was eating breakfast. "I think they would like that," she said, smiling once more. "And so would I."

CHAPTER 15

Randall parked his truck in front of the Trinity Trading Center. He left Adella at the restaurant to wait for him. The factory workers who ate breakfast told him about the new doctor in town. Randall knew the doctor would be coming here. He knew who the doctor was, and he knew that Dr. Linton would be easy to persuade. But could he be trusted? Why would Neil Elder send Dr. Linton here, to Trinity? There had to be a motive behind that decision. Dr. Linton knew too much to just let go.

Randall looked back at the front doors of the building. The trading center was a new facility, replacing a church that had been there for years until church meetings were banned in *Life Plethoricity*—a joke of a life plan. Eve had written the life plan, and Neil Elder had stolen it. Randall had made the way with the flames he was apt at using. Same kind of flames that he used to quiet the loud preacher making a ruckus in the colonies. He had been hired to silence the Apostle too, but he had never found her. He wondered if the rumors about the Apostle were true. Was she really a Life Therapist? The same one on the list that Dr. Linton gave to Eve after her Awakening in the Sleeper?

Neil had found Eve's life plan in two locations. It was, of course, on Eve's LPS. However, it was also found on Christina Straight's Portable. Eve must have gone to see her. But why would she trust a therapist she hardly knew? Did the Apostle soften Eve's hard exterior somehow? Eve Pallue trusted no one—not even him. And she was correct not to trust him. He snuffed out her life in an instant. Neil gave the order and he obeyed like a trained dog.

Randall noticed that his hands were gripping the steering wheel so tightly that his fingers ached. He let go and tried to relax his body. That was the old Randall Hunt. If the preacher's son, Zacchaeus Mark Daniels, could forgive him for killing his father in the church fire, then he was forgiven for what he did to Eve Pallue, and what he did to countless others.

Randall smirked. At least, Neil Elder didn't get off so easily. The life plan did the opposite of what he expected. Instead of increasing his ratings, they instantly dropped, as Efficientists left rank. Eve Pallue had written it based on an empty life filled with producing. Her life plan was as hollow as she, and it didn't sit well with the rest of the Efficientists. Now Neil was letting Ada Armel throw a gala to distract the masses. It seemed to be working, a little. The Colonials at the restaurant were talking about it. They were discussing the Shaman, or Bear, as his friends called him. Bear was friends with the preacher's son. He had seen them together when he was sent out to find and get rid of Zach Daniels. He never did tell Neil about the Shaman's relationship with Zach, and now the Shaman was in the city. If Neil knew the friend of the man who stole from the World Bank was under his nose, he would have him turned in for questioning and then killed.

Randall thought of the fighter. He wouldn't have admitted it then, but he had great respect for the man. Maybe that was why he never exposed him. He had punched through his truck window to get his wife back. Randall scratched at his eye patch. The glass that buried deep into his left eye caused him the greatest amount of pain he had ever felt. Bear protected what was his and didn't let a glass window get in his way. Randall was a bodyguard all of his life, but he never had risked his life to save anyone—not really. Maybe a few times he had to get Eve Pallue away from threats, but would he have punched through thick glass to save her? Probably not. He had never loved anyone like that. He didn't even know if he was capable of such love.

He noticed movement at one of the front doors. It was Dr. Linton. Randall got out of his truck quickly.

"Dr. Linton," Randall said. He kept his hands down and his palms open to show that he had no weapon. The doctor would be skittish to see him since he had been declared dead.

The doctor turned to him and looked surprised, but not as much as Randall was expecting. He seemed more relieved than anything. He let go of the door handle and let it close. Then he walked toward the truck where Randall stood.

"Hi, Randall. I was wondering when you would come to visit me," Dr. Linton said.

"You know I'm still alive?" Randall questioned.

"I know the World Government has declared you dead, but they do lie a lot, don't they?" Dr. Linton said. "I know a John Hunt owns property a little over an hour from here. I know that people have been talking about a new boss of that property—a grandson—who is amassing an army."

Randall half smiled. "Not quite an army. Just a few men to help me repair my property, which is why I came. One of my men is injured. We need a doctor. I'll pay you well. We just need you for the day. I can bring you back this evening."

Randall watched Dr. Linton think. He had a bag in his arms from the trading center that he shuffled to the other arm. Finally, Dr. Linton looked around to see if anyone was listening.

"Look, I'm a dead man. I know too much. Neil and Matt Coughlin sent me away from the gala. I don't know why, but it can't be good. Now I know too much about this place. Everywhere I go, clues come to me. I can't stop it. I'm a liability. I expect to be killed any day now. I'm this close," he said, holding up his thumb and index finger about an inch apart with his free hand, "to doing it myself. I can't live like this anymore."

Randall listened to Dr. Linton. The man did know too much, but Randall wasn't sure if he wanted to acquire that liability.

"Look, all I need is a place of my own. Just give me a cottage on your property, and I will take care of your medical needs. I just want to live in peace. The city has ruined me. All I ask is for food, shelter and safety. I would have come to you sooner, but I heard that your men carry bows and arrows and shoot at anything that moves. If I do die, I want it to be quick. Not with a bunch of arrows protruding from my body and draining my blood for several hours," Dr. Linton said, allowing his voice to rise.

"Keep your voice down," Randall hissed and leaned in. "I don't know if I can trust you. What if you were sent here by Neil just to find me and gather information? You are going to have to give me something that convinces me that I can trust you. The fact that you weren't surprised to see me makes me think you have been planted here to find me."

"If you don't trust me, then why come find me?" Dr. Linton asked, exasperated.

"Because I need a doctor. One of my men is hurt," Randall said. He wondered if he should have taken this trip in the first place. He could just let the man suffer. But he had promised his men that he would take care of them. He couldn't violate their trust. He would lose everything he had built so far, and Adella would probably never look at him the way she did earlier that morning.

"I promise you," Dr. Linton pleaded. "They all think you're dead. They are not searching for you. They got a report from Ted Stanton, the director of the factory, that you had died in an accident. Your case is closed."

Randall looked down to think. "They were supposed to get rid of me, but I was able to get away." He didn't mention that he was saved by the very man he was sent to destroy. He looked back at Dr. Linton. "Still, that isn't enough to make me trust you."

Dr. Linton brought the bag he was holding to the center of his chest and wrapped both his arms around it. "Okay, I have information that no one knows. I haven't told a single soul. Remember what you told me when we first met at the colonial hospital? You said to always act like you know less than you do. That's what I've done. I'm telling you information now that I have told no other. I am making myself vulnerable to you. I need your help. I need to get away from Neil and the city for good. I promise you if you don't take me in, I will kill myself anyway."

Randall examined Dr. Linton. His face was flushed, and his voice quaked a bit. He crossed his arms and thought. Having a doctor on his property would be a great benefit. What if Alex and Ana truly did get hurt or sick? Or if something happened to Adella? A doctor would be an asset, not a liability. Plus, Dr. Linton was right. Neil would eventually have him killed. He did know too much. He cleared his throat. "I doubt that you know anything that I don't know but let me hear what you have to say. I'll take you back to my property, and we will see about making arrangements for you."

Dr. Linton closed his eyes briefly and swallowed. "Eve Pallue did not die in the fire. I met her here in Trinity a while back to help with her dying mother. Her brother, or half-brother, Zach Daniels, is the one who stole from the World Bank."

Randall felt the air in his lungs being pushed out by unseen force. The heat of fear, relief and disbelief all wrapped into one powerful blow shot through his body like lightning. Then he thought of the woman, the Shaman's wife. She had seemed familiar to him, yet different. "The Shaman's wife," Randall whispered, lost in a memory.

"The Shaman at the gala?" Dr. Linton asked.

Randall shot a look to the doctor. "You're right. Clues do seem to come to you. Come with me. I'll take you back to my property. I want to hear the rest of those clues on the way."

"Can I get my stuff first?" Dr. Linton asked.

"No, it needs to look like your disappearance wasn't planned, like you have been kidnapped. Leave your stuff. I'll replace everything you lost."

"I guess all I really need is what's in this bag," Dr. Linton said, looking into the opening.

"What's in it?" Randall asked.

"Medicines I took from the factory clinic. I was going to trade them for credits at the trading center."

Randall nodded. "Good, bring them and let's go."

As they both walked back to the truck, they didn't notice the watching eyes and listening ears from the man inside the trading center. Pastor Tom hid behind the shelving that lined the wall next to the front doors of the building. Luckily, the wind had died down just in time for him to hear the last part of the conversation outside. Dr. Linton was leaving, and the rumors were true. Randall Hunt was in his family's estate, building an army.

CHAPTER 16

Shayla looked around the city flat. This was her first time in the city. First time in a high-rise. First time without her mother. Her mother had finally allowed her to stay—only after she asked her father—the Shaman, or Bear as he is called now—a million questions. She looked at her stepmother, Ruth, who was sewing thick fabric of a long skirt on an electric sewing machine. To Shayla, the woman looked like she could have been almost her age. Maybe a little older. Her mother berated her father for marrying so young, but to their astonishment, Ruth was in her thirties only a few years younger than Bear.

"Have you finished reading the assigned chapters?" her stepmother asked, stopping the needle's flow of thread.

Shayla looked back at the screen of the LPS and frowned. "It's boring. I don't want to do school while I'm here."

Ruth's face did not change expressions. "A biased assessment. Your mother has allowed you to stay on the condition that you continue your studies."

"Can't I go with you to one of the events at the gala, please? I can't go back home and tell my friends I was in the city, but I never got to attend any of the *Grand Opus Gala*. I'm tired of being stuck inside. I want to do something fun."

Shalya watched as Ruth placed her thin hands on her lap and thought. Ruth's face was slightly pale with dark hues under her eyes like she wasn't getting enough sleep. She had a very petite frame that made Shayla feel almost masculine since she looked a lot like her father who had a strong body structure. After several moments, Ruth used the back of her arm to wipe her forehead before looking at her. Shayla noticed that Ruth's face began to glisten with sweat.

"I will ask Ada if you can attend one of the events. The assigned seating is usually full. However, if you do want to attend, you will have to complete all your assignments each day and sew your own outfit," Ruth said. "I have enough to sew for Bear and me."

"Are you okay?" Shayla asked concerned, forgetting about the gala for the moment. "You look like you're getting sick." She watched her stepmother scoot her chair away from the sewing machine. Her face suddenly got even pastier than her already white complexion. "You're going to throw up, aren't you?" Shayla jumped from her chair. She scanned quickly for a container of some sort. She spied a small wastebasket next to the desk and lunged for it. She brought it to Ruth just in time.

Ruth vomited several times into the basket that was now on her lap. Shayla held her hair back and away from the putrid liquid. Earlier that morning, she had sat with Ruth at breakfast, and noticed she didn't eat much. She couldn't possibly have that much food in her stomach. Finally, after two more dry heaves, the retching stopped. Shayla removed the wastebasket and brought it to the sink in the kitchen. When she came back, Ruth was lying on the couch in a fetal position.

"*Aha-enah* said you might be trying to have a baby. Looks like he was right," Shayla said, grinning. "I have two brothers and a baby sister. My brothers are four and five years old, and my little sister is almost one. I helped my mom with each pregnancy and delivery. She'd get really sick too. I told myself I would never have kids when I saw how sick she got, but then Tucker was born, and he's so cute. Then she got pregnant with Tanner, and she had the same sickness all over again. But when she got pregnant with Taylor, my little sister, her sickness got even worse. I don't think she left her room for five months. I had to take care of my brothers, and they were definitely a handful."

Ruth looked up at her from the couch. "I had no symptoms the first several weeks, but my condition changed suddenly. I am unable to sleep. I feel nauseated all the time. I am scared to eat, but I know it is imperative. I feel helpless."

Shayla knew that the city doctors were always available and would even come to the Efficientists' homes. She didn't ask Ruth why she didn't just call the doctor, but she had a suspicion it had something to do with why she always wore a mask when she left the flat. "I
know what to do. First, it is way too hot in this place. Let me open the windows and let the winter air in."

"I do not like the cold," Ruth said.

"Believe me, you'll like it now," Shayla said, walking to the windows. They opened easily and the cool breeze flooded the room.

Ruth turned onto her back. "You are right. The cold does feel good."

Shayla nodded. "Now, how do I order food and supplies?"

Ruth pointed to the LPS. "You have to log into our temporary account."

Shayla walked to the LPS and gladly closed out her assignment. Maybe if she took care of her stepmother, she wouldn't have to do her schoolwork. The same thing happened each time her mother was pregnant. She was always relieved from schoolwork for a time. A letter appeared on the screen from a Levi Jones to Bear. "Hey! This is the letter from the baker to my father!"

"The letter arrived a day too late," Ruth said from the couch, "which is probably just as well. Ada wanted the entire world to watch our surprised expressions to boost ratings, and that is exactly what happened."

Shayla smiled. "Yep, I still have the highest-rated night at the gala so far. You would think that Ada would want me back again."

"Unless you can offer Ada further increases in ratings, she will not ask for you," Ruth said matter-of-factly.

"You're probably right," Shayla said. "But I still want you to see if she can squeeze me in at least one more night. I would like to watch my father perform." She closed out of the letter and scanned the screen. "There, I see the Runner services symbol," she said, pointing to the icon of a figure pushing a dolly. She ordered everything Ruth would need to feel better, and then she ordered several things for herself. There was so much more to choose from—lots of factory-made foods, which she never got at home. "You don't mind if I order a few things for myself, do you?"

"Help yourself. The World Government is paying the bill," Ruth said.

"Well, in that case," Shayla said. She began clicking everything that looked remotely good. When she finally submitted the request, she was impressed that her order would be delivered later that day. "Wow! Our groceries will be here in a few hours. I could get used to living in the city."

"You would hate it," Ruth said.

"Why?" Shayla asked looking at her stepmother who now seemed to be shivering. "Are you cold?"

"Yes, but I feel better."

"Your lips are turning blue," Shayla said. She looked around and spied several bolts of fabric. She reached for the thicker fabric and unrolled it. There was enough fabric for a small blanket. She walked to her stepmother and laid the blanket gently over her. "That will be better for you. Now try to get some sleep. I'll make you a brothy soup when you wake up."

"Thank you, Shayla. You have helped me today. I was sewing and praying to God for help. I did not feel well, but I do not want to call a doctor."

"That's okay. I'll be here," Shayla said and thought. "Why would I hate the city?"

Ruth did not open her eyes. "You dislike schoolwork," she whispered softly. "In the city, schoolwork takes up the majority of our day."

Shayla watched her stepmother drift off to sleep. She was probably right. She would hate doing work all day. She liked hanging out with her friends. She hated sitting down for long. Maybe getting factory-made food delivered to your door wasn't worth a lifestyle of sitting and working all day.

She heard the front door of the flat squeak open. She quickly put her index finger to her lips when she saw her father walk in. "Ruth is asleep," she whispered.

He nodded and quietly closed the door behind him. He was drenched in sweat despite the cold air. He had been using a small gym that had been set up in one of the spare rooms of the building. Although he was older than the video clips she had first seen of him, he still looked like that same Shaman. He had aged well. Besides the grey strands running through his long black hair and the deepened creases on his forehead and the edges of his eyes, he looked fit and healthy. He came and stood beside her.

"Was she sick?" he asked, staring down at her.

"Yes, I forgot about the wastebasket. I'll clean it out," Shayla said.

"How did you get her to sleep?" he asked.

"The cold air helps. I ordered her a few things to be delivered. I've helped my mom with all her pregnancies. I can help Ruth too," Shayla said and wondered what her dad would say. She had only been there a few days. Although she didn't know him well, she liked his upfront personality. She never had to guess what he thought. He stated exactly how he felt and what he was thinking. It made her nervous at first, but now it alleviated her anxiety. He would talk. She would talk. And together they would figure things out. Just like they did when they came up with a compromise for her to stay in the city during the gala.

"My wife is strong in her heart and in her mind, but when it comes to out here in the real world, she is very weak. If you can help her during this time, I will be grateful to you," he said and turned to her. "But I feel already indebted to you because I was not there for the first fourteen years of your life. I am now at a place where I don't believe I will ever make up for what you have lost."

Shayla felt a rush of embarrassment. Although her stepfather had always loved her, he was a reserved man and didn't show his emotions well. But this man, her real father, was honest and expressed his emotions easily. She didn't know if his bluntness was a personality trait, a trait of his Native American heritage or a trait of being a fighter, but she guessed it was probably a mixture of all three.

"Just being here has filled a weird void I've always had. It has been difficult growing up in a family that was so different from me. Don't get me wrong. I love my mom and my brothers and sister and my stepdad, but I've always felt like I didn't fully belong. When I met *Aha-enah* at your house, something in me clicked. It was like all my questions were suddenly answered."

He crossed his arms. "It is difficult not fitting in, but it forces you to find your own way and not rely on others. My best fighters are always the ones who have something to prove."

Shayla nodded and held her breath uneasily for a moment. "I—I was wondering. I've been avoiding it, but we never discussed what I should call you. I call my stepfather, Dad, because I've known him since I was three years old. But my mother called your grandfather *Aha-enah*, which I really liked. It means grandfather, right?"

"Correct," he answered.

"What would be the word for father in our language, the *Ka'to* language?"

"It is *Ah-nah*," Bear said. "I have never used that name. My own father was an Anglo fighter and didn't have much use for my mother's heritage."

"Oh," she whispered.

He stared at her waiting for her to continue, so she quickly asked her question. "Would you mind if I called you *Ah-nah*? I want to learn more about my heritage—even if just a little. And I like that word. It's easy to say, and it's different."

Bear kept his arms crossed for a long while lost in thought. Finally, he smiled and placed both his hands on her shoulders. "I would be honored to be called *Ah-nah* by you Shayla. I pray in time that I can prove to be better than my own father. I will be a father that you and my unborn child deserve."

Shayla felt her cheeks flush even though the breeze that swept through the room was cool. "Thank you, *Ah-nah*," she whispered. Even as she spoke the foreign words to address her father for the first time, they felt comfortable, like she had been speaking them for years.

CHAPTER 17

Bear sat on the sofa. His belly was full and warm with the soup and bread Shayla had made. Once the groceries arrived, she went straight to work in the kitchen. She baked a whole chicken and then deboned it for the chicken and vegetable soup. She kneaded dough and baked fresh bread. As of late, his meals with Ruth in the city comprised of either fancy gala food where everyone watched him while he ate or factory-prepared food in the flat. Ruth did not cook. He didn't mind doing the cooking, but the demands of the gala were occupying his time, and he feared Ruth wasn't eating well enough. She had just started getting sick from the pregnancy, and he didn't know how he was going to care for her.

He listened to the shower going in the spare bathroom. Shayla was still in there. He laughed. It was nice to have a warm shower. She probably had never had one before. When she had asked to stay with them during the gala, he had said absolutely not. He thought having her would be too much of a burden. But when she cried in front of him, he couldn't tell her no. He owed her too much to reject her now. He realized, though, that she would make his time in the city easier. She could take care of Ruth while he continued to train.

His gaze went to Ruth at the LPS that lined the living room wall. She looked better now. She had eaten and not thrown up after. She was reading all the correspondence she had missed the last few days. With her sickness and Shayla's entry into their lives, she was a little behind.

He leaned back on the couch and rubbed his left shoulder with his right hand. His muscles ached. He had been lifting heavy at the small gym in the building. He was not in fighting shape, and he knew it. He thought of what Ada had told him earlier that day. He needed to boost his ratings. His demonstrations were becoming boring and predictable. What she didn't realize, though, was that it was difficult doing demonstrations without sparing partners. With the sport of fighting, there always had to be at least two people—preferably more.

"Not good," he heard his wife say in a soft whisper.

He looked back over to her. He couldn't read her emotions, which meant something was wrong.

"What is it?" he asked.

Ruth turned to him. "Pilar is in prison. She was unable to leave. The officer who helped her take the video footage at the labor camp explained to Pastor Tom that another officer detained her. He had to escape."

Bear jumped up from the couch. "What is Pastor Tom going to do to get her out?"

"Zach has already left to try to get her."

Bear shook his head. "He can't. If he gets caught, they'll get him on robbing the World Bank. They'll torture him for information."

"He needs to prevent the Kill Switch from being used," she said. "He believes he has a way to stop it from working. Or maybe he is simply saying that, so he can try to save Pilar."

"What? What is the Kill Switch?" Bear asked confused. He thought he had heard her mention it or he read about it somewhere.

"Li and Zach's strategy to take down the Regional Integrated Banking System is in place. They plan on doing it on New Year's Eve because the more people tuned into the gala, the more destruction they can create. The only thing that will stop their plan is the Kill Switch."

"But how does he expect to escape with Pilar once this is all over? Does he even think ahead?" Bear asked a little too loudly. He heard the shower stop. He needed to keep his voice down. His daughter knew of none of their plans.

Ruth stared at him. He could see tears filling the lower half of her golden-brown eyes. "If he can take down the RIBS, then the World Government will be crippled or even destroyed. His plan is to walk out with all the prisoners once this is over."

Bear knew his wife was hurting, though she didn't express it very well. He noticed something else in her eyes. "What else is wrong? There's more, isn't there?"

"Yes, but it is confusing. Pastor Tom cannot make sense of it, and he is normally excellent at anticipating the actions of others. I do not understand it either, but I do trust that it is for our good and not harm."

"God, help me," he said and began to pace. He finally stopped and exhaled. "What else is happening?"

Ruth thought for a moment. He knew she was gathering her words. He didn't take bad news very well, and she must be trying to buffer what she says.

"Jonah—or Matt as he is called here—sent Dr. Linton to Trinity Village."

Bear could hear his daughter walking into her bedroom, so he kept his voice down. "Why on earth would he do that? It doesn't make sense."

"I do not know. He probably sent him away to prevent him from seeing me at the gala, but the reason behind sending him to Trinity is a mystery to me. I trust him, though. He has his reasons."

Bear inwardly questioned his reasons, but he quickly remembered all that he had done for his wife. She wouldn't be here today if Jonah hadn't risked his life saving hers. "We haven't even seen him yet. Is he hiding from us?"

Ruth shrugged. "He is trained to stay behind the scenes. I am certain, though, he has seen us."

Bear made a mental note to do a better job at seeking Jonah out at the events. He was a large man. It couldn't be that hard to spot him. "Do you think Dr. Linton will discover what Zach and Li are up to? People in Trinity talk too much."

"He is no longer in Trinity," she said.

Bear was confused. "What? Where did he go? He could have only just gotten there."

Ruth looked back at the screen she had been reading like she was making sure of what she had read. She sighed and returned her gaze to him. "Pastor Tom saw Dr. Linton leave with Randall Hunt, my old bodyguard. Apparently, Randall moved into his grandfather's estate and is amassing a small army. There is a rumor that he has oil there."

"You're kidding me," Bear said. He had lived through some crazy things, but never in his life would he have imagined the events that were taking place around him today.

"Dr. Linton is one of the few people who knows that I'm alive. It is guaranteed that Randall knows now."

Bear froze stunned. "Well, this just keeps getting better. That man can't be trusted."

"We just have to trust God," Ruth said simply.

"That's easier said than done when you have more at stake." Suddenly, Bear felt powerless. Pastor Tom, Pilar, Zach— they were all risking their lives, and what was he doing? Going to social events and performing for the cameras. He needed to do more. He had to help his friends. "What can I do, Ruth? Tell me. I can't go on doing nothing while the people I love suffer."

"We need to get as many people tuned into the *Grand Opus Gala* on New Year's Eve as possible. The plan to take down the RIBS will not work otherwise."

Determination filled Bear's body. He had not been giving his best at the gala events. If the Shaman was what they craved, he would give the crowd exactly what they wanted. He needed every Colonial out there with an HMS to remember

121

who he was. And he needed every Efficientist in cities across the world to stop working and watch what he could do.

"I need to use the LPS," he said, walking to Ruth. He helped her up and sat down. He moved his hands to type and hesitated. Then he looked back at his wife. "Show me how to use this thing. I need to contact my fighters. I have a show to put on."

CHAPTER 18

Pastor Tom watched as Levi pushed his palms against the basement wall of the trading center. He had a difficult time getting Levi to follow him downstairs and out of earshot of the shoppers. As a father himself, he knew the anger and grief Levi was feeling. This was the second time he had lost his daughter, Pilar. The first time she was taken by force. And now she left by choice. Infiltrating the labor camp was a risk that she took, and she knew there was a possibility that she wouldn't be able to leave. At least not right away.

"But why? Why was securing this video worth the risk she took allowing herself to be imprisoned?" Levi asked, rubbing his dark hands against the stubbles of his face. "So what! You're making prints of it on that machine of yours," he said, pointing to the printing press. "How is that going to help anything?"

Pastor Tom heard a soft knock at his office door. "May I come in, Tom. It's Li."

"Yes, please, please come in," Pastor Tom said, relieved. He would need help explaining the situation to Levi.

Li walked in and closed the door behind him. Pastor Tom could tell he wasn't getting any sleep either. Their plan to take down the RIBS was meeting up with resistance. He would push to give up on the plan if Pilar and Zach weren't in desperate need for the plan to work.

He looked back at Levi. "We know how to take down the World Government by destroying the Regional Integrated Banking System, but we need as many people watching the gala as possible. The polls are not good. People are only tuning into Bear and the birdman. They like the costumes that Ruth is creating, and they are somewhat enraptured by the themes Ada is creating for every event; otherwise, they are bored with this *Grand Opus Gala*."

"What's that have to do with my daughter being in jail!" Levi interjected.

Li cleared his throat. "We needed the images for two reasons. One, we are giving the prints to Jonah. He has found a way to disperse them at the final New Year's Eve event at the gala. All the regional magistrates will be there, and other Elite Efficientists. They need to see what is happening. The World News will capture their expression and more people will tune into the gala to see what is going on."

"That isn't enough reason to sacrifice my daughter's life," Levi said. "What is the second reason?"

Pastor Tom walked to Levi. "We all agreed—you included—that we needed to take down the World Government. The world will not understand our reasons unless they know their hidden corruption. We must expose these forced labor camps that Neil Elder is running because they are only going to get worse. Only then will our actions be justified."

Li walked next to Pastor Tom and faced Levi. "Our plan is ready. Pastor Gupta has old-style computers being spread all over our region. I have more being delivered across the other nine different regions. There are Colonials and Efficientist across the globe who are helping us. They are repairing old computers and plugging them into the system. I can't explain it, but it is like the hand of God is helping us. My virus to take them down is being installed into each computer. In a few weeks, we should have several hundred computers ready for the New Year's Eve event, but it won't work unless the world is tuned into the gala. Everyone who received money points from the World Government must be online. Right now, there are not enough Efficientists and definitely not enough Colonials who are watching. We need to do everything possible to cause a commotion in order to make people come online. These images will help that. Pilar knew the importance of the video from the labor camp, and she took a risk."

Levi's arms fell limp to his sides. "Fine, you now have the video. Can't we now just go in and get her?"

"If our plan works," Pastor Tom assured. "The World Government will fall, and she and Zach can walk out."

"What about the officer who helped her get the video? What does he say? Can he help us get her back?"

Pastor Tom shook his head. "His identity must remain secret. He would assuredly get killed if he is exposed. He did what he promised, and we can't expect more from him."

Levi leaned forward and pounded the top of Pastor Tom's desk with both fists. "I have a wife at home who will not rest until her daughter is home. You can't expect me to do nothing while my daughter suffers!"

"I'm not asking you to do nothing," Pastor Tom said, calmly. "But I'm asking you to trust us. Trust what God is doing."

"No!" Levi yelled. "You sit and do nothing. I will not sit by and not go after my daughter. Not again."

"Zach is on his way there," Li interjected.

"What can that boy do for her? He has proven he doesn't love her with his indifference. She should have moved on long ago, but she waited for love. Well, I'm not waiting. I will get my daughter whether you help me or not!" Levi walked to the door and yanked it open. He looked back and stared at Tom. "I won't mess with your plan, but I will get my daughter back even if I have to exchange my life for hers."

Pastor Tom watched Levi Jones, the founder of Levington, storm out of his office. He wondered what Austin Daniels, Zach's dad, would do in this situation. He was the pastor of Levington for many years before he was murdered in the church fire by the World Government. That fire could have easily been waiting for him at his church. He pastored Trinity Village beside Austin Daniels at Levington. He knew the World

Government needed to be stopped, but Pilar also needed to be rescued. He just hoped that achieving one wouldn't sabotage the other.

"Do you think Zach can really stop the Kill Switch from being used?" Li asked, bringing Pastor Tom out of his thoughts.

"I don't know, but I do know I'd feel better if Zach was with Pilar."

"If he turns himself in as Zach Daniels, they'll torture him. What if he tells them where I'm at?" Li asked.

Pastor Tom turned to Li. "Remember that ranch idea you had?"

"Yes," Li said.

"I talked with Gupta. He has begun setting up his trading center up north. He tells me that there is a ranch up for sale a few hours west of him. It's small, but it has some acres and horses that stay with the property," Pastor Tom said. He looked at Li, and he saw hope kindle in his expression.

Li stood quietly and then shook his head. "What about Esther and Deborah and the other Efficientists? Shouldn't I wait at least until after the New Year's event?"

Pastor Tom walked to the bookshelf lining one of his walls. He pulled out a worn, thick green book. He opened the book and instead of pages inside, it had a storage compartment. He pulled out a small bag and placed the book on his desk. "This is the last of the jewels you got from Ruth's vault. Zach already knows. His story will be that you stole the rest of the jewels and left. That's all he knows. That's all I need to know. Take this, take your horse and leave Trinity. You have risked enough. Now your presence here is a danger to us, especially since Dr. Linton was here. Who knows what that man found out."

Li stared at the small bag he held but finally reached out and took it. "I will bring my old-style laptop with me. You can count on me on New Year's Eve," he stopped. "You know, I just realized that I named my horse *Xin Nian Kuai Le.*"

Pastor Tom nodded. "Yes, and Xin for short."

"Do you know what that name means in Mandarin?"

"No, I never thought to ask," Pastor Tom said.

"It means *New Year*," he said simply.

Pastor Tom took in a deep breath. Finally, he placed his hand on the young man's shoulders. "Well, it looks like God had made this His plan long before we knew about it. It's time for you to explore a new life."

Li nodded. "Let us hope that we can all explore a new life once the new year begins."

CHAPTER 19

Pilar turned the lever. She was glad there were no mirrors in prison. She probably looked terrible. She slept on a cot, bathed with a basin of rainwater and a rag and worked all day doing menial tasks. She was grateful that, at least, it was winter, and she didn't sweat so much. The constant labor brought her heart rate up, but the cool breeze kept her from overheating. She knew she had already lost weight. Her jeans were getting looser. She had to force herself to eat the food they served. Their bread was factory-made, and she longed for her father's baking. Other than missing the things she enjoyed, the forced labor camp wasn't that bad as long as you obeyed all the rules and didn't get sick.

What was cruel, though, was the atmosphere of hopelessness. All around her were people saturated with discouragement. It was strange that the hope inside of her became stronger in such a depressing place. Never had she felt so safe and so secure. God's presence was so close to her now. She could hear His voice almost like it was audible. The beep noise and flash from the machine alerted her that it was time to turn the lever the other way.

She was part of a labor group that was dyeing fabrics. She was in charge of a lever that needed to be turned counterclockwise and then clockwise every few minutes. She really didn't know how the machine worked, but she could turn the lever. Her arms tired, but she eyed the young woman in front of her. She couldn't be more than sixteen years old, and she began turning the lever right when the buzzer sounded. Pilar had no right to complain. She had tried to talk to the young woman when the work began, but the girl wouldn't talk.

It was like she was lifeless and checked out from reality. Pilar looked around to the other workers. All of them were lost in their own inner worlds as they dutifully obeyed the guards surrounding them.

Pilar heard commotion. She looked over her shoulder and saw the main director walking into the factory from the corridor that led to his office tower. His name was Ted Stanton, and there was never a legitimate reason for him to come to the factory floor. As he continued to walk the path through the machinery, Pilar began to feel anxious. *Lord, please don't let him come to me*, she pleaded silently. She focused her gaze back on the lever she held in between her two hands and continued to turn it. She tried to ignore the sharp footsteps she heard that stopped near her.

"Are you Pilar Jones?" the man demanded.

She jumped. "Yes, sir. Sorry, you scared me."

He motioned to another officer near him. "Have a worker take her place. I need to ask her a few questions."

"Yes, sir!" the man yelled.

The director looked at her and gave a short command. "Follow me."

Pilar let go of the lever and followed Mr. Stanton back toward the door that led to his office towers. She didn't know if Officer Holten had been found out or not. If he had, she could be tortured or killed depending on what he told them. She resolved herself. God would not have brought her this far just to fail. She would not be intimidated. She followed him up the stairs to the top floor. When she entered the office, the breeze from the open windows swept across her, cooling her face.

"Have a seat," he said, pointing to a chair across from his desk.

As she sat down, she set her expression to indifferent. She didn't care who this man was. She would not be bullied.

"You can leave us," he said to the officer by the door. Then he walked around the desk and sat down. He put his elbows on the desktop and looked at her for a moment. "Welcome to our little family," he began.

"It's quite a family," she replied.

He straightened his back. "The officer who turned you in has been missing for several days. Do you know anything about it?"

"If I had, I certainly wouldn't be here talking to you. I'd find myself missing too," she said, flatly.

"Did you know Officer Holten?"

"I had never met him in my life until he picked me up and brought me here. Whatever charges you have against me are false. I have done nothing wrong."

He stared at her for a moment and smirked. Then he took up his Portable that was on his desk and pressed his thumb to it. When the screen turned on, he began to read. "Pilar Jones wanted for theft."

"What did I steal?" she pressed.

He set the Portable down. "It doesn't matter what you stole. I don't care what you stole. What matters is that you were caught, and you will serve your time."

"How long am I in for?" she asked.

His smirk transformed into a grin. "As long as I say you are." His grin faded, and she felt his gaze analyzing her. "I looked up information about you and discovered that there is a Jones family that runs a village bakery. Included in this family is a Pilar Jones. Is that by chance your family?"

Pilar didn't know whether she should answer him. She was off the hook for Holten's disappearance, but she sensed there was something else he wanted. "Yes, but we sold it a few years ago when my father died," she lied. Very few people if any in her hometown of Levington had an HMS. They were frowned upon. She was sure he didn't find out much information about her family. And if he did, he had very little from which to make assumptions.

He got up from his seat. "Here's the thing. For security reasons, I am unable to keep the factory's books online. I have to do everything by hand, and the job is taking more of my time than I have to spare. I need someone who knows how to keep the books of a business by hand, so my men are kept accountable. I'm being shorted somewhere, and I can't find the culprits. Missing cotton, missing fabric, food supplies are shorted—bit by bit, my men are stealing from me, and it needs to stop." He walked up to Pilar and stood over her. "So, tell me. Is there anything useful about you or should I just send you back to turn levers all day?"

Pilar kept her focus on the tattered, wooden desk in front of her. She felt Ted Stanton rearing over her like a wolf ready to devour. She knew he couldn't keep his books online because he was hiding the forced labor camp from the world. It had nothing to do with security reasons. Finally, she looked up at him. "Yes, I know how to keep the books of a business. This factory is quite larger than my dad's bakery was, but I'm a quick learner. I'll find where the leaks are."

Ted Stanton's shoulders relaxed and, instantly, a pleasant smile appeared on his face. "Good, good. Well, there's at least a little good news from Holten's disappearance. He's unimportant now. He'll show back up on our radar eventually. They always do," he said, walking to a row of filing cabinets. "Just start from January of this year. That's when the trouble really began. If you can get this year cleaned up before the next, maybe we can shorten the time you serve here." He grabbed a stack of file folders and pulled them out. "How long do you think it will take for you to find those leaks?"

Pilar thought of Zach and Li's plan to take down the RIBS on New Year's Eve. "If I'm thorough, it will take two to three weeks to have a complete assessment, but I'll need access to an HMS to make calculations."

He crossed his arms. "Sorry, that's not possible."

"Then it will take me at least four weeks. Maybe five if I have to do the calculations by hand," she said.

"As long as it's done before the new year. I want a clean slate starting January one, you hear me?"

"Yes, sir," she said. She'd make sure that the calculations would be done just in time for the new year.

Ted Stanton began to walk toward the door of the office but stopped and turned to her. "Best not to tell anyone what you're doing. I wouldn't want the other officers catching wind that there's an informant in the office. Let's just let them think that you're doing some secretarial work for me. And when you find out who's been stealing from me, I'll make sure they regret it."

CHAPTER 20

Ada Armel stood in awe of her creation. She wore a satin full-length bronze skirt that shimmered weightlessly as she walked. Her suit jacket of a muted bronze was structured with shiny, gold buttons going down the center and trimmed with brown, orange and yellow feathers. She looked upon the walls of the main gala room and did a slow circle taking it all in. The walls were adorned with festive drapery, lit sconces and baskets decorated with fruit, acorns and feathers. "This will be the most fantastical Thanksgiving celebration ever!" She had been doing her research. She discovered that during Old America in the 19th Century, Thanksgiving was a time to dress up and beg for treats. The poor would dress like the rich and the rich like the poor.

Ada had an entire line of clothing created for the celebration, and every piece sold overnight—mainly to those in attendance. She looked at Matt standing next to her. His presence seemed bigger than ever in the candle-lit room with additional low light from electrical chandeliers and wall lighting. She had appreciated his hand in the *Grand Opus Gala*. He acted as if the entire thing was a nuisance, but she sensed deep down, he understood the magnitude of the event.

"So, Matt, what do you think about my Thanksgiving resurrection?" She asked, truly interested in his thoughts.

She watched him inhale the view. "Ada, I do believe you have outdone yourself. Although, wasn't Thanksgiving almost two weeks ago? We are about to start the second week of December."

"No one cares about logistics. They just want a show," she assured. She brought the Portable she always held in her left hand toward her face. She began swiping the screen with her right hand. "You haven't seen the best of it. I have a Christmas ball planned. Then we will finish the climax of the *Grand Opus Gala* with a New Year's Eve event. I'm still working out the details of the final event. It needs to be spectacular."

"I agree," Matt nodded.

"The only problem is that all of the ten magistrates, including Neil Elder, want to be at the final event on New Year's Eve. They know that their individual polls are being boosted by my work in the gala, and none of them want to be left out." She swept her freshly cut blonde hair behind her ears. "What can I do? Having them all there will help the ratings of the entire gala to be greater. When one of the magistrates is present, everyone from his or her region logs onto their LPSs and watches."

The man's dark expression turned into an overly exhibited sigh. "You want me to talk to Neil about getting all the magistrates there? You know that will be a security nightmare."

"I have already implemented ideas to ease the threat—which, I don't even think there is in the first place. *The Grand Opus Gala* is by no means a political statement. It's an expression of beauty and enjoyment, but that is beside the point. With your astute security, I am sure nothing will go wrong. Could you please talk with him about it? I want every owner of an LPS logged onto my gala!"

He shrugged. "I'll talk to him about it. I think that the other magistrates have been pestering him anyway. He's almost about to give in, so my suggestion will probably be the breaking point."

Ada clapped her right hand on her hip. "Matt, you were holding out on me! I love when you do that!" Then she frowned. "Now, that takes care of the Efficientists, but I'm having trouble getting the Colonials to join the fun. I enlisted too many boring Efficientist contestants. They have no charisma. Nothing worth watching. I wish I would have brought in more Colonials. The only person who is getting views is the Shaman, and even he has disappointed me. If it weren't for his wife and her clothing designs, he would almost not be worth showcasing anymore."

"He has the highest ratings of all the gala contestants," he corrected. "And the bird of prey handler is getting views."

"I know. And how lame is that? A fighter and a birdman. Next year, I will make sure to pick only those who bring in an audience." Unexpectedly, Ada heard commotion around her, and several bodyguards ran to the front doors of the building. "What's going on? Is someone from the World News trying to sneak in again?"

She watched Matt crane his neck for a moment. He was tall and could see over the furnishings of the lobby to the doors. She waited for him to react, but his body stayed at ease. He looked back at her and gave her a mischievous smile.

She brought her hand to her mouth. "Are you holding out on me again? Please say yes!" she exclaimed.

"Bear has had a change of heart. He wants to put on a show for you at this Thanksgiving event. I know you told him that he couldn't invite guests, but I gave him the okay. Come and follow me. I think you'll enjoy what you see."

Ada tucked her Portable under her arm and followed Matt expectantly. She normally liked to know what was going on in her event, but she had learned to trust Matt's decisions. She had begun to enjoy his hand in the production. He had a warm demeanor and unassuming way about him like he would never do anything to harm her or her plans. Though she knew from experience, everyone had their secrets....and their price.

As they got near the doors, she saw a gathering of young, rough Colonial men. They wore similar outfits to what Bear—the Shaman—had come wearing the first day she met him, a gi. She had reproduced the outfit for men and women, and they sold out. "Who are they?" she asked when Matt finally stopped in front of the lobby doors.

"They are your answer to higher ratings with the Colonials," he said simply. "These are Bear's fighters. It is impossible to demonstrate a fighting sport without an opponent. Now he has plenty."

Ada grabbed onto Matt's thick arm and squeezed. Her heart raced as she watched the young fighters look around in awe at the building's décor. She could see the wonderment in their expressions, and the World News began to flash their cameras wildly. Finally, both Colonials and Efficientists would gain a true reaction to her work. Behind her, the elevator dinged. She ignored it until some of the paparazzi from the World News began to jog to it. She turned around and there stood the Shaman. He wore a charcoal-colored gi with a red sash around his waist. His long, black hair was braided. He looked toward her and Matt and gave her a nod. She gave only a slight smile back; though, she was overcome with excitement on the inside.

The Shaman walked over to where she stood. "I will need a few rooms for my men. They don't need a lot of space. They can sleep anywhere—bed, couch, floor, tub. Extra blankets would be good if you have them. Also, we will be training in the empty lot behind the building. You will not want the cameras to be there if you want our demonstration to be a surprise at your Thanksgiving event."

Ada released Matt's arm, quickly covering up her over-excitement. She cleared her throat and brought the Portable up to her face and began to give sharp commands while scrolling with her finger. "Of course, I will send you the room numbers to your LPS," she said, a little too loudly. The cameras were flashing in her face, and she knew that they were capturing her surprise.

Suddenly, the Shaman made a piercing whistle that sounded through the lobby halls. The young fighters instantly stood at attention.

"Grab your bags and follow me," Bear said.

"I'll join you," Matt said. "I need to do a background check of all your men and get their names into the system."

Bear nodded. Then he turned and walked back to the elevator, pushing the up button. Once the door opened, he held the doors open as his men filed into the elevator. Ada watched as each fighter walked by her, enraptured by the uniqueness of each man and wondering about his story. They were all young, fit and of every race. Most tried to look indifferent as the cameras captured their photos, but some of them smiled and waved, saying hi to family and friends back at their colonies. Finally, Matt squeezed himself into the elevator with the Shaman to the right of him. He looked like a giant wall, keeping the overflow of fighters at bay.

The World News captured the last shots just before the elevator closed. Ada could already imagine the headlines. The ratings of the gala would instantly go up once those images spread across the World Government sites. She quickly took the moment to evade the paparazzi. She went straight to the stairwell and shut the door behind her. She took off her high heels and began the long ascent to the faux ceiling above the Gala Hall. She had taken the stairs many times and enjoyed the exercise. She didn't mind the sweat that seeped through her satin blouse as she walked up the last level of stairs. This would be the last time she would ever wear this ensemble.

She opened the door to the rafters that spanned the length of the ballroom. She enjoyed walking the faux ceiling, so she could look down over her creation. She thought of the paparazzi capturing the fighters entering the gala building. The moment was gone, and the world needed a new one to devour. She would make the next moment even more spectacular. She had to. The world needed to see what she could create. And thanks to the Shaman, she now had the perfect tools to make her statement. She needed Matt to give her the names and backgrounds of each fighter. She would put her research skills to good work and find out everything she could about these men. Heartbreaking stories, horror stories, love stories – any story that would provoke the emotions of her viewers. She would find the heart of each fighter and exploit it to establish her presence firmly in the hierarchy World Government. They would finally learn how much they needed her expertise in order to maintain their control over the masses. They needed Ada Armel.

CHAPTER 21

Jonah waited, watching for Neil's reaction to the information he had just given him. He had left Ada at the Grand Opus Building where there was a bustle of excitement. Now he stood in Neil's dreary flat that smelled of pungent body odor. Neil sat at his desk. The glow of the LPS was off. His clothes looked haggard like he had slept in them. His belly hung over his leather belt and there were drips of whatever he drank the night before down his button-up shirt. It was still morning, and Jonah knew this was the best time to discuss details with Neil Elder. Any other time he would be too distracted by people and events. The *Grand Opus Gala* was feeding his self-image with fame and prestige. However, in the morning, Neil's insecurities were left exposed without anything able to conceal them. Neil got out of his chair and stared out the window of his living room. The streets below were busier than usual.

Jonah continued to wait. He was getting tired of playing this charade in the city. He didn't want to be Matt Coughlin, the bodyguard to Neil Elder, anymore. He wanted to be Jonah Goodman the Third. That was his family name. That was his legacy. But he had to be patient and continue to silently remind himself of his true identity. It was the only thing that gave him hope. The circumstances around him were accelerating, and one misstep would cause his carefully laid out plan to collapse. All would be lost, and the years he spent serving with Christina Straight, the Apostle, would be in vain. His mind wandered to her last few days on the earth. She shouldn't have lived so long. Every moment of wakefulness was filled in pain. She got a little relief at night when he would give her pain medicine. Even still, she'd wake up moaning in agony, and he would have to comfort her. If she could endure such torture for what she believed in, he would remain patient.

"Matt, are you telling me there is a worldwide planned attacked on the Regional Integrated Banking System?" Neil asked in disbelief.

Jonah nodded. "Yes."

"But how is that possible?" Neil asked. "We have seen no activity. Everything is quiet. There have been no hacks for months."

"Dr. Linton doesn't know how they are doing it. He just told me what he had heard. They are planning an attack on the RIBS on New Year's Eve right at midnight. I don't know what technology they are using, but it's different. I think Charlie Liu may have discovered a new method of infiltrating our systems."

"I thought Charlie Liu was out of the picture and spending the millions that he stole on a tropical beach somewhere. Why would he risk exposing himself?" Neil asked.

"Dr. Linton heard that both Charlie Liu and Zach Daniels are working on this project," Jonah lied. He kept his voice even.

"And you believe him?" Neil asked. His cheeks were scarlet and his breathing rapid.

Jonah exhaled. "Dr. Linton has a lot of secrets, but he doesn't lie very well. He wouldn't make something like this up because the information only puts him at risk."

"Then we need to go there. Find out what those two are doing and stop them!"

Jonah shook his head. "This plan is everywhere and involves all ten regions. If we stop one, the others will continue. We need to find out exactly what they are doing and how, so we can stop this plan from ever happening now and in the future. And if we get their technology, we may be able to use it to gain information about other possible threats."

"But how can we do that if we can't go there? We should have never let them steal from the World Bank!" Neil yelled. "This is all your fault for letting them get away."

Jonah stood quietly and waited for Neil to calm down. "You are forgetting that you took most of what was in Eve Pallue's vault. So, in essence, it is you who stole from the World Bank and got away with it. You are a very rich man who could retire to your own tropical paradise."

Neil strung his fingers through his thinning, grey hair. "Sorry, I don't mean to yell. I just have all the other nine magistrates watching me. They send gifts to the *Grand Opus Gala* with one hand, but their other hand is ready to destroy me if the gala doesn't bring up our ratings. We need people to believe in the World Government or I'm going to take the fall for it."

"I have the solution," Jonah said. "What we need to do is make a copy of the RIBS."

Neil sucked in air. "That would take months to do."

"We don't have months. We have weeks. They plan to attack New Year's Eve."

Neil rubbed the stubble on his chin. "Do you think they chose that time because more people will be plugged into the World Government for Ada's last event of the gala?"

Jonah shrugged. "It's hard to say when I don't know their plan and how they are able to infiltrate the RIBS, but it makes sense. If we let them destroy the original RIBS, we can see how they do it. Once we know what they did, we will replace the original RIBS that they sabotage with the copy. No one will know the difference."

"Money points change every second. We'd have to get the final count right at 11.59pm," Neil said. "That's impossible."

"The money points change so quickly, people won't notice if they are a little off," Jonah countered. "We can have the copy ready days before the attack. We simply have to put a freeze on large transactions for a few days. The World Government has done it before."

"Why don't we just use the Kill Switch right at midnight. That might be safer. They'd do their attack and there would be nothing there. The system would reboot right where it left off, and their attack will fail."

"Rebooting is too risky. We still don't know if it will recover the RIBS," Jonah said.

"I've already told you! It worked once, and it will work again!" Neil said loudly.

Jonah held up his hand. "Okay, if all else fails, the Kill Switch is our last option. But remember, we need to know how they are attacking the RIBS. For now, let us start making the copy."

"I can't tell the other magistrates because they'll want to know why," Neil said.

"Is there not a way you can make the copy without them knowing?" Jonah asked.

Neil turned to face him. "Yes, but it won't be legal."

"It won't matter when this is all over. You will be known for saving the Regional Integrated Banking System from sabotage and for protecting trillions of money points belonging to powerful people. They'll be so appreciative that they won't notice if there are subtle changes in the amounts."

Neil grinned. "And all those magistrates wanting my demise will now be indebted to me. This may not be a bad plan, after all. We can let Zach Daniels and Charlie Liu make their scheming plans; but this time, they won't be getting away with it. They will take the fall, and I'll have a copy of the RIBS and the Kill Switch if all else fails."

"Exactly," Jonah said.

"Why don't you bring Dr. Linton back to the city? I want to question him myself," Neil said.

"I was just getting to that," Jonah sighed. "He was either killed or kidnapped. A neighborhood girl reported that he hadn't come home from a trip to the trading center. All his stuff is still there in the house. I contacted the factory, and they confirmed that he hadn't shown up for a few days. I think Zach Daniels and Charlie Liu got wind that he was spying on them."

"You think they took him out?" Neil asked.

"I don't know if they could, but desperate times do call for desperate measures. My gut tells me they're simply holding him against his will, but you never know. It's the colonies. Anything can happen there."

"If he hasn't been taken care of when this is all over, make sure he's silenced. He's a liability now. The good doctor needs retiring...permanently."

"Yes sir," Jonah said. "Is there anything else you need me to do?"

Neil walked back to the window and continued to stare out at the building crowd below. "Prepare a team. No, not a team. I need an army. At least a hundred men. I will give you authority to take needed personnel from any of the factories. Get the best of the best and take over Ted Stanton's prison. Do you know where it is?"

"Yes, I've been there once. A long time ago," Jonah said.

"Good, you'll know what to expect. Have Ted Stanton turn on the electricity and turn off the generators. Also, get rid of the people there. Send them to other prisons in the area that need labor. Once the attack on the RIBS has taken place and we find out who and how they did it, you will take that army and destroy every person who had the audacity to attack the World Government under my watch. They will be an example to all the world of what happens when you oppose the World Government. They will also be my salvation. People will no longer just teach Arthur Pallue's name as the savior of civilization. My name will be right there with his as an equal, the protector of civilization."

Jonah nodded his head. "I will get my things ready and let my team know to proceed without me. They will continue to ensure the safety of the gala guests. They are trained well."

"You are dismissed," Neil said. "Just be ready for my arrival on New Year's Eve. I want my hand on the Kill Switch just in case the copy doesn't work."

"You won't be at the New Year's Eve event?" Jonah asked.

Neil sat down on his couch. "I have better things to do than to be entertained by Ada Armel's demonstrations. Let the pathetic be entertained. I'll be at the prison waiting for my act of salvation."

CHAPTER 22

R uth exited the elevator and walked next to her husband toward the lobby doors where the paparazzi and Ada awaited them. They had been in the city for weeks now, and she still had not seen Jonah. She wondered if he was avoiding her or if he had not found the right time to approach her. Bear was able to see him when his men arrived, but she seemed to miss every opportunity. She looked for him frequently at every dinner and presentation, but he must be staying in the shadows. She always ensured her inquisitive looks were hidden behind disguises. Today, her face was concealed by an ornately etched leather mask that she detailed with gold paint and turkey feathers. She wore a greenish-brown 18th-century silk, brocade, colonial wedding gown with intricate gold threading. The décolletage of the dress was low, but not as deep as was customary during that time. Her wedding pearl rested on the highest point of her sternum. The petticoat she created was also tweaked from the original design. It was smaller and allowed for her to move and sit easily. Ada had asked her to send her costume ideas for each event to her Portable before creating them. Although Ada did not copy Ruth's designs exactly, she would keep with a similar theme when she created clothing and accessories for the public. Ruth didn't mind, though. In return for her ideas, Ada would give Ruth any materials she needed to create her costumes.

Ruth looked up at Bear walking resolutely next to her. He wore a simple loincloth, but he left his pearl behind on the nightstand. He would be demonstrating fights for today's gala event, and he didn't want to lose it. He had shaved the sides of his head, leaving only a strip of silky, dark hair running down the middle and falling to the right side. His tan muscled frame contrasted with her petite, snowy figure. She knew he was uncomfortable, but he disguised his embarrassment with annoyance. He had difficulty concealing his emotions, so he would simply transform them into something he found more manageable. Anger and annoyance were easy for Bear to utilize, especially when training and fighting.

Ruth saw the bird of prey handler talking with the World News. His name was Sonnie Wood, and he was in his early sixties. He had grey, thinning hair, a stocky frame and a round mid-section. He laughed heartily and obviously enjoyed the limelight. A Bald Eagle rested on a leather sleeve around his left arm. The eagle's name was Uncle Sam. Ruth had to look up the name's meaning. It was the personification of Old America. The bird handler did not stay in the building with the rest of the gala contestants. Ruth guessed the building could not accommodate his dozens of birds. Instead, he drove into the city in a large, covered truck, pulling a trailer with a massive wooden housing structure for all his birds built upon it. He parked along the street, and Ruth could see him practicing with his birds outside every morning. He had owls, falcons, caracaras and eagles. Ruth would watch the birds and then research them on her LPS. She wondered what it would be like to touch one.

As they neared the buzz of reporters, Ada happened to glance their way. Ruth grew accustomed to Ada's excited reactions to her and Bear. The World News loved capturing her many ecstatic expressions. She quickly sauntered to them with open arms. Her colonial gown looked much like Ruth's except the décolletage was steep, the petticoat was large and the blue silk was layered and trimmed with lace. She suddenly slowed when she noticed Bear. Her face flushed a bit, but she recovered and grabbed each of their hands.

"Exquisite as ever!" Ada said, taking in Ruth's dress. "You must turn. Let me see all of your handiwork."

Ada let go of their hands, and Ruth obeyed, turning in a circle. "I see that we have left the Regency Era behind and now are jumping back a few decades to pre-Revolution America."

Ruth nodded.

"Yes, quite right! What better way to celebrate Thanksgiving? And speaking of Thanksgiving, the turkey feathers on your mask look stunning! And I love what you have done with the lambskin I gave you. That etching on the leather is marvelous! And you—" she turned to look at Bear. "I'm quite stunned. The Shaman has returned to us. A little more silver in the hair, but just as strong...maybe even stronger! You look so Colonial!" Ada stopped like an idea had just sprung into her mind. "Perfect! Follow me, both of you!"

Ada grabbed Ruth's and Bear's hands again. Ruth looked at Bear as he rolled his eyes. She knew he hated being paraded around, but the risks Pilar and the others were taking helped him to forfeit his pride—at least for the time. "Don't leave, Sonnie! We need Uncle Sam!" she yelled when the bird handler turned to leave. He was happy to oblige.

Ada brought Bear and Ruth to either side of her and faced the World News. She motioned for Sonnie to come on the other side of Ruth. When everyone was situated, she began her impromptu speech.

"As you know, the *Grand Opus Gala* is an attempt to unite the Ten Regions and to give us common ground from which creativity, beauty and loyalty can be birthed. Neil Elder wants nothing more than our world to be united in both cause and strength. Since our region is the first to host the *Grand Opus Gala*, I have delved into Old America's forgotten history, not to resurrect old mistakes but to highlight ancient holidays! Let us cut any entrapment of religion and superstition from these celebrations and allow the imagination, awe and inspiration of these festivities to permeate *Life Plethoricity* as a tiny, allotted time to celebrate the lasting productivity of our lives!"

Cameras flashed as a cacophony of questions exploded in the lobby.

Ada paused for a moment and smiled towards different angles so that each reporter could capture a frontal smile. "Before I answer questions," she continued. "I have a visual demonstration of my goal for the *Grand Opus Gala* here with me now." She turned to Sonnie. "Will you hold up your eagle, so Ruth can stroke its feathers?"

Sonnie smiled and nodded. He looked to Ruth. "Uncle Sam is old and gentle. He'll let you pet his back but let me turn his face away from you."

"Are you sure that is a good idea, Ada? My wife's hands are very vulnerable," Bear said.

"You have nothing to worry about!" Ada exclaimed. "I have already touched the sweet thing. It's harmless. Now stand next to your wife," she said, moving to the side. "I need them to capture this final shot."

Ruth waited until Bear was next to her. She felt safer now that he was at her side. She could feel the tension radiating from his body as if he was about to pounce. If the eagle took one misstep, Bear would seize it by the neck, like she had seen him do with chickens, turkeys and ducks. She stared at the Bald Eagle allowing her curiosity to fill her with courage. She had seen him flying earlier that day. He was massive, and she wondered how Sonnie could carry the weight of the bird on his arm so long.

"Go ahead, Ma'am," Sonnie said. "You can stroke his feathers. He's already been fed, so he won't hurt you."

Ruth nodded her head, though his words did nothing to soothe her. Finally, she reached her right hand to the eagle's back and allowed her index finger to glide along a feather. The bird did not stir, so she allowed all four of her fingers to slide along his silky plumes.

"And here you have it!" Ada said excitedly. "Feast your eyes on our Thanksgiving celebration visual for tonight! Our Native American, our Colonial and our Bald Eagle."

The rapid-fire camera flash surrounded them like a lightning storm. Ruth blinked and felt Bear's hands clasp her shoulders, backing her away from the eagle who had begun to flap its wings.

Ada was oblivious to the commotion behind her and continued speaking. "Tonight's celebration will include a fighting demonstration by the Shaman and his fighters. Plus, the Shaman will be singing for us, so you Colonials out there will want to spread the word," Ada said, pointing at the live video streaming to the World News.

The cameras continued to flash, but their position angled up as the Bald Eagle lifted off from Sonnie's arm.

"Uncle Sam!" he shouted. "We must get him out of this building."

Cameras continued to flash, and Ruth watched horrified as the eagle flew into one of the tall, vaulted windows of the lobby. The great bird crashed into the window, and gasps were heard all around them as the bald eagle plummeted to the lobby floor.

"Out of my way," the bird handler yelled. He ran to the eagle and carefully picked it up and brought it to his chest. "He's still breathing!" he said mainly to himself.

Ruth didn't know what overcame her, but she felt her feet fly toward Sonnie and the fallen eagle. The neck of the eagle dangled over Sonnie's hand as he held it close to his chest. The neck looked broken. Ruth looked into Sonnie's eyes for affirmation. They were filled with both shock and distress. Ruth felt a prompting in her spirit to pray for the bird, and an image of Jason, the little boy with cerebral palsy, came into her mind. He was the boy she had prayed for behind the Trinity Church when they were doing communion. She shook her head. *Why would God want me to pray over a bird?* She thought. But again, she felt the prompting even sharper. She needed to at least try. That was all she could do. She placed her hand gently on the neck and head of the Bald Eagle. "God, please heal Uncle Sam, so he may continue to fly for Your glory. I pray this in the name of Jesus, amen," she whispered.

Ruth removed her hand and stared at the bird waiting. Her back was to the World News, and no one could get a good shot of what was going on. Nothing happened for several seconds. Finally, she looked back at Sonnie.

Sonnie returned her gaze. His face became resolute, and he looked back down at the eagle. "Uncle Sam, did you hear Ruth here? You have more flying to do, so you've better wake up!" he said loudly enough for the World News to hear him.

Unexpectedly, the bird's injured head came up, and he flapped his wings. Sonnie deftly balanced the eagle back onto the leather covering around his left arm and stood up. Ruth moved out of the way from the flapping, and Sonnie held out his bird. Only a glimmer of tears barely shone in the corner of his eyes, and he held up his eagle proudly. "Uncle Sam is alright! He was merely stunned, but nothing can keep him down!"

The cameras again began to flash, and Ada quickly re-entered the shot. "That is right! No matter what hits we take, you cannot keep New America down!" She smiled for several seconds, giving the World News every angle. "Now please," she said, genuinely concerned. "No more photos. We need to get Uncle Sam back to the trailer to rest. There will be much more to capture later today. Matt, please escort the fine ladies and gentlemen out until the gala tonight."

Ruth hastily turned around just in time to catch Jonah's gaze. Finally, she could see him out from the shadows. She bowed her head slightly. He gave a slight nod before bringing up his arms to wave the paparazzi to the door. He had been there, watching over her.

"There's our friend," Bear whispered in her ear, coming up beside her.

"Yes," she said. She wanted to say more but feared someone was watching them. Someone was always watching.

"I better get Uncle Sam back home," Sonnie said. "I need to check every feather to make sure nothing is broken." He looked to Ruth. "Thank you, Ma'am. I'm indebted to you." Sonnie brought his left hand closer to his chest and made his way to the fire exit that led outside to his truck and trailer. Uncle Sam's claws wrapped tightly around the leather.

Ruth felt heated anger she had never experienced rise from the pit of her stomach and spread into her limbs and face. She knew that Uncle Sam had died. He had flown into a window to gain freedom away from the cameras, and he had broken his neck in the process. The World Government had exploited the eagle, and death was the result—regardless of the miracle that brought him back to life. She looked at her husband's face who was standing next to her. He was watching Sonnie and the eagle as they left. She would not let Ada Armel and the World Government use her husband to the point of injury. She didn't know Ada's plans for the continuation of this gala, but if it included Bear getting hurt, she would find another way to get the ratings they needed.

Jonah watched as Sonnie's Crested Caracara dove through the audience once more. The Efficientists smiled and cheered when the bird of prey landed on Sonnie's leather sleeve wrapped around his arm. The giant bird gulped down what Sonnie called a "pinky," a baby rat. He stood in the back and noticed Ada Armel clapping and nodding back at him, seeking his admiration and approval once more. He gave her a slight smile. Not too much to make her think he was too emotionally involved.

When Ada looked back at the stage, he closed his eyes. He didn't know who he was anymore. Was he still Christina Straight's confidante and sticking to the original plan they first developed when they met in prison? Or was he still Ruth's protector? He looked over at Ruth and the fighter sitting next to her. She wore another mask. Her husband was very protective of her. Jonah was glad, but it gave him little purpose in watching out for her. He looked at Neil Elder. He was enjoying the best seat in front of the stage. Who was he now? He was a mole in the World Government trying to stop the oppression of thousands of Colonials.

Jonah knew what he wanted, and he could achieve it at any time. But here he was living as Matt Coughlin second in command to the very man he hated most. Again, applause erupted. For being Efficientists and governmental leaders, the crowd was boisterous. Jonah knew that the pressure of production was finally getting to the masses. People could only busily produce for so long without knowing their true value and purpose. *Life Efficiency* was a volcano about to erupt. No number of galas could stop the inevitable. It only needed a trigger, and that was the plan he needed to implement. That was his purpose, and he couldn't get lost in the chaos around him.

He closed his eyes while the people applauded and whispered, "God, please help me stay on track. Every detail counts, and I can't afford to skip any step. Help me Holy Spirit. Amen."

When he opened his eyes, he saw Bear getting up from his seat. He was wearing his customary gi, and his hair was braided down the back. He commanded the men lining the back wall to join him. They were all wearing the same outfit. He knew the routine they would be doing. He had watched them in the back parking lot practicing. Impressive moves, but most of them were for show. He had watched the Shaman's fights. He would not only fight to win; he would fight to entertain. He had allowed his body to be abused in order to gain the crowds adoration. They loved him for it. But he disappeared from the circuit, reappearing one more time to let everyone know that he was a changed man. Very brave. Something that Jonah only wished he could do. Hopefully, the show would garner more views. For the plan to work, everyone needed to be connected to the gala the night that the World Government would fall.

CHAPTER 23

Zach huddled behind a thick lump of grass beyond the prison camp. It was a cold day, but the sun was out. He had been surveying the camp for two days. There was no way in without being caught. He had his binoculars and finally spotted Pilar the first afternoon he had arrived. She was working in the office at the top of the tower. It looked like she was going over the books of the prison camp. Ted Stanton would look over her shoulders every now and then and ask her a few questions. But he never harmed her. Relief washed over him. She wasn't using the LPS to calculate the books, so he knew she was probably biding time and doing all the calculations by hand. Pilar was a strong woman, but the fact that she willingly endured imprisonment for their cause moved him. He had been so weak. So consumed with anger and fear, and she had never left his side. He wished he could start everything over with her. He wondered if God could give him a clean slate.

God can do every good thing, he thought. *And he specializes in restoration.*

He had to smile. Those were his father's words. Pastor Austin Daniels was an anointed man. Zach prayed he could live up to him. The Portable that Li had given him bleeped. He looked at his battery power. He didn't have much power left. He would have to go back into town and charge it. Pastor Rohan had left his keys to his house and some supplies. It was a godsend for him. It gave him the ability to plan.

There was a message from Pastor Tom. Pilar's father, Levi, had gone to find Randall Hunt.

"Great," Zach said aloud, dropping the Portable on his lap. "Not only did I have to forgive the man who killed my father, now I have to work with him?"

Zach felt anxiety and fear begin to creep up his chest, and his breathing began to escalate. "No, this will not happen again. I have forgiven him. I am free from anger. I am free from hate. I am free from shame. God, You give me peace that surpasses all understanding. You give me grace to have peace upon peace. I claim your supernatural peace right now. Thank You, Jesus, for giving it to me."

Zach closed his eyes and envisioned Randall Hunt lying unconscious on the bed with the bandage around his head. He remembered the peace that washed over him as he stared at the man who had killed his father. He saw him through God's eyes. He saw a son whom God deeply loved and wanted in His family. God gave Zach the peace to forgive him then, and He will give him the peace to forgive him now. He needed to embrace love, not fear. Only then would he be released from his pain.

Zach focused back on the Portable. He finished reading the letter from Tom. Levi was going to try to bring Randall Hunt here to the prison camp. Zach knew that Randall had amassed an army. And word was that oil diggers were being set up on all his land. Randall had to know that the World Government would discover the oil diggers soon enough. Did he not think that they wouldn't come and take them from him? Would his small army protect him from a government desperate for oil?

Zach shrugged. "Maybe," he said aloud. The World Government was weak. The only power they had to control was persuading people to stay glued to their LPSs. It was all starting to backfire, and now the World Government was running out of oil, and Neil Elder was desperately trying to stop everything from caving in. Zach wondered if Randall Hunt would indeed help their plan to keep his own property safe. He shrugged again. "Maybe."

He typed an encrypted letter back to Pastor Tom. He had already told them that Pilar was safe for now. They couldn't break into the prison camp until after New Year's Eve was over. They had everything in place to take down the RIBS, and having Pilar there was a tiny safeguard that no one would touch the Kill Switch—though, he didn't want her to risk her life. That would be his job. This was their one chance. With the Money Point system out of the way, the World Government would topple. And people could truly live again. Zach just needed to formulate a plan to get into the prison camp and make sure Neil Elder did not use the Kill Switch.

Zach slid back and crawled out of view of the prison. He headed to the graveyard some distance behind the prison yard. The tombs were concealed by trees and tucked under wild grasses that grew over them. It was like the graveyard was concealed in shame. He didn't like going through it, but it was the safest route back to town. There was freshly dug up grass for a grave without a marker. It must have been the man who was shot when Pilar arrived or the dead body dangling for days from the fence. Pastor Tom had video of both atrocities and was currently printing copies with his printing press. They would disperse the gruesome copies to all the magistrates and their dignitaries at the *Grand Opus Gala* on New Year's Eve.

Zach looked around at the disheveled graveyard with only a few dozen grave markers. He believed that there were many more graves than there were markers. He had done some research with Li's Portable. Thankfully, Li had hacked the Portable into the World Government systems, and Zach was able to poke around through old, forgotten files. This prison camp had been used almost twenty years ago as a forced labor camp. It was headed up by Neil Elder as an experiment, he assumed. The World Government was already thinking about using prisoners as a work-force even back then. Something happened, though. All information about the camp abruptly stopped. It was like the lives of every prisoner were erased. Then it became a women's prison for Efficientists.

He walked by the few shabby tombstones. They each were hand-carved with names. He wondered why the World Government would take time to mark these particular graves. He looked closely at one tombstone. The name etched in the rock looked like it was done by hand. He looked around. In fact, all of the ones with names looked like they were etched by hand. One tombstone looked different from the rest. It was large and round like a giant stone rolled over and set in place. He didn't know why, but he felt like he needed to look at it. He looked at the name and his breathing instantly stopped. The name etched in big letters was Jonah Goodman III.

"That can't be," Zach said and squatted down, setting the Portable on the grass. He stared at the words. Yes, it was Jonah Goodman the Third, but he was alive. He thought of Jonah in the city pretending to be Matt Coughlin. He was now Neil Elder's bodyguard because he took a knife to the chest to save his life. Neil now trusted him. *Had Jonah been here in this prison? He would have been just a teenager or even younger.* He had a sudden thought and grabbed the Portable. He recognized that name. He went to his last search in the World Government's files. It was a list of the original prisoners' names. He scrolled down and almost dropped the Portable. He saw Jonah Goodman II, Mary Goodman, Jonah Goodman III, Isaiah Goodman and Maureen Goodman. The entire family had been sentenced to the work camp.

Zach stumbled back several steps. He looked at the smaller tombstones surrounding Jonah's large stone. Every name he had just read on the Portable had a grave marker hand-etched with each name of the Goodman family on it. "Oh no," Zach whispered.

Suddenly, he heard a loud thud and the large stone of Jonah's marker disappeared into the ground. Zach dropped the Portable and jumped. "What the heck is going on?" he yelled.

He looked around to see if anyone had heard him. He was too far from the camp to be heard. He stopped and waited to see what would happen next, but everything was silent. Finally, he slowly walked to the stone. It had fallen only about three feet.

Pick up the stone, he heard the voice of the Lord say.

"No way!" he exclaimed.

Pick it up and I'll show you a secret, the Voice said again.

Zach looked tentatively at the stone. It had Jonah's name on it, and obviously, Jonah was not dead. He planted his feet on either side of the hole and tried to reach his hands around the stone. The fit was too tight, so he dug out some dirt on either side. When he had made enough room, he reach down again and pulled the large rock up and rolled it on the grass. Indeed, the hole was only three feet deep. There was a rusty tackle box below. He grabbed it and sat with it on the grass. He clicked open the two latches. They were almost fused to the box. Rust dusted over him. He opened the lid and exhaled. There were photos and a large, folded parchment. He picked up one photo. He instantly knew who it was. It was a young-looking Jonah. He set the photo down. He knew the other photos would be of his family, and he avoided looking at them. The grief would be too much. He had lost his father, but to lose your entire family? Unbearable.

He picked up the large parchment and unfolded it. He saw some kind of map. He looked at it confused until realization caught up to him. He folded the map back up and set it in the tackle box. Then he set the tackle box aside and leaned over the hole. He reached his arm down and over. This wasn't a grave. It was a tunnel.

CHAPTER 24

Randall walked out on the porch. He sipped his coffee. He liked it hot and knew the cold air would cool it fast. Adella was leaning against one of the porch posts and staring out on the lawn. She looked beautiful in the morning light. Randall had never felt so at ease. His land was producing oil. Tal was an excellent leader and was managing his men well. He had all the provisions he needed. Dr. Linton had settled into his small cottage. Adella's girls were vibrant and thriving. Even Favian, the German Shepherd Wolfhound, had made this place his home. Favian protected the perimeter of the house daily. Randall wouldn't admit it, but he liked having that dog here. He had an attentive nose and alert ears.

He strolled next to Adella and took another sip of his coffee. He loved the way she made it for him. "What's so interesting?" he asked, trying to match her gaze.

She nodded her chin toward Dr. Linton's cottage. "The girls noticed that Favian was limping, so they brought him to Dr. Linton. He's on the porch right now with them. He has a thorn imbedded in his paw."

Randall squinted his right eye. He could see the figures of Alex and Ana sitting on the ground next to Dr. Linton. He was holding Favian's paw. He couldn't see from the distance, but he was sure Dr. Linton was holding some kind of tweezer to remove the thorn. "Dr. Linton is proving his value more and more every day."

Adella laughed. "You should have been here five minutes ago. It took a while for Favian to trust Dr. Linton. The girls had to prove that Dr. Linton meant no harm. Ana even started petting the doctor's head to show that he was a friend."

Randall smiled. "I wish I could have seen that." He sipped his coffee again and continued to watch the scene unfold. Then he heard Tal's truck come up the side of the house. He had gone out before dawn for supplies from the nearby town. Randall watched Tal park near the house. He quickly opened the door and jumped out. The way he walked to the house made Randall know that something was wrong. He gave his mug to Adella and walked to meet him. "What is it?"

Tal had gotten good at covering up his emotions since Randall first met him, but now worry was all over his face. "It's the World Police. They have patrols out in nearby towns and they are arresting people. They are making false accusations and taking them to a prison camp a few hours away. It's like a work camp. Entire families are being taken."

Randall knew exactly what camp they were being taken to. The same camp that he was rescued from by the band of Christians. The painful memories punched his gut, and he lost his composure for a moment.

"You've heard of this camp?" Tal asked.

Randall quickly regained his normal indifferent countenance. "Yes, I've been there. It is not a pleasant place. And if they find out what we have here, they may want to take our lands." Suddenly, Randall's peaceful mood vanished. He looked at Adella. Her face was filled with fear. "Don't worry, Adella. We are well protected," he said, not believing his own words. "Why don't you go inside and check on my grandfather?"

"I'll read more Scripture to him, and we will pray," she said, resolutely.

Randall watched her walk back into the house. She had been reading the *Bible* to his grandfather every day. He acted like he didn't enjoy it, but Randall knew better. Adella was softening the hard parts of John Hunt.

"What's our plan?" Tal asked after Adella closed the door behind her. "They will discover us eventually."

Randall thought. The World Government was so desperate for oil that they were using forced labor. However, production was much slower with human hands. Randall had heard that they had tried it almost twenty years ago, but it had failed. He was surprised a few years back when Neil Elder told him they were implementing the idea again.

"We are going to have to go there and fight," Randall said.

"But what can we do? Kill the guards? Even if the men agreed, which many won't, the World Government will hear about it and then we will have a much bigger fight on our hands."

Randall almost regretted purchasing all the oil diggers. He should have been just like his grandfather and lived a simple life. He shook his head. A simple life was just not in his nature. He now realized why his grandfather was so adamant about staying under the radar. He looked toward Dr. Linton's cottage. The girls were running in circles while Favian chased them. Dr. Linton must have gotten the thorn out of his paw. Randall suppressed the fear rising in him. He had been overly confident and now the people he cared about were in danger. He didn't know what to do, and he had a sudden urge to pray. He eyed Tal looking at him expectantly. He purged his pride. "I need to pray."

Tal's eyes widened, and he nodded. "Yes, that is what my mother would do."

Randall bowed his head. "Um, God. It's Randall Hunt. I've never asked you for anything. I'm a strong man. I usually don't need help, but I've had to accept help recently. And I appreciate it. You saved my life and freed me from guilt. So, I'm telling you that I need help now. Show me what to do to protect this place and these people. I pray this in, I think, in Jesus's name. That is what Zach said. Amen."

"Amen," Tal repeated.

Suddenly, alarms sounded in the air. Men from the towers were shouting.

"Intruder! Intruder!"

Adella raced out onto the porch. "What's going on?"

"Get the girls and Favian and go down to the basement with my grandfather. Lock the doors!" Randall yelled.

Adella sprinted to the girls who were now running toward the house behind Favian.

Randall and Tal ran around the house toward where the men were pointing. He regretted not having his gun at his side. He had gotten too comfortable. When Randall got to the front of the house, he saw an older black man with his hands up in the air being led in by two of his men. Several of his men surrounded them with their bows and arrows raised. He recognized the man. He quickly thought to himself: *The baker.* He shook out his hands by his side, calming his nerves. The baker was no threat.

He walked to his men. "Arrows down. This man is no threat."

The men looked relieved but still on edge. They lowered their weapons.

"You can release him."

The man fell to his knees. "Please, help me get my daughter back. She was taken into the prison camp a few hours from here. I know you can help her. I'll do anything!"

Randall recalled that the baker had two daughters. One was married and one had a relationship with Zach Daniels, or so he thought.

"My oldest daughter. Please, we need to get her out!"

"How did she get there? Your town is an hour away from here. Are the World Police patrolling that far?" Randall asked.

The man hesitated and shook his head. "No, she went there to film abuses and gather evidence."

Randall straightened. "Why? What are you planning on doing?"

"We have a plan to destroy the entire World Government system," the man said.

Randall laughed. "There is no way you can do that."

"No, it's true! Zach, Li, Pastor Tom and Jonah—they have developed a plan to erase the Regional Integral Banking System, the RIBS, as they call it. They have old-style computers all over the world now ready to implement the virus. It's going to happen on New Year's Eve. They just have to ensure the Kill Switch isn't used! And that switch is where my daughter is!"

A kindling of hope started to form deep within Randall's chest. He knew who Zach, Li and Pastor Tom were, but he had never heard the name, Jonah. "Who is this Jonah?"

The man hesitated again.

"If I'm going to help you, you need to tell me everything."

"He's the mole in the World Government. They call him Matt Coughlin. I think you know him."

Randall's thoughts halted. He knew there was something off about Matt. He could never figure his motivation. Now he knew what it was.

The man took the silence as an opportunity to talk more. "Look, do you have an HMS? You can talk to Pastor Tom. He will tell you all about it. You can help us take down the World Government," the man said, looking around. "They will find out about what you are doing here. We did and we are hours away. The news is spreading fast. The only way you can protect yourself and your land is if you take down the enemy before they come after you. This is your only chance."

"Stand up," Randall said. "What is your name?"

"My name is Levi Jones," he said.

Randall turned to Tal who was standing next to him. "Get us an HMS and an old-style computer ASAP. And see if you can find me a Portable—even an older model will do."

"Yes sir!" Tal said and ran back toward his truck.

Then Randall reached his hand toward Levi. "It looks like you have yourself a deal. Give me the details of this plan to take down the World Government, and we will do our part to get your daughter out."

CHAPTER 25

Pilar sat at her desk in the large, musty office that occupied the top space of the watchtower. Her eyes became tired from staring at numbers all day. She found several discrepancies in the books. She had a good guess at the different guards who were siphoning materials from the work camp. She looked up each person's profile. They almost all had large families who relied on them. They were stealing to help supplement their living. The officers barely made enough money points to support themselves. She made a choice that she would allow Officer Holten to take the fall. He was already wanted as a deserter, and this would be the explanation for his sudden departure.

Pilar hoped that Pastor Tom had ensured that Holten had disappeared. By adding theft from the World Government to his name, he would never make it out of the workforce camp alive. But she needed a scapegoat in order to free the true culprits—many of which watched her every move. None had threatened her, but they would come to her during a lunch break or when their shift was over and casually ask her how her work was going. She'd always put on a friendly smile and say, "It is going well. I see nothing of concern yet." To which they would reply, "Good, good. We wouldn't want any trouble here."

She heard the front door of the office swing open, and Ted Stanton, the prison director, walked in. She could see an underlying glimpse of excitement underneath his normally onery demeanor. She watched him walk to the main system of the work camp. He pressed a few buttons and flipped several switches. Suddenly, the loud hum of the generators silenced, and the lights overhead flickered a few times before becoming brighter. *He's turning on the electricity*, she thought. She continued looking down at the printouts in front of her, allowing her eyes to follow where Stanton was walking next.

Stanton walked along the main systems to where a large lockbox-like contraption was sticking out over the long, narrow built-in desk along the wall. He placed his thumb on the print-identifier, typed in a lengthy digital code and brought out his keys from his pocket. He found the right key and slid it into the keyhole. A short, loud beeping sound went off, and he gently lifted the lid. He turned his head toward Pilar, and she instantly placed her gaze back on the printouts and turned the page. However, she had seen what was under the lockbox. It was a large, red lever, and she instantly knew that it was the Kill Switch.

After several moments, she heard the keys jingle once more, and the click of the lockbox lid coming down. She guessed he was making sure the Kill Switch was still active.

After several moments, she heard Ted Stanton's footsteps walk up to her desk.

"Well, what have you found? I have given you plenty of time. You should have identified the thieves by now."

Pilar inhaled softly, preparing herself to lie, which she never did very well, but now she had a reason. "Yes, I have found many discrepancies. A little cotton here. Some food rations there. Nothing extravagant but just enough to stay under the radar."

Ted Stanton placed his hands on the desk and leaned toward Pilar. "I knew it. Who are the culprits?"

Pilar looked square into Stanton's eyes. "Officer Jordan Holten. I have discovered that everywhere there was a shortage, he was assigned to that area." Pilar waited for the news to soak in. Ted Stanton stood back up and crossed his arms, thinking. Pilar noticed that a few of the officers were at their workstations, listening intently to every word.

"Is that the only name you could find?" Ted Stanton asked, unconvinced.

Pilar nodded. "Yes, I could find no other discrepancies with any other officer." She noticed that the officers behind her seemed relieved and went back to their work. One of the officers, a young female officer Pilar had discovered had two children at home, quietly left the room. She assumed to tell the other officers or to thank the Lord she had been spared of getting caught.

Ted Stanton rubbed his chin and paced a few steps. "That makes sense. He has no family and nothing to lose. Once he made enough money off me, he left town. Not to worry, though. He'll run out of money soon enough and will wind up back on the grid eventually. Officer Holten is young and naïve. He won't make it in the colonies without help."

Pilar nodded, but she knew that if Pastor Tom was helping the young man, he would vanish for good.

"No matter," Ted Stanton said almost jovially. "We have more pressing matters to attend to. We are sending all the prisoners away. This prison is turning into a military base, and I will be commanding it."

Pilar was flabbergasted. "Which prison?" If she moved now, no one would be able to find her.

"It doesn't matter to you," he said. "You'll be finishing your prison sentence here. I'm enlisting you as my personal secretary. I have an army of soldiers coming here, and I'll need your keen eye and expertise to keep them in line. I won't let officers take advantage of me and that goes double for the World Police. No one exploits Ted Stanton. I want books on everything they eat and every stitch of clothing they wear. I want to know where they sleep. Where they go. I want eyes and ears on them at all times. Is that understood?"

"Yes, sir," Pilar said. She didn't know if she should be thankful or not. She was saved from having to move to a new location, but now she would be under the constant scrutiny of

Ted Stanton. The World Police was being sent to that complex, and she knew the Kill Switch was the reason. She wondered if Neil Elder had caught wind of their plan. If that was so, and the Kill Switch was being prepared, their plan to take down the RIBS would be thwarted.

"Now, file those papers," he said, pointing to the printouts on her desk. "You'll be using my LPS from now on—under limited access, of course."

"Yes sir," she said, getting up.

"And clean up this place. It smells of dust. I want this office sparkling clean before the World Police arrive in the morning."

Pilar nodded and gathered up the papers. She walked them to the filing cabinet and placed them in the correct order by date. Once she closed the cabinet, she walked to the large windows that overlooked the work area. She watched as the officers gathered up the people—men, women and children—all rounded up like cattle. She prayed silently that transportation was on the way. She couldn't bear it if the people were killed and buried in the graveyard she knew was behind the prison. Ted Stanton was a bad man, but she doubted he would have everyone killed. However, she knew that something must have happened long ago for there to be so many unmarked graves in the graveyard.

Under the tunnel, Zach could hear multiple trucks rumbling to a stop within the prison gates.

"What is going on?" he whispered. He began to crawl faster toward the prison. He thanked God that Jonah was a big man because the tunnel was roomier than it needed to be for his thin, long frame. The tunnel led to a large, old air conditioner duct. When he reached the entrance to the duct, he placed his hand on the vent. He could feel air moving inside of it. "They turned on the air conditioner," he said quietly. He could feel the cool breeze on his hand. He had opened the duct just yesterday and the large tube was filled with dirt and dust. He knew he couldn't crawl in there now without a face covering. He'd have to go into town and get goggles and a facemask or he would have to crawl blindly through the duct system of the old factory.

He used the extra room that connected the tunnel to the duct to turn around. He needed to go back and see what was going on. If there were large trucks at the prison, they were either changing the guards out or moving the prisoners. If it was the latter, he needed to follow the trucks quickly before they left. He couldn't lose Pilar's location no matter the cost. He may lose his sight on the Kill Switch, but that would be a loss he could deal with. He couldn't deal with losing Pilar.

When Zach finally made it to the grave where the tunnel started, he shimmied his way through. By now he had gotten the knack of getting in and out of the grave marked with a living man's name—a feat he never thought he would have to maneuver. He placed the tombstone over the entrance and jogged to the lining of trees that separated the prison from the graveyard. He could see prisoners lined up at each truck waiting for their turn to get in.

"No. No. No," he exclaimed. "What if she's already in one?" He looked back at the watchtower, trying to see if he could find her. He would have to leave soon. How would he follow the trucks on foot? He would have to hitch a ride on the back of one. *But they would see me?* he thought. *You'd have to get on the last one.*

"God, what do I do?" he asked in desperation. He would have to leave soon in order to be ready when the last truck left. But if he left now, he wouldn't know for sure if Pilar was still in the watchtower. "God, help me. Is she in there?"

He stared at the watchtower waiting while the trucks continued to load with prisoners. He would wait until the trucks were loaded before leaving. He looked quickly at the lines of people again. She was definitely not in line. She was either already in one of the trucks or still in the prison. Zach knew that Pilar had been working in the office, so they may have wanted to keep her there, but she could easily have been removed with the other prisoners. He continued to wait and stare at the watchtower windows, willing Pilar to show her face.

Finally, the trucks started pulling out. The first one was leaving the gate, so he knew he needed to gather his things and get ready to run. He was just about to turn away when he saw something white. He squinted his eyes. He saw a hand holding a white cloth and moving it in a circular motion on the windows. His breath let out. It was Pilar. She was cleaning the inside windows of the watchtower.

Zach fell to his knees. "Thank You, God. Thank You for showing me Pilar. Thank You for keeping her there." He felt his heart racing, and he tried to calm his breathing. He looked back up to the window. There she was—cleaning the next set of windows. Something big was going down if Pilar was told to clean the office. Someone important must be coming or something important was about to happen—or both. Zach looked up toward the sun. It was getting late. He needed to get into town and barter for goggles and some kind of face covering. He would be going into the prison tonight. It was the perfect time because the prisoners were gone and whoever was supposed to replace them had not arrived yet.

CHAPTER 26

Tal walked briskly along the perimeter of the ranch as the large wolf shepherd walked by his side. He allowed his eyes to look around behind the dark lenses of his glasses. He wanted to see if anyone noticed Favian jogging beside him. Favian had figured out the social ranks on the ranch, and he always stayed by Randall's side if he wasn't watching over the girls and their mother. When Randall was gone, the dog would either take a nap with Mr. Hunt, Randall's grandfather, or he would tag along with Tal while he did his rounds on the grounds. Today, the dog seemed eager to check the property, and his ears were alert to every sound that didn't fit into the busy commotion of the ranch.

Tal heard the static of his walkie-talkie come on. Randall had been impressed when he returned to the ranch with several dozen walkie-talkies. Now they could communicate without having to yell or send out messengers. He waited until the voice came on.

"Tal, this is Leonard at the second watchtower. We have something you may need to check out. Over."

Tal grabbed his walkie-talkie which was dangling from a clip on his belt. "Tal, here. Copy that. Headed there now."

Tal deftly clipped the walkie-talkie back onto his belt and turned right toward the back of the ranch. It would take him a good three minutes to get to the second watchtower, and he hoped whatever they found would still be there when he arrived. He picked up the pace, noticing that Favian began to gallop next to him. When he finally arrived, he saw one of his men hiding behind the watchtower pointing to him to get low. Tal instantly squatted and duck-walked to where the man was standing.

"What's going on?" Tal whispered.

"Leonard spotted a man hidden in the woods scoping out the ranch with binoculars. He's still there. We don't think he knows that we've seen him because he's still looking. James is up there acting natural, but Leonard is on the ground watching him through the scope."

Tal nodded his head and entered the stairwell of the watchtower. He looked back at Favian. "Stay," he commanded. The dog quickly obeyed and sat down next to the entrance. Tal made his way quietly up the winding stairs. When he got to the top of the lookout, he crawled on his hands and knees to where Leonard was lying down. The scope was poking through a small opening at the base of the room. Tal tapped Leonard's shoulders twice. Then he grabbed the scope, keeping it steady as the man moved over, so he could see what had been identified through the scope.

When Tal peered through the scope, he saw a man hiding behind the shrubs with binoculars. He couldn't make out his face because the binoculars blocked the view. He would have to wait until the man was finished with his surveillance. By the way the binoculars were facing, Tal knew the man was looking at the oil diggers. He wondered if he should send men out to detain the man. *No*, he thought. *I just need to know who he is. Then Randall will organize a plan.* Less than a minute later the man finally brought the binoculars to the ground before crawling backward into the forest. When he was out of view, Tal stood up. "You can get up now. The threat is gone."

"Did you find out who he was?" Leonard asked as he stood up.

Tal nodded. "I did. And I'll take the information to Randall right away. You did good," he said, patting Leonard's shoulder. "I'll make sure Randall knows that you discovered him and that you did a good job contacting me."

The man smiled. "Yes, sir!"

Tal walked back to the stairwell and made his way down. Favian was anxiously waiting for him at the bottom. "C'mon, boy. We got some work to do."

Favian sprinted by his side. Randall had gone to town with the old man, Levi Jones, and Adella. After Levi told Randall everything about what they were planning on doing to take down the World Government, they went into town to find some more old-style computers. Tal didn't know if he believed the old baker, but Randall did. He seemed to have a history with the other names the man mentioned – a pastor from Trinity, a Colonial named Zach and an Efficientist named Li. It all sounded far-fetched to him, but maybe that was because he didn't understand any of it. He had never heard of the RIBS— Regional Integrated Banking System. He had never heard of a Kill Switch or even these old computers they were trying to find. Tal was good at covering up his ignorance, though. He would never let Randall have any reason to doubt or mistrust him.

As Tal approached the house, he saw the young sisters playing outside while Mr. Hunt sat on the rocking chair on the back porch watching them. Favian instantly ran off to be with the girls. He began to head that way when he heard a truck coming up the driveway. It was Randall. He walked to the end of the driveway and waited for Randall to park. He wouldn't seem overanxious, but he needed to explain the situation to Randall right away.

After Randall parked, he must have noticed Tal standing there waiting because he instantly walked up to him.

"What did you find?" Randall asked.

"Leonard was at the second watchtower, and he spotted a man on the outside perimeter surveying the ranch with binoculars. When I got up there, I noticed that he was looking at the oil diggers."

"Did you get a look at his face?" Randall asked.

"Yes," Tal nodded. "It was Robbie, Adella's ex-husband. I would have sent men out to detain him, but I thought it better to tell you first."

Randall thought. "You did right. We have no grounds to detain him. Pick out two men to follow him. I want to know where he is at all times."

"Where who's at?" Adella asked, walking up to them.

Tal stayed quiet. He would let Randall decide if he would tell Adella or not.

"It's your ex-husband. He was surveying our lands with binoculars."

"What do you think he's planning?" Adella asked, looking to where Ana and Alex were playing with Favian.

"In my mind, he has only two options," Randall said. "He can either tell the World Government we are here or hope he gets some kind of payout."

Adella shook her head. "He wouldn't do that. He hates the World Government more than anything. He's lived his entire life staying under their radar. They could only give him money points, and he has no interest in those. What he wants is probably the oil."

"Then there is only one other thing he could be planning to get that oil. He has no money. He has no friends. He'd have to barter for the oil."

"But there is nothing he has that we would want," Tal said confused. He looked at Randall who was now staring at the front porch where the girls were lying in the grass, soaking up the winter sun.

"He would try to take one or both of the girls as ransom," Randall said.

"We must stop him! He can't touch my girls!" Adella exclaimed.

Randall looked back at Tal. "He will bide his time until he thinks we are most vulnerable."

Levi walked up to the group holding an old-style computer. "Where can I connect this?"

"Adella," Randall said. "Take Levi into the house and show him where he can connect the computer. I need to talk with Tal for a minute."

Adella hesitated but then turned to Levi. "Follow me. I'll show you where to connect it. Are you hungry?" she asked, leading him toward the house.

"Yes, ma'am," he said, following next to her.

Randall waited until the two were out of earshot. "We are going to have to coordinate two missions now. I will plan our attack on the prison camp on New Year's Eve, but I need you here to protect Adella and the girls. We need a foolproof plan to keep them safe and capture Robbie when he decides to sneak into the camp to take the girls."

Tal looked down disappointed. He was excited about going to the prison camp and taking down the World Government. He didn't understand all the details, but it was an operation that he knew he didn't want to miss. If Randall was right, he would be part of history and a new beginning for everyone. Now that would be something to be proud of.

Randall must have noticed his reluctance. "Look, I know that you were looking forward to fighting beside me, but there is no one I trust more than you. This is our home," he said, pointing to the ground. "And these are our people. If we don't protect this place and those entrusted to us, we lose the reason for why we are fighting."

Tal looked back at Randall. He could see the sincerity in his eyes.

"Now, I'm trusting you. I give you full reigns. I want a detailed account of how you plan on protecting Adella and her girls and this property, and how you will apprehend any intruder that dares to venture into our domain."

"Yes, sir!" Tal said. He felt a renewed sense of purpose fill his soul. Randall trusted him with what he loved most.

"If I know Robbie, he won't want to confront me again. His nose is probably still healing from when I broke it. He will lay low until he knows I'm gone. Keep a watch out for him. I bet we'll see him several times scoping out the ranch. I'll stay close by until we leave for the prison. Expect him anytime while I'm gone."

"Yes, sir," Tal repeated. "I'll start on that plan now." He was just about to walk back to the house when Randall stopped him.

Randall placed both his hands on Tal's shoulders and brought his face only inches away from him. "Look, I'm being honest with you. I like Adella—possibly," he hesitated. "I possibly love her, and I need to trust you to take care of them. All of them."

"Nothing will harm them. I promise," Tal said, firmly.

"Good," Randall said, releasing his grip. "Now formulate a plan and run it by me later today. I have to formulate my own plan on how to take on the World Police."

CHAPTER 27

Zach reached the air conditioning duct. It was around two in the morning. The few guards that remained were all asleep. He had only seen one guard walking the perimeter of the prison. Since the prisoners and all the raw materials had been shipped out that afternoon, there was nothing left to monitor. The AC was no longer running. They must have only turned it on to ensure it was working. The temperature outside was in the mid-sixties that day, but now it had plummeted to the low fifties. *Could be worse*, he thought. He could live in the upper part of New America where the temps were below freezing.

He opened the vent that led into the air conditioning duct. He had to squeeze through and wondered how Jonah had made it. From the photo he had found in the rusty tackle box, Jonah was a much younger man, but he was still big—definitely not as big as he was now. He didn't know where the duct led, but he would get out the first chance he got. Pilar was staying in the upstairs office. He had seen her through the window fluffing out a blanket. He hoped no one else was staying there with her.

Zach crawled through the duct, trying not to make too much noise. He left his goggles and face mask around his neck. There was dust and debris all over the duct from lack of use. Even the time they turned it on today couldn't rid it of the years of filth that had gathered. His clothes would be filthy. He needed to make sure he didn't leave tracks. He finally made it to a large vent and listened for several seconds. He didn't hear anything, so he quietly pushed the vent out and laid it on the floor of the prison. He scooted onto the floor, hoping the dirt that clung to his clothes didn't make too much of a mess. He would have to find some way to clean it. He got up and placed the vent against the wall over the opening. He didn't lock it fully in place, though. A few lights were on, illuminating the factory just enough so he could see the stairs.

Once he reached the stairs, he quietly made his way up each step. It was several flights until he made it to the office where Pilar was. When he finally got to the top entrance, he heard a man talking from inside an adjacent room. Zach almost bolted down the stairs, but he could tell the voice was talking into something—probably an LPS. There was no other voice to be heard. He crept to the door of the room and listened.

"Yes, Mr. Elder. The Kill Switch has turned on and seems to be in working order. My thumbprint is needed to open the encasement, and I've sent you the encrypted code to open the systems. There are two keys. One is in a safe in the office and the other is on my person. Yes, sir. I'll make sure to give you the spare when you arrive. And when will that be? December 31. Roger that, we will be expecting you. And I received the list of soldiers you are sending over. All very solid individuals. It will be nice to work with Efficientist soldiers again instead of the riffraff ones from the colonies. Copy that. We will keep the factory on lockdown. Stanton out."

Zach deftly ran to the office door and opened it. He slipped in without a sound. He hid under a desk waiting to see if Ted Stanton entered behind him. After several minutes of waiting, he assumed the director went to bed. The call was late. Neil must be busy doing gala appearances. The fact Neil Elder was coming to the factory on New Year's Eve meant that he knew there was a planned attack. How he discovered it and what all he knew, Zach didn't know. But his future arrival meant he was willing to use the Kill Switch. Zach knew that if the Kill Switch was used, all their efforts would be in vain.

He quietly walked to where he had seen Pilar laying out her blanket. There she was, sleeping soundly on a cot. He crept

178

up to her and softly whispered her name. Her eyes sprang open and just before she could yell out, he covered her mouth.

"Shhh, Pilar. It is me. Zach. Don't yell," he whispered into her ear.

Pilar's breathing was rapid, but she nodded her head with understanding.

"I've come to bring you home. I have a way out," he said. "Get your things, we are leaving."

Pilar sat up on the cot and looked toward the door. "Ted Stanton is able to turn on the Kill Switch," she said, quietly.

"I know," Zach said. "Somehow they have discovered our planned attack on New Year's Eve. Neil Elder himself is planning on coming here that day."

"How did they find out?" Pilar asked.

Zach thought. "I don't know."

"Dr. Linton?" she asked.

"I don't think so. He is staying with Randall Hunt now."

"What?" she asked in disbelief.

"Long story. I'll get you caught up when we get out of here."

Pilar went to grab her small backpack and then paused. "Maybe I should stay."

"What? No. I came here to bring you home. You can't stay here."

"But I have to find a way to disable the Kill Switch or at least prevent them from using it. How much time does the attack have to last to take down the RIBS?"

"I'm not certain, but at least five to ten minutes. If the Kill Switch is used too early during the attacks, the systems will reboot, and all our work will be erased. But if the attacks can take down all ten of the RIBS, even if the Kill Switch is used, the damage will be done, and the money points will be lost."

"Then I must stay here," Pilar said. "It is the only way."

"But what can you do with the World Police surrounding you?" Zach asked, desperate. "There is no way I'm leaving you here. Please, Pilar. I've been waiting outside of the prison for days. Please, come with me. I need you to leave."

Pilar grabbed Zach's face and looked into his eyes. "Look, there is a reason God put me here. There is a reason I didn't get sent off with the others. I need to stay here and do what I can."

Zach hesitated. "Your dad is going to kill me."

"Just tell him what I told you. He'll understand," she said.

"You and I both know that isn't true," he said, trying his best to sound light-hearted. "I've lost his trust long ago."

Pilar put her hands back down with a sudden thought. "How did you get in here without being seen? The doors all have alarms."

"That's another long story, but I found a tunnel leading from the graveyard to a vent inside the factory."

"Really?"

Zach nodded. "And you'll never guess who dug it."

"Who?" she said, leaning in.

"Jonah Goodman the Third."

"What? I don't believe it."

"And there is more," Zach said. "I saw the tombstones of his entire family. They either all died at once or they were killed. They were buried in the back with hand-carved names etched into their tombstones. I found a tackle box with Jonah's photo in it and all his family. He was very young. I'm thinking in his early to mid-teens, so around fifteen to twenty years ago."

"Whoa," she exhaled.

"It gets more interesting than that," he said. What he had discovered during his research of the prison, he hadn't shared with anyone yet, not even Pastor Tom. He still couldn't make heads or tails of it.

"What else did you find?" Pilar asked, wide-eyed.

"I discovered that this is the same prison that Christina Straight was sent to when she wouldn't disclose her patient's information. Remember her? She's the one they call the Apostle and the one who helped Ruth after her Awakening."

Pilar nodded.

"And guess how long ago she was here?"

"Around fifteen to twenty years ago," she whispered.

"Bingo."

"Do you think this is where she and Jonah met?"

Zach shrugged. "I don't know. The records of Jonah's family, including his, completely disappeared. She may have arrived after he vanished. That's when this place became a women's prison for Efficientists. We can't be sure without asking him. But there's something else."

Pilar shook her head. "You're kidding? There can't be more."

"Yes, and this one is the kicker." He paused and looked around the office making sure no one was watching them.

"Guess who was the director in charge of this facility when Jonah's family died and while Christina Straight was sentenced here."

"Who?" she asked.

"Neil Elder," he said.

Pilar covered her mouth in disbelief but recovered quickly. "There is more to Jonah than we originally believed. He's not just a good Samaritan helping us. He has ulterior motives."

"Yes, he does," Zach agreed.

"That settles it," Pilar said. "I'm staying here. There is too much at stake. Tell me where the vent is that leads to the tunnel. I promise if things get too dangerous, I will leave. And talk to my father. Let him know that I can escape whenever I need to. But you need to go back to Trinity. Give this information to Pastor Tom and my father. There is much more going on than we originally believed. Pastor Tom will know exactly what to do."

Zach didn't want to leave Pilar. He wanted to grab her hand right now and take her with him. But he knew she was right. There was too much at stake. Plus, knowing that she could leave through the tunnel at any time gave him a sense of peace.

"Okay," he said. "Grab some cleaning supplies and follow me downstairs. I will show you where the vent is. I just need you to clean up the trail of dirt I'm leaving behind. I will get my Portable. It's hidden in the graveyard. I will leave it for you in the AC duct. Just make sure they don't turn on the AC again. It's pretty dirty in there, and the dust will damage the machine. That way you can let us know what's going on here." He grabbed her hand. "Just don't get caught, okay?"

Pilar squeezed his hands tenderly. "I won't get caught. I promise. I'll be careful. And if you haven't noticed. It's too cold to turn on the air conditioning right now."

He looked at her face one more time. He didn't want to leave her here, but he knew she was right. Her father wouldn't be pleased by her choice to stay, though, and he wasn't looking forward to telling him.

Pilar let go of his hands and glanced at her desk where she left the spray bottle and rags after cleaning the office all morning. She got up and walked to the desk, grabbing the cleaning supplies. "I'm right behind you."

CHAPTER 28

Adella was done waiting. She could tell that Randall liked her, but he continually kept her at a distance save the small moments of conversation she could manage between his busy schedule and hers. She needed to get him away, and a picnic lunch would do just that. He would still be on his property, but they would, at least, be a distance from the men and their constant questions. She had already arranged for Mr. Hunt to watch Favian and her girls, and Tal knew to give them at least an hour, if possible, to eat lunch and enjoy each other's company without distractions. She wore a long flowing, floral skirt, belted at the waist with a tight-fitted yellow knit sweater. Her tan skin looked fabulous in yellow, and her smokey eye makeup enhanced her dewy, brown eyes. Plus, the weather was unusually warm for winter, and the skies were clear. A perfect day for a picnic.

She held the picnic basket in her hand waiting for Randall's reply. She didn't understand why he looked hesitant, even displeased.

"Did you not want to spend time with me?" she asked, trying not to sound hurt.

"Yes—I mean no," he fumbled his words. "I mean, yes, I want to spend time with you. It's just I had a bad experience with a picnic a while back. I guess it still brings uncomfortable memories."

"Well," she said, rousing her confidence. "Let us make new memories and replace them, shall we?" She offered her hand and waited, hoping he we take it into his. "I've already made arrangements with your grandfather and Tal. They know we will be away for an hour or so. I found a little spot that would be nice. I've made us hoagies—your favorite—along with fruit salad and two slices of sweet potato pie."

He hesitated again. She wondered what he was thinking, but she knew it would take a lifetime to unravel his layers. All she knew was that Randall Hunt was where she belonged, and she needed him to understand her cues since he seemed to be missing them.

He looked out of the screen door to see if anyone was out there. Adella knew all the workers were at lunch. He was having trouble letting his guard down. She would just have to help him.

"Look," she said, taking his hands into hers. "I'll take the picnic basket and you take the new Portable thing you bought," she said, pointing to the table. "Tal knows how to use the HMS you got him. Plus, you have your walkie-talkie. If anything happens, we will only be five minutes away. No problem."

That information seemed to alleviate his worries. "Okay. I am hungry. And I do love your hoagie sandwiches," he said, squeezing her hand. He grabbed the Portable with his free hand and led her through the backdoor.

She couldn't hide her smile. Finally, she was going to have some alone time with this man, Randall Hunt. His grandfather had told her a little bit about him. He was a bodyguard in the city. In fact, he had worked for Eve Pallue for many years. She wondered if his bad picnic experience was with her. She doubted it, though, because from what she could remember from school, picnics were not part of *Life Efficiency*. Whatever happened in his previous life, those moments were gone for good. She forgot the verse, but she knew that the *Bible* said it was better to start badly and end well than to start well and end badly. Whatever skeletons Randall had in his closet, she knew that in his heart, he wanted to end well. And she would be there to help him.

She felt his hand relax around hers. Little by little, as they got further away from the main house, the tension seemed to evaporate from his body. She stole a glance his way several times. Even with his eyepatch covering a large portion of his face, she could see his countenance was relaxed and even contented.

"It is a nice day," he finally commented.

"Yes, it is. In fact, everything is nice. The girls are thriving. They keep your grandfather busy, and he seems to love it. The ranch is doing very well. Tal is growing into quite a leader under your direction. Under your leadership, there has been absolutely no fighting, no tension and no uncertainty. I haven't felt this secure and safe for a long time. It's nice."

She looked his way again. She could tell her words hit their mark because his cheeks reddened a bit. Then his face hardened. "I will not let the World Government steal what I've built."

She slowed and let go of his hands. She had more to say, but she needed to take her time. "Here is the spot. Will you help me lay out the blanket?"

He nodded and set his Portable on the ground. She set the picnic basket down and grabbed the blanket, handing him the two corners. "Let's spread it out here."

Once the blanket was spread, she took her basket and set it on the corner. Then she sat down. "Come join me."

Randall moved his Portable to another corner and sat down next to her. "It is difficult for me not to worry," he admitted.

Adella pulled out the plates and set them down in front of them. Then she began to unwrap the cloth around the hoagies and set the sandwiches on the plates. She scooped out a portion of fruit salad onto each plate and then leaned back on her palms. "I believe God gave you this ranch for a reason. You have stewarded it well, and it has blessed the people around you with food, shelter, safety and work. God sees what you're doing, and He is working behind the scenes in ways you can't comprehend. Just look at what we've discovered so far. There are people out there who have the same mind as you. They want to take down the World Government, so they too can live in peace. You have to trust that God knows what He's doing."

Randall took a bite of his hoagie and listened. When he didn't reply, she continued.

"I've learned long ago to only allow my mind to concentrate on the things in my control. Other than that, worry can do nothing to help the situation. Worry robs you of peace and joy and doesn't add a single good thing to your life."

He swallowed and nodded. "I look back at my life. I thought I had everything under control. Now I see that I was the one being controlled. I was controlled by my fears, by my desire to be esteemed—even by a desire to be known. Those emotions ruled me and caused me to do things that I regret. But that's all in the past. I've gotten a new start, and I don't want to mess it up."

"So," she said, placing her hand on his. "Why not do it the right way this time? Do what you can today and trust God with what you can't do today."

"It's easier said than done," he said.

"I guess it just depends on how real God is to you and how much faith you're willing to carry," she said. "I just finished several years of hardship and questioning God. Now that I'm here, I see what took so long. I see why God had me wait."

Randall looked away. He began to fidget with his eye patch, which he usually only did when he was alone and agitated. She had found him many times reading the *Bible* in his office and fidgeting with it. Again, she wondered what he was thinking. He was a very intelligent man, but his faith was just maturing. Adella knew, however, that it was during great difficulty that faith could grow the quickest, and he had been through great difficulty.

He finally looked back at her. She could see the sincerity in his expression. "Why did God have you wait?"

"I was waiting for you," she said. She wanted to blush and look away, but she knew that he needed to see her confidence. She would not back down on how she felt—even if she was uncomfortable saying it.

"I'm glad you like being here," he said.

"It's more than that. I like being with you," she said honestly.

He stared at her for several seconds. She could tell he was trying to read her. She had nothing to hide.

The Portable next to him beeped loudly, and she blinked, losing eye contact with him. He picked up the Portable and pressed his thumb to the print identifier. She watched him read whatever had been sent. After a moment, his face became rigid.

Randall stood up. "I need to speak to that doctor right now!"

As Randall walked toward Dr. Linton's cottage, he reminded himself of Pastor Tom's words. They didn't know for sure who had leaked the information about their plans to take down the World Government. As of now, their old-style computers have not been discovered—only the plan against the RIBS. However, someone had leaked their plan because Zach had just contacted Pastor Tom and told him that the prisoners were being removed from the work camp. The World Police was taking their place. Randall felt his fists tighten. Why would they need the World Government to protect the Kill Switch if there was no threat? Obviously, someone had spoken to Neil Elder, and that someone had to be Dr. Linton. There was no other explanation.

"What's wrong?" Adella asked, breathlessly behind him.

"I don't know," he said, keeping his voice calm. "But I will find out."

When he got to the cottage, he saw Levi Jones and Dr. Linton chatting in the shade of the porch. *Good*, he thought. This information concerned both men. Better just get it out of the way.

Dr. Linton was the first to watch him walk up the steps. "What's wrong?" he asked.

Randall looked for shame or fear in the doctor's eyes but saw none. The doctor had been good at covering up his feelings, though.

Randall walked up the steps and stood before Dr. Linton and Levi. Adella made it up behind him and leaned against one of the porch support beams, catching her breath.

"Neil Elder knows about the plan to take down the RIBS," Randall said flatly.

Levi stood up. "That's impossible! Everyone has kept the plan under tight wraps. No one would tell because it would compromise their very lives!"

Randall stepped directly in front of Dr. Linton. "What did he promise you for you to squeal?"

Dr. Linton stood up, looking eye to eye to Randall. His face and neck were blotchy red. "You don't intimidate me."

"Did you tell Neil Elder the plan to take down the RIBS?"

"No!" Dr. Linton said firmly.

"Did you tell anyone the plan?"

"No!" he repeated just as vehemently.

"Then why have the prisoners been moved to another facility? Why are the World Police coming to protect the Kill Switch?"

Levi stood up from his chair. "Where are they taking her? Where are they taking Pilar?"

Randall regained his composure. "Pilar is still there. Zach found a way in and spoke with her. Director Ted Stanton is keeping her there to help keep his books."

Levi began to ask a question when Randall interrupted him.

"She is fine. Zach wanted her to leave with him, but she insisted on staying. There is too much at stake. I doubt there is much she can do, but she will at least give us intel. Zach left his Portable in a secret place where she could contact us."

Levi fell back into his chair. "That girl is too headstrong."

"Look," Dr. Linton began. He eyed both Levi and Randall, waiting until they were both looking at him. "I told Neil Elder nothing. The time I spent in the city felt like a death sentence to me. Now. Here," he said, pointing to the ground. "I finally feel free. Don't you think I know that I've already been blacklisted by Neil Elder? If he wasn't so busy with this gala, I would probably be dead by now. I want the World Government destroyed—maybe not for social or moral reasons. I'm selfish. I want it destroyed, so I can live in peace, so I can be free."

Randall listened to Dr. Linton's words. The nonchalant doctor had spoken passionately. He was a selfish man, but weren't they all?

"So you did not contact Neil Elder or anyone in the World Government about the attack on the RIBS?" Randall repeated.

"Don't you remember what you told me that day in the hospital when I first met Eve?"

Randall thought of the time Eve was sunburned and had to be taken to the colonial hospital. That was the day he met Dr. Linton. It felt like a lifetime ago, and he was an entirely different person. "No, I don't remember what I told you."

Dr. Linton paused, calculating his words. "I told you when you found me at the trading center. You said to keep information to myself, and that I shouldn't give people a reason to distrust me. I am here at this ranch. I like it here. I would do nothing to sabotage it. I was contemplating suicide before coming here. And I would especially not contact the man who wants me dead. You can look in my house. Tear apart my room. I have nothing to contact him with anyway, nor do I want anything to do with LPSs, HMSs, Portables or even those old-style computers. I want none of it."

Randall took in Dr. Linton's speech. He knew the man was telling him the truth. "I believe you," he finally admitted.

Dr. Linton let out a sigh of relief. "Good," he said, sitting back down in his chair.

"But what are we going to do about my daughter?" Levi asked, still standing.

Randall looked at Adella who was quietly listening next to him. "Go get Tal for me, will you?"

She nodded and quickly went down the steps toward the main house.

"Don't worry about her," Randall said. He lifted his gun from his holster. Ever since Adella's ex-husband was spotted on his property, he carried his weapon every he went. "I'm going to get more guns, and come New Year's Eve, I will take down every last soldier in the World Police who gets in my way. They won't have time to hurt your daughter because they'll be too busy dealing with me."

CHAPTER 29

Esther wiped her hands on the apron she wore. She was glad Zach was back at the ranch, even if it was only for a little while. He sat at the kitchen table working on one of the old-style computers while she fried up bacon and eggs. The house was comparatively quiet that morning. Most of the Efficientist houseguests had left earlier for a big market they had heard about further south.

"Feels quiet around here," Zach said, looking up from the screen. He smiled. "I kind of like it."

Esther gave a deep sigh. "I'm sorry. I don't mean to be rude, but it's nice having a break from Efficientists. Don't get me wrong. They are each dear to me, but they get bored easily and complain quite a bit. Since its winter, there is not much to do besides organizing and cleaning, which they find disagreeable."

Zach leaned back in the wooden chair, stretching his arms. "I'm glad I get you and Deborah all to myself. And that breakfast smells wonderful. I haven't eaten much in several days. I will eat everything and anything you set before me, especially bacon."

Esther giggled and blushed a bit. She hadn't been complimented properly for her culinary capabilities in a while. Efficientists were not good with common etiquettes, and she felt unappreciated by them—though, she knew that wasn't true. She was sure they did appreciate all her work. They simply lacked the foresight to share their appreciation. Again, she had to fight the urge to feel sorry for herself. *They don't know any better,* she thought. She glanced out the kitchen window. Deborah was coming in from feeding the animals. She wore a thick, wool robe wrapped tightly around her. The wind was chilly that morning, and she could see by the way Deborah was walking that the wind was also strong.

"Would you mind getting the backdoor for Deborah? The wind seems fierce, and I don't want the door to fly out from her hands."

Zach nodded and quickly got up to open the door for the other aged sister. "Come on in, Miss Deborah."

"Oh, thank you, Zach. How nice of you," Deborah said, walking into the warm kitchen. "Esther, breakfast smells amazing as usual. You do know how much I love bacon, but I have a feeling you made it for our guest this morning."

Deborah smiled. Her sister was in a particularly good mood. Esther assumed that she too needed a break from the constant serving of their Efficientist guests. "I've been saving the bacon. We only have a little left, so I didn't want to make it for our Efficientist friends when there wouldn't be enough, but there is plenty for our three here this morning."

Deborah shook off her wool robe and folded it over one of the empty kitchen chairs. "So, what have you found?" Deborah asked sitting at the table.

Zach joined her back at his seat. "I checked the HMS this morning. Pilar says that the World Police are at the prison now. It seems like they are preparing for something." He shook his head. "Well, it's more like they're preparing for us."

"But how could they possibly know our plan?" Esther asked, setting three plates down at the table. She looked at Zach. "There is a lot more where that came from, so please eat as much as you want."

He shrugged his shoulders. "I haven't a clue. I received a message from Levi before going to bed last night, and he insists Dr. Linton hasn't told a soul."

Deborah noticed concern filling Zach's eyes. "And what about Randall Hunt? Is it true he's going to help us?"

Zach picked up his fork and stared at his food for a moment. "He's not really helping us. He's helping himself, which in turn will help us." He took a bite of egg and chewed slowly, thinking. "He must have a lot of oil on his land to willingly defy the World Government. We have reason. We see how they oppress the Colonials. We just want to be free."

Deborah waited for Zach to take a big bite of his bacon. "You know the Efficientists are oppressed too, but in another way. Their entire lives are built around those LPSs and being productive. It's another form of oppression taught since their infancy, and they too need to be set free."

Zach shrugged again. "You may be right, but it does seem that Efficientists enjoy life on the backs of our labor."

"I'd rather milk a cow than be stuck at one of their LPSs all day, and that's the truth," Deborah interjected between bites.

"You may be right," Zach admitted. "Is that the wind?" he asked, looking toward the living room that led to the front door.

Esther listened. "No, it sounds like someone is here. Oh, I hope that our Efficientists haven't returned. They've only been gone for a few hours. They're not supposed to come back until late this evening."

"Let me go look through the peephole," Deborah said, pushing away from the table. She walked to the front door and peered into the tiny hole. "It's Pastor Tom!" she exclaimed while opening the door. "Come on in from the cold."

Esther instantly got up to get another plate. She was thankful there were still a few pieces of bacon and a large spoonful of eggs left. "Come on into the kitchen," she said, loudly. "You came just in time. I have breakfast ready for you."

Pastor Tom followed Deborah into the kitchen and took off his jacket.

"Here, I'll take that," Deborah said. She grabbed his coat and her wool robe from the chair. "Sit here and make yourself comfortable. We haven't had you over in ages. How are Cindy and the kids doing?" She asked before laying the coats on a chair in the living room.

Pastor Tom took a seat where Deborah had indicated. "They're fine. Cindy is at the trading center, and the kids are playing outside with friends. Cindy and the other homeschool moms have decided to let the kids have the next several weeks off from homeschooling until the holidays are over."

"You mean the *Grand Opus Gala* is over," Deborah said, winking.

"That too. We are all busy watching and praying. No one really wants to work when there is so much going on right now."

Esther placed a plate of bacon and eggs before the pastor. "Here you are. Straight off the griddle."

Pastor Tom clapped his hands together. "I have to admit. I was hoping you'd have something hot cooking for breakfast. Cindy had the kids eat cereal this morning, so I took my chances that you would be cooking."

"Your gamble paid off," Esther said. Now she felt tripled blessed. She was so discouraged this morning, but God was letting her know that she was still appreciated by those she cared about most. She sat down with her table of four. Today was the perfect day, and she thanked God for blessing her with it.

They all began to eat. Deborah knew that Pastor Tom only came over when he had news or when he was worried about something, but a peaceful meal with friends was overdue for them all. No one wanted to spoil the moment.

"And I forgot. I have a fresh pot of coffee and some buttered toast," Esther said, getting up. She grabbed four coffee cups and filled each one with the black, aromatic liquid. Once she served the coffee, she placed a large platter of toast in the middle of the table.

"Esther, I can smell the aroma from the coffee, and it smells like heaven," Pastor Tom said before taking a piece of toast and placing it on his plate.

"Freshly roasted coffee beans, as well. Thanks to the Trinity Trading Center for supplying the beans."

Pastor Tom bowed his head slightly. "Never in a million years did I think I would be running a store, but I actually enjoy it."

"It's grown quite a bit, hasn't it?" Deborah asked.

Pastor Tom nodded. "Yes, once people trust you, the news spreads fast. I'm fair, and people respond to that."

Once they all finished eating, they sipped their coffee, making small talk. Finally, Pastor Tom took out two folded pages from his pocket. The other three at the table watched him as he reread both pages to himself.

Zach finally broke the silence. "Did you find out who alerted the World Government to our plan?"

Pastor Tom nodded. "I did."

"Was it Dr. Linton after all?"

He shook his head. "No, it wasn't him. I doubted it would be. He gains nothing from the information."

"Then who was it?" Deborah asked. "Someone from the factory?"

Esther said nothing and listened. She silently prayed it was no one she knew, but she knew almost everyone from Trinity and the surrounding areas.

"Did someone overhear us at the trading center?" Zach asked.

Again, Pastor Tom shook his head. He looked at Zach. "I knew exactly who it was when you found that tunnel at the prison camp."

Zach sucked in air. "It can't be Jonah."

Pastor Tom looked back at the two pages and held up one. "I wrote him right away when you told me what you found over there and how you found Jonah's box of photos. I don't know what happened. All the records were erased from what I can find, but Jonah lost his entire family at the camp around fifteen to twenty years ago."

"But that doesn't make sense," Zach said. "Then why would he alert Neil Elder to our plan?"

"Neil Elder was the director in charge while Jonah's family was at the camp. Jonah was a teen. Apparently, Neil Elder does not remember him. He only knows him as Matt Coughlin."

Zach stood up from the table. "Does he have some kind of vendetta planned against Neil Elder that we don't know about? But how would sabotaging our plan to take down the RIBS—compromising all of us—help get back at Neil Elder?"

"It's not simply a vendetta. Don't forget. Jonah took a knife for Neil Elder. If he simply wanted him dead, he could have let the knife reach its mark."

Esther noticed that other paper in Pastor Tom's hand. "What does that paper say?"

Pastor Tom sighed. "It's Jonah's response to my letter."

"What did he say?" Deborah asked, eyeing the page.

Pastor Tom didn't need to read it. "It says to trust him and stick to the original plan."

"A plan that Neil Elder knows about," Zach said, his voice rising.

"There is one more thing," Pastor Tom said. "And this is the reason why I have chosen to trust Jonah. We will continue to follow the plan, regardless of who knows."

"What did you find?" Deborah asked. She knew from experience that Pastor Tom's research was extensive and meticulous. It was like he had a sixth sense when it came to finding information. He was the only one who discovered Ruth's true identity without anyone hinting to him.

Pastor Tom cleared his throat. "Christina Straight, the one we called The Apostle, she was sent to the same prison when it was upgraded to a prison for Efficientists. Probably just after many of the colonial prisoners disappeared from record, including Jonah's family."

"I can confirm that information. I discovered the trail that led them both there on my Portable while I was camping outside of the prison for days," Zach said, sitting down. "But I found one additional piece of information that you missed."

"What else did you find?" Pastor Tom asked, placing his napkin on his plate.

"Neil Elder was director of the prison when Jonah was there and all those prisoners went missing, and also he was still the director there when they changed it to a women's prison," Zach said.

"So what do you think it all means?" Deborah asked.

"I can't be sure," Pastor Tom said. "But let's just pray that Jonah has a plan we know nothing about."

"Those were my thoughts," Zach added. "I just hope his plan coincides with ours, or else all our work will be wasted."

Zach lingered next to Esther as she pruned her winter flowers. Zach watched Esther work and had to smile. Even in the winter, Esther would find something to plant and grow. It was an unseasonably cold day, but she wore her winter coat and tended her garden, nonetheless.

She held a batch of weeds in her hands and finally looked at Zach. "What can I help you with? I can tell you have something pressing on your mind."

Zach felt anxiety rise in him—an emotion he used to live with but now found mostly annoying because he had trouble concealing it for some reason. "It's about Pilar."

"Are you scared for her? Well, you shouldn't be. Fear does nothing to help the situation. Only prayer does." She threw the weeds into a pile she had formed. "You must continue to pray for her."

"I do pray for her, but it's not that specifically. I know she can get out whenever she wants. That tunnel I found has made sure that when things get too heavy, she can leave. And Ted Stanton trusts her. She is able to move around where she wants, as long as she gets his books done."

"So what it is?" Esther asked.

He massaged the tension at the back of his next. "It's my relationship with Pilar. Leaving her at the prison has me more conflicted than ever. I wish I could start over with her. We've had so many years and so much has happened. And mainly I've been a fool for so long. I really don't know why she has stayed around. She could have found someone a long time ago. Now when I look at our relationship, I see a mess of good and ugly all mixed together."

Esther took off her garden gloves and walked over to Zach. She grabbed his hands into hers. "Look, when your father was murdered in that church fire, you experienced trauma. Some people get over it better than others. You, on the other hand, have been struggling with the same pain for so many years."

"I guess I just don't understand why my dad was taken from me so soon. It's like I try to fit the information into my brain, and it doesn't compute," Zach confessed. "Even now, it still doesn't make sense, and I fear that once this is all over, I still won't have the peace I need."

"That peace you are looking for won't come from external circumstances. It's an inside job. You have to choose to trust God without understanding."

"It's easier said than done. I have lost all trust in myself, and that truly feels like the worst thing ever," Zach said. He hated admitting his need. He always claimed indifference. It was an easier burden to bear. But he couldn't even claim that anymore because he did care.

"Listen to me, Zach. I know that the heart can be deceitful above all else. But let me tell you, a heart submitted to God's Spirit will reach for His gifts and blessings. And, Pilar, she's a gift. You don't want to let her go."

"I know," he agreed. "It just so hard asking for that gift when you've taken it for granted, messed things up and pretty much don't deserve it."

Esther released his hands. "Don't take offense to this, Zach, but you can be overanalytical when it comes to the things of the heart. The past is gone. We are talking about the here and now. You are laying too much information on the table with your decision-making, which makes everything too confusing. Do you want Pilar or not? That is the only question that needs answering."

"You're right," he said. "And I feel like I have the answer, but I can't seem to rid myself of all these other emotions, like discouragement, fear, insecurity, unworthiness—they are all pressing into me. I feel like those emotions are crushing my only hope for happiness."

Esther reached down and scooped up a pile of weeds she had pulled. "You see these weeds? I know they will find their way to my flowers, but does that stop me from planting something I find beautiful? No, I simply must steward my flowers by pulling out the weeds. You are carrying a lot of weeds in your relationship with Pilar. Throw them out. Give them to God. They are doing nothing but choking out your happiness."

"But how do I do that?" he asked. He truly wanted to know. He was so tired of living under the heavy cloak of defeat.

"You simply have to trust that Jesus has already taken those weeds on the cross. You make a mockery of the cross every time you pick those weeds back up. I can assure you that Pilar is not thinking about the weeds. She's one of those people who forgives and trusts easily."

"I forgive and trust easily too—just not myself."

Esther placed her hands on her hips. "Zach, that is pride. There are two sides to pride. One is arrogance. The other is insecurity. You can't be perfect, so that fact makes you insecure, which is pride. You've made mistakes. We all do, but once we repent, God doesn't see them anymore. And you shouldn't either, and you especially shouldn't wallow in them. You will miss out on all the blessings God has for you."

Zach didn't feel a load lifted from his shoulders, which he had hoped for, but at least now, he had a game plan. He would give God the weeds and keep giving them until he learned to stop picking them up again. "Thank you, Esther. I needed this chat," Zach said. "I better head out. Pastor Tom is probably ready to get back to the trading center."

"Before you leave, Zach. I have something to tell you," Esther began.

"Yes?" he asked, turning to her.

"I hope you don't feel pressured by this, but my sister and I have already agreed to give you our mother's ring if, or should I say when, you finally decide to propose to Pilar. We offered it to Ruth, but she and Bear wanted their pearl necklaces. But now we know we want you and Pilar to have it. Just let us know. It is all yours."

Zach walked to Esther and gave her a hug. "Thank you, Esther. And tell Deborah thank you, as well. Pray for me. Pray that I'm able to let things go and simply take a step of faith."

CHAPTER 30

L i looked out of the window of his new ranch house. The ranch was small—only twenty acres or so, but it was enough for him and his horse, Xin. Xin now had a few other horses as companions who came with the ranch. He watched as Xin grazed on dry grasses in the round pen with his friends. He would exercise him later that day. He hoped the sun would come out by then. It was colder up north where his ranch was located, but he liked it. The cooler atmosphere made it easier to stay in the warmth of his home where he could sneak around the World Government on all the electronics he had. He laughed to himself as he looked around his living room. He had one LPS, two HMSs, four old-style computers and one Portable—all in working condition. He was a one-man force of intelligence gathering. He would send everything he could glean to Pastor Tom who would then make projections and assumptions from it all.

He liked snooping about, especially on the old-style computers because no one could detect him. He sent a message to Pastor Rohan earlier that day. They had received more old-style computers and Rohan had a question about one of them. Each computer they found was a little different, but Li had become a master at working on all of them. The differences were subtle, and he helped Pastor Rohan with information that would get his new one running.

Li went to Matt Coughlin's LPS. He could easily infiltrate his systems without being caught. He looked over his shoulder like someone may be watching him.

"Look, if Jonah is on our side, he will have nothing to hide, right?" he asked himself.

Li thought for a second longer and then went ahead and opened Matt Coughlin's LPS. He wanted to see his search history. Li scanned. There were many messages from Ada Armel, mostly about gala stuff. Nothing interesting. There was a list of security guards under his authority. He could go into each of their LPSs, but that probably wouldn't do any good. They didn't have as much clearance as Jonah. There were no messages from Neil Elder. Why would there be? Neil could talk to Jonah face to face without leaving even the slightest trace.

He saw several deletes messages. Another LPS wouldn't notice them but searching with an old-style computer was like wearing 3D glasses. He could see breadcrumbs everywhere. Each bread crumb had an identifying feature. He could see the messages that were sent to Pastor Tom and deleted. There were many of those. He saw a few to Pastor Rohan's HMS. He recognized those by entering his own LPS with an old-style computer. Jonah didn't send many messages out. Too many deleted messages would eventually be detected if done from the same LPS repeatedly. Li was just about to log out when he noticed something peculiar.

"Why does Jonah have two of you?" he asked out loud.

Li knew that every LPS and HMS in both the city and colonies was implanted with *Life Plethoricity*. Neil Elder made sure that everyone had a copy of it. The new life plan was his crowning moment, and he installed it everywhere—in all the World Government sites, research sites, bank sites and personal sites. Little did he know that the plan would backfire, forcing him to put on the *Grand Opus Gala* as a distraction which happened to go against everything *Life Plethoricity* preached. Li rolled his eyes. The World Government was so duplicitous that one would have to be completely ignorant or brainwashed not to see it.

He clicked on the first *Life Plethoricity* link. The file opened and looked like all the other files he had seen: A detailed life plan written in T-variety. Too bad Neil Elder made the links impossible to remove. In his zeal to steal and publish the life plan, he ensured that they would remain forever unalterable. That was, of course, if someone didn't find a way to bring down the World Government. If that happened, everything would be removed. Li sighed. He just hoped their plan to bring down the RIBS would work.

He got out of the file and clicked the other *Life Plethoricity.*

"What in the world?" he whispered. He held his breath, thinking that if he moved even a centimeter, the code being revealed before his eyes would disappear. "What is going on? Why haven't we seen this before?"

He quickly clicked the link to the other *Life Plethoricity* file.

He read them side by side. They looked almost identical. Same sentence structure. Same number of words in each sentence. Same number of letters in each word. However, the second file was not English. It was code. A code he had never seen before. He looked deep into the second file's history. With his old-style computer, he could see things others could not. The second file had been copied from the original *Life Plethoricity* file and then altered. He looked at the first one. It was an original. He checked the origination of the file. Every *Life Plethoricity* file should have originated from Neil Elder's LPS from a secured World Government site. But this one did not lead there. It led to an LPS or Portable that had been completely wiped out. He began a search to find any breadcrumbs that would lead him to its original source. His search led him to an undisclosed Portable and then to the same LPS that had been erased.

Li let out a breath he had been holding. "Whose Portable did this come from and why did Jonah have it on his LPS?" He wondered, staring at both files. "Someone went through a lot of trouble to hide their origins." He looked at the date of the copy with the code. Then the fire in the city came to his mind. It was around the same time. "I bet you anything these two files came from Eve Pallue, but how did Jonah get the original? Either Eve gave it to him willingly or he stole them from her. It doesn't matter," he said to himself. "If Ruth thought it was important, she would have mentioned it by now." He pushed back in his chair. "But then why does Jonah have them sitting on his LPS? Both of them, side by side, looking innocent but holding secrets? It's like he wanted them to be found."

Li thought for a moment and examined the other three old-style computers at his workstation. He went to the one closest to him and began typing. He got into Jonah's LPS and clicked on both links of *Life Plethoricity*. Neither one revealed the code. He quickly went through the same process on the other two remaining computers. None of them revealed the code either. He analyzed the first computer. It didn't seem any different than the other three, but something about it exposed the code that the rest couldn't. "Let me try something," he said to himself. His fingers swiftly typed on the keyboard of the first computer. He got out of Jonah's LPS and went into a random Efficientist's LPS. He clicked on *Life Plethoricity* link. "What?" he whispered. "There's the code again." He got out of that LPS and went into a Colonial's HMS and clicked on the *Life Plethoricity* link. The code was there too. Then he went to several LPSs and HMSs and even a few Portables and clicked on the *Life Plethoricity* links. The code was everywhere, but it could only be seen from this computer.

He took a screenshot of the code and then stared at the computer in wonderment. How could a regular old-style computer reveal something that nothing else could? He didn't understand it, but he knew he had stumbled onto something big. He thought over the endless possibilities, but nothing seemed to make sense. He'd have to send the information to Pastor Tom. Maybe he could discern the clues. He began typing again. He searched the computer's data to find the make and model and date produced. Once he gathered all the details, he opened an encrypted message to Pastor Tom. He sent him the computer's information and the screenshot of the code. Maybe there was another computer out there with the same make and model that also exposed the code—or maybe, it just so happens that he had the only one.

Deborah flipped the pancake. Esther was still sleeping. She rarely slept in, so Deborah decided to make breakfast that morning. Besides, it wasn't like she had a lot of nursing calls lately. Families would visit their ranch occasionally for colds or scrapes. She'd administer first aid well enough. Whenever Pastor Tom received medicines or medical supplies at the trading center, he would alert her. He kept her nursing hobby well-stocked, and she would in return give him canned goods or a few of Esther's baked goods. Nothing worth what he gave her, but he was appreciative of her food offerings. Plus, he knew that she cared for the people of Trinity and the surrounding area free of charge. People would give her what they could, but she expected nothing in return for her services.

She thought of the morning she and Esther found Ruth in their barn. She was burned badly and dehydrated almost to the point of death. She brought her back to life by the help of the Good Lord, and she and Esther cared for her. Their lives had turned out so differently than what they ever imagined, but she wouldn't change one single thing. She knew beyond a shadow of a doubt that she was fulfilling her God-given destiny. Esther too. They had both been obedient to the point of not understanding, but trust was a much easier burden to bear than understanding everything.

She missed Ruth. She prayed for her and Bear continually. She also prayed for Shayla, Bear's daughter. What a sight it was to see her on the HMS at the *Grand Opus Gala*. There was no disputing that she was his daughter. She and Esther already knew about Shayla before she was introduced, but the way Ada Armel introduced her was not right. The look of surprise on Bear's face was captured and spread everywhere by the World News. Bear's grandfather had met her first. He had told Pilar's sister, Reyna, and Reyna told Pastor Tom, and Pastor Tom told her and Esther. News traveled fast from Levington to Trinity, especially since Levi Jones and his family delivered their baked goods to both villages.

"I can't wait until this whole thing is over, so we can get back to normal," she said to herself. "Whatever our next normal will look like." She realized that in all her years of life, normal changed with the will of God. She had to learn to find peace outside of her circumstances. "Okay, Lord. I see what You are doing. I understand that there is no such thing as normal—just Your will. And Your will is good and perfect and right where we need to be."

She checked on the sausages. They were done. She turned off the stove and set each sausage on a plate with a spatula. Then she placed the final pancake on the stack. She cooked extra, knowing that the Efficientists would be up soon. She'd go wake Esther, so they could have a quiet breakfast before the hustle of the day began. She pressed down the French press that had been sitting for a good seven minutes. "Fresh coffee will entice Esther's eyes open," she said with a nod.

She washed her hands and dried them on her apron before taking it off and hanging it on the hook. She adjusted her skirt and headed to her sister's room in the front hallway. She knocked gently on the door. "Esther, dear. Breakfast is ready. I brewed us some fresh, hot coffee."

She opened the door. She saw her sister sleeping soundly on her bed. Deborah couldn't help but notice how pretty her sister looked. Even in her old age, she had a graceful beauty that defied time. She walked up next to her and went to pat her shoulder but stopped. Something was very wrong. Her sister looked peaceful, but the slow rise and fall of her chest was absent. She wasn't breathing. Her face looked more pale than usual.

"Esther," she whispered. She felt a deep fear slice through her chest. She placed her two fingers on her sister's neck, feeling for a pulse. There was none. "Oh, no! No! No! No!" She sat down next to her sister. "Esther, please don't leave me. Not yet. Esther, please wake up!" But in her heart, she knew Esther was gone. She had seen death before. Her sister was no longer with her. She was with her Father in heaven.

The fear she felt exploded in pain, and she grabbed her sister into an embrace and began to rock her back and forth. She couldn't stop the tears, and she didn't realize she had been crying until several of their houseguests ran into the room.

"Deborah, what happened? Is Esther alright?" one of them asked.

She held onto her sister and continued to rock. "She's in her eternal home now. She is planting fruits and vegetables in the rich soil of heaven. She is surrounded by little ones who died too soon, telling them stories about all she has experienced in this life. She's at the throne of God where Jesus sits at His right side, and she is worshiping, dancing and singing. She feels no more pain, and she is filled with such joy that she can hardly contain it."

None of the Efficientists spoke a word. Deborah continued to rock her sister, allowing her heart to release some of the heartache building up. However, she knew she would feel her sister's loss until she saw her again in heaven. This is one normal she could never get used to.

"Would someone mind driving to Pastor Tom and letting him know?" she said, finally turning to the Efficientists.

"And please. Don't let the breakfast get cold. I will be out in a bit. Just let me say my goodbyes."

The Efficientists nodded and slowly backed out of the room, gently closing the door behind them. Deborah turned back to her sister and continued to imagine all the amazing things she was doing now that earth was no longer her home.

CHAPTER 31

G randfather sat in his chair just outside of the shed that housed his grandson's stored goods. He held the large rifle that he had shot the night before. His grey hair was pulled back, but many of the silver strands blew with the wind. Someone had tried to break into *Ne'aw-ze's* shed, and he had fired a warning shot. He wouldn't leave the shed now. He would not allow his grandson's goods to be stolen under his watch. *Ne'aw-ze's* young fighters had left earlier that week, and he was sure news got out that the house was being watched only by an elderly grandfather. Everyone knew that Bear, or as he called him by his *Ka'to* name, *Ne'aw-ze*, had most of his winnings stored in that shed.

The air was cool, and he had draped a thick, woven blanket over his lap. He didn't have a coat. They weren't necessary so far south, but his thin frame quivered in the cold. He looked up to the sun. It was covered by a thick layer of grey clouds. If the sun would simply come out, he wouldn't be so miserable. Didn't matter, though. He would protect the property regardless of the weather. He would not let his grandson come home to a house that had been stripped of its wealth.

He jerked the shotgun into both hands when he heard tires slide over gravel. He recognized the baker's truck. He squinted his eyes to see who was driving. It was Pilar's little sister, Reyna. Grandfather licked his lips. She always brought him sweet treats. He watched as she parked, looking for a small paper bag that she would be holding in her hand once she got out. To his surprise, she brought out two large bags.

He watched her as she walked over to him. She looked more like her mother. Lighter skin than Pilar with her mother's Latina features. He wondered how her marriage with Javier was going. He looked at her midsection. Not pregnant. Still as lean as usual. She wore a bright smile—though, she couldn't hide the exhaustion she must have been feeling. He could see the dark circles under her eyes. Having Pilar and now her father gone must be taking its toll. He wondered how Levi's wife, Maria, was doing. Both her husband and her daughter were fighting an invisible war against the government, and she had to continue the family business.

He greeted her with a nod. "There is a chair next to me. Please join me for a talk," he said. He was glad she wore warm clothes including a coat. He reprimanded himself for not having a fire going. He didn't need one, but a beautiful young lady may enjoy the warmth.

Reyna set the two large bags next to his chair and reclined into the chair next to him. "Did you hear about Esther?"

Grandfather shook his head.

"She died during the night. Deborah said she was lying peacefully on her bed. I delivered to her just before coming here."

He stared at the ground. "I'm sad to hear she is gone, but I am glad she died in her sleep. That is how I want God to take me. No pain. Just to wake up and see the beautiful faces of my wife and daughter again."

"Pastor Tom doesn't want us to spread the news just yet. He and Deborah will have a small funeral at the ranch, but we will have a grief gathering once this is all over," Reyna said.

"Yes, I agree. Now is not the time to mourn. Now is the time to fight. We will mourn our losses once the battle is won."

The two sat in silence, allowing the breeze to flow over them, like a reminder that things were constantly changing, but change didn't have to be difficult. It could be as peaceful as falling asleep and waking up in eternity surrounded by the loved ones who have gone before.

"I wish I could stay longer. My mom and I are swamped at the bakery. Javier is making all the runs, and she and I have been baking nonstop. The winter is always so busy for us. The harvest is done, and people are at home—especially now with the *Grand Opus Gala*. People are staying in and watching for Bear and Ruth. I don't know how we are going to make it to New Year's without my dad. Javier said he would ask his family for help."

Grandfather said nothing, allowing the young woman to speak her heart seemed like enough. Finally, she sat up as if shaking off the gloom. "I've been so busy that I haven't been able to come by. So..." she said, grabbing one of the bags. "I brought you treats to last for days."

Grandfather set the shotgun next to his chair. "I do love your treats."

"As an apology for not coming sooner, I brought you your very own pecan pie." She used a piece of tissue already in the bag to pull out a pre-cut slice of pie and handed it to the grandfather. "I cut the pie into slices, so you won't be tempted to eat the entire thing in one day. It is very sweet. The slices should last you at least a week so don't overdo it or you'll be in a sugar-induced coma, and it will be all my fault. I can't live with that guilt," she jested.

"Yes," Grandfather said, grasping the small slice of pecan pie into his fingers. "I will make it last."

The smell of the pie was enough to fill his senses with delight. Suddenly, the day didn't seem as gloomy. He took a bite, and instantly his mouth was filled with sticky sweetness and hearty chewiness—and something more. He looked up at her. "What else is in it?" he asked.

Reyna giggled. "I wondered if you would taste it. We soaked the pecans in vanilla and bourbon to make them a little softer for you to chew and a little friendlier too," she added.

Grandfather took another bite and nodded. "Yes, it is bourbon. You have made this old man very happy."

Reyna leaned back into her chair. "I'll let Mom know. It was her idea, after all. I honestly think she wanted an excuse to have a little drink herself. She's been under so much pressure. There isn't anything that Javier and I can do to help her. We wait by our HMS for information, and we tell her what we find out. It's like a waiting game, but she prays constantly."

"*Aha-enah*!" a shout sounded across the river.

Grandfather dropped the last piece of his pie and grabbed his shotgun before standing to attention. He looked across the river and saw half a dozen men. They were fighters. The man who shouted looked familiar.

"How do you know that name?" Grandfather demanded.

"My name is Watchman. I used to fight the Shaman or Bear as he is known now," the man shouted. "May we come onto your property? We intend no harm."

Grandfather squinted to see the man who called himself Watchman. He remembered him now. He was the aged, dark-skinned fighter who lost his final bout against his grandson. *Ne'aw-ze* had torn his shoulder and finished his career in the fighting circuit for good. "Is that your son with you, Watchman? Is he the one who trained with my grandson?"

"Yes! This is Sentinel and a few of his men. May we come and rest for a while? We have been walking for days."

Grandfather thought for a moment longer. Then he set his shotgun down against his chair and waved the men to come over. He sat down and looked at the last bit of pecan pie on the ground. He turned to Reyna. "Do not worry about these men. They are honorable."

Reyna looked relieved. "I remember them from my wedding. My sister talked with Sentinel, the fighter. I thought they may become an item, but her heart will always be elsewhere," she sighed before continuing. "Sentinel has been fighting in the circuit, and he's winning every bout. I wonder why they are here."

"I don't know," Grandfather said. "But we will find out shortly. May you offer some pecan pie to the men? I know they will be hungry after so much walking."

"Yes, of course," she said, getting up. She still held the bag with the pecan pie slices.

"Could you give me another slice?" he asked, extending his hand. "I dropped mine on the ground when I heard the shout."

She eyed the small morsel of pie resting in between patches of dried grass. "Why not?" she asked, reaching in the bag with the tissue paper and handing him another slice.

When the men arrived, Grandfather stayed seated and continued to eat his new slice of pie. Watchman stood in front of him. "I apologize for using the name that Bear calls you, but I saw that you had a shotgun ready, and I wanted to make sure you knew that we meant you no harm."

"You did good," Grandfather said in between bites. "I have no seat to offer you, but you are welcome to pull the logs over here. There is kindling to start a fire. I have not been able to do my daily routine. Someone tried to break into my grandson's shed early this morning, and I must keep watch."

Sentinel surveyed the lands. "All Bear's men are gone into the city, I heard. You must watch the lands alone?"

Grandfather nodded. "I will protect what's mine."

While the two aged men chatted, several of the younger men grabbed bulky, long logs and pulled them around the firepit. Another young man took the fire-starting elements and quickly produced flames on a small pile of firewood. He carried a few larger logs to the firepit from the stockpile of firewood leaning against the shed. He added one log and left the others nearby.

"Here, take my seat," Reyna said to the old fighter. "I'm just about to leave."

"Thank you," he said, sitting down. "I appreciate the rest. I forget my age sometimes. Our travels have been rough on me. I fear I am slowing down my son from his assignment."

The other men sat down on the logs, allowing their legs to rest near the warm fire.

"This is Reyna, the daughter of Levi Jones. He is the founder of Levington."

"Yes, we know him," Sentinel said. "He owns a bakery. We enjoyed the quality of food at your wedding."

"Thank you," Reyna said, still holding the bag of treats. She looked down at the bag like she had forgotten it was still in her hands. "Oh, Grandfather asked me to share this with you." She pulled out the first slice and set it in Watchman's hand. Then she pulled out a piece for Sentinel and the other men. "It does have bourbon in it, but it's not enough to do much. It's mainly for flavor."

The young men ate their slices in three bites, and Grandfather could tell they were still hungry. "I have dried meats in the shed. Do you have anything to trade for it?"

"Yes," Watchman said. He was still enjoying the final bite of his pie, which he took time to savor. "We can offer you information."

Grandfather looked at Watchman. He wouldn't waste his time unless he had information *Ne'aw-ze* needed. He wondered if he knew anything about what Zach and Pastor Tom were planning. Probably not. Colonials weren't really involved in whatever they were scheming with those old computers—at least, Colonials who didn't care much about the government. Most fighters were indifferent about life outside the fighting circuit.

"You tell me the information, and I will tell you how much food it is worth," Grandfather said, noticing Watchman glance at his son, Sentinel.

Grandfather also eyed the young man. The information must be about him. He could tell that the young fighter was bigger and stronger since he saw him last. Bear had trained him a few rounds in the ring in exchange for his help to build a casket for Naomi when she passed away. He was a good fighter then, but from what Reyna had said, he was now an excellent fighter. He wondered what assignment brought him to his doorstep.

"We were told not to tell anyone, but I find it only fair to prepare my son's opponent for the inevitable. No one knows anything about the assignment besides the faces you see before you now," Watchman began.

"Should I leave?" Reyna asked, standing uncomfortably. "I don't want to get anyone in trouble."

"No, stay," Grandfather insisted. "I don't have one of those HMS things here. You will need to notify my son."

"Notify him of what?" Reyna asked confused.

Grandfather took a deep breath and stared at Watchman. He knew now what was going on, and for the first time ever, he feared for his son's life. "Sentinel is to fight my grandson."

"What?" Reyna asked. She looked to the young fighter. "Is that true? You are like half his age."

The young man nodded. His muscles on his chest and arms tensed, causing his shirt to crease in layers. "Yes, on New Year's Eve I will be fighting Bear. They want it to be a surprise to boost the ratings of the *Grand Opus Gala* on the final night. And I just can't win. I must make a show of it and then win. I tried to decline, but the World Government has insisted. I'm to arrive in a few days—quietly like a thief about to steal everything. I don't like it. Bear should know and prepare."

"Will you notify him?" Grandfather asked Reyna.

"Yes," she nodded. "I will message Ruth right when I leave here. Then I'm headed to the trading center."

Grandfather got up and pulled keys out of his pocket. He walked to the shed and began opening the locks. "I will give you and your men some dried meat. You have given my grandson a fair chance."

"I don't know how fair it will be," Watchman said. "I must be honest. I have fought Bear before, and he was the best. But now I know that my son is the best. He is younger, stronger and now because of Bear's advice, he is a better fighter."

"You may be right," Grandfather said, continuing to open the locks. "But at least my grandson can face an opponent willingly. He would have a sour taste if he had to fight against his will. At least this way, win or lose, he is still the one in control."

Grandfather walked into the shed where the dried meat was stored in crates. He grabbed several handfuls before closing the lid. When he exited the shed, he tossed several pieces to each man. They all ate hungrily. He went back over the locks and secured each one before sitting back down.

Watchman held his meat and looked around. "I have one more proposition for you."

"I am listening," Grandfather said.

"Let me stay here with you. I'm only slowing down my son and his friends. I will help keep watch until Bear returns. All I need is a place to sleep and food to eat. They asked me to join my son—probably some ploy to talk about my shoulder and my son getting revenge. I don't want to be any part of it."

"What will I tell them, Father?" Sentinel asked.

Sentinel swallowed his bite of the dried meat. "You worry too much about what they think. The World Government only has the power that we give them. Don't forget. God is in control of your destiny. You just follow His lead. Just tell them the walk was too much for me and I became sick. You had to leave me behind."

"Yes, Father," Sentinel agreed.

216

Grandfather felt relieved, though, he wouldn't show it. "You will take the first shift at night. I like to sleep early and rise early."

Sentinel took another bite. "Fine by me. I like to sleep late and wake up later." He leaned back in his chair. "I didn't want to go into the city anyway. I've only been there once, and I vowed to never go again. Let the young men fight, and let the old men defend."

Grandfather nodded. Now that his lands were secure, his thoughts turned to his grandson. He only had less than two weeks to get ready for the fight of his life. The only problem was that unless *Ne'aw-ze* could turn back the aging process, there was little chance he could win.

CHAPTER 32

Ruth pulled the black wool hood of her cape down over her head. The wind was strong today, even though towering buildings were all around her. She didn't want to wear a mask since she wasn't at the gala, but she still wanted to cover her face. She looked to Shayla who was quietly walking beside her. She had finished her schoolwork quickly that morning, so she could enjoy an outing in the city for an early lunch. Ruth liked Shayla. She too was quiet and only spoke words of purpose. She had helped her greatly during her morning sickness. She still got sick every few days, but the worst of it was fading now.

The streets of the city were more populated than she remembered. Even though it was lunchtime, she was surprised so many Efficientists were eating outside of their homes. She passed the small café where the little girl had tripped and fallen from when she walked this street with Jonah. Ruth remembered the mother's tenderness in picking the young girl up and holding her while she cried. She felt for the pearl strung with nylon around her neck. That time felt like ages ago, yet it had been a little less than a year. So much had changed since then. That was the same day she and Jonah went into her safety deposit box—or room, as it was. The day the pearl necklace broke, and she shoved all the milky gems into her pant pockets.

"There are a lot more restaurants than I remember," Ruth said.

Shayla turned toward her. "You used to live here? Were you an Efficientist? I see you working on the LPS. You are very fast."

Ruth almost regretted her words, but she had been so comfortable around Bear's daughter. "Yes, I was an Efficientist all my life."

"I read that many of you guys left *Life Efficiency* when Neil Elder introduced the new life plan...*Life Plethoricity*. It's stuck on every HMS in the colonies. I've noticed it's also on the LPS in our flat."

The mention of *Life Plethoricity* caused a surge of guilt to permeate Ruth's midsection. Her chest also tightened. She hadn't had this response to the life plan before, but she guessed being in the city and seeing the full effects of what she created had her feeling shame she wasn't accustomed to. "Yes, Neil Elder anchored it to everything."

"It's obviously not working," Shayla said. "Why doesn't he take it down?"

"He cannot remove it," Ruth said. She had tried to take it off the LPS in their flat, but Neil and his team had figured out a way to burn the life plan into every system of the World Government, and there was no way to undo it. He used it to his advantage, though. He passed new laws that gave him more power, while severely limiting the power of the individual. That is why so many Efficientists dropped rank.

"I wish he would have given it to the Colonials in Long English. I can barely read the T-variety," Shayla said. "He's enforcing a new life on us that we can't even comprehend."

Ruth looked at the young lady. Her features were much like Bear's, and she tended to be just as stubborn. "It would not matter. I can read it, and it makes no sense. It was written from a point of view that is not real or logical."

"Really?" Shayla asked. "Then why would he publish it?"

Ruth thought of her own reasons. "The life plan only makes sense from the security of the home, working on the LPS. It makes no allowance for the complexities of life."

"You mean the messiness of life," Shayla interjected.

Ruth smiled. "Yes, life is messy. My life before was pristine and perfect, yet it lacked color and energy. It was not until I almost died that I realized I was not truly living."

"You almost died?" Shayla asked shocked. "But how? Weren't you safe in your home?"

Again, Ruth regretted speaking so honestly. "Are any of us truly safe from death?"

Shayla thought for a moment. "You're right. Death comes after us all eventually. Sometimes, I'm scared of dying. Then I think of Jesus. I imagine his dusty feet walking this earth. It helps me to know that He died and is waiting for me."

An image of Uncle Sam, Sonnie's Bald Eagle, flying into the window crept into Ruth's mind. Death was inevitable, but she would not allow it to force itself into her small family so quickly. She would protect her husband, her baby and now her new stepdaughter from harm. She knew the city intimately, and she knew Ada Armel and Neil Elder would do anything for high ratings. The chase for public approval never ended. She personally had to reinvent herself so often that her only true identity was when she was sitting at her LPS, but even then, that was taken from her.

"Ruth, are you okay? You got quiet," Shayla asked, concerned. "How are you feeling?"

Ruth lightened her expression, though, her face was still hidden behind the hood. At least, her voice would sound more upbeat. "Let us get lunch for your father and his fighters, as well. They have been training all morning behind the building. They will be hungry."

"Do you mind if we sit at the restaurant and eat before bringing them lunch? This is my first time to really walk around and experience the city. I get tired of staying at the gala building all day."

"You know how your father does not want my face to be seen?" Ruth said, knowing it was a loose argument. She too thought it would be nice to eat out instead of inside their flat.

She was feeling much better today. Her morning sickness was alleviating a bit.

"Why is that?" Shayla asked. "Mine is seen every day."

"There was nothing your father could do about that. Remember, he did not know you existed until Ada introduced you to the world. That was a choice you made. I choose to stay anonymous."

Shayla looked embarrassed. "You're right. I wanted to be seen. I think I just wanted to finally fit in."

"Did it work?" Ruth asked.

Shayla recovered her emotions quickly—something Bear still had troubled doing. "Yes, it did. Not really in the city but with you and my father. I finally don't feel like an outsider. *Ah-nah* looks like me."

Ruth nodded. "I like that name you call him. He says *Ah-nah* means father in the *Ka'to* language. It suits him," Ruth said.

"Even though I might have come here for the wrong reasons, I really like my father. And I like you too," Shayla said.

Ruth stopped. "Thank you. I like you too."

Shayla hesitated. "Don't take this the wrong way, but you are just as weird as I am."

Ruth thought for a moment and began to laugh. "I have had many labels throughout my life, but *weird* was never one of them."

Shayla's cheeks brightened red. "I didn't mean to offend you. I like how you are. It makes me feel better about myself. I am so different from my mother. She has lots of friends. She loves to be around people. We are very different, and she doesn't understand me—though, I know she loves me."

Ruth continued their slow walk. "Shayla, I am not offended. In fact, out of all the labels I have been given in my life, I like *weird* the best."

"What label did you like the least?" Shayla asked.

Ruth enjoyed her inquisitiveness. "Perfect," Ruth said, resolutely. "That is by far the worst label I tried to carry."

Shayla nodded. "That would be an impossible one to live up to."

"And yet, that label has already been carried for us," Ruth said. She lifted her hand from under her cape and pointed a slender finger toward a bistro. "Let us eat here. I have read great reviews for it."

Ruth led the way into the outdoor seating of the restaurant. It was a cool day, but the wool cape she wore kept her warm. She received many stares from the other customers seated at their tables. Once the onlookers saw Shayla walking behind her, they knew she was the Shaman's wife. She could hear them whispering, but she ignored their talk. While living in the colonies, she had trained her mind to listen when it was required and to block out when needed. Their voices became like a distant hum. She set her attention on the breeze that flowed through the city streets.

She sat down at a round, metal-framed table with a glass top. The chairs were also wireframed with small cushions resting on the seats. As she sat, her feet barely touched the ground. A waiter came directly to their table.

"We are honored to have you both at our humble bistro. We have a full coffee bar, and our special today is a turkey, apple and brie open-face sandwich with chips and sun-dried tomato dip. Please order whatever you both want. It is on the house."

"For a photo?" Ruth asked.

The waiter floundered a bit but recovered quickly. "The paparazzi will be along shortly. But don't worry. We have given special rights to only one cameraman. He will not bother you. He must stay outside the enclosed patio."

"We will also need food to be delivered to my husband and his men. Can you have that ready before we leave?" Ruth asked without looking up. She did not want to expose her face.

She wished she would have brought a mask, but she did not think they would be eating out. She would have to eat carefully.

"Yes, of course," the waiter said, eagerly. "In fact, we will have the food brought to him ASAP."

"With the cameraman, as well?" she asked.

"Yes, but he will stay a distance and snap photos of the men receiving their food. Believe me, the last thing the cameraman wants to do is make those fighters angry."

Ruth smiled to herself. The paparazzi had been good at staying clear of Bear and his men. "What would you like, Shayla?"

Shayla turned to the waiter. "I would like the special and a caramel latte."

"I will bring you water, as well," the waiter said. Then he turned to Ruth. "And you?"

"I will take the special also. I will have a hot green tea and a side of honey. Thank you."

The waiter grinned. "Good choices." He turned and walked back through the patio and into the restaurant. Ruth knew he was going straight to his Portable to contact the paparazzi assigned to his restaurant.

Shayla leaned forward. "You definitely know the ways of the city."

"Restaurants have to keep up their public ratings just like the rest of the Efficientists. I never worried about it because I hired others to maintain my public ratings. I see now how time-consuming it is."

"Kind of goes against Efficiency, doesn't it?"

"Much of *Life Efficiency* goes against itself," Ruth said. She wondered how she never saw it before. Once her value was set on a life of production, she overlooked many dichotomies about *Life Efficiency*, including her own father's attraction to the colonies and the women he found there. Eve Pallue may have been considered the Top Elite Efficientists, but she had to construct a lot of closets in her mind to embrace that title.

"Can I ask you a question?" Shayla asked hesitantly.

Ruth nodded.

"Why do you look so young? I mean, you don't look much older than me, but *Ah-nah* says you are only a few years younger than he is. And he looks old!"

Ruth turned away and gazed toward the direction of the sun. The day was cool, but at least the light of the day fell brightly around them. "I believe I look young because I did not laugh nor cry for most of my life. Emotions stopped when I was very young and lost my mother."

Shayla sat quietly. "I'm sorry."

Then Ruth did something that went against her natural tendencies. She reached over the table and gently grabbed Shayla's hand. "Life has both joy and sorrow, which is why I did not want to be pregnant at first. However, it is the emotions of life that verify we are truly living. Laughing and crying mark our faces, as our lives gather memories with those around us. You cannot have one without the other."

Ruth felt a reciprocal squeeze from the young hand she held.

"Maybe that's why God gave me two families," Shayla added. "He knew my heartache, and He gave me *Ah-nah* and you."

A shadow fell across her body and the table. She looked up and saw a familiar face. She checked herself before speaking and brought her hand back to her lap. She almost said his true name out loud. "Matt Coughlin. It is very nice to meet you, at last."

Jonah stood above them. He smiled briefly before it was cut off by the waiter behind him.

"Can I help you, sir?" the waiter asked.

"No, I oversee the security of the *Grand Opus Gala*, and I am making sure that this place is secure. You have two of our best participants at your restaurant."

"Yes," the waiter said, slightly bothered. "And their lunch will be out shortly. We have a single cameraman coming to take a few photos. However, we care about our customers, and we will make sure they are not bothered."

"If you don't mind, I have posted two of my men there and there," he pointed to either side of the outdoor patio. "They too will make sure that these ladies are not bothered."

The waiter looked put out. "If you insist. Will you be dining with them?"

Jonah shook his head. "No, I will be leaving in just a minute. I just need to have a word with Bear's wife."

The waiter understood the hint. He turned to Ruth. "I will be back with your drinks momentarily."

Jonah waited for the waiter to go back into the restaurant. Then he brought his attention back to the ladies seated at the table. "I am letting all of the gala participants and their significant others know that I will be leaving the security of the gala in the capable hands of Rogers. He will take over security from here on out. I am needed outside of the city for a pressing situation."

Ruth knew that everyone around them was listening. She wondered why Jonah chose a public place to tell her this, but maybe this was his only chance. "I am sorry to hear that. Your security has been flawless so far."

"Thank you," Jonah said. "Ada Armel will be pleased to know that her favorite gala attendee has felt safe."

Ruth could tell that Jonah was hiding something. Or was he trying to reveal something?

"I wanted to let you and your husband know to continue as normal. This new security is no cause for any changes to your gala plans," he said.

There it was. Ruth looked up at Jonah and pushed back her hood just a bit. The cameraman had not arrived, and she wanted to get a better view of him. She knew where he was going, though she did not yet understand why. His expression was earnest. He did not want them to alter their plans on attacking the RIBS.

"I understand," she said.

"No matter what you hear or what people say. Stick to the original plan," he repeated. "I have made sure that all the security is in place. Neil Elder has made two copies of the security plan, so there won't be any last-minute changes."

"Thank you," she said, noticing the waiter coming through the backdoor with their drinks. She pushed the hood of her cape forward. "I will let my husband and his men know."

Jonah turned to the young lady sitting across from Ruth. "Shayla, I was hoping to get your assistance on something. I know you were told that the seats at the New Year's Eve event at the gala were completely full. However, I can get you backstage access, but I will need you to check on one thing for me."

Shayla's eyes opened wide. "I will do anything to go— even backstage will be better than watching on the LPS from our flat."

"It is a simple task, but one that needs to be done at the precise moment. Come by the front desk when you get in and ask for me. The front desk attendant will have your name and will inform me when you arrive. I will go over the details then."

"Yes, Sir! Thank you for trusting me Mr. Coughlin," Shayla added, unable to hide her excitement. "I will do my part to help with the security of the gala."

Jonah eyed someone on the other side of the fenced patio. "Looks like your cameraman is almost here. I leave you to enjoy your lunch," he said and turned to leave.

"Matt!" Ruth called. She waited for him to look at her. "I hope it all goes well with your new assignment."

"So do I," he said and walked through the patio door just in time for the paparazzi to begin setting up.

CHAPTER 33

Pastor Tom scooted one of the poinsettias further away from his HMS screen. His wife, Cindy, was in the throes of decorating for Christmas. She had placed the two bright red and green plants on each corner of his desk. He didn't mind them, but they were a constant reminder that New Year's Eve was right around the corner. Cindy once loved decorating Trinity Church for the holidays, but now she'd settle for decorating the trading center. He rather liked the greenery strung with green and red ribbon lining the doors, shelves and molding of the walls. He could tell that the locals enjoyed the evergreen she decked out in the store window. She even gave out hot cocoa along with the coffee they made available at the entrance table of the building. Her offerings seemed small, but they created a sense of Christmas Spirit that the town's people needed.

His basement was barren except for the two Christmas plants she placed on his desk. However, the basement was for researching, thinking and planning, not celebrating. At least, not yet. He looked back at his HMS and marveled at the *Life Plethoricity* link fixed to his screen. Why hadn't he noticed earlier that the file could not be removed? Maybe he took its presence for granted as an inevitable demand from the World Government to pile on the rest of the demands they had forced on them that year. No more church. No more Bibles. No more Christian resources. They had even tried to institute a government religion by establishing the *Unum Vernum*, which not even the Efficientists would accept. Suddenly, realization sparked a fire of understanding. "That's it!" he yelled. "Li was able to erase the *Unum Verum*, so Neil Elder irrevocably fixed *Life Plethoricity* to each site. That way it can't be removed!"

He glanced at the printout on his desk next to his HMS. It was a copy of the code that Li had discovered. From what Li had told him, every *Life Plethoricity* link had the code imbedded in it, and only Li's computer could reveal it. He checked every computer that had come through Trinity Trading Center. Li had the only computer with that make and model. Was the code created by the World Government? Was it a code to prevent it from being removed? And would that affect their plan to take down the RIBS? Would the web of *Life Plethoricity* links prevent the World Government sites from collapsing? He moaned to himself. "So many unknowns."

Finally, Pastor Tom's thoughts went to Jonah. Why did he have two links to *Life Plethoricity* on his LPS? One with the code and one without. Pastor Tom pushed away from his desk and stood up. "What is he telling us?" he asked himself. "And why did he leave the city?" Did he leave willingly? Did he have a Plan B?" He shook his head and began to pace. Too many what-ifs. Ruth had messaged him that Jonah made it clear to her that they should stick to the original plan. What did Jonah mean by saying that Neil Elder had made two copies of the security plan? Two copies? Was it the two copies of the *Life Plethoricity*—one with the code and one without?

Pastor Tom rubbed his pulsing temples. He felt a headache coming on. Li had too much faith in him. He couldn't figure it out, and Ruth's message confused him even more. His gaze drifted to the crates stacked next to his desk. He had finished making copies of the images that Pilar and the young officer retrieved from the forced labor camp. The printing press from Pastor Rohan had come in handy. He had used it to make copies of several books of the Bible, and now he used it to make copies of the gruesome images from the prison. He put the prints at the bottom of the crates and covered them with hundreds of balloons. They were to be shipped to the city that evening. If Jonah was not at the New Year's Eve event at the gala, who would make sure the prints got distributed? "Keep to the plan," he reminded himself.

Pastor Tom sighed. Then his thoughts turned to his conversation with Reyna. She had come bringing baked goods and information with her. She told him that she and Bear's grandfather had just seen Watchman and his son, Sentinel. Ada Armel was planning on springing a surprise fight on Bear at the New Year's Eve event. Bear would be fighting Sentinel. Pastor Tom had just finished watching Sentinel's last several fights before he got the message from Li. Sentinel was a good fighter. Maybe even better than the Shaman when he was in his prime and definitely better than Bear was now. He could try to dissuade Bear from fighting, knowing that it would be more than just a fight. It had to be a show. But Tom realized that this fight would draw in crowds to watch the bout; and the more people plugged into what the World Government was doing on New Year's Eve, the better chance they had to completely take down the RIBS. Could they expect Bear to risk his health— maybe even life—when he had a bride, a baby on the way and a new teen daughter relying on him?

Pastor Tom felt fear begin to grip his chest. He had received too much disconcerting news all at once. Jonah leaving the city. Bear's surprise fight. And the news of Esther's death that came earlier that morning. He slipped out of his chair and fell to his knees. He couldn't take it all in. Their plan rested on too many variables, and the loss of Esther felt like a low blow in an already tense situation.

He rested his elbows on the seat of his chair and began to pray. "Dear Father, I am at a loss of what to do. There are so many moving elements that are out of my control, and I fear if I try to grab them all, I'll mess up what You are trying to achieve. Help me to know what to do. Or if You want me to do nothing, help me to trust You." He felt the tension begin to ease up, and he let out a long exhale. "Thank You for the peace

I know that I already have through Christ. I will steward that peace and not let the worries of this world choke it out. Thank You, Jesus, for dying on the cross for me. Thank You for making me more than a conqueror. I know that You are greater than everything I face. And let Esther know she will be missed greatly. I pray this in Jesus's precious name, amen."

Pastor Tom remained on the floor for several moments on his knees. He didn't care that his legs were going numb, and his lower back began to ache. He wanted to hear from the Lord. Finally, he heard a whisper. The voices didn't come from outside but from within. "Stay the course." He could feel those three words rise from his spirit. "Stay the course. Don't look to the left or the right. Keep going straight with the directions you started with. Don't alter plans regardless of what you hear or see. Stay the course."

Pastor Tom leaned his hand on the desk and pulled himself up. "Okay, I will stay the course."

He sat back into his chair and opened his HMS. He was thankful Reyna had notified Ruth about the upcoming fight. He needed to stop sending out so many correspondences. It would endanger his family and all of Trinity Village if anyone from the World Government discovered his encrypted and deleted messages. He was on their radar more than anyone because of his occupation as a pastor—though they believed he had retired. "This will be my last one," he said to himself. "I will let Ruth know that the crates of balloons will be mailed to the city. Best not to mention the photos. I'm sure Jonah notified them. Hopefully, he also left them with a plan to distribute them." He thought about letting Ruth know about the passing of Esther. Several of Deborah's houseguests had driven to the trading center that morning to let him know. He shook his head. "No, now is not the time to burden Ruth with further loss."

Once he sent off the message, he heard the footsteps of his wife coming down to the basement. He swiveled his chair, "Hey, honey. Is it time?"

Her eyes were puffy from crying. "Yes, they are ready for us. I've already had the casket and headstone sent over."

He knelt down to retrieve one of the crates. "Let me bring these upstairs for the Runner, and I'll meet you in the car."

"Okay," she said. "I'll pack the car with the food Reyna brought over and wait for you there."

Pastor Tom, Cindy and Deborah stood in front of the small grave located under the sprawling oak tree some distance from the main ranch house. The sun was setting, and they had about thirty minutes of daylight left. Pastor Tom had a tombstone quickly, yet carefully, etched that afternoon after he was notified of Esther's death. Luckily, he had a beautiful marble headstone and a basic casket already at the trading center. Esther's name, years of life and a small dedication that read: "A beloved sister and friend" adorned the headstone. Deborah was pleased with it, and now it rested at the front of the grave, shaded by several thick branches. From Pastor Tom's point of view, it looked like the tree was guarding and protecting Esther's grave.

He glanced at his wife, Cindy. She stood next to him, wearing a simple black dress. She had her arm around Deborah's waist who also wore a black dress. He realized that Deborah and her sister almost always wore bright, cheery colors. It didn't feel right to see Deborah wearing black. He thought of Esther. He would miss her pleasant demeanor, and he knew that Deborah would not be the same without her. Yet, she still had a house full of guests from the city to keep her busy. The Efficientists were getting used to working with their hands around the ranch. They even volunteered to dig the grave where Esther's body now lay.

He looked back at the grave. He was glad that he and Zach went to visit the ranch when they did. Who would have known that she would die only a few short days later? She had seemed so healthy and full of life, but God had His ways. Although she died peacefully in her sleep, Esther would be sorely missed. He hadn't notified anyone of her death outside of Trinity. Deborah agreed to keep it quiet until the new year. Then they would have a grief gathering for her when everyone could attend.

"Would you like me to say a few words, Deborah?"

She held a handkerchief and dabbed under her eyes. "Yes, Pastor Tom. Esther would love that."

Pastor Tom cleared his throat. "It is during such great loss, that we can cling onto such a great hope. Because of Jesus's Finished Work on the Cross, we know that we will see Esther again. We know that she is in a better place. And we know that there is no sorrow or pain where she is. That is our hope. That we too can join her someday. We can reunite with all of those we have loved and lost."

He took a breath, allowing the Spirit to guide him in what to say next. "Not only that, but I can also say with firm conviction that when Esther embraced Jesus for the first time, He told her, 'Well done, my good and faithful servant.' Esther lived a life of passion and purpose, and her faith and service have touched so many lives, including the foster children she and Deborah cared for and now the Efficientists they have taken in. The full impact of Esther's work and love on this earth will not be fully realized until Jesus comes back to bring all of us home. I can speak for all of us here that we are better people today to have known her. We love you, Esther. Your legacy will continue through each life you have so lovingly touched."

Deborah held a bouquet of winter flowers that Esther had planted and cared for during the cool winter months of the southern colonies. Pastor Tom watched her pray silently for several moments. He could see his wife praying next to her. Finally, she spoke. "Thank you, Pastor Tom. Your words have said it all. May my sister rest in peace with our Father in heaven." With that, she kneeled and placed the flowers on the grave. "I will miss you, little sister. Don't have too much fun without me. I'll be there soon enough."

Cindy helped Deborah back up. "Come on into the house. Reyna came to the trading center just before we left and brought us extra baked goods from their bakery. We put it all in your kitchen. There's enough to feed all your houseguests for a week. By now, I'm sure our Efficientist friends have all showered and are ready to eat dinner. I can guarantee that they are hungry from all the work they did." Cindy placed Deborah's arm between hers, and together they began to walk back up the hill toward the house.

Deborah nodded and continued to dab her eyes. "It was so sweet of them to dig Esther's grave. I told them it could wait, but they insisted."

"I think they wanted to show gratitude to your sister," Cindy suggested.

Tears continued to flow down Deborah's cheeks as she walked away from the oak tree guarding her sister's grave. "I believe you are right, Cindy dear."

As Pastor Tom watched the two women walk away, he prayed. He prayed that the plan to take down the World Government's power was the right plan. Right now, when faced with death, he wondered if anything was worth the risk of life. However, deep in his spirit, he knew that risking life would always be part of following God's will. Jesus sacrificed His life for the world's salvation. And His followers risked their lives to spread the Gospel. He felt like the lives of so many were on his shoulders, but he knew he had to let that weight go. The risk of death was a choice that each person had to make.

CHAPTER 34

Ada was irritated. "And who are you again and why are you up here so late?" She had discovered the day before that Matt Coughlin had been sent away on a special assignment by Neil Elder. She instantly went to Neil's flat to complain. She needed Matt to be here with her at the gala. Only he understood her mission to bring beauty back to the empty canvas of *Life Efficiency*. He anticipated her needs, and she even enjoyed his company. But Neil was insistent, leaving her with the bland Rogers as Matt's replacement. He too was an empty canvas with no opinion and an unmovable sense of duty.

"I'm Shayla. Don't you remember me? I'm Bear's daughter," the young lady said.

Ada examined her. She wore plain denim jeans and a grey sweater. Her long, black hair fell to her mid-back. She did look a lot like the Shaman—though, much less pronounced. Even more so, she looked Colonial, and Ada disliked the look immensely. "And what are you doing up here?" Ada asked. "This is a restricted area, and it is also dangerous. You could fall off the rafters and bloody up all my hard work below. Do you know how difficult it was to decorate the Gala Hall with Christmas embellishments? First, I had to research how they look because Christmas decorations haven't been seen in the city since the Second Civil War. Next, I had to design my own line. Finally, I had to get them mass produced. Shouldn't you be in bed or something? It's late."

Shayla cleared her throat. "Let me be straight with you. I think I'm safer up here wearing my sneakers and jeans than you are wearing those heels and that pencil skirt. I grew up climbing trees and old buildings. Have you ever climbed anything?"

Ada stopped for a moment. She liked the girl's frankness. She was surrounded all day by yes-people, and she could trust none of them. "I do climb my exercise stair machine, but you're probably right. Oh! I'm just at a loss," she said, placing her Portable to her chest and swishing her short blond hair dramatically. "I'm missing something. I know it. The Christmas event is tomorrow, and it's absolutely perfect. I will stun the world with so much holiday spirit, as they say, that everyone will wish they were here. But then I only have less than a week to plan the New Year's Eve finale, and I have lost my confidant. I have a few surprises planned, but the nostalgia of New Year's is absent. I asked for fireworks. But, no, they say. It's too much of a risk, they say. We cannot pop fireworks in the city because of a threat to start another fire, like the one that killed Eve Pallue."

Ada felt a sting in both her eyes. "What is this?" she asked theatrically, wiping away a tear. "Oh, I do miss my muse, Eve Pallue. Did you follow her?"

The young girl shook her head. "Not really. I learned about her in school, but my mother was very strict about what we watched. I wasn't allowed to watch PR events."

Ada crinkled her nose. "And why not? Eve Pallue was the trendsetter. She was the Top Elite Efficientist!"

The girl nodded. "I know. After she shaved her head, many of my friends shaved theirs. It was cool for the first few days, but I think most of them regretted it."

Ada leaned toward the girl's face. "Shayla, is it?"

She nodded.

"That was my trend. I was Eve Pallue's image consultant. She did everything, and I mean everything, I told her to do. That day when she wore the crystals on her scalp and down her body was my crowning moment. Her ratings skyrocketed, as did mine."

The girl stared at her blankly, so Ada quickly composed herself. "I wouldn't expect you to understand. You're just a Colonial girl. Now, why are you here? Let me guess. You can't get a seat at the gala, so you are looking for another way to watch the event, I suppose. Of course, you would like to come, but I just don't have room for nobodies."

"Ah, actually, Mr. Coughlin sent me," she said.

"What do you mean? My Matt sent you up here, but why?" Ada asked, incredulously. Matt was her confidant. How dare he confide in this child.

"Uh," the girl paused. "He had a surprise for you for New Year's Eve. He has already arranged it, but he said if I could make sure everything went smoothly, that I could watch from up here."

Ada quickly turned on her Portable. "I don't believe you. Matt would have told me, and I don't see anything planned besides what I have already decided."

The girl gave a speech as if rehearsed. "He told me that if you were to find me, which he confessed you probably would because you don't miss much, that I was to offer his apologies. He only wanted to surprise you with a parting gift."

Ada felt a tingle of excitement rise in her throat. "Did he really say that? He left without saying goodbye, and to be honest, I was quite miffed. I believed he was different than all these other bland bodyguards, but then he was gone without a word! He was the only one who actually understood me and what I'm trying to achieve here. Shayla," Ada said, grasping the girl's hand. "What surprise did he leave for me?"

"It is for your New Year's Eve event," Shayla said, confidently.

"He knew. I remember telling him that the New Year's Eve event was missing a key element. Something reminiscence of New Year's Eve from Old America. He couldn't get me fireworks, so he said he would think of something. What did he come up with?" Ada almost didn't want to hear the words just yet. She wanted to revel in this moment of anticipation. She held onto the young girl's hand, watching her dark eyes focus on an image in her mind. The image was her answer to make the New Year's Eve event spectacular.

"He had it designed, and it is being installed after the Christmas event," Shayla said, slipping her hand away and moving toward the edge of the rafters where a large chandelier decked out with faux candles hung. She gathered herself and began her speech. "Large troughs will line all the rafters with a metal dispatching mechanism that will dump the contents of the troughs over the ledge, allowing the contents to pour over the audience just before the clock strikes twelve o'clock."

Ada squealed and brought her hand to her mouth. "What will these troughs be dropping?"

Shalya looked at her puzzled. "You don't know?"

"No, should I?" Ada asked. "We don't celebrate New Year's Eve in the city. It's against *Life Efficiency*."

"It's in all the old New Year's movies," she added.

"I've been so busy watching Christmas movies from the 1950s to prepare for this event," Ada scoffed. "Each event takes my full attention. I'll do further research for the New Year's event after the Christmas one is a success."

Shayla giggled. "Balloons! Hundreds and hundreds of balloons always drop on the crowd at midnight."

"Balloons?" Ada thought. "Yes, I know what those are. And you have them?"

"I received the crates of them today. Sonnie, the birdman, is holding them for me in his trailer."

Ada touched the rafter near her and looked down the length of it. There were several rafters that ran down the façade of the massive ceiling. She had grown accustomed to coming up here before each gala event to ensure that every detail was in place. There was nothing like a bird's eye view. Matt would often tell her it was too dangerous, but she needed to ensure her creation below was perfect. Plus, she enjoyed taking in her creation. Now, not only was her Christmas event going to be splendid, but the missing link to her New Year's event has finally been solved. "And you say there will be workers here after the Christmas event to set up those troughs to hold the balloons?"

Shayla nodded. "Yep and Mr. Coughlin put me in charge."

Ada stared at the young lady. She'd just prefer to take over from here, but she wanted to respect Matt's wishes. He did, after all, leave her this wonderful parting gift. "How about I make a deal with you?" she began. "I normally am the one who chooses who does what for this gala, but Matt has so delighted me with this surprise that I don't want him to think I am ungrateful. Why not let me handle the workers who Matt hired to assemble the balloon-dropping machine? I'm very particular about who comes into my building, and I need to get all their names under surveillance. But I will be far too busy on New Year's Eve to oversee the actual dropping. Can I trust you to drop the balloons on cue? I want the troughs filled to the brim with balloons hours before my guests show up, but you can't let one single balloon fall or it will spoil the surprise."

Shayla nodded enthusiastically. "Yes, I will get them blown up and everything ready. Sonnie has an air machine that I can use. I'll set it up here and blow balloons all morning long until the troughs are full. Then I will stay out of sight until it's time to drop them. I won't bother anyone. My friends at home won't believe I got to be here for this! And, if you don't mind me offering you a suggestion for the New Year's Eve theme, I think you will love it."

"Doubtful, but I'm all ears," Ada said with indifference.

"Three words," Shayla said in an excited whisper. "*The Great Gatsby.*"

Ada felt annoyed, but she would at least listen to the girl. She didn't have a clue of what she was going to do for the final event. She had thought of doing a masquerade, but she felt like that would be giving too much credit to Bear's wife. Plus, it had to be extravagant, and masks were old news.

"It's a book about Old America that I had to read last year for school. It's about the excessive lives of those who lived in the 1920s. Flappers, gangsters, champagne, dancing—everything was so over-the-top!"

Ada put her hand to her chest and breathed a theatrical sigh of relief. "I think I remember reading something about that era. Shayla, it has been divine providence that I ran into you up here. I will begin my research this very evening. By tomorrow afternoon, I'll have an entire line of clothing and accessories ready for production. Is that book, *The Great Gatsby*, a movie? I have very little time to read these days.

Shayla thought. "Yes, I think so. I'm sure there are several old films about the era. I've seen patterns of the dresses too. They seem to have a lot of fringe, beading and feathers if I remember correctly."

Ada's spirits lifted. The worry she carried about Matt leaving vanished. Shayla made a great sounding board for her thoughts, and the young Colonial even gave insightful ideas. "Make sure, though, you don't whisper a peep about this to anyone. Except, let Ruth know. And have her send her designs to me before the Christmas event tomorrow. I want to see what she will be creating."

"I promise to keep it quiet," Shayla said.

"Does Bear know about the balloon dropping?" Ada asked. There were a lot of surprises she was keeping from the Shaman.

"He knows about the balloons, and he tried to dissuade me from dropping them. He was going to have one of his fighters do it, but Mr. Coughlin enlisted my help. If my father had his way, I would be sitting in our flat all day, not enjoying anything from the city. All I want is to be a part of the first *Grand Opus Gala*—even if it is from the ceiling."

"So true," Ada agreed. "And I can't wait to see the faces of those boring magistrates as balloons fall all around them. The paparazzi will have a field day, and every Efficientist and Colonial alive will be plugged into my event, wishing they could be here. Believe me, Shayla. It is better to be up here in the rafters than watching the festivities from an LPS or, worse yet, an HMS. And who knows. Keep up the good work, and I just may include you in the second *Grand Opus Gala*."

"Thank you," Shayla said. "That would be amazing."

"Now run on back to your father before he gets suspicious. Remember to keep everything quiet. If you lose my trust, you will never be able to gain it back. You'll miss out on many more opportunities that I can offer you."

"Yes ma'am," Shayla said, earnestly. "I excel at keeping secrets."

Ada placed her Portable back to her chest with her left hand and flicked her blonde hair from her shoulders with her right. "Good," she said, looking at the girl's wardrobe with disdain. "And, Shayla. Please do try to dress more appropriately. We are making history here. This is not a Colonial high school party you are attending. You are at the *Grand Opus Gala*, so please play the part."

"Yes, I totally agree," Shayla said and started making her way slowly to the exit that led to the stairwell.

When Shayla closed the door that led from the ceiling rafters to the stairwell, she leaned against it. Her heart was racing. Mr. Coughlin had been right about everything. He knew that Ada Armel would be up here right when he said she would. At first, Shayla didn't understand why he wanted her to fake the balloon surprise when, in actuality, he wanted Ada Armel to know, but she quickly understood his angle. Ada Armel would never have let her, a young Colonial girl, be in charge of anything at the gala. But because Mr. Coughlin had surprised her, Ada felt obligated to let Shayla at least drop the balloons.

She pushed off the door and began to make her way down the several flights of stairs to her father's flat. Mr. Coughlin told her she could tell her father and Ruth the full truth of what she was doing, but she knew exactly what *Ah-nah* would do. He would say it was too dangerous for her and send one of his fighters to do it like he already suggested. "No way," she whispered. "Mr. Coughlin gave this job to me." She wouldn't tell anyone about the printed images, which is why she asked Sonnie to keep the crates from the Trinity Trading Center in his trailer. Underneath several layers of balloons were stacks of printed images from a forced labor camp she had heard whispers about in the colonies. Shayla remembered one image in particular: A dead man dangling from a wire fence. It was repulsive.

All *Ah-nah* and Ruth knew was that she was going to drop balloons from the ceiling. This was her backstage access. They didn't know about the hundreds of images from a prison camp that would also be poured over the audience. Shayla grinned. Ada Armel was right about one thing. She couldn't wait to see the faces of all those magistrates who allow forced labor camps and think that no one will ever find out. The paparazzi would capture it all, and the whole world— Efficientists and Colonials—will see that the rumors were true.

CHAPTER 35

R uth finished the last stitching on her winter cape. The fabric was red plaid with faux white fur trim around the hood and the outer lining of the cape. The dress underneath was also plaid made in a basic 1950s pattern, which Ada had chosen as the time frame for the Christmas event. She wouldn't be showing the dress, though. The 1950s fashion relied on creating an hourglass figure, and though she had lost weight from her bout of morning sickness, her midsection did look thicker. A keen eye would guess that she was pregnant, so she would leave the cape on for the entire Christmas event of the gala.

She looked toward the bed where she had placed Bear's ensemble. He would not like it one bit. She made him red plaid pants, which matched her dress, along with a white button up shirt, red tie and green cardigan. She was not in love with the outfit either, but Ada insisted that Old America's Christmas traditions were supremely influenced by the 1950s. He would only have to wear the outfit to dinner. He would replace the Christmas outfit with either a gi or his fighting loincloth. She picked up the Portable she had been given by Ada and examined the old photos from the Roaring 20s, as they called it. She didn't know how she would cover her pregnancy in any of those dresses. They were all form-fitting. She would have to think of something. Ada expected her design before the Christmas event that evening. She laid the Portable on the bed and rubbed her temples. She was tired of being in the city. She was tired of sewing. Bear was preoccupied and gone almost all the time. She missed her brother, Zach. She missed Pilar, Deborah and Esther. She missed the slow pace of living by the river with Bear. She had to laugh to herself. The colonies were once revolting to her, but now all she wanted to do was go back home.

"Bear," she said. "Are you here?" She looked to the open door of her bedroom, waiting to hear his voice from the living room or kitchen. She had not heard anyone enter their flat, but when she was sewing, the world around her faded away.

"I'm at this LPS thing," he said.

Ruth sensed that he was irritable. He was always irritable lately. He hated the city more than she, but there was something else in his voice. A note of fear? And why was he on the LPS? He almost never got on.

She exited the bedroom and walked toward her husband sitting at the LPS. He was watching another fight. "Are you preparing for your demonstration tonight?"

He didn't answer. She walked up behind him and peered over his shoulder to the screen. "I recognize that fighter. He fought with his team at the bazaar near Levington. His name is Sentinel, I believe. You were his father's last fight. Was he the young fighter you trained? The one who helped build my mother's casket?"

Bear nodded, keeping his eyes on the screen. Ruth cringed at the bloodied fighters. Both men were hurt and tired. Suddenly, Sentinel grounded his opponent, clasping his arms around his leg and pulling back with all his might. Then the screen went black.

Bear got up from his seat. "He has him in a knee bar. You don't need to see the rest."

"Did he win?" she asked. "When was this video taken?"

"Yes, Sentinel won. This video was taken a few weeks ago. His opponent won't tap out. Some fighter's carry too much pride. They would rather be injured."

"What will happen to that man's leg?" she asked.

"His knee is hyperextended, and the surrounding ligaments and tendons are damaged, maybe even torn. I doubt Sentinel will break anything, but his opponent won't be able to walk for several weeks."

"Brutal," Ruth said, thinking. "You tore his father's shoulder, correct. That is why he retired."

Bear ran his fingers through his black and silver hair. He hadn't braided it yet. They needed to get ready soon, but her husband was extremely distracted. He was never good at hiding his emotions, which Ruth appreciated. All she needed now was to help him to open up to her.

"I did tear it. He and I knew it was going to happen. He wouldn't tap out, and we both knew I had become the greater fighter."

Ruth looked back at the dark screen where she had witnessed Sentinel's most recent fight. "Is Sentinel now better than you? Is that why you are upset?" she asked. She walked up to her husband and clasped his chin. He had not shaved yet, and she could feel the black and silver stubble coming through his face. "There is nothing wrong with that. He is a young man. You are not. Your place is to train young men, not to fight them. It is part of the movement of life. There is nothing to be ashamed of. You have a beautiful young daughter and a baby on the way. We have everything we need. There is no need for you to miss the fighting circuit."

Bear grabbed her hands and took them into his. Ruth loved the way his calluses felt against her smooth skin. She knew he would protect her from anything. "I'm not upset about not fighting anymore. I did my last fight before we met, and I vowed I wouldn't fight again. Once I met you, my fight became something different. My fight is now to protect you and my family."

Ruth stared into his dark brown eyes. "Then what is bothering you?"

"I just got word from Pilar's sister, Reyna. She was visiting my grandfather, bringing him the treats that he loves," he smiled in memory.

"How is everything at home?"

He let go of her hands, got up and began to pace. "Not good. Someone tried to break into our shed, so my grandfather has been sitting outside in the cold with his shotgun. All my men left him. I didn't think of asking any of them to stay."

"Can Levi help?"

"No, Levi left. He's with Randall Hunt."

Ruth inhaled. "What? Why is he there?" She knew that Randall had taken over his grandfather's ranch in the colonies. There was a rumor of oil diggers being spotted there, but he had kept to himself.

"Levi has asked for Randall's help. They are going to the prison camp where Pilar is on New Year's Eve to prevent the Kill Switch from being used."

"But how can two men stop them?" Ruth asked. She had been so consumed with keeping up with the gala that she wasn't keeping up with their plans to take down the World Government. She was being torn between keeping up the gala ratings and keeping up with the morphing landscape of their plan. She had at least messaged Pastor Tom from her Portable about what Jonah said about the security plan and leaving the city to go to the prison camp. She needed to research what he was trying to convey and not expect Tom to figure it all out. She knew that *security plan* was code for something, but she hadn't had time to analyze it. Time was slipping away, and New Year's Eve was only days away.

"Randall Hunt has an army," Bear finally said. "They have guns and bows and arrows. They leave for the prison camp in a few days."

"I cannot believe Randall Hunt would risk his estate to help us," Ruth said. "He may have changed a little, but that is a bit extreme."

"He's not helping us to be nice. He knows we have a formidable plan, so he's probably helping us to help himself. It will only be a matter of time before the World Government catches wind that he has oil on his property. We all know, and he's only been there for a little over a month."

Ruth thought. "You are right. That must be his motive. Can we send some of the fighters back to help Grandfather keep watch?"

"There is no need. Watchman is staying with him," he said.

Ruth noticed that his features grew dark again. Why would that bother him? "That is good news," she suggested.

He turned from her, setting his hands on his hips. "Yes, it is. Watchman is greatly feared—even in his old age. No one will mess with my property while he is there."

"Something is still troubling you," Ruth said, coming alongside him. She strung her arm through his.

"When Reyna contacted us, she also sent other news. We've both been so busy that I'm just now reading it. It's news which Ada Armel was going to keep secret until the final event on New Year's Eve."

"She surprised us with Shayla, and we handled it well. In fact, I rather like her. She reminds me of you, but a little less animated. She learns quickly and is very resourceful."

Bear looked down at her and laughed. "She is a great young lady. Her mother did well raising her. Where is she now?" he said, looking around.

"She is with Sonnie, helping to feed his birds. She enjoys helping. She is like you in that she has to feel needed. I know she has assisted me tremendously during my sickness."

"I'm sorry I haven't been available. I was angry when she came because I felt like she would be just another person I needed to provide for and protect, but she has shown herself to be very independent and capable. I am glad she has cared for you while I've been training," he said. Ruth could see a tenderness wash over his face.

"So tell me the surprise. Let us work it out together."

Bear went to the kitchen table and sat down in one of the plain white chairs. "This is something only I can work out," he whispered.

Ruth felt fear rise up in her stomach. She had never seen her husband look this helpless before. "What is it?"

He rubbed his face for several seconds and finally looked at her. "I am to fight Sentinel."

"What? How can that be? He will surely win," she said.

"I don't fear losing," he said. "But in order to get the ratings we need for our plan to work that night, we will have to make the fight last all twelve rounds. And I am sure Ada Armel will mention that I tore his father's shoulder, causing him to retire."

"What are you saying?" Ruth asked, not wanting to hear the answer.

"I will get injured during this fight. I don't know how bad. Sentinel is good about not overdoing it, but he will be fighting for the first time in the city. His adrenaline will be pumping. There is no telling what he will do, and I can't tap out."

"No!" Ruth screamed and then covered her mouth. An image of Uncle Sam's broken neck came into her mind. "I will not let them hurt you just to get ratings."

He stood up. "And if I say no, I will be labeled a coward. And the plan to take down the RIBS will fail. No one signs on to watch a loser run from a fight. They sign on to watch him face his opponent, regardless of winning or losing."

Ruth placed her hand on her growing stomach. "What about our baby?"

Bear walked to her and placed his hands over hers. "I want our baby to grow up without fear of being sent to a forced labor camp. Once the World Government gets away with what they are doing now, there is no telling what they will do next. I will not have him growing up as a slave. Trust me on this. I will heal. I know I will. I will do everything in my power to put on a show and not get too hurt. We all have to do our part, and this is mine."

Ruth nodded, but she began to feel anxiety wrap around her heart like a noose.

"And we can't let Ada Armel know that we know her surprise. I don't want to get the Sentinel and his father in trouble. They were sworn to secrecy, and they risked a lot by telling my grandfather."

"I understand," Ruth said. But her understanding did not help alleviate the weight of fear that was now pressing against her chest.

CHAPTER 36

Sonnie took the cage from Shayla. Inside the cage rested a snowy owl wearing a small, red Christmas hat with a white pompom on the end, which was connected to a thin red scarf. He held another snowy owl on his leathered wrapped arm. "You did a wonderful job, Shayla. I know having your help tonight will make my birds of prey demonstration even better. I do love a Christmas theme." He opened one of the many large bird pens he set out near his truck and trailer. He allowed the first snowy owl on his arm to jump in. Then he opened the small cage he was holding and took the hat and scarf ensemble off the other owl. The second owl also hopped into the pen and stood next to its sibling.

"Here, why don't you feed them a pinky each? Just one. We don't want them to be too full tonight or they won't perform for us," Sonnie said, handing Shayla an ice chest with several dead baby rats.

Shayla picked up two pinkies. "Here, Aeolus," she said, throwing the first bird a treat. The owl quickly snatched the food between its strong beak and gobbled it down. "And you too Boreas," she said, throwing him a treat, as well. "They are very easy to handle," Shalya admitted. "They weigh much less than they look. And their feathers are so soft. They almost feel like fur."

"Awe, yes. Their feathers do make them look bigger than they really are, and they are as soft as a kitten's fur. You did very well, and I believe both birds have gotten the routine down. And they both trust you. Now that usually doesn't happen so quickly."

"The routine is simple. I open the cage to let Boreas out and Aeolus knows to come in. Then Boreas flies to you with his Christmas outfit on. I love being around animals," Shayla said. "I once took care of a black-bellied tree duck that was abandoned by its mother just before a storm blew in. Maybe I can do what you do someday."

Sonnie grinned. "That would be something now, wouldn't it? I honestly couldn't ask for a better life. I'm glad I saw you up on the ceiling. I wanted a Christmas trick to perform that would fill the audience with a little holiday cheer. I've done this trick before but never for Christmas. Tell Ruth thank you again for creating the hat and scarf on such short notice."

"She didn't mind. She's very quick at sewing with her electrical sewing machine. She's glad I have something to do. I have no more school until after the New Year, so I have the time to help you. I'd much rather be here helping you than on that LPS doing schoolwork."

"If you're willing, I need help cleaning out some of the pens and cages tomorrow. I've fallen behind on my chores with the demonstrations I need to prepare. I know Uncle Sam would like to see you again. Maybe you can hold him this time."

Shayla's eyes widened. "That would be awesome. Yes, I'll come first thing in the morning. Can I bring you breakfast?"

"I normally eat with Bear's fighters before they start training, but I think breakfast with a young lady sounds even better. Is he ready for his demonstration tonight?"

Shayla looked at her feet. "He's angry with Ada Armel."

Sonnie breathed a sigh. "Why? What has she done this time?"

"I don't know for sure, but I heard him yelling after he read a message from her on the LPS just before I left. She changed the plans for the demonstration tonight last minute. I don't think she wants another fighting demonstration. She says it doesn't fit the Christmas theme or something like that."

"So what is she telling him to do?" Sonnie asked, slightly amused. Ada Armel had switched things on him more than enough times. Thankfully, she hadn't bothered him for this event. She had her focus elsewhere.

"I couldn't quite catch was he was yelling, but Ruth said something about him singing a Christmas song."

Sonnie laughed but stifled it quickly. Shayla was his daughter after all, even though they had only recently met. "I think I remember hearing something about the Shaman singing and playing a drum."

"Yeah, I've seen videos. I don't know how Ada plans to pull this off without making *Ah-nah* look like a fool."

"*Ah-nah?*" Sonnie asked.

"Oh, it means Father in my native *Ka'to* language."

"Ah, I see. Well, don't you worry about him. Ada Armel has worked very hard to ensure Bear keeps high ratings. She wouldn't sabotage it right before the final event on New Year's Eve."

Shayla nodded. "That's what Ruth said. I'm glad your demonstration is first, so I can leave before my father starts singing. I'll bring Aeolus straight back to the pen."

"And I will meet you here, and we can celebrate with a few pinkies for the birds and some Christmas cookies for us."

Shayla looked at the two owls. "You know, they don't look exactly the same. Do you think the audience will notice that it's two different birds?"

"As I said, I've done this trick plenty of times, and everyone thinks they are only one bird. It happens so fast that all they see is a white, snowy owl. The fact that Boreas is a little bigger and Aeolus has a grey patch on her chest are small details that they'll miss at first glance. Just make sure you send off Boreas right when Aeolus arrives. The less time in between, the better."

"I will be ready," she said, confidently.

"I know you will be," Sonnie agreed. He looked toward the city streets. He had moved his trailer to behind the Gala Hall building to get out of the way of nightly paparazzi. He enjoyed his new location. He could watch Bear and his men train. He'd always been fascinated with the fighting circuit. Normally the streets were fairly bare, but tonight lines of limousines waited their turn to drop off their prestigious guests at the gala. "It looks like the show is about to start."

Shayla followed his gaze. "I better go take a shower. I don't smell very nice. I was able to finish my Christmas dress," she said. "It's very pretty and not what I usually wear, but I want to make a good impression for your demonstration."

Sonnie grinned. "I'm due for a shower, as well. And I know you will look just beautiful in your new dress, especially since you made it yourself."

Shayla turned to go, but Sonnie reached out and touched her shoulder. "Uh, before you go, I have a quick question for you."

"Yes," she said, turning to him.

"Um, I opened one of the crates that you delivered to my trailer. I wanted to see how many balloons there were in each crate, so I could give you an estimate of how long it will take to blow them all up for the New Year's Eve event."

"And," she whispered, staring at him.

"Ah, I noticed those printouts on the bottom, hidden underneath the balloons. Are those real?" he asked.

Shayla nodded. "They were only taken weeks ago at a prison up north."

Sonnie scratched his chin. "So the rumors are true. The World Government is using forced labor?"

"Yes," she nodded. "And I am going to help expose them."

"You plan on hiding them under the balloons in those troughs they plan on building in the ceiling?"

"Exactly. And all the magistrates' awful deeds will be known to both Efficientists and Colonials. If we don't do something about it now, it will only get worse."

He thought for a long moment. "You'll probably get in trouble. Did you ever think about that?"

"Well, no," she confessed. "I was asked by a very powerful person to help out, so I am doing my part."

"Do Bear and Ruth know?" he asked.

She shook her head. "They only know that I'm in charge of dropping the balloons. They don't know about the images."

"And did that very powerful man tell you to keep it a secret from them?" he asked. He had a sneaking suspicion on who this powerful man was, but he didn't know if Matt Coughlin, the bodyguard in charge, could be trusted or not.

She hesitated. "Yes, he told me I could tell them." Then she quickly added, "But if I did tell *Ah-nah* what I am doing, I know he would never let me be in charge. He'd make one of his men do it!"

"Maybe that would be better," Sonnie explained. "You are just a young lady. You don't want to get on the wrong side of the World Government."

"Look," she pleaded. "Please don't tell anyone. I promise that I will be careful."

"Did you ever think that you will not just get yourself in trouble? Both Bear and Ruth will be questioned, as well."

"I was told that everything would be fine. Something big is going to happen that will create confusion. What I'm doing is only a small part of a much bigger plan," Shayla said. "And I trust the person who put me in charge. And I know that Ruth trusts him too."

"She told you that?" he asked. This would change his mind a bit.

"Yes, he came to us while we're having lunch. He told Ruth to stick to the original plan," she said. "I was there. He said he was leaving but for her and Bear to stick to the original plan."

"So Ruth and Bear are already involved in whatever is going to happen," he said, mainly to himself. "I wondered why Bear started to raise up the ratings of the gala. It didn't make sense to me why he even cared. It was obvious he didn't want to be here, but then he began to give the audience exactly what they wanted."

"Look," Shayla interjected "I don't know the plan. All I know is that I'm to drop the printouts and balloons on New Year's Eve just before midnight."

Sonnie had to admit that he would love to see something happen to the World Government, especially after being in the city and seeing how the Efficientists interacted. He didn't think much of the plan, though. Images could be altered and even denied, but it would be fun to see the printouts floating all over Ada Armel's creation. But, truly, what could a couple of Colonials, a bodyguard and a young woman do to hurt the World Government? He had to admit, though, that it would be fun to have the last laugh on the way out of the city. "Okay, I won't say a word. Just make sure you hide the images under the balloons. You don't want anyone finding them like I did."

"Yes, sir," she nodded.

"And," he said, making sure he had her full attention.

"Yes," Shayla said, waiting.

"Let's make an escape plan," he finally said.

"What do you mean?"

"I will leave right after my show on New Year's Eve and get the trailer ready to leave. Once you drop the balloons, find Ruth and Bear and meet me right here. Hopefully, in the confusion, no one will see you all leaving. I have room enough for three more people. Just get them out here, and we will be on our way back to the colonies."

"You would do that for us?" Shayla asked.

"I owe Ruth a debt of gratitude. I don't know how she did it, but she brought my Uncle Sam back to life. This is the least I can do."

CHAPTER 37

Ruth brushed past the other attendees in the audience. Bear had already made his way to the middle seats of the row. Her thick, full-length plaid cape rubbed against the knees of everyone seated, and Ruth wished that Ada would have placed fewer seats in the Gala Hall. However, she knew that Ada wanted as many people as possible to watch the Christmas gala event live.

She looked toward Bear and giggled under her breath. He did, in fact, look comical in the Christmas outfit she made him. The plaid pants and green cardigan did not match his muscular frame and long black and silver hair braided and cleanly shaved on both sides. His expression also didn't match the Christmas feel that Ada Armel was trying to create unless one considered Ebenezer Scrooge from *A Christmas Carol*. She had translated that book into T-variety when she was just a young teenager. She knew that Charles Dickens would be severely disappointed in her abridged version. She cut his novella down to a few pages of condensed English. So many adjectives were unnecessary, so she thought.

Ruth adjusted her white, laced mask. She normally placed a lot of time adorning her masks or creating something unique, but she felt the Christmas cape that she wore needed no further embellishments. When she finally got to her seat, she was relieved to sit down. They had eaten a rich dinner that included squash soup, stuffed turkey, cranberry and pea salad with walnuts and spiked eggnog, which she politely denied. She was glad her appetite was coming back, but now her skirt felt even tighter around the waist. She hoped that after the event began, she could undo the top button of her skirt without being caught by the cameras.

"Where is Shayla? Did she go back to our room?" he asked, looking around the audience.

Ruth was glad to see his protective mannerisms were now spreading to his newly discovered daughter. Ruth liked Shayla very much and would not mind if she would come to visit their house by the river on occasion. She had shown herself to be a tremendous help, and Shayla kept her company since Bear was occupied with his fighters.

"I believe she has a surprise for us," Ruth said. "She would not tell me what, but she seemed very excited. I know she has been helping Sonnie since school has been out."

"Great," he said looking up to the ceiling. "Will she be dropping snow from the ceiling on us?" Bear asked.

"No," Ruth said, amused. "Now sit down. She is an extremely capable young lady. She will be fine at whatever she does."

Bear sat down next to her. She could feel him fidgeting with the thick fabric on his legs. "Are your pants too tight?"

Bear exhaled. "I didn't want to say anything because you worked so hard to sew these, but they do feel tight around my thighs."

"How about the waist?" she asked.

"No, the waist feels fine," he said. "They just feel tight in the thigh area. And I must admit, the shirt is tight around my shoulders. Did you get my measurements wrong?"

"No, they are the exact measurements I always use. I have them memorized. I think I know what is happening," Ruth said, giggling again. She wondered why she was in such a good mood. Maybe because her morning sickness was finally abating.

"What? Is it the water? Or that electric washing machine? My other clothes are starting to get tight too."

"No, you have been training non-stop for weeks, Bear. You are doing what your fighters say, *bulking up*."

Bear stared at Ruth for several seconds and started laughing. "I guess I am. I haven't trained this hard in a while, and those young men are pushing me to my limit. I guess my body is adjusting."

"Just like my body is adjusting to pregnancy," she said. Her giggles vanished. "Do you think this will help your chances with Sentinel? He has not arrived yet. I have had Shayla keeping surveillance for me."

"It definitely won't help him," Bear said. "But I've looked at his videos repeatedly. I can tell he studied my moves from when I was in the fighting circuit. We will do all twelve rounds; he will win and Ada Armel will get her show. Then the ratings will go through the roof, and by God's mercy," he leaned in to whisper in her ear, "Zach and Li will take down those RIBS."

Ruth stared at her husband. She loved him unendingly. His fiery spirit may not be easy to handle, but he made up for it with his intense loyalty. The fact that he would risk bodily harm without any material gain showed just how much his capacity to love selflessly had grown. "The doctors in the city may be better than the ones in the colonies," she said, quietly. She wanted to broach the subject earlier, but she couldn't find the right time. Since they were already discussing his inevitable physical harm, they might as well get this part out of the way.

"Whatever you do, do not take me to a city doctor. Take me back to the hospital near Trinity or just to Deborah if I'm not too bad off. I want out of this city right at midnight, regardless of my condition. I'm done playing Ada Armel's puppet."

"Sonnie has offered to take us home," Ruth said. She was glad he didn't want a city doctor. He would get cared for immediately in the city but at the risk of being detained.

"Why wouldn't we just go in my truck?" he asked.

"I think it will be better if we are not followed. People know how we arrived. Leave the truck here. We will get another one, and there is not much in our flat that we need. We could leave before the attack on the World Government is found out by the media and be gone before anyone spots us."

"Let me think about it," he said.

Finally, the lights of the Gala Hall went black, and a single light showed on the stage. Ada Armel walked up the short steps, holding up the long train of her form-fitting green velvet gown with a deep neckline. She wore a shimmering ruby necklace and earrings and white satin gloves to her elbows. Her hair was pulled back in a French twist. She looked very elegant, like a 1950s movie star, which was probably the angle she was going after. The paparazzi had loved her look tonight, and she overshadowed Ruth for once. Ruth did not mind. She tired of planning, creating and sewing. She was ready to get back to the simplicity of her rural life with Bear. Ada droned on about Christmas traditions until finally, she introduced Sonnie.

The crowd laughed when they saw him donning a white beard and wearing a Santa outfit while holding his snowy owl on a leather sleeve. He was the perfect 1950s Santa Claus. He had a round belly and a cheerful expression. The bird clung to Sonnie's left arm and with his right arm, he gently clasped Ada's hand and kissed it. Then he brought his snowy owl to her hand. She moved back in fear, but the owl simply brought his beak to her hand, like a kiss. The crowd clapped and the cameras flashed. Suddenly, Ada's hesitation was replaced with a beaming smile as the camera lights sparkled off her light eyes.

When Ada finally exited the stage, Sonnie's robust voice echoed across the hall. He introduced his owl, Aeolus, and gave details about snowy owls: where they live, what they eat, how they mate, their life span, etc. Ruth found it all fascinating. She had studied them before, but never while actually looking at a living specimen. When he was finally done describing the snowy owl's characteristics, he had a glint in his eyes like he was keeping a secret.

He looked at the owl on this leathered arm. "Aeolus, are you feeling left out of the Christmas fun?"

The owl turned its head and hooted.

"Would you like to get dressed up like me?"

The owl hooted again.

"But not in front of all these nice folks, right? We want to be discreet. We have some high-ranked Efficientists here and even magistrates from all over the world," Sonnie said, looking gravely at the audience.

The owl flapped his wings and hooted again.

"Why don't you go somewhere secret to change into your holiday best? We will wait here," Sonnie said, lifting his left arm into the air. Aeolus took flight, flying straight up to the ceiling.

Ruth watched the snowy owl flying toward the chandelier, and she wanted to cry out for the owl to stop. She didn't want it to hurt itself like the Bald Eagle, Uncle Sam. However, the owl disappeared into the ceiling façade. The audience was quiet, and each person strained their neck to see where the owl had gone. A few seconds later, the snowy owl came back down, wearing the hat and scarf duo that Ruth had made. The bird grabbed Sonnie's arm with his talons and came to a stop.

"Now you are ready for the Christmas ball!" Sonnie shouted, jovially.

The crowd cheered and the cameras flashed. Ruth looked toward Ada. She had her hand on her chest in awe. Ruth knew that Sonnie's presentation would greatly add to the gala's ratings. Ada Armel had done a good job choosing Sonnie to represent the colonies. Ada stood up and clapped. The audience took the cue and stood up, as well. Finally, Ada joined Sonnie on the stage.

"Sonnie, you have epitomized the whimsical magic of Christmas," she began, allowing the cameras to take photos of her next to the holiday decked-out bird and Santa handler. "Please, do let us know your secret! How did Aeolus magically transform into our Christmas snowy owl?"

"I must confess," Sonnie said, soaking in the anticipation of the audience. "I have two snowy owls, a brother and a sister. This here is Boreas."

"So where did our fair Aeolus go?" she asked, looking at the faux ceiling.

A spotlight followed Ada's gaze to the ceiling.

"It's okay, Shayla. Show them Aeolus," Sonnie shouted

Ruth saw a small figure appear from the rafters, holding a birdcage with a white owl inside.

"Look who it is?" Ada gushed. "It is Bear's long-lost daughter. I introduced her at our very first gala event. Now look at her! She shines! Take a bow, Shayla. You are indeed a valuable member of our team!"

Shayla took a small bow. The cameras flashed their photos. They wouldn't get a great shot of Shayla because of the distance, but they had technology that could clean up photos and make them seamless. Shayla disappeared back into the shadows.

Ada turned to Sonnie. "Thank you for your demonstration this evening. You have definitely set a jolly atmosphere."

Sonnie took that as his cue to exit. He bowed to the audience. Then his snowy owl bowed.

"Aww, aren't they simply divine? One more applause for our favorite birdman and his snowy owls!"

Again, the crowd clapped as Sonnie made his way down the steps.

"Shayla did a good job, didn't she?" Bear whispered in Ruth's ear.

"She was magnificent. I believe she practiced all morning because I did not see her," Ruth said.

"Do you think she's still up there?" he asked, concerned.

Ruth shook her head. "No, she will be taking the bird back to Sonnie's trailer."

"Good," he said. "Now Ada needs to introduce me, so I can get my singing over with before she comes back. I don't want her to see her father looking like an idiot."

"Singing is not a foolish talent, Bear," Ruth said. "I fell in love with you even more when I heard you sing at Reyna's wedding. I wish you would do it more often. It's much less dangerous than fighting."

Bear sat silently. "I guess I have mixed feelings about singing because I used it to exploit my heritage and to gain popularity."

Ruth stroked his cheek. "Now you can do it to sing about the birth of our Savior."

He nodded. "I will. When I'm finished, I will go straight to our room. Meet me there when you can."

"I will," she said. "I'll only listen to a few lectures."

Bear got up and began to make his way to the aisle nearest the stairs of the stage.

Ada's voice once again echoed through the Gala Hall. "We have one more Christmas treat for you before we go into the presentations from several esteemed Efficientists who have research that will transform your view on life as we know it." Ada tried to sound excited, but Ruth could tell her enthusiasm was forced.

Ruth knew that the Efficientists were receiving terrible ratings, which is why Ada chose the two most popular Colonials to go first. Much of the paparazzi would depart after Bear's song, leaving behind only a few photographers to take photos of the Efficientists to add to the short synopsis of their findings. Ruth had learned long ago that rank was based on production, and rating was based on popularity, and Efficientist had to excel in both. Ruth hated PR events when she was Eve Pallue, but now she truly knew how important they were. It didn't matter how hard she worked, if she was not popular, her work would not have mattered. Ada Armel had done an excellent job keeping her ratings up, and she realized that she had never thanked her for anything she did.

"We all know Bear, previously known as the Shaman, can fight, and fight he does well! But did you know that he also sings?" she paused, making a circle on the stage to look at the entire audience. "To add to the Christmas spirit, Bear has chosen to sing the classic song, 'White Christmas.' We don't receive much snow in the city, so a song about a white Christmas will have to do!"

Ada spread her arms out, and one by one, small, electric candles started popping up from the perimeter of the stage floor. The candles made an opposite domino effect, rising consecutively around the circular stage. The effect was spectacular. Then, Ada exited down the stairs and grabbed something from under the stage. It was a large red drum. "Bear, please honor us with your song," she said, holding the drum out to Bear who was waiting in the aisle.

Bear grabbed the drum from Ada and bowed. She clipped a tiny microphone to his sweater. Then, she smiled and went back to her front row seat. He walked to the middle of the stage and sat down with his legs crossed. He brought the drum on his lap. The lights dimmed, and several cameras flashed. He closed his eyes and breathed in several breaths, relaxing his body.

Finally, he opened his eyes and spoke. "I regret to inform you that I was unable to learn the song, 'White Christmas.' However, I promise to make up for it. I will play another valuable Christmas song for you from the 1950s Old America. It is entitled, 'Little Drummer Boy,' and I hope it speaks to the true heart of Christmas."

Ruth looked toward Ada. She kept her expression neutral, but Ruth knew she was not happy. Bear would have to give a spectacular performance to gain her good graces once again.

Bear began to beat on the drum. One loud burst every few seconds. Then he added a deep hum that resonated with each beat. His eyes were closed, and Ruth knew he was pouring all his emotions into the drum and his voice. He continued to beat and hum, building the expectancy of the crowd. The audience was completely silent, and Ada looked around pleased.

Finally, Bear's voice cried out the song's lyrics. He sang about a King being born and how gifts should be offered. He sang about being poor with nothing to offer the King besides the beating of his drum. He sang deep and loud—every syllable enunciated with power and meaning.

Ruth felt tears sting her eyes, and tears began to flow under her mask. Bear was singing a true Christmas song, and she wondered if anyone in the audience would notice that this song was about Jesus, the very Savior they chose not to celebrate for Christmas.

When the lyrics ended, he continued to hum and beat the drum. Next, all that could be heard was the slow, rhythmic beating. Then, silence hushed over the crowd, as Bear held onto his drum. Not a single camera flashed. It was as if the crowd held their breath, waiting for what was coming next. Bear opened his eyes and gave a slight bow. Suddenly, Ada stood clapping, enthralled by Bear's song. The crowd too stood and applauded loudly, and the cameras once again began to flash.

Ruth leaned over the sink and splashed her face with cool water. Bear's performance had her crying, and she made her way to the gala bathroom to freshen up before returning to her seat. She wanted to hear the recent research of several of the Efficientists. She was only slightly curious about the research, but she realized that her true intention was to see how the Efficientists were getting on without her. She knew everyone speaking that evening—though many only from her LPS. It was unique to have so many Elite Efficientists from other regions at one place, and she didn't want to pass up the opportunity of hearing them and analyzing their research.

She dried her face with one of the cotton towels with the gala seal on it that were rolled up and stacked on a Christmas platter. When she finished, she picked up her white laced mask to put it back on.

Then a voice she recognized surprised her.

"Eve Pallue? Is that you?" the voice asked.

Without thinking Ruth turned to see Ada Armel staring at her. She quickly turned away and put her mask on over her face.

"I can't believe it! It is you! I knew there was something familiar about the way you talked. Very formal for a Colonial." Ada walked up to Ruth. "They said you were dead. Why haven't you come back? We need to tell Neil right away."

"No!" Ruth said, grabbing Ada's white-gloved hand. "He is the one who tried to have me killed. You must not let him or anyone know that I'm alive!"

Ada gave a nervous laugh. "He wouldn't do that," she said. "You're Authur Pallue's daughter, the founder of *Life Efficiency*. You're untouchable."

"And yet I am here," Ruth said. She brought her hand up so Ada could see the burns. "You see this? I got these burns from the fire. I barely made it out alive."

"But they found a tooth in the fire," Ada said, unconvinced.

Ruth opened her mouth and pointed to where a tooth was missing. "You mean that one?"

Ada stepped back a few paces. "I can't believe it."

"Ada, please do not tell anyone. If Neil finds out that you know the truth, he will have you killed too. He tried to have Randall killed, as well. He cannot afford loose ends."

"What do you mean tried. Is Randall still alive?"

Ruth adjusted her mask. "The less you know the better. Neil is dangerous. He will stop at nothing to be in charge. He has a history of violence."

"Was that your life plan that he published? *Life Plethoricity*," Ada asked. "Is that why he tried to kill you?"

"Neil wants power. He can have that life plan. I disowned it a long time ago. Trust me when I say this: You do not want him to know that I am alive. You will be another body in his way."

Ada slowly nodded. "Your life plan opened the way for me to do the *Grand Opus Gala*."

"*Life Plethoricity* is unrealistic and founded in logic not reality. I disagree with every word of it."

"That makes two of us," Ada agreed. "I can't believe that you married a Colonial. Isn't it scary out there?"

Ruth shook her head. "I miss it. I want to go back when this is all over."

"Well, I don't know what you're missing, but I'll take your word for it."

Ruth stared at Ada. "Please promise me that you will not tell anyone. I do not want you to get hurt. It will only compromise your life and everything you have built here."

"Okay, I give you my word. Besides, I don't want to go back to being just an image consultant. I'm enjoying my new position as director of the *Grand Opus Gala*."

Ruth sighed. "Thank you, Ada. I will return to my seat now." She walked to the bathroom door and just before opening it, she turned back to Ada who was still staring at her. "I never told you thank you for all you did for me. You kept my ratings up, and I was ungrateful for your work. I sincerely apologize for my behavior. You were the best image consultant that I ever had. Truly, no one can surpass your creativity, imagination and work."

Ada brought both her gloved hands to her mouth. "Oh, Eve! You don't know how many years I longed for you to say those words. It was my pleasure working with you. We created many magical moments together."

"Yes, we did. And I believe the *Grand Opus Gala* will be the best moment yet. Please remember, my name is Ruth now." With that, she opened the door and left the stunned Ada in the bathroom. Ruth thought of how her words of thanks encouraged Ada. How long had she herself longed to hear similar words from her own father? He never did utter them, but she found joy in another Father's words for her.

CHAPTER 38

L i allowed Xin to gallop at his own pace. The air was chilly, but the cloudless sky shined down much-needed warmth. The clouds had been thick for days, and he was beginning to wonder if the dreary days would ever give way to a bright one. Li worked all morning trying to decipher the code implanted in *Life Plethoricity*. However, his efforts were fruitless. The code was designed for something very specific. He had seen nothing like it. The code seemed almost irrelevant, like a made-up code young kids sometimes use to talk to each other without anyone understanding. He wondered if the World Government had created the code and why. And more importantly, would the code sabotage their plan to take down the RIBS?

He had tried to get back on Jonah's LPS, but his personal site was closed like Matt Coughlin had been erased. Pastor Tom said that he left the city because Neil Elder assigned him to oversee the Kill Switch at the prison. Whether he was forced to go or chose to go was unclear. Li then tried to contact Jonah on the Portable assigned to Matt Coughlin, but that too had been erased. When he did a search for Matthew Coughlin, there was nothing of him anywhere. Matt Coughlin, the bodyguard for Neil Elder, vanished without a trace.

Whatever Jonah meant about two copies, Li could not figure out either. Something else really nagged at him. Jonah told Ruth that there were two *copies* of the security plan. Two copies did not mean an original and a copy. It meant a copy of two different originals, right? The more he thought about it, the more confused he got. Pastor Tom was at a loss, as well.

Jonah may have chosen his words carefully, but no one could infer their meaning.

"Let's call it a day," Li said to Xin, pulling his reins to the right. He didn't particularly want to go back to his ranch. He really loved it, but the loneliness was beginning to set in. And New Year's Eve was only a few days away. Once this was all over, he was planning on opening his home to Efficientists who dropped rank. He experienced first-hand how Deborah and Esther helped him acclimate to the colonies. He could do the same for others. His ranch house had six rooms. More than enough room to take in several boarders. They could bring in more horses, chickens and cows. He even saw what looked like a garden in his backyard. They could add to it. So much he could do, but only if the threat of the corrupt World Government was gone. The World Government was like the dreary, grey clouds that prevented the sun from shining on the land.

As Li neared his ranch, he saw a van parked in the driveway. He had not been notified of any visitors, and fear clenched his stomach. He didn't have anything to protect himself. Why hadn't he at least bought a shotgun? He was about to turn Xin around to make their way to the forest, but he saw a man step out of the van. He was an aged man with white hair and tan skin. He began to wave. Li's pulse began to calm. It was Pastor Rohan Gupta. Li waved back and leaned forward, so Xin would know to sprint.

When Li came alongside the van, he jumped off his horse. "Pastor Rohan! What a surprise to see you. Why didn't you let me know you were coming? I would have been more prepared."

Rohan reached his arms around Li's shoulders and gave him a hearty hug. "Some things must be spoken face to face, my boy. Plus, there's not much going on at home. We have the old-style computers ready, so I thought we would come for a visit. It only took us about four hours to get here. Not a bad drive. Here, let me introduce you to one of my sons, Christian Gupta."

A young man around Li's age came out of the passenger side of the van. He was a little lighter than Rohan but had better looks. Li had seen a photo of Rohan's entire family, and the young man favored his mother's appearance. "Good to meet one of Rohan's sons. We are grateful for all you have done. You are a wizard when it comes to working on these old-style computers."

The man shook his hands. "I must confess, you have my father to thank for it. He would never let us have an HMS, so I would salvage any old computers I found. I had to teach myself how to work them and put them together, and I am glad of all I learned."

"We have benefited from your expertise. Please, make your way into my house. I have restrooms. There is food in the kitchen. Take whatever you find. I'll put Xin in his pen and meet you both inside."

The young man nodded and looked toward his father. "Go on in first, Dad. I'm going to grab my computers and meet you in there."

"Good," Rohan said. "I need to use the bathroom, and I don't think I can wait one more second."

"Come on, Xin," Li said, taking the horse's reins. He led him around the side of the house to where the horse pens were located. Li knew something was going on. Rohan had a good-humored nature, but for him to drive all the way down to his ranch meant they had found something. He opened the door of the first pen and led Xin inside. He looked at the pile of hay and the water trough. There was enough for him until the morning. "Good," Li said. He unlatched the bridle and reins and took them off. Then he unbuckled the saddle and carried everything out of the room, closing the door behind him. He set the gear down on a table. He would have to hang them up later.

Li walked to the back of the house. He could see Rohan already at his kitchen table, enjoying a slice of bread with jam. He walked in the back door. "Does your son need help setting everything up?"

"You better not," Rohan said in between bites. "Christian has a way of setting things up to his liking. He went to use the bathroom. He'll be right back."

"Okay," Li said. "Then I'll fix him a plate of food. Do you both like cashews and pecans?"

"Yes, please. And water if you don't mind."

"I have plenty of everything," Li said. He was glad he brought in a gallon of water from the well that morning. He poured three glasses and added extra food to the plate that Rohan had already prepared. Then he made a plate for Christian and himself and sat down next to Rohan. "The generator is right there," he said, pointing to the wall behind the table. "Christian can set up there on the table."

"That's what I figured," Rohan agreed.

Li went to take a bite of his bread but set the slice back down. "I can't help but be curious. Your son found something, didn't he?"

"That he did," Rohan said. "But I can't steal his thunder. It took him over a week to fully understand what he was seeing. He'd explain it better than I could anyway."

"Let me ask you this," Li said. "Is it good news or bad news?"

Rohan shrugged. "I would think it was bad news if we hadn't caught it earlier, but Christian believes he found the copy that Jonah told Ruth about."

Li was a little surprised that Rohan knew about the conversation Jonah had with Ruth before he left the city, but Pastor Tom made it a priority to keep everyone up on current events. He believed that the more people who saw the puzzle, the more pieces could be seen.

Li grabbed several cashews and placed them in his mouth. Then he drank down the cool water. He examined the equipment that Christian brought in from the van. Several old-style computers, a Portable and a very old LPS. "Your son has quite the collection, doesn't he?"

Rohan laughed. "There is way more where that came from. His wife doesn't know what to do with it all." Rohan leaned forward. "Between you and me, I think Christian has a hardware hoarding problem, which has been aggravated since we began our little plan here."

"Everyone needs a hobby," Li said and smiled. "I found Xin, and now I want to collect more horses."

Rohan spread his arms. "You have quite the ranch to collect them. How many horses does the stable hold?"

"I have three now, but I can have at least twelve total. However, building more stables would be simple. Maybe your son simply needs to get a bigger house for his collection."

Rohan slapped the table and laughed. "That would work, but I'd rather have more grandbabies than hardware."

"What have I missed?" Christian asked when he walked into the kitchen.

"We were talking about having more grandbabies," Rohan said, winking at his son.

"I've already given you one. Now it's my brother's turn."

"Ah yes, but you forget. He needs to find a wife first."

"Can't you just arrange it? Wasn't that our tradition in Old America," Christian said, sitting down in front of his hardware. He began to assemble the large pieces together.

"I couldn't even force you boys to eat all your food. How could I force you to marry?" Rohan asked in jest.

"You are right, Father. And you did an excellent job allowing us to choose our own paths."

"As long as it was God's path," Rohan interjected.

"And obviously God wanted me to work on these old computers, despite my father's displeasure in them."

Rohan held up his hands. "You are right, my son. I should have encouraged your curiosity more. I would have never realized that your hobby could be used for something like this, but God's ways are higher, and He sees what we cannot."

"Are you attaching all of those together?" Li asked, getting up.

Christian grinned. "Why, yes I am. I have found that I can create a supercomputer. I can see everything and because the main hard drive is in the old-style computer, no one can detect me."

"I can't believe it," Li said, stunned. He stared as Christian assembled two old-style computers, a Portable, an HMS and the old version of the LPS.

"I have a newer LPS you can disassemble and use," Li offered.

"Nope, I've tried all of them. It is only this LPS that is compatible with the rest of my system."

"That makes total sense," Li said. "There have been upgrades added. It is a perfect bridge from the old-style computers to that newer model Portable you have."

"Bingo," Christian said, excitedly. "I had to find the perfect combination of hardware to make my supercomputer, and I've had many weeks of trial and error, but, finally, here it is. I give you the Gupta Computer."

Li stared at the supercomputer in awe. "The Gupta Computer," he repeated.

"I don't know if I love the name. It tells everyone that my family created the very thing that can infiltrate the World Government," Rohan said.

"That shows a lack of faith in our mission, Dad. When we win, we will have a legacy of defeating evil. Is that not something you want your family to be known for?" Christian asked.

"Again, my son, I stand corrected. I have raised you well," Rohan said with obvious fatherly pride.

"Who knows about this supercomputer?" Li asked.

"Only the three of us at this table," Christian said.

Li didn't want information about this supercomputer to get out. "Maybe just inform Pastor Tom. He'll know who to tell and who to keep it from."

"He's taking a break from receiving and sending messages. He feels like he's had too many, and he doesn't want to compromise his family and the people of Trinity," Rohan said.

"He's probably right," Li said. "I will go there tomorrow. It will take longer on Xin, but I can't leave him here alone."

"If you don't mind," Christian said. "My father and I would like to stay here until New Year's Day. We also don't want to jeopardize our family. You can take our van. We gassed it before we came here, and we will watch over your horses."

"It's a plan, so what do you have to show me?" Li asked, walking behind where Christian was sitting.

Christian attached the monitor to his supercomputer and turned it on. "You will see for yourself."

Li stared at the screen as Christian snuck into the World Government site. Then he went to the link for the RIBS, and Li instantly noticed it. "He couldn't. There hasn't been enough time."

Christian shook his head. "He must have been working on it for weeks. It was like he knew a while back that we were going to attack the RIBS. Who do you think told him?"

Li shook his head. "The only one I can think of is Dr. Linton, but Pastor Tom insists that he didn't do it. The only other person who could have told Neil Elder so early is Jonah, but that doesn't make sense. Why would he jeopardize the very mission he risked his life to be part of?" Li looked back at the screen. "Neil Elder copied the entire RIBS."

Christian nodded in awe. "Yes, he did. And after he reboots the system with the Kill Switch, he will have a brand-new RIBS to install that is almost identical."

"It's not identical?" Li asked.

"Since I knew that it was only Neil Elder who could order a copy of the RIBS to be made, I checked the difference between his account on the original RIBS and on the copy. His wealth has more than quadrupled on the copy."

"Wait," Li said with understanding flashing in his mind. "Is that what Jonah meant about two copies? Was he saying there is a copy of *Life Plethoricity* and now the RIBS?"

"That might be the two copies he was referring to," Rohan said. "But how are they connected?"

"That's it!" Li shouted. "That is why Jonah has gone to the prison. He knows that the Kill Switch must not be used. If Neil Elder is able to use the Kill Switch, not only will our plan be thwarted, but we will be responsible for making Neil Elder the most powerful and the richest magistrate alive."

"Isn't there another army going to help? Pilar's father was able to get that bodyguard we found at the prison camp to help. The one missing his eye," Rohan said.

"Yes, Randall Hunt is also going to stop the Kill Switch from being used," Li said. "And Pilar is still there. I'm sure between the three of them, they will make sure that switch is not pulled." Li had another thought. "Can you hook up my computer to the supercomputer?"

"I can hook up anything to it," Christian grinned. "That's the beauty of the Gupta Computer, but I don't think it will make a difference. I already have two old-style computers routed in the system."

Li quickly went to his workstation. "No, this computer is special. It is able to see a code that no one else can see." He brought the computer to Christian. "You'll have to make this computer the main hard drive."

"Okay," Christian said. He unplugged the computer that he had been working on and plugged in the one Li had given him. "It's ready."

"Now go to any LPS," Li said.

"Just anyone?" Christian asked.

"Yes, and click the link to *Life Plethoricity*, and you'll see it," Li answered.

Christian typed slower than Li, and it took him several seconds to open the link.

"Whoa!" Christian said.

"What is it?" Rohan asked.

"I don't know," Li answered. "But it's imbedded in every single *Life Plethoricity* on all LPSs, HMSs and Portables. Now check to see if that same code is on the copy of the RIBS. If it is, we will know for sure that the World Government created it."

Christian continued to type. He opened the copy of the RIBS he had discovered. "There's no code."

Li stared at the screen. "Great. Either the World Government didn't create the code, or they only wanted it inserted in *Life Plethoricity*. Either way, we are no closer to finding out who created it and what it does."

Zach felt the truck come to a stop. The pillowcase over his head was suffocating him, and his breathing was rapid. He was seconds away from passing out. Last thing he remembered was that he was headed to Bear's house to talk to his grandfather, but the World Police stopped his truck and pulled him into the van.

"Get out of the truck, Zacchaeus Daniels," a voice yelled.

He tried to get up, but having his wrists taped together didn't help the situation.

"I said get out!" the man yelled again. This time he yanked Zach by the arm, throwing him onto the ground. He kicked Zach in the ribs, and pain exploded in his chest.

"Mr. Stanton wants to see you," another man's voice shouted.

Zach groaned. He was back at the prison camp, but this time he was not able to hide behind the graves.

Hands grabbed him and pulled him to his feet. "You may want to say your prayers now, preacher boy. What you're about to experience will have you squealing like a pig."

"I don't know anything," Zach shouted, as he was being pulled by both arms. His feet dragged along the dirt behind him.

"That's what they all say, preacher boy. Just you wait. They all confess. It's only a matter of time, so you'd better think quickly about how much pain you truly want to endure."

Zach indeed did pray. This time he didn't ask God why. Instead, he asked God for courage. His father endured being burned alive by the World Government for what he believed in. If his fate ended like his father's, he couldn't be prouder. He would rather stand side-by-side with his father in heaven than confess a single word to the World Government.

CHAPTER 39

Hunt looked over the guns and ammo spread across his kitchen table. He rubbed the stubble on his chin with his knuckles. There still wasn't enough to take on the World Police that had been sent to the prison to protect the Kill Switch. He and his men were preparing to leave, and they needed as much protection as possible. He resisted the temptation to fidget with his eyepatch, a habit Adella said he did when he was worried.

He looked at Tal. "Tell the men to also bring their bows and arrows. They may not be as accurate, but they are quieter. If we are going to get through this tunnel that is supposedly there, we will have to go single file. I'll have to leave half the men behind and let them in once I get inside."

Tal strung his fingers through his dark hair. "Are you sure you don't need me there? I can oversee the second team waiting outside."

Randall shook his head. "Absolutely not. I need you here. We have a perpetrator trying to get onto my land, and he will know that I'm gone. You need to protect Adella and the girls." He grabbed one of the guns on the table. "Here, take this. It's loaded, but I can't afford to leave another magazine. Only shoot when absolutely necessary."

"Yes, sir," Tal said.

"Get these guns out of here before my grandfather comes down and sees them," Randall said.

"Too late," a voice came up from behind.

Randall turned to see his grandfather coming into the kitchen. He closed his eyes. He knew a lecture was inevitable.

"You see now? This is why your father and I had so many arguments when you were a boy. This is exactly what I feared. I knew if the World Government found out about the oil on this land, it was only a matter of time before they confiscated it."

"They don't know, Grandfather. That is the point. We will stop them before they come after us. And I know you still harbor anger towards my father, but he never did tell, did he? I didn't even know there was oil here. He kept his word and kept this mouth shut."

"Yes, but at what cost? I never saw him again. And I lost all those years with you."

"Well, I'm here now, and I will fix this."

His grandfather came up to him. Randall could tell he was trying to hide his emotions. His eyes were red like he had been crying.

"Look, Randall," he said, putting his hand on Randall's shoulders. "I don't want to lose you again. I like what we have here. I've grown fond of Adella and her girls. Even Favian has grown on me. I don't want to lose what we have."

Randall hesitated but finally reached up and grabbed his grandfather's hand. "I don't want to lose any of it either, which is why this is our chance to protect what is ours before it becomes a target. You let me worry about the World Government. I need you to keep an eye on Adella and the girls. Tal will be in the house to protect you."

Randall's grandfather removed his hand and regained his composure. "Why do you think Adella's ex-husband is scoping out our lands? He is no threat to us."

"He is a threat if he takes what we care about," Randall said, simply.

"You think he'd kidnap Adella or the girls? But why?"

"He's a volatile man that has lost everything, and he knows I have oil. He would try to kidnap Adella or the girls and keep them for ransom—pure and simple."

A noise came from the back door. "May we come in?" Levi Jones asked. Dr. Linton was standing next to him, holding a Portable. They both entered the kitchen.

"We have news from Li," Levi began. "He's the Efficientists who is Zach's friend."

"Yes, I know him," Randall said, impatiently.

"Oh, I forget how involved you are in all of this. He sent us two encrypted messages. I learned how to decode them when I was monitoring the bakery's HMS."

"And what do they say?"

"He says that Neil Elder sent Jonah—or Matt Coughlin, as you know him—to the prison. So be careful. We have a good guy on the inside. Don't shoot him. We think he's going to try to prevent them from using the Kill Switch."

Randall put his hands on his hips. "Whether Matt Coughlin is a good or bad guy is still to be decided. And that is why I am going to the prison. I will stop that Kill Switch from being used, so Matt—or Jonah—better not get in my way."

"Trust us," Dr. Linton interjected. "When I was in the city, I was close to suicide. I didn't want to live anymore. Life was getting complicated and the stress of it all was wearing down on me. Then Matt gave me stacks of papers—illegal papers about God, faith and Jesus. Why would he jeopardize himself for me? Then he sent me to Trinity Village."

"He sent you there to gain information," Randall insisted.

"No, he knew I wouldn't jeopardize myself by taking sides. He sent me away, so I could leave the city. The city was killing me. Jonah is not a bad guy."

"Fine, I won't shoot him unless he shoots at me first. He better stay out of my way."

"Also, there is one more thing," Levi said. "And it's not good."

"What?" Randall asked. He hated that his simple plan was being altered by the new information, but he knew it was better to be prepared.

"They have Zach," Levi said, simply.

"What do you mean *they have Zach*? Who? Where?"

"They captured him in Trinity. Pilar saw him come into the prison yesterday and messaged Li last night from the Portable that's hiding in the tunnel. They are going to torture him for information," Dr. Linton said.

Randall thought of Zach. Would that man break? And how much information did he know? Probably almost all of it. "This is not good." He turned to Levi. "Do you think Zach will talk?"

Levi shook his head. "No, I don't think he will. That's what I fear. If Jonah doesn't find a way to get him out, Zach will die. And Pilar, she may expose herself to save him."

"Tal, tell the men we are ready to leave," Randall said.

"Yes, sir," Tal said and ran out the backdoor.

"We are coming too," Levi said, resolutely.

"No, you both are a liability," Randall insisted.

"That is my daughter in that prison, risking her life. I will not stay safely in this ranch while you go fight my battle."

"And you may need a doctor too!" Dr. Linton said. "I won't get in the way. I'll keep my supplies at the ready and make myself available to help the wounded."

Randall stared at both men. "I understand why Levi wants to help, but why would you risk your life, Dr. Linton?"

"For the first time, I found a place where I can rest and not live in fear. I want to keep this place from being taken over by the World Government just as much as you do. I will go and do my part—even if it is a minor one."

"Fine, but no weapons for either of you. You are not trained, and I don't have enough to waste. Go get your stuff ready. Levi, you will help Dr. Linton carry what he needs."

Randall watched the two men leave. A baker and a doctor, wanting to help him keep his lands. Only in the colonies would such a diverse group of people unite together like this. He turned to his grandfather. "Where are Adella and the girls? I want to say goodbye."

"They're downstairs."

Randall turned to the table and grabbed a smaller gun. He slipped out the magazine and made his way to the stairs. "Adella, it's me. Can I come in?" he said once he got to the basement.

"Of course," Adella's voice called out. "We are in the living room. The girls are playing with the toys you got them for Christmas."

He entered their small basement apartment. Adella had decorated it for Christmas. There was a small tree with ornaments and garland with ribbon around the door frame. Plus, the girls had made a few decorations of their own. This was the first Christmas he had celebrated since he was a boy visiting his grandparents. He almost forgot to get them presents until his grandfather mentioned it.

The girls were on the floor of the apartment playing chess. The board was handmade with carved pieces that he purchased in town last minute. It was quite expensive, but he didn't have much to choose from. Obviously, though, the girls loved it. Adella laid on the couch reading one of the books he bought her. Favian rested at her feet on the edge of the couch. He wagged his tail and it thumped against the cushion. Randall went to pet the dog, buying time.

"You're about to leave, aren't you?" she asked, closing the book and eyeing the gun he held in his hand.

He still didn't look at her. "Yes, we must leave soon. My grandfather and Tal will be staying here to protect you and the girls if your you-know-who decides to show up."

"Alex. Anna. Come say goodbye to Randall. He will be leaving for a few days, but he'll be back."

The girls instantly stopped their game. He quickly squeezed the small gun he had brought between the couch cushions.

"Hurry back," Alex said, giving him a big hug. "We will be bored without you."

Randall smiled. "Grandfather and Tal will keep you company."

"I hope so," Alex said, giving room for her little sister to come.

"Are you going to stop the bad guys?" Ana asked in her innocent voice.

"Yes, I am. Then we will all be safe," Randall said, receiving her hug, as well.

"Why don't you take the game carefully into your bedroom? I need to talk to Randall alone," Adella said, sitting up.

Randall watched as the girls carefully picked up either side of the chessboard and carried it into their bedroom.

"Shut the door, please," Adella called out.

A second later their door was quietly closed. Randall sat in between her and Favian. He finally stared at the woman he had begun to fall in love with. "I will miss you," he said. He wanted to say more but found it difficult.

She leaned into him. "I'll miss you more. I'll miss seeing you every morning. I'll miss seeing you bossing around the men. I'll miss the way you fidget at your eyepatch. I'll miss your smell, and the way you kiss."

He embraced her. She wore another soft sweater she was fond of wearing. He loved the way it felt on his skin. He would have to buy her more when he returned. "We've only kissed a few times," he added, grudgingly.

"Kiss me then," she teased.

He turned her toward him and kissed her softly. He wanted to kiss her with more intensity, but he was sensitive to the girls in the other room. It was best to move slowly.

He felt a tongue on his face and opened his eyes to see Favian wedged between them, licking their faces.

"Gross," Adella laughed. "His breath is so bad."

"I was wondering what smelled," Randall teased. Then his countenance became serious. He reached to get the gun he had placed in-between the cushions. "I want you to keep this gun with you. Sleep with it. If your ex-husband comes, it will most likely be at night. We have a few men staying behind to man the watchtowers, but they won't be able to see everything. He has scoped out my lands, and he may have found a way in that is out of sight."

"But I don't know how to use it," she whispered.

"It's simple. Plus, it's mainly just to scare him. You don't need to hit him. It will warn Tal, and he can take care of him. But watch," Randall said, placing in the magazine. "You see. Once you put in the magazine the gun is ready to shoot. And you just push this button to release it." He pushed the release button and the magazine slid into his other hand. "So keep the magazine out of the gun until you are ready to shoot. Just push the magazine up and it's ready. Here try."

He watched her shove the magazine in and press the release button several times until he was sure she had it. "I hope you won't have to use it," he finally said.

"Me too," she agreed. "Do you mind if I pray for you?"

He felt a little awkward receiving prayer, but he was so desperate to keep his new family and his new life that he would do anything. He bowed his head like he has seen her do so many times.

"Father, God," she began. "Protect Randall on this mission. He is a warrior for You, Lord. Through Jesus, he has the victory. Greater are You than all the enemies of the world. Thank You for his presence in my life. I love him. He is a good man. Give him supernatural help when he needs it and give him supernatural insight at just the right time. I pray this in Your name, Jesus, amen."

"Thank you," Randall said, looking away and getting up. He didn't want her to see the tears running down the side of his cheek. He wanted to be that man she saw in him. He wanted to be the words she spoke over him. This was his chance to right all wrongs. "I will be here after the New Year, and we will finally be safe for good."

Randall Hunt left the room and began to make his way up the stairs, but now he felt like a new man. It felt strange, but he wouldn't shy away from it any longer. He was the good guy for once, and he would take down the enemy.

"Favian, where are you going?" Adella whispered. She heard Favian whimper and then he jumped off her bed. It was late— maybe around three in the morning. She had read her book until midnight and then turned off the lights. Her girls had been asleep already for several hours. Tal and John had checked on her several times, and she reminded them both that she was fine, but now she didn't know. Favian was gone. She sat up and grabbed the flashlight that was next to her bed. When she turned it on, she located the gun. She quickly inserted the magazine like Randall had taught her.

"Favian," she called out again. "Where are you?"

Suddenly, loud barking could be heard upstairs. Then a crashing of glass and a man yelling in pain. She jumped out of bed and ran to the door of her girls' room. "Alex! Ana! Stay in there. Do not come out. Make sure the chair is still wedged under the door handle. Do you hear me, Alex?"

"Yes, Mother! The chair is still there. I'll make sure Ana stays with me."

Adella's hands shook. She carried the flashlight in her left hand and the gun in her right. Both hands were shaking so bad that she knew she couldn't shoot anything, but Randall said all she had to do was scare him. She began to make her way up the stairs. She could hear Favian growling and a man crying out. When she made her way to the kitchen, Tal ran past her into the living room.

"Put that rifle down or I will shoot you!" Tal yelled.

"Here take it!" the man cried. "Just get him to let go!"

Adella recognized the voice. It was her ex-husband, Robbie. Randall had been right. He would try to break in the instant he knew Randall was gone.

She heard noises upstairs. It was Randall's grandfather coming down. "Don't worry, John. Tal has him," she called out.

He didn't listen to her and continued to make his way downstairs.

"Adella, can you call off Favian?" Tal yelled from the living room. "He's ripping apart Robbie's arm."

Adella placed the gun she held onto the table. She didn't want to risk shooting Tal. She grabbed the flashlight now with both hands and walked into the living room. She saw Tal holding his gun and the rifle that she recognized as Robbie's. Favian had his jaw clamped around Robbie's right arm.

"Favian, come here!" she shouted. Favian pulled harder and more blood gushed out, as Robbie's skin ripped apart.

"Ouch! Get him off me!" Robbie screamed in pain. "He's killing me!"

"Favian!" she shouted louder. "Come here right now!"

Finally, Favian let go of the arm and came to her. Crimson blood smeared across his large muzzle.

"Just let me go!" Robbie cried. "I promise you I will never come back." Blood pooled all around him.

"I'll have to take him to the hospital," Tal said. "Dr. Linton is gone, and his injury is bad. I think I can see his bone in there."

"Indeed," John Hunt said. "I'll stay here and watch over things. It shouldn't take you too long."

"Can you get up?" Tal asked. "I'll take you to the hospital, but you best get out of town. Once Randall Hunt finds out you broke into his property, he'll be looking for you."

"I promise!" the man yelled. "Just get me to the hospital, and I'll get far away from here!"

Adella looked at both men. "Please don't tell the girls about this. Just tell them it was an intruder. I don't want them thinking so poorly of their father."

John and Tal both nodded. Then they got back to work removing Adella's ex-husband from the living room while Favian continued to growl and bark.

CHAPTER 40

Jonah stepped out of the limousine. Riding in one wasn't his preference, but he needed to make a statement at the prison. The symbol was necessary to show the World Police that he was now in control. Ted Stanton had already been sent the message to his LPS to expect him and cooperate. Jonah knew there would be a power struggle, but he didn't wait this long to back down at the end of things.

He began walking the trek to the front of the factory, a path he knew well. He glanced briefly beyond the wire fence to where the forest began. Tombstones were hidden under the trees. Tombstones he had painstakingly etched in the names of his father, mother, brother and sister. The Goodman family all gone in one day, and he happened to be recovering from a rattlesnake bite—left for dead by the security guards yet picked up and cared for by an outsider who would change his life forever. He looked beyond the forest to where he knew the road led away from here back to Trinity Village.

He would not let anything stand in the way of taking down the World Government. He had many chances to kill Neil Elder, but Christina Straight had been right. Someone would simply replace him. Better to take down the monster that allowed the corrupt to rule, and that monster was a government spawned out of fear. He had taken a knife to save Neil Elder in order to gain his trust, a trust he would soon exploit. As he walked, soldiers saluted him. He didn't bother saluting them back. He was beyond such protocols.

The door in front of him opened. He saw Ted Stanton, the facility director, step out to meet him. This was a good sign.

Jonah spoke first. "I'm Matt Coughlin. I was sent by Neil Elder to protect the Kill Switch and relay information."

Ted Stanton looked unamused. "Yes, I got his message. I don't know why he sent extra help. We have everything secure, but I'll respect his wishes. I tried to look you up. I can't find Matthew Coughlin anywhere."

"My files have been erased for security reasons," Jonah said. He knew that when the year began, Matt Coughlin would be dead. He looked around for Pilar but didn't see her. He hoped she would be good at pretending not to know him when she saw him face to face. He continued. "I would like to inspect the Kill Switch first. I want to make sure it is in working order. If we have to use it, I don't want it quitting on us." Jonah made his way past Ted Stanton and headed to the stairwell that led to the tower offices.

Ted Stanton walked beside him. "I can assure you that I have already had a team of the best engineers looking at it. Many of them are still here if you want to ask them for yourselves." He walked silently for a few seconds. "However, I think there is something, or should I say someone, you would want to see first."

Jonah stopped. "Who authorized you to take someone captive."

Ted Stanton grinned. "You may have taken a knife for Neil Elder, but you aren't the only one who he trusts. He asked me several days ago to find this man. I'm surprised you didn't catch him sooner. We found him two days ago. He was so easy to find."

Jonah felt like his guts had been slammed by a two-by-four. He knew instantly who he had captured. He hadn't spoken to Pastor Tom since he closed down all his accounts, which was exactly two days ago. He quickly masked his pain with anger. "And does Neil Elder know that you have acquired the target?"

Ted Stanton looked stressed. "I have not said anything yet."

"And why not?"

Ted Stanton hesitated. "The man won't say a word about the plans to attack the RIBS. All he does is spout these sentences about God and his religion repeatedly. We have tortured him in every way I can think, but he won't break. Frankly, my men are getting spooked. They don't want to enter his cell anymore. I don't want to contact Neil Elder if I can't get the man to speak."

Jonah looked in the director's eyes. He could see fear. "What is something he repeats?"

Ted Stanton shrugged. "I don't know exactly. Words like being *more than a conqueror. The victory has already been* won by this deity named Jesus. And something like, *though a thousand fall, I will stand strong.* Whatever he's doing, it's working. He hasn't said a word. I'm having my men take him out back to execute him for treason this evening. He robbed the World Bank and now he is trying to take down the RIBS. If he won't talk, he will die."

"You have detained Zach Daniels, I'm guessing. Let me talk with him. I know religious guys like this. I can get information from him, and then you can execute him in the morning."

"If you do, don't forget this was a team effort. I broke his body; you break his will," Ted Stanton said. "Follow me."

Jonah followed behind the officer. His insides were hot with fury. He had to flick his hands to alleviate the tension. He silently prayed that Zach hadn't been beaten so badly that he wouldn't survive. They continued walking to the stairs that led down. How many times had he walked up and down these stairs when he was a teenager? His family had been taken when he was fourteen, and at age sixteen he was orphaned and alone. They worked two years in the forced labor camp before a snakebite almost killed him and his father revolted with the other families. They were all killed. And what was his father's crime to be sent to the prison with his entire family? They claimed he had broken into a government factory and stolen several HMSs. Jonah knew that wasn't true. His father was a fisherman, like all the Goodmen family members before him.

When they neared the cells, Jonah cleared his mind the way Christina Straight had taught him long ago. He wouldn't be of any use if he carried bitterness in his bones. He would have to let it go and trust God to attain vengeance but letting go and trusting God didn't mean he would have to stand by and do nothing. He would do everything in his power to allow God room to redeem the life and the family that had been stolen from him.

As he passed the first cell, he heard a woman's voice cry out. "Please, Mr. Stanton, don't hurt him anymore! He won't survive one more beating. Please! Please! Don't hurt him!"

Jonah stopped. "You have a second prisoner?" He peered through the barred opening of the door just over the deadbolt. He could see Pilar huddled on the ground.

The tension came back to Ted Stanton's face. "Shut your mouth, Pilar, or the officers will come in there and tape it shut!" He turned back to Jonah. "She was one of the prisoners we had here before they were sent to another camp. I kept her here because she was good at doing the books. Her father owns a bakery or some sort of family business. How would I know that she knew Zacchaeus Daniels?"

"Did you check her records? Where is she from?" Jonah said, allowing anger to fill his voice. Ted Stanton avoided eye contact with him.

"She is from Levington."

"You must know that Trinity and Levington are neighboring villages, don't you?" Jonah asked, mockingly.

"It doesn't matter. The mere fact that she knows him makes her an accomplice. She is to be executed, as well."

"I guess you'll have to execute the entire population of both villages next. You are leaving a trail of bodies that is going to gain notice from the Colonials. You'll have rioting outside of these prison walls. It's happened once before, and it could happen again. The graveyard in the back is already full enough."

"We just need room for two more," Ted Stanton shot back.

Jonah took that as his cue to make a deal with the officer. He knew he now had the edge. "Look, I won't say a word to Neil Elder that you found Zach Daniels and that you kept a prisoner here without telling him. Give me the key to his cell, and I will get the information you need. Then you can execute them in the morning, and we can keep our focus where it belongs on the Kill Switch."

Relief flooded Ted Stanton's face. "This is the master key for all the cells. Just bring it back when you're done. I doubt you will get the information we need anyway, but you can try. He's in the last cell to the left."

Jonah took the key. "You can tell the other officers to leave me. I doubt Zacchaeus Daniels poses much of a threat to anyone."

"I know he doesn't," Ted Stanton said. Then he looked to the other officers. "Take a break. Let's see what magic he can do on our prisoner."

Jonah waited until the sound of the officers' footsteps faded upstairs. Then he went to the first cell and put his face next to the barred window. "Pilar, it's me, Jonah. Please don't yell. I'm going to open your cell now."

"Jonah—Ruth's Jonah?" he heard a shaken voice ask.

"Yes," he said and opened the door with the master key that Ted Stanton had given him. Instantly, he was met with an embrace by Pilar. "Thank you, Lord, you are here. Zach's screams. They were horrible. I've prayed and prayed, but they kept coming into his cell." Pilar began to cry. "Is he still alive? I haven't heard anything from him."

Jonah took her hands. "Listen carefully, we don't have much time. You both are to be executed in the morning. I will give you a key to open the cells. You'll have to reach carefully through the bars and open it from the outside, but it can be done. Just don't drop the key. Take Zach and get to the tunnel. I was planning on helping you escape anyway; though, I thought under better circumstances. Don't worry about the Kill Switch. I'll take it from here. I left a small car hidden under debris off the side of the road behind the graveyard. Get Zach to Deborah. She's at the ranch. She'll take care of him. And there are a few of my things in the back. Just keep them until I return."

"But if you give me the key, they'll know you helped us," Pilar said.

Jonah let go of her hands and reached into his pocket. He pulled out a ring of old keys. "I still have my set of keys that I stole when I was seventeen after I dug the tunnel leading inside the prison. Let us see if any of them still works." He took the master key and compared it to each of the old keys. "Here it is," he said, taking the key off his key ring. "Wait here." Jonah closed the cell door and opened it with the old key. "Perfect."

"Hide it so no one can find it," he said, handing it to her.

"Can I go see Zach?"

He shook his head. "Not right now. When everything quiets down tonight, open his cell and get him out. I'll make sure the coast is clear. I sent the coordinates of the car to the Portable you have hidden in the tunnel just in case. Just follow it if you lose your way."

She nodded and hugged him again. "Thank you. You are an answer to my prayers."

"Keeping praying," he said. "We still have a plan to finish."

She nodded and he closed the door and locked the deadbolt. He placed his old set of keys back into his pocket and walked to the last cell on the left. He prepared himself for what he would find. When he opened it, he heard Zach moan. All Jonah could see was Zach's blonde hair and a bloodied face. "Zach, it's me, Jonah. No one is going to hurt you again."

Jonah walked to Zach and kneeled to inspect his body. He prayed there weren't any broken bones. "Can you speak, Zach? Did they break anything?"

"Jonah, is that you?" he mumbled. "My face hurts so much."

"Yes, I gave Pilar the key to the cell deadbolts. She is going to get you out of here tonight. I have a car waiting on the side of the road behind the graveyard. Do you think you can make it through the tunnel? What did they break?"

Zach held up his hand. "They broke two of my fingers, and I believe my wrist is broken. My nose is broken. Definitely some ribs. I may have internal bruising in my abdomen. I think my jaw is fractured. It hurts to talk."

Jonah winced. He hoped it wasn't internal bleeding in his abdomen. "Let me look at your stomach." He tried to gently pull up his shirt, but the fabric was stuck to his skin in many places because of the dried blood. Zach moaned quietly. "I see bruising. Does it hurt to move?"

Zach sat up. "It hurts, but I can do it."

"How about your legs? Can you walk?"

"They pulled out most of my toenails. I don't have shoes, but my legs aren't broken—maybe a few toes, though."

Jonah finished checking Zach's body. He was beaten up badly. His face was unrecognizable, but with Pilar's help, he could leave tonight.

"I'm sorry this happened to you. I never meant for anyone to get hurt."

"It's not your fault. We all took this risk," Zach said, breathing heavily. "Are you going to make sure Ted Stanton doesn't pull the Kill Switch?"

"Listen, don't you worry about anything. I will make sure we accomplish our mission. The World Government will fall. Promise. Get to the ranch. Deborah can nurse you back to health. You have done your part. Make sure Pilar lets Pastor Tom know that you both are safe and out of harm's way. I'll watch over the Kill Switch. Tell him to stick with the plan."

Zach nodded. "Thank you, Jonah. I was ready to meet my father in heaven tonight, but I think he won't mind me staying here for a little while longer."

"Rest up and try not to talk," Jonah said. "Pilar will get you when everything is silent."

"What if I make a track to the tunnel?"

Jonah nodded his head. "I'm planning on there being a trail. But try as they may, they won't find you. You two will be long gone. Make sure to take the Portable with you that Pilar has been using. I sent the exact coordinates to where I hid the car. Also, do me a favor, leave the key in the air conditioning duct where it can be easily seen."

"Thank you," Zach whispered.

"Godspeed, Zacchaeus Daniels. Your father would be proud of you."

Jonah made his way to the door and locked it from the outside. He cleared his mind and walked down the hallway of cells to the stairs. When he reached the factory floor, his mind was focused on the mission ahead. He walked the length of the floor to the winding steps that led to the tower offices. He walked up the steps in a medium cadence. He didn't want to be winded when he made it up to the top.

"Well," Ted Stanton said when Jonah entered the office.

Jonah walked straight up to him and handed him the master key. "They are using old-style computers to attack the

RIBS. They can't be detected by our systems. They have them set up all over the world."

Ted Stanton stood stunned. "I can't believe it."

"Believe it. Now send out the World Police to find old-style computers. We need as many as we can get," Jonah said, sitting down at the LPS. "I need to notify Neil Elder. Can you turn this thing on?"

"Ah, yes," Ted Stanton said, pressing his thumb against the print identifier. "Are you sure we need to send them all out?"

"They are going to attack the RIBS on New Year's Eve. That is only a day away. We need those computers now. The Kill Switch will be safe with you and me and just a handful of officers to monitor the premises from the watchtowers. Then they can take care of the prisoners in the morning. They aren't going anywhere. I don't want to see any of the World Police come back empty-handed. Or shall I tell Neil Elder it was I and I alone who got the information out of Zach Daniels?"

"No, we are a team in this. I'll send them out. They are bored anyways. At least this will keep them occupied until tomorrow."

"Good," Jonah said and began his letter to Neil Elder.

Pilar didn't know how long she held the key to her chest, listening at the door of her jail cell. She heard a ruckus earlier that day. It sounded like people leaving the prison. She could hear the echoes of the trucks pulling out. She didn't know how Jonah did it, but he sent the World Police away. Now all she could hear was silence. There were probably a few security guards watching the premises outside, but they wouldn't see them. They would be traveling underground through the tunnel.

"God, please help me," she pleaded. Finally, she took the key and reached through the bars and down to where the deadbolt was. The fit was uncomfortable, but she held onto the end of the key with all her might. If she dropped it, they would be stuck in the cells and executed. She breathed a sigh of relief when she got the key into the lock. She carefully turned the key, and a click could be heard. The cell door was unlocked. She opened the door and made her way to Zach's cell. She knew from his screams that he was down the hall to the left.

She peered through the last few cell windows until she found him lying there. He was in the last cell. She carefully opened the door and crept in. She knelt next to Zach. She gently stroked his face. It was so swollen that she didn't recognize his features with her fingers. "Zach," she whispered. "It's time to go."

"My face is throbbing," he muttered.

"Don't talk," she whispered. "Just lean on me, and we will get out of here." She put his arm around her shoulder and squatted to a standing position. He felt like dead weight. "Please, Zach. You are going to have to help a little. Try to walk."

"My feet hurt," he muttered again.

"I know everything hurts, but we are going to Deborah and Esther's Ranch. They will make you all better. Just think about that. We will be out of here, and Jonah will take over."

She felt Zach standing stronger as he walked beside her out of the cell and down the hallway. She didn't bother closing the cell doors. They would be gone before anyone noticed. Luckily, the air-conditioning duct was right up the stairs in the main factory room. She could feel Zach's legs trembling as he made his way up every step. He was using everything in him to move. "Just a little more, Zach. You can do this."

Finally, they made it to the main floor, and she saw the large air-conditioning duct. She gently set Zach down and moved the vent, placing it against the wall. "I'll have to get in first, so you will follow my lead."

Zach looked at her. "Jonah said to leave the key in the duct where it was visible," he whispered, flinching with every word. "And take the Portable. It has the coordinates to where he left the car."

"Okay, I'll get it. Now you are going to have to crawl behind me. Just listen to my movements and follow me. You will have to be strong for just a little longer. Stay quiet and keep crawling forward. Once I get to the end, I will pull you out, okay? Then we will find Jonah's car. I'll get us home."

He nodded.

"And just leave the vent on the ground. Jonah will get it in the morning."

She crawled into the vent, silently praying for God to give Zach supernatural energy. She grabbed the Portable she had hidden several feet into the air-conditioning duct and began to crawl. She listened for Zach. He made it in and was crawling behind her. She remembered his screams from when they tortured him. When she had found out Zach was there, she pleaded for Ted Stanton to let him go. She gave herself away without letting him know she knew his plans. Stanton thought they were simply old sweethearts, never considering she could be part of the plan. How could she be? She had been in jail when it all began.

Every time they would torture Zach, they would leave frustrated. He would scream out Bible verses, never revealing a single thing about how they planned to attack the RIBS. He wouldn't even say his own name. When Zach would scream, she would pray out loud. She would pray that the armies of heaven would come down and rescue Zach. With her praying and Zach declaring Scripture, the men started getting nervous. They didn't want to torture Zach anymore. Besides, it hadn't worked. He wouldn't break.

When Pilar finally made it to the opening of the tunnel to the graveyard, she reached up and scooted the headstone. Then she threw the Portable gently on the grass. She waited for Zach. He was almost to her now. When he reached out his hands, she pulled him to a standing position. He winced in pain. Some of his fingers felt broken. "We are almost done. Now, I'm going to boost you up."

She placed a knee out for him, and for the first time, noticed he wasn't wearing shoes. In the moonlight, she could see blood across his toes. He was missing toenails. She wanted to cry but now wasn't the time. He placed his foot on her knee and pulled himself over the empty grave where the tunnel began. He rolled onto the grass. Finally, she pulled herself out and covered the hole back with the headstone. She could see searchlights from the prison towers in the distance, but none of the lights were pointing at them.

"Let's go," she pointed. "Is the street that way?" She was confused. Everything looked different in the dark.

"Turn on the Portable. Jonah sent you coordinates for the car," Zach said in labored breaths.

She quickly surveyed the ground. When she spotted the Portable, she picked it up and pressed it on. The first thing that popped up was the coordinates. Relief filled her. She grabbed Zach's arm and put it around her left shoulder. Then she held the Portable in her right hand and led the way. She would get them to the car and drive all the way to the ranch. She and Zach would finally be safe.

CHAPTER 41

Randall watched as the two people escaped through the tunnel with his binoculars. His men were behind him in the forest, but he crept up first to get a good look at the prison. He was glad he came when he did. He got to see first-hand the tunnel he had heard about being used. He was thankful for the full moon. He could see that one of the people coming out of the tunnel was the baker's daughter. He would let Levi know right away that his daughter was free. The man she half carried with her favored the build of Zach Daniels—though, from the looks of him, he was in really bad shape. Randall would wait a few minutes to make sure they weren't noticed by the security guards. They made their way to the street he knew was just beyond the woods. He hoped they had someone waiting for them with transportation. By the way Zach was limping, he wouldn't make it very far.

Randall looked back at the prison with his binoculars. Most of the trucks were gone, and there were only a few security guards watching the perimeter. Now would be the best time to attack, but it was too early. They would have to wait until almost midnight the following night. If they stood guard at the Kill Switch too early, Neil Elder would send reinforcements. Best to keep his attack a surprise for just the right time. He wondered where the World Police were and when would they be coming back. All their trucks were gone. It would be nice if they stayed away, but he knew Neil Elder wouldn't leave himself so vulnerable. They'd be back in the morning; he was sure of it.

Maybe Neil Elder would even leave the *Grand Opus Gala* to come to the prison. He would have to be the one to pull the Kill Switch, right? A smirk fell across Randall's face. Wouldn't Neil be shocked to see Randall Hunt back from the dead and with an army of his own? Randall fidgeted at his eyepatch for a moment before thinking of Adella. She would always move his hand away from his eyepatch. Even with a missing eye, he preferred his life now to how it used to be. He thought he had all the control, but, in fact, he was merely a pawn used by Neil Elder and the rest of those power-hungry Efficientists. Now he had Adella and the girls. He even enjoyed his grandfather's company. His life was rich. All that needed to happen now was for the World Government to fall, so they would leave him alone for good.

He felt someone coming up behind him. It was Dr. Linton and Levi Jones.

"I thought I told you all to stay put?" Randall said, exasperated.

Dr. Linton lifted his hands in defeat. "You told me to stay with Levi. When he left, I followed."

"I have to know about my daughter. Is she there? Do you see her?" Levi asked.

Randall looked at both men. "Look, I saw Pilar and, I believe, Zach leave over five minutes ago. I was waiting here to make sure no one saw them. As of now, they have made it away. I'm sure whoever picked them up has them by now."

"Let's go get them!" Levi demanded. "How do you know there is someone waiting for them?"

Randall shook his head. "You will just bring more attention to them and jeopardize their escape. I saw Pilar with a Portable. She was following directions. I could see her looking at the screen as she made course corrections. Wherever she is going, it's not by accident. There is a plan to get her and Zach out. Leave them be. They are safe. Now it's our turn to finish what they started, or do you want to leave now?"

Levi thought. "No, I trust you. She is safe. I want to stay here and help. We need to get rid of the threat once and for all—for my family's sake."

"Agreed," Randall said. "Let's eat and get some sleep. Tomorrow morning, we will make our plan. Some of us will go through the tunnels with our guns, some will make their way through the perimeter with bows and arrows and cause a distraction and you two will stay here to care for any of the wounded. You got that?"

Both men nodded.

"We have to make sure that the Kill Switch isn't pulled, so the plan to take down the RIBS is successful," Randall said. He didn't know if the plan would work. There seemed to be a lot of what-ifs and unknowns, but at least it would cripple the World Government for a time, so he could figure out a better plan to protect his family if need be.

Jonah drank his coffee. He wasn't normally a coffee drinker, but he needed to stay busy in the office. The two officers had gone downstairs to take Pilar and Zach out to execute them. They would be severely disappointed. He had gone early himself to ensure they were gone. They left the key in plain sight in the tunnel. Jonah moved the air conditioning vent back onto the duct opening. He glanced at Ted Stanton working at the LPS.

"Any word from the World Police? Have they gathered enough old-style computers?"

Ted Stanton swiveled in his chair to look at Jonah. "Not all of them have Portables, but the ones who have communicated with me say that they have found parts, nothing more. No one has found one intact. I hope you have a plan to find someone who can put them together."

Jonah took a sip and kept his expression indifferent. He knew it would be difficult to find any computer parts in the surrounding area, let alone complete computers. Pastor Tom and his team have been collecting them since he anonymously dumped a bunch of them at the Trinity Trading Center so many months ago. He had waited patiently for Pastor Tom to mention them, so he could offer them as a solution for penetrating the World Government, but he didn't have to. Charlie Liu, or Li, as they call him now, discovered them and their hidden uses. The first part of his plan fell into place like a ball kickstarting a contraption of moving parts that he designed. "If Zacchaeus Daniels wasn't beaten so badly and about to be executed, I would say he could probably be useful at putting them back together."

Ted Stanton stood up. "Why didn't you mention this before?"

"Does it matter? You couldn't get him to talk. Do you think you could actually get him to comply? Things would have been different if I knew you had captured him. If you'd notified us, I would have had him talking and working for us by now. Looks like you really messed this one up. Now, you'll just have to find someone today who knows how to work these machines."

"No Efficientist knows how to work them! They are antiquated and of no use! New Year's Eve is tonight. What you ask is impossible!" Ted Stanton yelled.

Jonah waited for Ted Stanton to calm down. "I guess you are in luck then. I happen to know how to assemble and use them."

"Why didn't you say something?"

"I just want you to fully understand how much I'm saving your career," Jonah said.

"They are gone!" an officer yelled, breathlessly once he made it to the office. "We are looking for them, but their cells have been opened. There is no sign of forced entry."

Jonah placed his undrunk coffee down. "That is impossible."

Ted Stanton stared at Jonah for several seconds and they both made their way down the stairs to the cells. When they arrived, both cells were unlocked and opened.

"They must have gotten a key!" Ted Stanton yelled. Then he pointed at Jonah. "You were the last to see them!"

Jonah chuckled. "Have you already forgotten? I handed that key to you."

"Then you must have given them another key!"

Jonah allowed his anger to rise. "How dare you accuse me! I had just arrived at the prison when I saw the prisoners. Do you think I had a key to the cells already in my pocket? You know what I think? I think one of your officers sympathized with the prisoners, and before he left, he slipped a key under Zach's door. And I bet you that officer will not be returning."

"There would be no way they could make it out," Ted Stanton insisted. "I had officers surveying the premises like you said."

Jonah walked to Zach's old cell. "I see his trail. It's not hard to follow since you beat him to a pulp. Follow me. They are probably still in the factory hiding since they weren't discovered last night on the premises." Jonah followed the trail of dried blood and dirt. He knew where the trail would lead, but he made a show of analyzing the floor. When he finally got to the air conditioning vent, he stopped and pulled the gun from his holster. He motioned for the other officers to get ready, and they pulled out their guns, as well. Jonah silently prayed that Zach didn't forget the Portable. That would be difficult to explain.

He used his free hand and tore the vent off. Every officer pointed their gun at the empty vent. After several seconds, Jonah peered in. The Portable was gone, but the key was right where he wanted it. He picked it up. "It does look like we have a sympathizer," he said handing the key to Ted Stanton. "Send an officer in there."

"Get in there and find them," Ted Stanton said to the officer nearest him. The officer went headfirst into the vent and started to make his way down. Suddenly, he stopped and began to backtrack to the opening.

When he crawled out, Ted Stanton yelled. "Who told you to come back? They're in there somewhere. Go find them!"

The officer's face contorted with anxiety. "Th-there's a tunnel," he stuttered.

"What do you mean a tunnel?"

"There's a tunnel that veers off from the air conditioning vent. It goes through the dirt. I don't know where it leads, but it's long and dark."

Jonah put his gun back into his holster. "Let me guess. That tunnel leads under the premises and out the other side." He looked at Ted Stanton. "How long has this tunnel been here and you did not notice?"

CHAPTER 42

Ruth couldn't eat dinner. Her abdomen starting cramping earlier that morning, and she knew it was from nerves. She had spotted a little blood, but nothing that seemed out of the normal. She researched on the World Government's medical website, and spotting happened in 20% of pregnancies. Ruth looked to her husband sitting at the right side of her. He too hadn't eaten much. The dinner of lamb, baked fish, black eye peas and an assortment of cakes tantalized the guests, but few people were eating. Ruth looked around the room where dozens of ornately decorated tables sat holding eight guests each. The faces at each table looked the same except for Ada's table. Neil Elder was missing. Ada invited Shayla to take his place last minute, but her displeasure was obvious.

The atmosphere vibrated with restlessness, not anticipation. The excitement of the gala waned, and both Colonials and Efficientists were ready to get back to their lives. Ruth wondered if Ada knew the impatience to be finally done with the gala would happen, which was why she was planning on surprising her guests with a real fight. She still hadn't told Bear who he would be fighting. She'd probably introduce Sentinel in much the same way she introduced Shayla, so the World News could capture Bear's surprised expression. The paparazzi would be disappointed this time. Bear would not be surprised in the slightest. The bell finally jingled for them to make their way to the Gala Hall.

Ruth sat her napkin on her plate, relieved to finally be finished with the last meal of the gala. She wanted to go home. Bear had not decided if they were to take his truck or go with

Sonnie. It all depended on how badly he was wounded in his fight. Ruth felt Bear pull at her chair, so she stood up. She wore a silver flapper-style dress with lace and draping fabric. The dress was looser and boxier than she would normally create, but she had to hide her small, but noticeable pregnant belly. She wore layers of sashes around her midsection and feathers in the silver mask she created. Shayla swept her chestnut hair into thick waves that were pinned to her head.

Bear wore his gi and his long dark hair pulled back into a tight ponytail. That afternoon he refused to wear the outfit she had created for him. Ruth didn't argue about it. She followed him into the Gala Hall, noting that Shayla left her table and made her way to the stairwell that led to the faux ceiling of the Gala Hall. As Ruth entered the hall, she couldn't help but feel awe for Ada Armel's final design of the *Grand Opus Gala.* Extravagant Art Deco themed furnishings filled the large space. A white, cream and gold art deco façade was placed from floor to ceiling on every wall. A gold cascading chandelier fell from the center ceiling of the room above the stage. The chandelier was smooth, so hopefully the balloons Shayla would be dropping at midnight would not pop as they fell onto the gala guests.

This time Ada had placed their seats next to hers right in front of the stage. There were several empty ones next to them, and Ruth knew who they were for. She and Bear sat down. He was looking around at all the faces entering the Gala Hall. Ruth knew he was looking for Sentinel, but she had a feeling that Ada was going to save introducing him until last. Ruth looked directly behind the stage, and a large sun-like clock with silver and gold rays hung on the wall. It was only ten in the evening. Two more hours left. Ruth felt her chest tightening and pain shoot through her belly. She needed to calm down or she wouldn't make it through the fight.

Once everyone was seated, Ada Armel made her way onto the stage. The seat next to her own was empty. Neil was nowhere to be found, and Ada must have known his absence did not look good for her or her gala. The fact that the nine other magistrates were in the Gala Hall without the tenth, Neil Elder, was a show of condescension. She looked at the nine magistrates seated by the stage, and their expressions appeared extremely displeased.

Ruth thought of Jonah. He was also at the prison. She had looked for messages on the LPS in their flat all day, but everything was eerily quiet. Pastor Tom had stopped sending out communications several days ago. Li sent nothing nor did Zach. Ruth realized silence was probably the best thing now. They had done all they could. There were elements of the plan they could control, but there were many more they couldn't. God was ultimately in control.

Ada Armel walked to the center of the stage wearing a strapless gold-laced gown that hit just below her knees. The gold lace was transparent, so she also wore a nude, full-body slip. The bottom of the dress shimmered with tassels that reached almost to her ankles. Her blonde hair had thick, pinned waves much like her own, but she wore a gold headpiece with several white feathers on one side. Several strands of pearls roped loosely around her neck. Ruth instantly felt for her single pearl. That pearl meant more to her than all the pearls in the sea.

Ada waited for all eyes to be on her before she began speaking. "Today is the final day of our *Grand Opus Gala!* I want to thank every contestant who presented his or her work for the world to see. You are each a valuable member of the World Government and humanity. We will wait to see after midnight which contestant has the highest rating!" She waited for the expected applause to die down, and it didn't take long. "Each contestant has five minutes to wrap up his or her work, and every demonstration is assured to inspire your own research. Sonnie will start our evening off with a short demonstration from his beloved Uncle Sam, Old America's national bird! Then we will end the gala with a surprise that all of you and those watching from their LPSs and HMSs won't want to miss." She waited and did her slow circle to build the anticipation of the audience. The crowd seemed mildly interested. She overcompensated by allowing her voice to become too animated.

"I have planned for your viewing pleasure this evening an actual twelve-round fight between Bear and Sentinel. Most of you have seen Sentinel in the Colonial fighting circuit!"

Many of the faces from the crowd looked toward Bear, and the paparazzi flashed their cameras, but Bear kept a stoic face and gave a subtle nod.

Ada floundered a bit. Apparently, she was expecting more of a reaction from Bear. "Ah—oh, yes! Sentinel is the son of Watchman. Bear—or the Shaman as he was known at the time—retired Watchman from the fighting circuit by tearing his shoulder. Now it's Sentinel's turn to get retribution on his father's behalf."

On cue, the front doors of the Gala Hall opened, and Sentinel along with three other fighters came out. A nameless man Ruth didn't recognize stood up at the back of the room and began to play the electric guitar. He must have been plugged into the speaker system of the entire hall because the music poured out of all the speakers. Ruth had to cover her ears because a speaker was right over them, tucked in next to the base of the chandelier. Sentinel had light black skin and muscles protruding from his entire body. He was around the same height as Bear and powerfully stocky. He was young, but not naïve. He had a strength about him that reminded Ruth a lot of Bear. Sentinel and Bear would be equally matched if Bear was twenty years younger.

Sentinel sat in the empty seat on Bear's row but on the edge. The other three fighters sat in the chairs between Sentinel and Bear. Ruth glanced at her husband. He was unreadable. She then stared at the young men sitting next to him, and she felt her chest tighten again and another pain shot down her abdomen toward her pelvic area, but this time the pain made her wrap her arms around her waist and lean forward.

"What's wrong?" Bear asked, concerned.

"I do not know. I started having cramps this morning. I know it is because I am worried about you, but they are coming in stronger."

"Ruth," he said, putting his hand on her knee. "You don't need to be here for this. My fight won't start for another hour or so. I will be the last demonstration before midnight, and then this will all be over. You are putting too much stress on your body. I don't want anything to happen to our baby."

"But I do not want to leave you," she said.

He looked into her eyes. They were filled with concern. "This isn't my first rodeo, and I honestly don't want you to watch me fight. Please go to our room and lay down. If you want, just turn on the LPS and watch from there."

Ruth nodded. She really didn't want to watch him fight. "Okay, I'll go lie down. Everything is packed and ready for us to go right when the balloons drop. Will you be driving your truck or are we going with Sonnie?"

He exhaled. "I would like to say I will be driving, but I must be honest. I don't know what shape I'll be in. We may have to go with Sonnie."

"Good," Ruth said. "When the fight is over, I will come down. Shayla knows to meet us behind the building. Sonnie will be waiting for us."

"Get some rest," he said, placing his hand under her chin to give her a kiss. Several cameras flashed. They caught the kiss and they caught Ruth leaving the Gala Hall. Luckily, Ada Armel didn't see her leave. She was too busy introducing Sonnie and his bald eagle, Uncle Sam, for the last time.

As Ruth walked to the elevator, the piercing pain in her stomach shot through her again. She buckled over, leaning on the wall while she waited for the elevator to open. Luckily, it was already on the bottom floor. Once she got in the elevator and the doors close, she let out a cry. She felt a gush of hot liquid flow between her legs. Something was not right. She was cramping. When she made it to her flat, she could barely walk into the room. She looked down at her dress, and deep red seeped through the delicate silver lace. She entered her room and tried to get to the bathroom but fell on the bed instead. The cramps were coming hard now, and she curled up in a fetal position. She had never felt such excruciating pain.

Blood continued to flow, but there was a lull in the cramps. She instantly got up and turned on the LPS with shaking hands. She didn't want to miss her husband's fight. She needed to pray for him. Sonnie was already done with his demonstration, and the Efficientists were all getting their five minutes to wrap up their research. Ruth looked away from the screen and writhed in pain. She thought of getting Shayla, but she had no way to contact her. Another pain shot through her abdomen, and she cried out louder. No one would hear her. They were all downstairs watching the gala. She began to hyperventilate, and she felt dizzy. She began to sweat. More pain hit her, and her breathing became erratic and rapid. The last thing she remembered was crying out to God before passing out.

When Ruth awoke, blood was all over her dress and bed. She moved a fold of the fabric and screamed. She saw a baby fetus lying next to her. The fetus was the size of her pinky. She instantly closed her eyes. She didn't want to see it. "Bear!" she yelled out loud. She looked toward the screen. Bear's face was bruised and swollen, and he was receiving side hits from Sentinel. His head was also bleeding profusely. When the bell sounded, he staggered back to his side of the stage and leaned on the ropes Ada must have added to form a fighting ring. Ruth saw the round card. They were only on round seven.

Bear would have to endure five more rounds, yet he was so weak, he could barely keep from swaying.

Ruth looked at Sentinel. Although he too looked tired and had several bruises, he was not nearly as bad as Bear. She got up and looked at the number of people watching the fight on the LPS. The ratings were extremely high, but at what cost? She felt very weak herself. Too weak to change out of her bloody dress. She walked to the dresser where Bear kept all his personal belongings. He placed his survival items in the top drawer—things he would take with him everywhere he went, including matches. She grabbed the matchbox with shaking hands. She calmed her breathing and steadied her hands. She looked back at the LPS screen. Round eight was about to begin. Then she saw the single pearl strung with nylon that he wore around his neck. He must have taken it off before his fight. She quickly took it and placed it over her head and around her neck. Bear's pearl rested gently next to her own.

She walked back to the kitchen and looked through the cupboards. Shayla had cooked several meals for them, so she knew there had to be cooking oil. When she found it, she placed the small bottle under her arm. Wooziness threatened to wash over her as she neared the bloody bed. She wouldn't look at the tiny baby. She would have to process the loss later. She wrapped the sheet into a ball and carried it to the bathroom. She placed the red-stained white sheet into the bathtub and poured cooking oil over it. Then she took the matchbox from her hand and tried to light a match. Her hands began to quiver intensely.

"God, help me. I can't leave him like this," she whispered. She lit another match and this time the flame burst forth. She dropped the lit match on the wound-up, bloodied sheet. The small flame traveled quickly down veins of oil. Ruth watched. She watched as the fire consumed the fabric and everything within. Finally, when the white and red burned into blackened ash, she turned on the shower. The flames instantly sizzled and died.

"I see heaven opening up, and my child running into the arms of Jesus. I don't see these ashes. I only see beauty." She stared for a moment longer, allowing the ash to grow into a flowered meadow in the imagination of her mind. Finally, she turned from the tub while a portion of her heart stayed behind.

Round eight and Bear was already ready to fall. His eyes were swollen almost completely shut, and he could barely see his opponent swinging at him. He took several hits to the other side of his ribs. Sentinel was trying to be nice, not hitting the same ribs repeatedly, but to no avail. Several of his ribs were broken. Sentinel had stopped beating his face, knowing his nose was broken, and blood continued to flow. Bear reached out and grabbed Sentinel around the neck.

"We can stop. Just fall," Sentinel said.

Bear shook his head. "No, we need to last all twelve rounds. We must get to midnight."

"I don't think you'll make it another two minutes, let alone ten. I've beaten every part of your body. I'm running out of places to hit."

Bear pushed him away and punched Sentinel in the jaw.

Sentinel's eyes became angry, and he came at Bear with several hooks to his already inflamed cheek. Then he brought his hand up into an uppercut to the chin before the bell sounded for round eight to end. Bear fell to the ground. The referee started counting, but he crawled to the ropes and forced his way back up. He had never felt so much pain everywhere. Sentinel was an amazing fighter—the best he's ever fought.

The audience cheered, rooting for Sentinel, the new up-and-coming fighter. Sentinel went back to his corner only after doing a half-circle with his arm raised. More cheers from the audience. Just before the bell rang for round nine to start, a hush fell over the crowd like a blanket of clouds. A woman wearing a bloodied silver dress entered the front doors of the Gala Hall. She limped slowly to the ring, blood trailing on the floor behind her. Bear couldn't see who it was. As she drew closer, she crawled onto the stage next to him. He leaned down, holding the ropes so he could stay standing. The woman gently cupped his face. "That is enough. I won't let you fight anymore."

Bear yelled out, "No!" but she pushed him away. In his weakened state, he fell over the ropes and landed on the gala floor, knocking himself out.

Ruth walked to the center of the stage and motioned for Ada to bring her a microphone. Ada hesitated, but Ruth pointed to the floor and mouthed, "Now!" The crowd began to murmur, whispering and pointing to Bear's maskless wife.

Sentinel stood confused in his corner of the ring. He looked to his friends seated near the stage. They shrugged. His opponent had just been knocked out by a woman.

Ada made her way into the middle of the ring, trying to avoid the blood that splashed across the ground in a gruesome design. She finally handed Ruth the microphone and whispered in Ruth's ear. "Your mask is not on. People will discover who you are."

"That is the point. I'm giving you the ratings you desire," Ruth said, taking the microphone. It was her turn to be on center stage.

She looked at the clock behind her. Less than eight minutes before midnight. She placed the microphone close to her mouth. "My name is Ruth, but my full name is Eve Ruth Pallue."

Voices erupted as cameras flashed wildly. Several paparazzi ran up to the stage to get better shots.

She paused allowing the cameras to capture their images. She waited almost a full minute, trying not to squint her eyes from the blinding flashes of light. Finally, she began her speech. "Almost a year ago, Neil Elder had my flat set on fire."

More murmurs erupted from the crowd. She ignored the noise and continued. "I managed to get out with help, but I was left with burns," she said, showing her hand. "And a missing tooth." She opened her mouth to let everyone see the empty space. "Neil Elder stole my life plan, *Life Plethoricity*, and forced it on Efficientists and Colonials alike. I want to tell you right now that I reject that life plan. It does not speak truth. It is only a counterfeit to the true meaning of life, which is to know and love our Creator and to have a relationship with Him through His Son, Jesus Christ."

More cameras flashed. Many in the crowd began to yell, "Treason! Treason!"

Sentinel walked up to Ruth and looked at the crowd, yelling, "Silence!" He balled up his fist and stared at each face as he moved in a circle on the stage. His face was filled with disdain. "We have listened to each one of you drone on about things that don't matter. Now it's time to let Bear's wife speak or I will come out there and pummel each and every one of you!"

The crowd instantly became quiet. Even the cameras stopped flashing. Ruth looked at Sentinel, "Thank you." Then she stared back at the faces in the crowd. "My father wrote *Life Efficiency* out of fear. He wanted to prevent a third Civil War, but he allowed safety to usurp freedom. Neil Elder continues my father's efforts to gain control and maintain peace, but true peace is not achieved by separation and control. It is achieved by people learning to love others and to live in harmony despite our differences. That is what I have learned from living in the colonies."

She looked back at the clock. Three minutes left until midnight. She silently prayed that Shayla would remember to unleash the balloons, so they could meet Sonnie who was waiting for them next to his truck and trailer of birds.

CHAPTER 43

Neil Elder inspected the mass of old-style computers scattered on the tower office of the prison. "So that is how they've been doing it? Ingenious. And this is all you could find?"

"Yes, sir," Jonah said. He was sitting at one of the computers, trying to finish assembling one more. "I believe Zach Daniels and Charlie Liu have confiscated most of them in this area, but we can find more." He looked to Ted Stanton. They did not tell Neil Elder that Zach had been found and got away. Ted agreed to tell Neil Elder that Jonah had discovered the computer information on his own.

Neil Elder looked at the clock. "Looks like we have three minutes before I pull the Kill Switch. Ted, please ready it."

Ted Stanton looked at Jonah confused. "If we have discovered how they will attack, why would we pull the Kill Switch?"

Neil looked at Ted and scoffed. "Because, you imbecile, we have no way to stop them now. Does it look like these computers are ready to be set up?"

"Actually, Jonah has set up quite a few of them," Ted countered. "And we have enough time to alert the World Government of their plan. We can send them the algorithms of these old-style computers, so they can block the attack on the RIBS. Jonah said he can do it, but we must act now. We've just been waiting for you. What if the Kill Switch doesn't work? We can lose everything. I've been saving my money points, and I'm too close to retirement to lose it all."

Neil Elder thought for a second. "That's a risk I'm willing to take. Just open the Kill Switch case."

Ted Stanton looked at Jonah, but he said nothing. Finally, he threw up his hands in defeat and followed Neil's directions. He opened the Kill Switch encasement with his thumbprint, and he placed the key in the correct keyhole. The encasement opened. "There! Are you happy?"

"Quite," Neil said, and he removed his gun from the holster at his hip and pointed it at Ted Stanton, shooting him twice in the chest. "That's another risk I'm willing to take."

Jonah watched the scene unfold, and he wasn't surprised—though watching Neil kill Ted Stanton greatly unsettled him. He knew that Neil had added so many money points to his account that the Kill Switch had to be used or else the discrepancy would be blaring. Neil kept the amount to himself, but Jonah had been patiently waiting for him to increase his wealth, which was exactly what Jonah had wanted. He had dropped subtle hints, and Neil took the bait. Now he had no choice but to pull the Kill Switch.

Suddenly, the sound of more gunfire could be heard, but this time the noise came from downstairs.

Neil pointed his gun at Jonah. "What was that?"

Jonah looked to the door. "It sounds like the shooting is coming from the factory floor."

"How did they get in?"

"Did Ted Stanton fail to tell you? He found a tunnel leading from one of the vents to the graveyard out back."

"That's impossible!"

"It's true," Jonah said. "And the tunnel is old. In fact, I believe it was dug when you were director of this prison."

"Impossible! That was years ago!"

"Doesn't change the fact that it's the truth," Jonah replied.

More gunshots were heard from downstairs, and something different, like a whistle, sounded outside the tower walls. Jonah walked to one of the open windows and looked out. "We are under attack, and they are shooting arrows." As he finished speaking, one arrow zipped past his face and stuck into the adjacent wall. "Looks like they have an army trying to stop you from pulling the Kill Switch."

Neil Elder placed his gun back in its holster and retrieved the keys clipped to his belt. "It will be too late to stop me. Cover the door!"

Jonah grabbed his gun from his holster and walked to the door. He looked at the clock. "You can't pull it now. We still have two minutes left. If you pull it too early, there won't be an attack on the RIBS, and the other magistrates will wonder why you pulled it without an imminent threat."

"I know!" Neil Elder yelled, looking through his keys. "Do you think I'm an idiot?" Once he found the right key, he went to the nearby desk and retrieved his Portable and walked to where the Kill Switch waited unlocked. He placed his key in the second keyhole. "There. Now, I can pull it just a few seconds after midnight to give those Colonials a few attacks before I reset everything. Then I'll upload the new copy of the RIBS, and I will become the wealthiest man alive."

Neil took out a small, shiny storage device from his pocket and set it on the Kill Switch encasement. Jonah recognized the cartridge. It was the one used to upload information to the Kill Switch. It had never been used before to the World Government's knowledge, but Jonah knew better. He watched Neil grab hold of the Kill Switch with his left hand and turn on his Portable with his right hand.

"Let me see how the gala is going. Ada's surprise fight must be a spectacle because I've never seen this many people logged in," Neil said. He stared down at the small screen on his Portable. "Wait. This can't be!"

"What is it?" Jonah asked from the door where he stood guard.

"It's Eve Pallue. She's alive!"

"Let me see." Jonah walked over to where Neil stood and looked at the screen. "That's Bear's wife, Ruth."

Neil closed his eyes. "Ruth! I should have known. Eve's middle name is Ruth! All they found in the fire was a missing tooth. That's it! Somehow, she got out. I don't know how, but she got out!"

"She must have had help," Jonah said. He looked at the clock. "Less than a minute left."

More gunshots sounded, but this time they were in the stairwell.

"Get back to the door! Shoot anyone who comes in!" Neil threw the Portable on the floor and carefully picked up the silver cartridge with the copied RIBS. "I will have to deal with her when this is all over. She can't be allowed to live. She'll ruin everything!"

Footsteps were coming rapidly up the stairs. "Someone is coming," Jonah said. "Be ready."

"Only ten seconds left. It will take him more than that just to break that lock."

Finally, when the footsteps made their way to the door, Jonah opened it wide.

"What are you doing?" Neil Elder yelled. Then his face froze. "Randall Hunt? You're supposed to be dead!"

"Surprise," Randall said, squeezing the trigger of his gun three times. Two shots to the chest and one to the head for insurance. Neil Elder slid to the floor as blood spilled from his body. The Kill Switch remained unpulled.

"You came just in time," Jonah said.

Randall looked around the room with his gun ready. "Anyone else here?"

"Just me, you and two dead bodies," Jonah said.

"When I found out you were playing both sides, I couldn't believe it," Randall said, putting his gun back into his holster.

"I have only played one side," Jonah countered. "And that is my Father's side." He then walked to the large, red Kill Switch and pulled it.

322

Randall quickly took out his gun and pointed it at Jonah. "Why the hell did you do that? You pulled the Kill Switch! I came here to protect my property and my family by ending the World Government once and for all!"

Jonah coolly looked at the dead body of Neil Elder. "This man killed my entire family when I was sixteen years old. We were sentenced to work at this camp. I've had many chances to kill him, but my Father wouldn't allow it. Now he is dead." He looked at Randall. "You've rid the world of a killer. He would have gone after Ruth."

Randall stood stunned. "But why the hell did you pull the Kill Switch?"

Jonah smiled. "Because a friend and I planted a coded virus in it almost fifteen years ago. The entire World Government system is disintegrating as we speak."

"But how?"

Jonah grabbed the Portable that Neil threw on the ground. It was still on. "What do you see?" he asked Randall as he handed him the Portable.

Randall kept his gun up but stared at the screen. "Nothing. I see absolutely nothing. How could you pull that off?"

Jonah then leaned over Neil's dead body and took out the shiny cartridge from his hand. He showed it to Randall. "A similar cartridge to this one was given to me by one of the creators of the Kill Switch. It had a virus on it, and I uploaded it to the Kill Switch in this very room over fifteen years ago."

Randall stood stunned. "Even if that were possible, it still doesn't explain how you erased the entire World Government."

"I waited for many years for three things. I needed someone to have a reason to pull the Kill Switch. I needed as many people plugged into the World Government as possible. And I needed a platform for the virus to spread. A link that could be found on every system."

Randall thought and, suddenly, his eyes widened with surprise. "The *Grand Opus Gala* and *Life Plethoricity*!" He put his gun back into the holster. "You're the one who leaked the information about the attack on the RIBS to Neil Elder."

Jonah's smile broadened. "I needed him to have a reason to pull the Kill Switch, but I also needed him not to suspect me. I had to be very intentional about everything I did and said, so I wouldn't be found out. Neil Elder was an extremely suspicious man."

"But how did you get Eve's life plan? She never showed it to anyone?"

"Before Eve Pallue became Ruth, she gave my boss, Christina Straight, *Life Plethoricity*, and we encoded it with the virus. The only problem was that we needed Eve Pallue to erase the original because our copy was the one with the code. Luckily, Neil Elder stole both the original and our copy, and he destroyed Eve's and used ours."

"I remember Christina Straight. She was Eve's Life Therapist. And you—you were her bodyguard, weren't you?" Randall asked in amazement.

"Yes, she was the one who they called the Apostle. We met outside of this very prison when I saved her life. I had finally finished digging the tunnel you came in through. It took me almost a year, but the timing was perfect. That was when this place became a women's prison for Efficientists. Once Miss Straight and I planted the virus into the Kill Switch, she took me to the city, made me her bodyguard and we waited for a long time for Eve Pallue to come to us."

"I can't believe it. You knew she would be caught in an Awakening?" Randall asked confused.

Jonah shook his head. "No, my Father gave me no further instructions than to wait for Eve Pallue to come to us, and she would help us defeat the World Government that her father created. I was worried when Christina Straight became sick, but God prolonged her life longer than it should have gone. She was in pain most days, but she quietly waited for the Lord to move, and He finally did."

Randall looked back at the empty Portable screen. "What you say doesn't make sense to me. I didn't know that God could talk to us like that—show us things in the future. But whatever you did, it worked. It's all gone."

"It took over fifteen years, but God's promise to take down the World Government has been fulfilled. I am done pretending. My name is Jonah Goodman the Third. I come from a line of proud fishermen. My father was wrongly accused by the World Government, and we were sentenced here to perform forced labor. My dad revolted, and Neil Elder killed every single prisoner. The only reason I wasn't among them was that they had left me for dead after a rattlesnake bite, but an outsider took me in and healed me. And he is the one who gave me the code."

Randall walked up to Jonah and reached out his hand. "When I hired you, I knew you were trustworthy. Yet, it never dawned on me that the trust I felt for you was from another Randall Hunt. The one who lost his eye yet gained his life. The Randall Hunt I am today."

Jonah took Randall's hand and shook it. "I must be honest. I believed you to be the worst of men, but now my Father calls you His son. So that makes you my brother in Christ."

Randall shrugged his shoulders. "This faith thing is new to me, and you and I look nothing alike. But, Jonah Goodman, I'd be honored to be your brother."

More arrows sounded around the building.

"You may need to get on the intercom and call your men off," Jonah said.

"We need to tell both our men to stand down. We are now on the same side. The World Government is dead," Randall said, walking to the intercom and clearing his throat before turning it on.

Shayla dropped the balloons and the printouts about ten seconds too early, but she didn't care. Her father was on the floor and Ruth was standing in the middle of the stage, telling the world she was Eve Pallue. She needed to get her family out of there and quickly. She ran down the steps by twos and busted through the Gala Hall doors. Chaos abounded. Ruth had just told everyone that the World Government had forced labor camps, and the images of the dead man on the fence scattered the floors along with silver, gold and white balloons. Cameras flashed, people screamed and Neil Elder wasn't there to control the situation.

"Now what?" Shayla asked herself, as she made her way through falling balloons and running bodies. She bumped into a man. She saw it was Sentinel. "Please, help me find my father! Take him out back. There is a birdman there with a trailer. We are going home with him. I'll get Ruth."

"You mean Eve Pallue," Sentinel corrected.

"Yes, whatever. I'll get her and meet you out there!"

Sentinel left her. He seemed happy to have a mission now that his competitor was knocked out. She could see his friends were trailing behind him. They went around the stage to look for her fallen father. She trusted that he would do as she asked. Shayla then rolled onto the stage floor. Ruth was still standing there. The microphone from which she had been speaking was turned off.

"Ruth, come with me! We are getting out of here." She noticed Ruth's blood-stained gown. She must have just miscarried. She had seen her leave the Gala Hall but thought she simply didn't want to watch Bear fight. It wasn't a fun bout to watch—though the audience reveled in it.

"What about your father?" Ruth asked.

"Sentinel and his friends are getting him. They will meet us at Sonnie's trailer. Let me help you." She put Ruth's arm around her shoulder and began to half carry her to the end of the stage.

"My ratings! My ratings!" a woman yelled. "They are gone! They are all gone! Everything is gone!"

Shayla looked at the seats at the front of the stage. Ada Armel stood in her stunning gown holding her Portable up to her face. Fear tore through her expression as she screamed hysterically. Shayla had only been in the city a few weeks, and the people had become stranger and stranger to her. She was glad they were leaving. She couldn't wait to tell her friends what the city was really like.

She carefully sat Ruth on the surface of the stage and jumped over the ropes. Then she scooted Ruth onto the main floor of the Gala Hall. All the Efficientists were leaving out the front door, and she had to push through the commotion to make her way to the backdoor. Once she got to the parking lot behind the building, she could see Sonnie standing next to his truck and trailer. Relief flooded her body. Her father was awake and began running toward them. "Ruth! Shayla!" he yelled. His face was badly beaten, and his ribs must have been in pain because he kept his arms tucked against his torso and winced with every step he took.

"I've got her, *Ah-nah!* Let's just get into the truck. Something happened. Everything is crazy and that Ada lady is screaming about her ratings being gone."

"Something happened to the World Government site," Sonnie said when they got close to the trailer. "I heard people out front yelling about it."

Shayla handed Ruth off to her father, and together they made their way into the back of the truck. She turned to Sentinel and his friends. "You guys have a way out?"

"No," he said. "We walked here."

"Here, take my father's truck. It's parked over there," she said, pointing. "Can you get my father's men? They don't have a way home."

"We will go back and get them all," Sentinel answered. His friends nodded their agreement.

"Go before things in the city get even crazier," Sonnie said. "Make your way back to the colonies where it's safe."

Sentinel bowed, and he and his men ran back to the gala building.

Shayla made her way around the trailer and got into the passenger seat of the truck. Sonnie got into the driver's seat and started the engine.

"You two ready back there?"

"Yes," Bear yelled. "Go!"

Sonnie put his truck in drive and began his way onto a back road, towing his trailer filled with dozens of birds of prey. He avoided the front of the gala building where the magistrates and Efficientists were running to their limousines to go back to their dark, blank LPS screens.

"I can't believe it!" Pastor Tom said, standing up with a Portable in his hands. "It's gone. Everything is gone!" He and Li were in the basement of the Trinity Trading Center. They were communicating with Pastor Rohan and his son, Christian, trying desperately to decide if they should attack the RIBS with the supercomputer or wait for another time. Either way, they knew they had missed their opportunity, making Neil Elder more powerful in the process. However, Pastor Tom held onto hope by remembering Jonah's words: *there are two copies*. There had to be an alternate plan.

Li looked at the HMS and the older version LPS they had acquired. "And not just the RIBS! Everything is gone. There's nothing. It's like the World Government has been wiped clean!"

Pastor Tom stared at all three machines, trying to understand. "What about the old-style computer?" he asked.

Li swiveled his chair and started typing on the computer keyboard. "I'm sending a message to Rohan and Christian."

They waited as the words he typed blinked back at them. Suddenly, they got a reply. "We are still here. Supercomputer still working."

Exhilaration rocketed through Pastor Tom's body. "Does the LPS and Portable work? The ones connected to their supercomputer. What do they see?"

Li began typing.

They both stared at the screen holding their breaths for the answer.

Li stood up when he saw what was written. "They can get on them, but there is nothing there. It's like the World Government has been erased!"

Pastor Tom's brain began firing with understanding. "The copy of *Life Plethoricity*. It had the code, and it was placed irrevocably on every site of the World Government. Jonah must have known that. And the Kill Switch..." he looked at Li with realization. "The copy of the RIBS gave Neil Elder a reason to pull it!"

Li's eyes widened with understanding. "Jonah *wanted* Neil Elder to pull the Kill Switch all along! He's the one who imbedded the code into *Life Plethoricity*, not the World Government." Li then thought. "But how did he get the anchor code into the Kill Switch without being detected? Neil Elder has a team of scientists monitoring it. They would have noticed."

"He must have done it when they weren't looking," Pastor Tom said.

Li shook his head. "No, the Kill Switch is monitored every second of every day. Arthur Pallue mandated around the clock surveillance when it was created."

Pastor Tom snapped his fingers. "Jonah must have done it when he was in the prison camp. Zach found his tunnel. Somehow he got in and uploaded it."

"But still, he would have been detected," Li said, unconvinced.

"Christina Straight must have helped him. She was at the prison too. That's where Zach said they probably met after he found the tunnel and lockbox with Jonah's photos. I don't know how they developed the code, but they anchored it within the Kill Switch fifteen years ago. Then they wrote that same code into *Life Plethoricity*, which Neil Elder fixed to every LPS, HMS and Portable because he didn't want it to be removed. Then all that was needed was for as many people as possible to be plugged into the World Government when the Kill Switch was pulled."

"The Grand Opus Gala," Li said in amazement. Then he shook his head again. "But even if she helped him, they still would have been detected when they uploaded the virus unless they uploaded it when the system was rebooting."

"Has the Kill Switch ever been used?" Pastor Tom asked. He didn't know much about the Kill Switch. There was little information he could find about its history and use.

Li thought. "I heard rumors of it being used when the World News was attacked by an underground Christian group. I was just a kid at the time."

"That's it!" Pastor Tom shouted. "Christina Straight was also known as the Apostle. She was sent to prison. She organized the Efficientist Christian Sect to attack the World News to force Arthur Pallue to use the Kill Switch, and she and Jonah somehow managed to upload the anchor virus! That's why Jonah leaked the information about us taking down the RIBS. The entire plan was already set in place. All he needed was for the Kill Switch to be pulled again!"

Li shook his head. "He had to wait patiently for years while all the pieces fell into place. It's a miracle. It's an absolute miracle. There are so many things that needed to happen in order for his plan to work. One missing element would have ruined it all."

Both men sat back down stunned. Jonah had carried the weight of this plan for many years. Once Christina Straight passed away, it was up to him to carry the plan to the finish line. They sat for several minutes quietly, each in his own set of thoughts. Finally, they heard footsteps coming downstairs. It was Pastor Tom's wife, Cindy.

"Well, did it work?" she asked.

Pastor Tom nodded his head. "Yes, but not in the way we planned."

"Jonah had an ace up his sleeve, didn't he?" she asked.

"Yes, he did," Pastor Tom said. "He had a big ace up his sleeve."

"One big enough to wipe the World Government's sites clean. No more ranks. No more ratings. No more money points." Li added.

"And no more forced labor camps," Cindy said, relieved.

Li looked at the clock. "It's past midnight. Happy New Year to you both."

Pastor Tom stretched his arms behind his back and leaned into a great sigh. "I believe this year will start a new beginning for us. And this time, instead of establishing our country on fear, we will be like our ancestors, and establish it on faith."

CHAPTER 44

Jonah stood behind those who stood around Esther's grave for the grief gathering. He had known most of these people only by name, and he had relied on each of them with his heart and soul. Now he knew their faces, and they knew his. Ruth stood next to Deborah. Both women were quietly weeping. Bear stood slightly behind Ruth with his hand on her shoulder. His eyes were still swollen, but the deep purple bruises on his face had turned a shade of green. He wore a nose cast, and his other arm was in a sling. Despite his appearance, though, he had a calm strength that seemed to encompass his wife's sorrow.

Bear's daughter, Shayla, and his grandfather stood beside him. He heard stories about Shayla's heroism in the city. Bear and Ruth, both dealing with massive injuries, wouldn't have made it out without her quick thinking and delegation skills. She already displayed many of her father's leadership skills at such a young age. He understood now why God wanted him to entrust her with such an important and risky task at the gala.

Jonah listened as Pastor Tom gave his eulogy. The pastor had known Esther and Deborah since he first began preaching in Trinity. Jonah couldn't help but smile. He had attended Pastor Tom's first sermon after the World Government banned all religious activities. The Trinity Trading Center was now both a trading center and a church. Next to Pastor Tom stood his wife, Cindy. Jonah enjoyed her company. She asked about his childhood and about his family. He was able to open up about his past to her—something he could only do with Christina Straight.

Next to Cindy stood Zach and Pilar. Zach looked just as bad as Bear—maybe worse. He too had a broken nose, but it wasn't until later that they found that he had tiny fractures along his jaw. He wasn't supposed to talk or eat solids for several weeks. Jonah watched as Pilar stroked the side of his cheek gently. He found out later that she had to practically carry him to the car that he had hidden for her to escape. She was a woman of strength, for sure. They both had shown so much resilience that it could only be the power of God in them. Jonah smiled as he observed the couple. Pilar's dark brown eyes and hair and dark skin contrasted against Zach's blue eyes, light skin and shaggy blonde hair—but the contrast made for something beautiful and complete, like green trees swaying in a backdrop of a clear blue sky. God's love for variety was evident everywhere.

Jonah then turned his eyes to Charlie Liu, or Li as he was known in the colonies. He was standing next to Rohan and one of his sons, Christian. When Jonah had dumped the batch of computers at the Trinity Trade Center, he hoped that Pastor Tom and Li would figure out what to do with them. He and Christina Straight had been working with old computers for years—a gift from the man who saved his life from the snake bite. They had held that secret for over fifteen years, which kept Christina Straight's writings and other illegal activities untraceable. But the time came for others to know about it. The young man, Christian, had even thought to construct a supercomputer, or the Gupta Computer, as he called it. It never occurred to him or Miss Christina to wire the old devices with the new. Now Li and his friends had a way to fill up the empty space of the erased World Government using the supercomputer. As of now, they could only post words. The first manuscript published was the Bible. Next, they published the writings of the Apostle. Jonah had given them the scripts for all of Christina Straight's writings. She would be pleased that her work continued to be read. Then they put up writings from Pastor Tom and finally from Ruth. They would continue to add more truth to the void as they found more manuscripts.

When Jonah had anonymously dropped off all the old-style computers at the trading center, he had prayed that one particular computer would find its way into discerning hands. Thank God it made its way to Li. This computer was the one that created the code that Christina Straight had implanted into the copy of *Life Plethoricity* that Eve Pallue sent to her Portable. This code would be the anchor on all World Government sites for the virus that he downloaded into the Kill Switch over fifteen years previously. The man who owned the computer and who wrote the code died never knowing if his plan to destroy the World Government would succeed. He had trusted a seventeen-year-old with his dying wish and detailed plan to stop the corruption. The man's plan seemed impossible to Jonah's young mind, but, thankfully, he met Christina Straight. She knew how to get Arthur Pallue to order the Kill Switch pulled, so they could upload the virus without detection. It would be up to him years later to find a way to get that same switch pulled for a second and final time.

Jonah gave a sigh of relief. His planning had finally come to an end. His gaze then drifted to Randall Hunt and his girlfriend, Adella, and her two daughters, Alex and Ana. Randall was definitely a surprise twist to his plan. Who would have thought that he would be one of the good guys? He had shot Neil Elder to prevent him from pulling the Kill Switch. Jonah realized that Randall had arrived at the prison when he heard the arrows flying past the tower. Pastor Tom had warned him that Randall's men carried bows and arrows. When those footsteps sounded up the stairs, he knew in his gut that Randall was out for blood. He had the chance many times to take Neil Elder's life, but vengeance wasn't his. It was God's, and God used Randall Hunt to pull the trigger. Probably better that way. Jonah had never killed a soul, and he understood now that he desired peace over revenge. In killing Neil Elder, he would have killed himself in a slow death of remorse.

Behind the two girls, stood another young man named Tal. He was Randall's second-hand man. He held a leash with a large wolf-looking dog attached to it. The dog curiously observed the people standing around him, probably wondering why everyone was standing still. Finally, Jonah saw Dr. Linton. The man who was there from the beginning. He was a great help at the prison once the fighting was over and everyone realized that the World Government was taken down and they were all now on the same side. Thankfully, the only causalities were Neil Elder and Ted Stanton. They buried both bodies in the graveyard behind the prison. Jonah ordered for the tunnel to be imploded. It was strange watching something he aggressively dug for almost a year being demolished in seconds. But that was another account to be told. Maybe, someday, he would write down his side of the story and tell the world about the real Matthew Coughlin—the man who helped build the Kill Switch and then create the code to destroy it, but not today. This was the day to start his own story as a free man.

"What do you say?" a tender voice asked, bringing him out of his reverie. "Are you hungry?"

Jonah blinked and looked down to see the aged face of Deborah. She was the one who was nursing both Zach and Bear back to health. Even though her sister had died, she carried a joy that was indestructible. He hadn't realized the grief gathering was over. "Yes, thank you, Miss Deborah. I am a little hungry," Jonah said, offering his arm.

She took it. "A big man like you? I bet you're more than a little hungry."

He laughed. "Maybe so. It's been a long, long—" Jonah was at a loss for words.

She nodded. "Yes, it has been a long journey, hasn't it?" She followed his lead up the path of the ranch to the main house. They passed Pilar and Zach heading to the winter garden that Esther meticulously planted and maintained. She said nothing for several moments as she watched the couple. "You know," she finally began. "I have a house full of Efficientists and more on the way who need help acclimating to rural life."

"There is a great need right now. People are leaving the city in droves," he agreed.

"And now that my sister went on and left me for Jesus, I'm at the ranch all by myself to handle a house full of guests."

"You'll probably be needing help," he admitted.

She stopped. "I was wondering if you would like to stay with us at the ranch. You can have my sister's old room—we'll redo it, of course. Don't think you'll be liking cat figurines and floral prints," she laughed.

Jonah thought of the paintings he took from Christina Straight's home after she died. Before leaving the city to return to the prison where he lost his family, he erased all record of Matthew Coughlin and had taken all the paintings he kept from Christina and placed them in the car he hid by the prison for Pilar's escape. Pilar and Zach were holding the paintings for him until he found a place of his own. "I have a few paintings that a friend gave me that might look good," he said, smiling.

"Well, now it's settled!" she said, clasping his large, dark hand under her aged, wrinkled hand. "You will stay here in Trinity at the ranch! Ruth will be thrilled! In fact, everyone will be thrilled that you are staying!"

The freedom that Jonah felt earlier swelled with love. He had a family. He was known. He belonged. He didn't have to pretend anymore. He could even take up fishing again. The Trinity River ran right through the back of the ranch. Some fried catfish or blackened bass sounded good right about now. "Let me ask you a question, Miss Deborah."

"Yes?" she asked with a knowing glimmer in her eye.

"How long has it been since someone has fished that river in your backyard."

"Oh," she said, patting his hand. "It's been ages. I'm sure it's chocked full of fresh fish just waiting to be caught."

He nodded. "Well, then. I guess I'll be staying." He looked up at the ranch house with new eyes. This was now his home. As he thought those words, half a dozen doves came flying over the roof of the house toward them. Once overhead, they made a slight turn and soared over the Trinity River. "I'm home," he whispered with a grateful exhale. "Thank You, Father, for bringing me back home."

"Esther's flowers smell so beautiful," Pilar said, as she walked with Zach away from the gravesite down the path to what they now called Esther's Garden. "She could grow anything during any season—even winter!"

Zach walked beside her and nodded. The rest of the people from the grief gathering made their way to the house for lunch. Zach wasn't supposed to talk. His mouth should be wired shut, but Deborah didn't have the tools to perform the procedure. So she told him that unless he stopped talking, his jaw fractures would not heal properly. Pilar made him liquid meals daily that he could sip. He had lost a lot of weight, and his normally lean frame was even thinner. Pilar knew he would gain it all back once he healed and regained his strength.

Pilar looked at Zach. His face was more familiar than it had been in days. She actually liked him quiet. He didn't overthink things out loud. Sometimes, she wished he would just be impulsive—even just a little bit. But she had been impulsive and it almost got her killed. Maybe caution was better. "I can't wait for spring," she said, interrupting the silence. "I'm tired of the cold weather." It really wasn't that cold compared to the northern colonies, but still, she was a warm-weather soul.

When they reached the center of the garden, Zach handed her a note. Then he took something out of his pocket and held it out, slowly kneeling to the ground. She looked at what was in his hand. It was a ring. She brought her hands to her mouth. "Zach! What are you doing?"

He pointed to the note with his free hand.

With shaking hands, she unfolded the letter and began to read aloud.

"Dear, Pilar," she began, trying to hold back the tears. "I hope you don't mind that I talked about our relationship to Esther before she died. She gave me wise advice to stop overthinking. I've really messed things up, and I can get caught up in all the things I've done wrong. When I was being tortured in the jail cell, I received a strange but divine sense of peace. I finally understood what my father had experienced at his death. He died for what he believed in, and nothing could be nobler. His death was not in vain. I know now that he had peace when he passed. I could have easily died in that cell to be with him. But when I heard your prayers, they gave me a sense of purpose that I haven't had in a long time. Though the life I believed I wanted died with my father, God is giving me a new life, a life I would have never imagined could be so full of love and joy." She stopped and looked at Zach who was still kneeling before her holding the ring out. He motioned for her to keep going.

"I've already asked, or wrote, your father for your hand in marriage. He said yes, but I had to endure a lecture, which I did since I can't say anything back. I guess, I deserved it for all I have put you through. I also asked Deborah, and she gave me this ring. It was Esther and Deborah's mother's ring, and Esther promised it to me when we last talked. I love you, Pilar Jones. I always have. My love for you had to become stronger than my wounded heart, and I'm sorry it took so long for me to heal.

I've learned that some things can't be understood. They have to be trusted. And that is my love for you. I don't understand it all, but I know how I feel about you. I want to share my life with you. I can't imagine living any other way. So will you marry me Pilar Jones?"

Pilar fell to her knees on the grass in front of Zach. Thick tears dropped from her cheeks onto Esther's Garden. Tears also fell from Zach's blue eyes, as he waited patiently for her to respond. She gently took the ring from his hand and slipped it onto her ring finger. It fit perfectly. "Yes, Zacchaeus Mark Daniels. I will marry you. I love you."

Zach took Pilar into his arms and held her. Even though he couldn't talk, Pilar felt his vulnerability toward her. No more indifference. No more hiding. He had confronted his greatest fears and had overcome them.

Zach placed his hand under her chin and lifted her head. He stared into her eyes and softly mouthed the words: *I love you too.* Then, he gently brushed his lips across hers. It wasn't a real kiss, not yet. Soon his physical healing would match his emotional healing, and they could start a new life—restored as one, both body and soul.

Onoma Series:
Eve of Awakening: Book 1
Bear into Redemption: Book 2
Mark within Salvation: Book 3
Hunt for Understanding: Book 4
Straight to Eternity: Prequel Novella

I hope you enjoyed this fiction series. If you like this book, please write a quick review on Amazon. Also, if you enjoy my writing, check out my other non-fiction and fiction works on my website, www.alisahopewagner.com.

www.ingramcontent.com/pod-product-compliance
Lightning Source LLC
Chambersburg PA
CBHW071524260626
47170CB00002B/494